THE HIDDEN SCROLL

To ASHLEY
AN OUTSTANDING
    PHYSICAL THERAPIST

SOME HISTORY
    SOME ADVENTURE
        AND SOME IMAGINATION

ENJOY

[signature]

AVRAHAM ANOUCHI   5/5/2017

THE HIDDEN SCROLL

IN SEARCH FOR THE LOST MACCABEE SCROLL

Avraham Y. Anouchi

To order additional copies of this book, contact:
Xlibris Corporation
1-888-795-4274
www.Xlibris.com
Orders@Xlibris.com
67222

TABLE OF CONTENTS

PROLOGUE

T HE HISTORICAL EVENTS that occurred in 70 CE are still with us in the 21st century. They inspired the writing of this book on the search for those events.

THE HIDDEN SCROLL is a historical novel spanning from 1930 to 2015 on an archaeology professor's impassioned search for ancient parchments and artifacts from the time of the second Temple of Jerusalem and the revolt of the Maccabees. He encounters obstacles raised by a radical Islamist organization dedicated to undermining the Jewish claim to the land of Israel— obstacles that include murders, kidnappings, suicide bombers and forged parchments.

Numerous legends tell the story of the golden candelabra, the golden Ark of the Covenant and other religious vessels used during the performance of priestly ceremonies in the Temple. The legends gave birth to the popular Hollywood production of the Raiders of the Lost Ark. Visitors in Rome can see the Triumphal Arch of Titus depicting an engraved image of the golden candelabra, known as the Menorah, being carried by Roman soldiers. Whether the Romans took the Jerusalem Menorah to Rome, or the defenders of the city hid it from the Romans, is still a puzzle that historians have not been able to determine with certainty.

To reach readers who are not familiar with Jewish history, I elected to structure the book in the form of a historic thriller. It includes fiction as well as references to events accepted by the literary world as historical facts. I have also included short historical notes about relevant events that are part of the book.

CHAPTER 1

1929 The Jerusalem Mufti

O N THE OUTSKIRTS of Jerusalem, the central square of the Bikamalyah village hummed with saber-rattling young men welcoming their leader, Ibn Najad.

"When shall we go to Hebron?" shouted one of the volunteers.

"Tomorrow is the day," answered young Ibn Najad who entered the square with his group of twelve hot-blooded young Arab volunteers. "We have been ordered to start street riots in the Jewish neighborhood of Hebron."

"Finally, we'll kick the Jews out of Hebron," shouted one of the volunteers.

"We'll meet here at noon tomorrow," Ibn Najad announced. "You will travel by bus to join the other groups. I'll bring more groups from other villages. Do not forget your knives and clubs. You will use them extensively in the name of Allah. You'll be the pioneers of the new Jihad against the Jews."

"Allah Hu Akbar," shouted the volunteers, starting to dance in the village square, some waving the short versions of their scimitar-like knives.

"Allah Hu Akbar"

*   *   *

"Allah Hu Akbar," shouted the thirty volunteers as they exited the bus which brought them back from the riots. They gathered at the village square, formed a circle and danced again waving their bloody stained knives in the air.

"Allah Hu Akbar."

*   *   *

Haj Amin Al-Husseini, the Grant Mufti of Jerusalem, sat in his home waiting for Ahmad Ibn Najad, the intelligent young man who earned his degree in Middle East studies at Oxford University. He was a dedicated revolutionary who demonstrated outstanding organizational talent.

Ibn Najad didn't understand why the Grand Mufti summoned him. His village Mukhtar was his commander who had provided him with all the operational instructions. He was never informed who provided the Mukhtar with higher-level instructions on organizing the riots against the Jews of Jerusalem. The Mukhtar himself informed him that the Grand Mufti wanted to meet him. He did not ask any questions and arrived at the appointed time, sporting a light black jacket and a distinctively large black moustache. A secretarial aide met him and escorted him into the Mufti's office.

Haj Amin stood up from his desk and walked toward the door, extending his hand to welcome Ibn Najad. They sat on both sides of a small circular table covered by a red tablecloth on which several words from the Koran were embroidered with gold thread.

"I am very pleased with your recent activities," Haj Amin greeted him with a smile. "I received reports about your success in organizing the riots last year. With the help of Allah, you managed to purge the city of Hebron of all of its Jews. The few Jews who survived will never be allowed to return. I also heard about your success in recruiting young Arab men to join us for fighting in our upcoming struggle in Palestine. Your accomplishments are very impressive."

"Thank you for your compliments," answered Ibn Najad.

"Your academic credentials, your organizational skills, and your impressive record are the reasons for considering you to become my advisor on a special project.

"The Council of Imams in Palestine decided to establish a new organization. I am looking for an advisor whom I can trust and who will help me in building it and operating it. The 1917 Balfour Declaration by the British Government to establish a Jewish homeland in Palestine indicates that the Jews have a great influence on British and other European leaders. The mission of our new organization will be to define and implement a plan which will undermine the popularity of the Jewish people in the world and will reduce the prominence of Jewish leaders in European political and financial circles. I believe that you can assist me in this project."

Ibn Najad didn't know how to respond, but he knew that this meeting with the Mufti could be the opportunity of his lifetime for a great personal career.

"I am honored to be a candidate," he finally responded with a surge of confidence. "I have admired you and I consider you a great leader of the Arab cause in Palestine. You have inspired many young Arabs to follow you in the fight to throw the Jews out of Palestine. I will be ready to offer my services to our cause to the best of my ability."

"To achieve our objectives," continued the Mufti, "our new organization must be non-violent. It will be legitimate with social goals. We will distance its association from the Arab struggle in Palestine by promoting social goals. It could be a research center of political scientists, or a religious seminary or any other organization with a front that will be effective in hiding its true mission."

Haj Amin stopped talking. He looked at the facial expressions of Ibn Najad trying to decipher his poker face. *He must have learned poker at Oxford.*

"I know that your recent accomplishments were in fighting and organizing riots. However, the Council of Imams decided that we need an exceptionally talented person to advise us on how to establish, manage and administer a new organization. They instructed me to find a person who can distance himself from any of the Arab violent activities against the Jews in Palestine.

"I have to determine if you can be as successful in our new non-violent operation. If you'll convince me that you can, I'll offer you the opportunity to contribute your talent and expertise to this important project."

Ibn Najad was dumbfounded. The Mufti was right. His experience was primarily in organizing riots and training young Arabs to kill. He was an expert in violence and now he was being offered a position requiring him to build a non-violent operation. He never dreamt that he would be chosen to undertake such an assignment and to report directly to the Grand Mufti. Listening politely without showing any enthusiasm, might convey an impression that he was not ready for such a responsibility. His facial expression changed when he decided to take the initiative and present himself as the most qualified candidate for this position.

"My first reaction is to ask two questions. Has anyone written any preparatory work in planning the creation of the new organization? If it must be recognized by the public as non-military, its nature will depend on many factors. Before we create the new organization, we must establish a center to gather and document information on the Jewish leaders in Europe, their family backgrounds, their financial status, their strengths and their weaknesses. We must understand what makes them prominent and influential and what makes them vulnerable to external pressures."

Ibn Najad was amazed at his courage in expressing his opinion in the plural form. He seemed to have succeeded in impressing the Mufti with his self confidence and his courage. He acted as though he were already part of the Mufti's inner circle of advisors.

"You asked a very a good question with a very good suggestion," commented Haj Amin. "What is your second question?"

"My second question is logical. The project will require a considerable amount of money. Has anyone prepared a budget?"

"This is also a good question. It demonstrates why I need you. I want you to prepare more questions and to propose answers to your questions. I have some ideas on how to create and how to operate the new organization, but I want your suggestions. I want you to think about this project carefully and to prepare a proposal with ideas, schedules and budgets. After I review your proposal, I will decide if you are the right candidate to be my advisor. If the proposed budget is reasonable, I'll raise the money for the initial establishment of the organization. Future funds will have to be raised later."

Ibn Najad appeared to have another question, but he hesitated to ask it.

"Do you have a third question?"

Ibn Najad shook his head, hesitating, but not responding.

"Then it is time to have coffee," the Mufti announced after not getting a response.

He pressed a button on his desk and a young man walked in with a shiny engraved copper tray on which were two decorated Finjan-type coffee cups and a steaming copper coffee pot. Without saying a single word, the young man poured coffee into the cups and left the room.

Ibn Najad interpreted this invitation for strong Turkish coffee as an approval of his performance during the interview. It elevated his self confidence and he asked a third question.

"Did the Council of Imams decide on a name for the organization?"

"I have considered several names," responded Haj Amin. "But adding new ones to my list would be desirable. Maybe you can suggest one."

Ibn Najad identified an opportunity to advance his chances of becoming the Mufti's advisor. He decided to act on this instinct immediately.

"How about calling the new organization '*Bismillah*'?" he replied with hesitation. "It could be a good name to inspire Arab men who will be recruited and to encourage others to support us financially. While in Arabic it means 'in the name of Allah', it may just be a name for the British and other infidels. If you like this name, I'll prepare a few ideas which will provide the new organization with a cover for its main goal; a '*raison d'être*'," he added in French.

"It sounds like a good idea," said the Mufti. "I'll add your suggestion to my list, but I'll decide on a name after you submit your proposal."

Ibn Najad accepted the challenge and returned to his village.

The next day, he stayed at his desk several hours listing ideas for his proposal. He structured it in the format of a dissertation for a PhD degree to convince the Mufti that he was the best candidate as the director of the new organization. He called his proposal "The Bismillah Charter", with a sub-title of "Operational Guidelines for Success".

*   *   *

A month later, Ibn Najad submitted the draft of his proposal to the Mufti. He highlighted the importance of carefully selecting a well-qualified and dedicated leader for the new organization. He proposed to locate his headquarters outside Palestine to keep its operation away from the eyes of the British and the Jews. Operating away from the region would avoid being associated with the struggle of the Arabs in Palestine, especially knowing the effective operation of the British Intelligence. He also had a self-serving agenda. He wanted to have complete freedom of operation without interference from other Mufti personnel.

The Bismillah charter included the main objectives, the mode of operation, the plan for a welfare network in several countries and the critical need for not being associated with any violence used by other Arab organizations in the Middle East. As he hoped, his proposed name was accepted by the Mufti and he was appointed to be the creator and the director of the new organization.

*   *   *

Ibn Najad established his new operation in a small office in the central business district of Baghdad. His proposal to Haj Amin was returned with positive comments on the charter, marked with remarks and suggestions for modifications, without altering the main theme of the document. The amended proposal was approved by the Mufti with a doubling of his proposed budget.

He recruited several intellectuals who had survived the Great World War. He also hired a few merchants and young non-radical Arabs. He gradually assembled a group of individuals who became the team that he needed at his headquarters. Bismillah became known for its social work in providing assistance to the poor and the small merchants in Baghdad, which was still recovering from the hunger and devastation of the Great War. Haj Amin provided the initial funding for the operation. Later, Ibn Najad published a news release on his plan to launch an international search for the lost parts of the Koran. He quoted several Islamic scholars at the Al Zahr University in Cairo, claiming that Mohammad had a second revelation, the details of which had not been included in the Koran. He urged Muslims to support his project to help finance the hiring of qualified scholars. He was successful in meeting his initial financial objectives, but the operation did not become self-sufficient. As his operation expanded, he hired additional personnel and subsequently submitted an ever-increasing budget to the Mufti. Haj Amin continued to provide additional supplemental funding.

Ibn Najad held weekly meetings with his senior staff. He didn't reveal to his staff the details of his plan for the Mufti's approval. He presented the confidential report to Haj Amin during a meeting in Beirut. It was done in the form of a written letter.

"To the esteemed Grand Mufti of Jerusalem, Haj Amin Al-Husseini.

"I am pleased to submit this report on the recent operations of Bismillah.

"It was not easy finding and recruiting qualified candidates for our Baghdad headquarter. I determined that candidates must be fluent in at least three languages, Arabic and French are imperative, with the third language being English, German, Italian or Spanish. These are the languages that are used extensively by the Jewish communities in Europe. Arabic and French are used by Jews in

North Africa and by their merchants in international trade. I didn't think that I could find an Arab who would be fluent in Hebrew, but I found one who grew up in Jaffa near a Jewish synagogue. He is very familiar with Jewish customs and traditions.

"I selected six senior members and I met with them daily. I wanted to know them well, to understand their way of thinking, to determine their dedication to our cause, and to decide how each can be assigned to specific tasks. When I determined that they were ready, I assigned each one to gather information from Jewish communities in several countries. I instituted a set of procedures to document the information which we gather to facilitate my analysis and to prepare action plans.

"In preparation for expanding our operation, I prepared a draft of an action plan to create Bismillah branches in major European cities. Initially, I will start with Berlin, London, Paris, Rome and Warsaw. These are non-Arab cities in which most of European Jews are concentrated. At a later date I will open branches in Casablanca, Tunis and Aleppo where we can provide social assistance to the poor Arab neighborhoods and be close to centers of Jewish communities.

Respectfully submitted,
Ahmad Ibn Najad."

CHAPTER 2

1930 Tel Aviv

T HE HOT DAYS of summer along the shores of the Mediterranean Sea slowly gave way to the approaching cooler days of autumn. The sweet smell of the lemon tree that he had planted floated through the upstairs window, mixing with the slight warm sea breeze. Benjamin breathed a sigh of relief that he had finally been able to move his family from his former home in the crowded city of Jaffa. The beautiful clear October sky in the Tel-Aviv suburb did not help him solve the problems that occupied his mind, nor did he find understanding of the disturbing dream of the previous night. He glared at the night in worry, took another deep breath. The bright moonlight lit the sand dunes that surrounded his home, trying to reveal their secrets and chase away the darkness. If only life's problems could be lit with solutions as easily, but his frightening dream told him otherwise.

Benjamin Amram stood in front of the open window in his new home facing the night, lost in thought. The news from Hebron brought new reality to his life. The massacre of innocent men, women and children in broad daylight, planted fear and anxiety. The British mandatory police did not intervene to protect the Jewish residents from a pogrom, just like the Tzar's soldiers did not stop pogroms in Jewish villages. His own uncle had moved from Hebron to Jerusalem six months before the riots.

How should the Jewish people react to such atrocities?
We cannot rely on the British to defend us.
We need a Jewish defense force of our own . . .
We have to teach our children war as well as the fear of G-d.
Our next generation must be followers of the Maccabees.

Pacing the floor of his new home, Benjamin was also preoccupied with the frightening problems affecting his family.

Gazing at the small grove he had planted in his garden, he examined and counted the trees—two orange, three grapefruit, one pomegranate and one sweet lemon. He especially liked the lemon tree with its exceptionally sweet-as-honey lemons

His mind jumped to his wife, Sima, and the future of their child about to be born.

Life given to a newborn arrives with great expectations and joy. Unfortunately, it also arrives with great suffering and sadness.

"Lord in Heaven above," he lifted his eyes to the star-studded skies. "Why should every mother on earth bear the punishment for the sins of Adam and Eve?"

He thought of his own life and the lives of his three young daughters who were sleeping in the house. He remembered the pain his wife Sima endured to bring children to the world. She was about to endure birth pains again.

The anticipation of birth pains brought with it great fear. He walked toward the bedroom to see if Sima was sleeping peacefully or if in labor, realizing there was nothing he could do to help her. He opened the bedroom door and found her sound asleep.

Benjamin sat in his armchair feeling exhausted after not being able to sleep well during the last three nights. His struggles with the troubling thoughts subsided slowly until he fell asleep. After a short nap, he woke up with great fear caused by the man who appeared again in his dream. The man was his father Avner, who appeared with his white beard just like he was before he returned his soul to his creator. With trembling lips, his father delivered a message to his son.

"Benjamin," his father said in the dream. "I came to tell you that a son will be born to you. I know you intend to call him Avner to carry my name. However, if you name your newborn son after me, you will not live more than two weeks after his circumcision. I am pleading with you to select another name."

Benjamin woke up, his face damp with sweat, his heart racing and his hands shaking. He remembered his youth when his parents told him about the family tradition to name the first son after the paternal grandfather and the first daughter after the paternal grandmother, whether the grandparents were still alive or deceased.

How can I break the tradition now? How can I face my relatives and friends by not naming my newborn son after my father? How could I live with my conscience after deviating from my family tradition?

The next day was the eve of Yom Kippur, the Day of Atonement. Benjamin's father appeared once more in a dream. This time, a white bearded old man holding a large scroll appeared with him.

"Benjamin," the old bearded man said while waving the scroll. "I accompany your father to inform you that your persistence in wanting to honor your father has been rewarded. Tomorrow, a son will be born to you and you can name him Avner, in honor of your father and in the tradition of your family. Because you were not willing to compromise your convictions regarding this tradition, the heavenly 'Bet Din' tribunal reversed its decision. You will live a long and fruitful life.

"Your newborn son will be determined and deliberate.

"He will be as our heroes of old. As ingenious as
Joshua—bringing down Jericho's walls with 300 trumpets,
Gideon—chasing Medianites with 300 trumpets,
David—battling Goliath with a shepherd's sling,
Judah—routing Greeks with a handful of Maccabees.
"Your newborn son

> Will raise his head up high,
> Will know his purpose,
> Will be ingenious,
> He will be a new Maccabee,
> But not the Last Maccabee."

The old man concluded his message and left. Benjamin was
puzzled, still not knowing who the old man was until his father
revealed his identity.

"Rabbi Akiva!" his father said. "The man who accompanied me
tonight was Rabbi Akiva—the spiritual leader of the Bar-Kochva
revolt against the Romans in the 2nd century, the great rabbi of
the Tanaitic period and one of the ten rabbis who were executed in
public by the Romans."

The day after Yom Kippur, Benjamin's son was born. Relieved
after his last dream, Benjamin gave his newborn son the name of
'Avner Akiva Amram.' The first name in honor of his father as the
tradition dictated, and the middle name in honor of Rabbi Akiva,
who interceded on his behalf at the heavenly court of justice.

Benjamin did not understand the significance of the scroll waving.

I'll teach my son to defend the Jews from pogroms.

CHAPTER 3

1931 Stranger in Oran

"THE NEWS FROM Morocco and Algeria is very alarming," Rabbi Navon addressed the group of men in Marseilles. "Vandals had broken into synagogues in Casablanca and Oran."

"Did they damage any Torah scrolls?" asked Rabbi Azulay. "This is always the most important issue."

"We are fortunate. All the Torah scrolls were in locked cabinets. I am afraid that the intruders were after more than damaging Torah scrolls. In both cases they tried, but did not succeed in breaking the door of the Rabbi's chambers."

"The publicly announced purpose of this meeting is known to you all," continued Rabbi Navon. "But the true purpose is confidential. You have been selected to go on a mission to accomplish an important task."

The Rabbi stopped talking and looked at the men who were listening to him.

They had arrived from Paris to meet with Rabbi Yossef Azulay, the Chief Rabbi of Marseilles. The group came with Rabbi Navon, the Chief Rabbi of France. It included his secretarial assistant, a rabbi and a merchant from Rouen, a rabbi and a merchant from Grenoble, one merchant from Nantes, one merchant from Troyes and two community leaders from Strasbourg. The visitors sat on both sides of a table at the center of the synagogue conference room.

"The two synagogues have large libraries," continued Rabbi Navon. "They both contain valuable ancient documents, manuscripts and Torah scrolls. Most are stored in locked chambers to protect them. Many scrolls were brought to North Africa by refugees from Spain and Portugal in the 15th century. During the last three years I have been concerned about the safety of these documents and the way they are stored."

"Why safety?" asked a merchant from Rouen.

"The two break-in attempts were simultaneous. I suspect that they were planned by an organized group and not by individual vandals or robbers."

"Do we know which group could have planned the robberies?" asked the Rouen merchant.

"We don't know. There are rumors that the riots in Palestine between the Arabs and the Jews may have encouraged some radical young Arabs to intentionally damage them or even destroy them. I suspect that it is an organized action."

"This is a matter that should be brought to the attention of French authorities," interrupted Rabbi Azulay. "The Jews in both Morocco and Algeria are full citizens of France. They should be protected by France."

"I have already talked to the security director of the '*France d'outre Mer*' Department, the government authority responsible for French territories in North Africa. However, your mission is not a matter of security. Your mission is to save the ancient documents.

You have been selected to go on a special mission to locate all documents that are older than 300 years, and to place them in a safe and protected environment."

The meeting lasted three hours with every rabbi presenting his opinion on the importance of the mission.

At the closing session, Rabbi Navon presented his concluding statement.

"It is agreed. I will return to my duties in Paris, and you will go on your mission in two groups. One will go to Casablanca and the other to Oran. Each group will spend at least five days reviewing the contents of each library with the cooperation of the local rabbis. Each group will prepare a written report of its finding and a detailed action plan. We will all meet in three weeks in Paris to review the two reports. I have already invited the Chief Rabbis of Casablanca and Oran to join us at the meeting next month."

On the next day, members of the Oran group embarked on a passenger ship and sailed from Marseilles across the Mediterranean to the Port of Oran. They traveled by bus along the coastline to the town of Mostaganem. A local delegation met them and placed individuals at the homes of local members of the Jewish community. They were invited for dinner at the home of the Mostaganem rabbi where they met the Chief Rabbi of Oran.

*   *   *

Saadia Leon arrived in Malta on a merchant ship from the Port of Jaffa in Palestine. He boarded another merchant ship to Oran. The sea was calm, the skies were blue; but he sensed that his visit in Algeria would be parched by hot Sahara desert winds.

It was a very hot Friday afternoon when Saadia disembarked at the port of Oran. He presented his French passport at the passport control desk.

"Do you live in Palestine?" asked the French passport control officer.

"I live in Jerusalem," Saadia responded.

"Your French passport was issued in Paris. How did you become French?"

"My grandfather was born in Oran. All Jews in Oran are French citizens."

The French officer looked suspiciously at Saadia and recorded his passport number. After writing the details of his conversation, he waved him to enter without checking his luggage.

Horse-drawn carriages, old trucks, street vendors and a few merchants wearing pony-tailed red Turkish tarbush hats crowded the port area. Saadia felt strange to see tarbush wearers. These hats had been very popular in Jerusalem, but they disappeared after General Allenby's British forces defeated the Ottoman Empire armed forces during the Great War.

He retained a porter to carry his luggage to the Oran bus station. An attending porter placed his luggage on the roof of the old and crowded bus. Passengers carrying their own luggage, bags and food, filled the bus to its full capacity. Two passengers carried live chickens causing great commotion. He sat next to an old man who continuously counted his Muslim beads. Saadia was right about the weather. Sahara desert winds brought the heat to an unbearable level in the crowded bus.

At the Mostaganem bus station, Saadia retained a private horse-drawn coach to take him to a hotel in the Jewish quarter of the town. He registered as a visiting merchant from Palestine and asked the concierge for the address of the local Jewish synagogue. Dressed in traditional Sabbath clothes, he walked to the synagogue and arrived half an hour before the evening services started. At the entrance to the sanctuary, the rabbi greeted him.

"Welcome to our synagogue," said the rabbi. "You are a stranger here. I have not seen you before. Where do you come from?"

"*Bon soir, Monsieur le Rabbin,*" answered Saadia nervously in French. "My name is Saadia Leon, I am a merchant from Jerusalem and I came to Algeria on business."

"It is a great honor to welcome a visitor from Jerusalem," said the rabbi, observing the mustached stranger and wondering if he was Jewish or an impostor. "It is not often that we have such a pleasure. What news do you bring from the land of milk and honey?"

"I regret that the news from Palestine is not as white as milk, nor is it as sweet as honey. When General Allenby entered Jerusalem with the British army, we danced in the streets of Jerusalem to celebrate the departure of the Turkish soldiers. We looked forward to a better future under the British, but we had chaos, especially after the massacres of 1920 and 1929.

"Many are unemployed in Palestine. There is a great shortage of flour, sugar, rice, cooking oil and many other necessities of life are scarce. Life is very hard. There are rumors that the British are planning to bring more supplies soon and that they are planning to initiate new construction projects which will create jobs for unskilled laborers."

The rabbi nodded his head, excused himself and left.

"How long will you stay in Mostaganem?" Asked David Attias, a local merchant.

"I have two business meetings in Oran," Saadia answered with a twitch. "I plan to depart on the next ship scheduled to sail to Jaffa on Wednesday."

"My daughter will be married on Monday," said Attias. "We will have a festive celebration to honor the bride and groom tomorrow night after the evening services at the synagogue. I hope that you will be able to join us."

"Is this an invitation?" asked Saadia.

David Attias often hosted out-of-town visitors in his house. He was a generous man, always ready to help the community and to invite visitors to his house. His house was very large with many rooms in which guests could have privacy and comfort.

"It certainly *is* an invitation. I am also inviting you to stay in my house during your visit in Mostaganem. If you accept my invitation, I can make arrangements to move your belongings from your hotel to my house on Sunday morning."

"Thank you for your hospitality," responded Saadia. "I'll be happy to accept your invitation to the celebration of your daughter's wedding, but I won't impose on your household as a house guest. I prefer to stay in my hotel. I'll be happy to visit your home before I leave."

The celebration party at the synagogue was very elaborate as befitted a successful merchant like David Attias. The social hall was large with a wrought-iron French crystal chandelier at the center of the domed ceiling. The guests were engaged in joyful conversations. The bride and groom at the center of a long head table covered with a blue tablecloth and a multitude of white flowers. On each side of the couple were eight chairs apparently for their parents, grandparents and dignitaries. A long food counter was set up along the opposite wall of the social hall with light summer dishes that seemed to have been prepared by a royal chef. They included a collection of oriental pastries, spinach-filled burekas, stuffed grape leaves, royally decorated salad plates, fruits, pistachio nuts, walnuts and other Middle Eastern delicacies. Waiters offered guests wine and arrack, the North African version of the Greek ouzo, the anisette flavored liqueur.

"This is my guest, Mr. Saadia Leon," David Attias introduced him to two guests. "He is visiting us from Jerusalem."

He stood aside listening to the conversation with a suspicious look. He wanted to know more about the stranger. The guests showered Saadia with questions about Jerusalem.

"Jerusalem is a most beautiful city," recited Saadia. "It is especially captivating when seen through its different shades of sunlight at different hours of a summer day. Prior to sunrise, the city's stone buildings are covered by soft and pale light from the eastern Judean Mountains, gradually changing shades from a grayish tint to white and finally to bright natural light as the sun appears in full view with a background of its clear blue skies. At sunset, the color of the buildings changes to full bright gold as the skies gradually change to red prior to disappearing at the western horizon. The golden reflection of the Jerusalem stones has been credited for calling the city 'Jerusalem of Gold'."

David Attias was impressed with the details of Saadia's responses and his familiarity with the Jerusalem Jewish customs that were very similar to the ones in the Oran community.

After the dinner and the celebration, Saadia and David Attias walked to join a group of four other men who were whispering among themselves. As they approached the four men, their whispering stopped.

"Please meet my guest, Mr. Saadia Leon," repeated Mr. Attias to the group. "He is visiting us from Palestine." Addressing one of the four men, he added "If you want to send a message to your uncle in Palestine, here is your opportunity. Mr. Leon will sail to Jaffa next week."

While the conversation with the four men was cordial, Saadia felt that they were trying to hide something from him. It seemed to him that they did not trust him. He started to worry. Are they questioning his identity as a Jerusalemite or as a Jew? Are they suspicious? Gradually he gained confidence. After all, he concluded, he was a stranger and they might have had some local secrets that they did not want strangers to hear. David Attias noticed the expression on the face of the visitor.

On Sunday, the man calling himself Saadia visited the Attias family at its elaborate house joining other guests and dignitaries at the continuing family wedding celebration. There was an extravagant display of dishes that included meat casseroles, baked fish casseroles with pine nuts, more stuffed grape leaves, stuffed cabbage, sautéed eggplant, meat stuffed pastries, baklava and many other delicacies, some that Saadia had never seen before.

David again engaged Saadia in a conversation concerning Jerusalem and listened patiently to his responses. There was something strange about him. He seemed to know the Jewish customs very well, but he lacked knowledge of Jewish history. David wanted to learn more about the stranger, but his responsibility as a host kept him occupied with other guests. David had some doubts about Saadia's honesty, but after hearing Saadia's tales about Jerusalem, he concluded that he had been wrong to doubt him.

Before his departure from Mostaganem, Saadia asked David Attias many questions about the Jewish Community in Oran. He wanted to know how many Jews lived there and if they had contacts with the Jewish community in France.

"We have very close contacts with the Jewish communities in Paris and in Marseilles," said David.

"Do you know any merchants in Marseilles?" asked Saadia. "I want to establish new contacts in France and to import French perfumes to Palestine."

"This is quite a coincidence. I have a cousin who lives in Marseilles. He can help you in making contacts with a perfume exporting merchant."

David was forthcoming in providing his guest with many details about the Jewish communities in Mostaganem, Oran and Marseilles. He bragged about the team of Jewish delegates from Paris who had visited Oran and spent three days in the Mostaganem Synagogue archives. They were looking for old documents which were stored there more than 300 years earlier.

Saadia knew what they were looking for.

CHAPTER 4

1931 The Tibet Parchment

A GREAT RESPONSIBILITY *was placed on my shoulders, a burden that is heavier than any load carried by the strongest slave.*

In preparation for the monthly council meeting in Lhasa, Tibet, Thubten Gyatso thought about his responsibilities to the Tibetan people. His health was gradually deteriorating. Since his selection in 1879 as the thirteenth Dalai Lama, he was the uncontested spiritual and political leader of the Tibetan people during the previous fifty-four years.

The day is approaching in which my advisory council of monks will have to select the next Dalai Lama.

He thought back to the time when he was a child in training under a regency council before assuming his office.

Thinking about my health is an exercise in futility. It just consumes time that I cannot afford to waste. My health and my life span are in the hands of Buddha. I am just the re-incarnation of a mortal Dalai Lama. I have many important projects that I want to accomplish before ending my time on earth.

*   *   *

"I prepared ten copies of the agenda for today's meeting," whispered Zinchu, the secretarial aide, as the Dalai Lama entered the conference room.

"Is it any different than what we agreed on yesterday?" asked the Dalai Lama.

"It is different. I added three items at the request of two members of the advisory council."

"Do not distribute the copies of the agenda. I want to discuss only one subject this morning."

Three monks dressed in copper colored robes and three laymen with traditional Tibetan robes entered the conference room, followed by Tsarong Dzasa, the Dalai Lama's aide, his diplomat and military advisor. They took their places at the conference table, talking quietly. They all stood up in silence when the Dalai Lama arrived accompanied by his secretarial aide Zinchu, until he gave them a signal to sit down.

"The council meeting scheduled for this morning will be postponed," the Dalai Lama announced.

"With your permission, your holiness, I would like to state an important matter," one of the council members dared to interrupt.

"You have my permission."

"Just a reminder that the messenger from India is scheduled to meet with you tomorrow, and we should discuss his visit."

"I did not forget. The matter is on the agenda and we will discuss it later this afternoon.

"Only one subject will be on this morning's agenda. We are facing a multitude of new complex problems that we must deal with soon. They may not seem urgent today, but we did not consider them in the past. We are receiving troubling news from many sources, news that is of great concern to Tibet."

"What is the urgency?" asked a council member.

"A decade ago the Great War ended and its ripple effects have not subsided," continued the Dalai Lama. "The economic recession in America has resulted in a major depression. A severe worldwide economic depression is on the horizon. There is hunger in Africa, political instability in Europe, political disputes between China and Japan—just to list a few.

"I sense that a greater war is looming on the horizon, a war in which many nations will be fighting. It may be a larger and more devastating world war. Such a war, if it will occur, will surely have great impact on the Tibetan people. Tibet could fall into an international trap between China and India. It is only prudent for us to be concerned, to examine our situation and to prepare contingency action plans for the future. We must implement these actions in preparation for harder times. This is the subject that I want to discuss today and to hear your opinions and your suggestions on how to address my concern in an open discussion."

The council meeting was still in full session two hours later when a knock on the door interrupted the discussion.

A messenger entered the room, approached the Dalai Lama and handed him a note. The Dalai Lama read it and immediately suspended the meeting.

"We will re-convene this evening," He announced. "An unexpected visitor is waiting for me in my chambers. Be prepared to present your recommendations tonight."

He left the conference room in haste, followed by his secretarial aide.

Returning to his office, Thubten Gyatso found the messenger from the British Governor-General of India waiting for him together with Shamar, the Tibetan Ambassador to New Delhi. He had anticipated their arrival in Lhasa, but it was scheduled for the following day. *His sudden appearance does not bode well. He probably brought important news, maybe a message from the King of England.*

"Welcome to Lhasa," the Dalai Lama greeted the highly-placed British guest. "I did not expect to meet you today, but I am always pleased to see a distinguished representative of his majesty, the King of England."

"I regret that I arrived earlier than planned," stated the governor. "I had no choice in the matter. I arrived late yesterday and I must leave Lhasa today to meet with our trade agent in the city of Gyangze."

"I hope that your journey from New Delhi was not too difficult. India is our next door neighbor, but crossing the Himalaya mountain range is not a simple journey."

"It was a long journey, but I am in the service of His Majesty, and I follow his orders."

"I hope that you brought good news from London."

"His Majesty, the king, sent his regards to you. He considers Tibet an important friend of the British people. In response to your request, the British Prime Minister has instructed me to provide you with all the assistance that India can offer. India will increase the shipment of the rice and oil, but only by twenty five percent and not by the fifty percent that you requested. We will supply all the medical supplies to your Medical College in Jokhang, but we will not be able to appoint this year the two professors that you need at the college."

"Well, that is not the good news that I expected, but it is not bad news," said the Dalai Lama. "Please convey my gratitude to His Majesty, the King, and to the Prime Minister."

"Yes it is good news, but I am afraid that I also have other news. There is great turmoil in India. Mahatma Gandhi has initiated civil disobedience to protest British Empire laws. The Viceroy of India is concerned that it will encourage a violent uprising, especially among radical Muslims in the Kashmir territory of India. Such violence may spread to our neighbors in Nepal and even to Tibet. His majesty, the king, instructed me to assure you that the British will provide you with the assistance needed to fight such insurgencies."

"That is bad news for us," the face of the Dalai Lama paled with worry. "We are not equipped to handle violent intruders from India."

*   *   *

After reviewing the opinions of his advisory council, the Dalai Lama appointed a senior council member to prepare a contingency plan on how Tibet could defend itself by supporting the British against insurgents or invaders. He wanted to protect the autonomous independence of Tibet and its unique culture.

"We must learn from other nations," he said to his Council members. "We must gather information about other nations which have been overrun by invading armies. To avoid losing our Tibetan culture, we must learn from them how to conduct our life, if Tibet ever becomes occupied by foreigners."

"Shamar should be consulted on this matter," interrupted his aide Tsarong Dzasa. "He is the most experienced diplomat that we have. With his wisdom, he could bring new ideas and draft guidelines for such a contingency plan."

"I already assigned that task to Shamar last night," responded the Dalai Lama. "As our Ambassador to New Delhi, he escorted the British messenger from India. He is waiting to be invited to join us."

He instructed his secretarial aide to bring Shamar to the meeting.

"Your present visit to Lhasa is of great importance," said the Dalai Lama to Shamar after his arrival. "You have already been informed about the reason for this meeting. Please repeat to our council members your advice on this matter and how we can learn from the experience of other nations."

"Your holiness, you have taken the proper first steps," responded Shamar. "You are our great leader, and you are also a philosopher who has studied and written many words of wisdom. I want to provide information about a unique people."

"Which nation do you refer to?" asked the Dalai Lama. "Are you thinking about the Indian people?"

"India is only one of the protectorates of Britain. India certainly has a long history of peace and war that is known to you. However, none of the British protectorates has a documented history that could compare to that of Palestine. It is a small territory that was part of the Ottoman Empire until the Great World War. The League of Nations gave it to Britain after the war with a mandate to prepare it as an independent homeland for the Jews who were exiled from it by the Romans. The Jewish people have a documented history dating back to Biblical times over a period of more than three thousand years.

"When I arrived in Lhasa yesterday, one of my assistants in Tibet gave me two items which I brought with me. They are surely of interest to us because they are about the Jewish people. He informed me that they were found last week in a cave in a Tibetan mountain."

Shamar retrieved a small package from his bag and presented it to the Dalai Lama.

"What are these items?" asked Thubten Gyatso.

"The cylinder includes an ancient document," responded Shamar while opening it. "It includes a parchment with an inscription we cannot decipher. I inspected the strange letters that appeared on the parchment, but I cannot read them. I think that it is an ancient Hebrew inscription."

"How do you know that it is in Hebrew if you can't read it?" asked the Dalai Lama.

"I *do* know that the other item found with the parchment belongs to the Jewish people," responded Shamar. "It is an ancient Shofar, the ram's horn that Jewish people use as a musical trumpet on their High Holidays. It is similar to the ones used by Joshua during the battle of Jericho."

"What is your recommendation?" asked the Dalai Lama.

"The parchment may have significant information," said Shamar. "We should keep the two items in a safe location until we find a Jewish scholar who could evaluate them and decipher the parchment inscription."

The Dalai Lama instructed his aide to find such a scholar. He wanted to learn more about the findings, but other matters of state took priority.

Thubten Gyatso was familiar with the history of the Jewish people, but he wanted to learn more on how they survived during two thousand years of exile. He knew about their Biblical history, about their exile to Babylon and their return to rebuild their destroyed temple. He was always amazed by the ability of the Jewish people to endure and survive twenty centuries of wandering from country to country as refugees. He knew that they suffered many pogroms in many countries, tortured by the Spanish Inquisition and expelled from Spain and Portugal in the 15th century. However, he knew very little about their recent history, and he wanted to know how that nation survived all these catastrophic events. He wanted to learn more.

The thirteenth Dalai Lama, Thubten Gyatso, never had his question answered. He died in 1933.

The new Gyatso was chosen to be the next Dalai Lama in 1935 when he was still a child. In 1940, he started a ten-year regency period under the tutorship of monks selected by his predecessor.

In 1950, the new Gyatso assumed full responsibility as the fourteenth Dalai Lama.

CHAPTER 5

1931-1945

1931

"DO YOU HAVE any good news for me today?" The Grand Mufti asked when Ibn Najad entered his office in Jerusalem.

"Yes. At our last meeting, we discussed my plan to send several of my senior members on fact-finding missions to Jewish communities. Since then, I sent one man to Rome, another to Cairo and Alexandria, and a third man to Casablanca and Oran. My spy brought important information from Oran.

"Kassem Ibn Masood is the man. He was born in a Jaffa street where many Jews lived. His Jewish friends invited him often to their homes and the neighborhood synagogue, where he learned Jewish holy days customs. He speaks fluent Hebrew and is very intelligent."

"Kassem's background sounds important," interrupted the Mufti. "But I am more interested in the news, which you say is 'good news'."

"He visited a synagogue in Casablanca and another one in a town near the City of Oran. In both places, he introduced himself as a Jewish merchant from Jerusalem. In Oran, a local merchant invited him to his home where he heard rumors that may be of interest to us.

"During the last nineteen centuries, the Jews have been searching for the gold Menorah and the Ark of the Covenant from the Jewish Temple in Jerusalem. Nobody knows if the Romans took them or if the Jews hid them before the Roman army entered the city.

"Kassem reports that a delegation of Jewish scholars from France visited the archives of the Casablanca and Oran synagogues looking for some old documents and manuscripts which were in sealed chambers. He overheard a man whispering about a rumor on a recent discovery of a manuscript from the time of the Greeks with information on the Maccabees. Another man claimed that it was not a rumor and that another sheepskin scroll was found. The rumor is that one of the documents includes information on the location of the golden Menorah hidden by the defenders of Jerusalem.

"If the rumor is true, the discovery of any information on the Menorah site will be of great psychological value to the Jews, especially if the parchments confirm that the Jewish Temple was on the present site of the Dome of the Rock, known to the Jews as the Temple Mount. Consequently, it would damage the Arab claim that the Temple was elsewhere. It would also embolden the Jewish claim to the site of the Al-Aksa Mosque in Jerusalem. They may even start planning the construction of a Third Temple on the site of the Dome of the Rock, which, as you know, was built in the seventh century by Al-Maliki, the Caliph of Baghdad."

"Allah is great," the Mufti burst into explosive laughter. "You have a very rich and fertile imagination. Do you really expect to find the Menorah? Neither the Jews nor we will ever find it. I don't believe *you* will find it, no matter how much money we invest in this project."

"Finding the Menorah is not my objective. I am only interested in the parchment and the scroll. I can use them to advance our cause. Naturally, if we find the Menorah, we will melt it and the gold will help finance our operation."

"Well, well," Haj Amin laughed even louder. "You really have an exceptional imagination. You will never find the Menorah, and the Jews will never build a Third Temple because they will argue endlessly among themselves about it. More importantly, they won't be here much longer. We'll throw them into the sea. Soon there will not be a single Jew in Jerusalem, just as we killed them in Hebron."

"I plan to send Kassem back to Oran," Ibn Najad ignored the Mufti's laughter. "I want to confirm the rumor and to obtain as much information as possible about the documents. If we succeed in learning where the documents are located, I'll send a team of operatives to steal them and bring them to me. If they are in Aramaic, I could read them. If they are in ancient Hebrew, or in ancient Greek, I will find a scientist to decipher them.

"If we have possession of the documents, we could use them to our advantage by modifying them, destroying them or even creating fake ones to replace the originals."

"Such a project will require a considerable increase in our budget."

"With your consent, I will prepare a proposal with details on the financial requirements to implement this plan."

"It is imperative that your plan on this matter is kept secret." Haj Amin interrupted him again. "To keep this project from being discovered, you should periodically issue news releases on our search for the lost parts of the Koran. It will be a tactical diversion to keep the world attention on the Koran research and not on your secret search of the ancient Hebrew documents."

"I will also expand our operation in other countries. To gather information from different languages, I will not limit our staff to Arabs. We could include other Muslims from Turkey, Serbia, Pakistan, India, China, Tibet and other Asian countries for recruiting individuals who are interested in joining us to promote Islam."

Following a series of questions and answers, Haj Amin praised Ibn Najad and assured him that the he will review and approve his proposed new budget favorably if it is reasonable. He only demanded a detailed monthly written report on the operation and a monthly meeting with him in either Jerusalem or Beirut. Ibn Najad left the meeting with an exhilarating feeling of success.

*　　*　　*

Ibn Najad returned to his headquarters in Baghdad. He entered his new private study at midnight and locked the door behind him. As he sat at his desk, he contemplated the pros and cons of his schemes. He had not revealed all their details to the Mufti.

> *No one, but me, could take the credit for these*
> *schemes when they succeed. Haj Amin would*
> *undoubtedly elevate me to a more prominent position.*
> *Eventually, I might even become his successor. Now,*
> *wouldn't that be something?*

As he clarified his thoughts, he opened a bottom drawer of his desk. He took out one of the six old parchments he had purchased from an antique dealer in a Beirut flea market. He passed the palm of his hand gently on the surface of the sheepskin parchment as though it were the soft skin of a baby. He walked back to the door to check again that it was locked. He walked back to his desk, again inspecting the surface of the parchment, this time with a magnifying glass. He concluded that its yellow tint gave it the apparent authenticity of an old parchment.

He retrieved the draft of the Aramaic text he had prepared several days earlier. He had learned the ancient Aramaic language at Oxford University. He started to copy the text to the yellow parchment using the old ink that he still had from his university days. He distorted most letters and slanted others so much that he had difficulty reading them. When he finished writing the inscription, he again inspected every letter with a magnifying glass. He then took a match and lit the candle on his desk. Lifting the parchment, he passed it over the candle flame until many of the letters were faded and hard to read. He passed the rims of the parchment above the flame until they were party burned. He passed his hand over the warm surface of the parchment to cause additional distortion of the letters.

Ibn Najad sat quietly at his desk, looking at the finished product with great satisfaction. While waiting for the ink on the parchment to dry, he got up and walked back and forth in his room, like an expectant father waiting for a newborn baby. Many schemes presented themselves in his mind on how he would best use the new "ancient" parchment. They appeared and disappeared, one following another, like a row of ducklings following their mother on a lake. He suddenly smiled. He figured out how he would use this parchment in his first scheme.

After the ink on the parchment was completely dry, he concluded with a smile that his new creation was ready to be stored in a controlled environment to enhance its appearance as very aged. Ibn Najad rolled the parchment and placed it in his office safe. It was time to put this first of his six parchments to use in his grand scheme.

* * *

1932

Ibn Najad met with his former deputy Mu-alem from the days of the Hebron riots. He invited him for dinner during one of his visits in Jerusalem.

"It is good to exchange memories from the days of the Hebron riots. We were three years younger and thought we could conquer the universe. Now we are mature and know that we can't conquer the world."

"I still consider myself young, Ibn Najad. I know that I can't conquer the world, but I want to conquer Palestine."

"You can help us in our struggle."

"I am too old for riots. I now have a family to feed."

"I have a small job that must be done this week. You won't need your scimitar or your brass knuckles."

"I am always ready to help you, Ibn-Najad".

"I have six important documents. I know that you have an open pit in the basement of your father's farmhouse. I want you to keep them for me in the ground until I am ready to take them back. I want to accelerate their appearance as ancient documents."

"I have a better place in my own home. It will be safer where I can check them often. I'll be happy to help you."

"Mu-alem, I know I can rely on you."

"When will you need them?"

"I don't know now. I will send you a messenger when they are ready. He will use the same code word we used in Hebron. Do you still remember it?"

"How can I forget it? We used it on the night we killed the old Rabbi in Hebron."

*   *   *

1936

It was Friday morning at the Jerusalem Makhane-Yehudah farmers market.

Ibn Najad walked to survey the Jewish vendors and the shoppers.

"Oranges! Grapefruits! Eggplants! Try our watermelons on the knife!"

A produce vendor announced his products to the constantly moving march of women and old men who came to buy fruits and vegetables in preparation for the Sabbath.

"What are watermelons on the knife?" a young woman asked the vendor.

"You never heard of the knife?" the vendor asked back. "Have you been living on the moon?"

"It's my first visit to Palestine. I am a visitor from Turkey."

"Here in Jerusalem we have a special way to please our customers. I guarantee my watermelons' sweetness. If you want, I'll cut piece with my knife for you to taste. If it isn't sweet, you won't have to buy it. This is what we call a knife guarantee."

Ibn-Najad walked on, observing the mass of shoppers. A touch of a smile spread on his face. He was pleased with what he saw.

He stopped at another fruit stand.

A husky young man had a large basket on his back strapped by a rope around his shoulders. A middle-aged woman placed in his basket a large bag of potatoes, twenty oranges, a few grapefruits, bananas, lemons and an assortment of candies.

He remembered his youth. He sometimes worked as a porter at the farmers market. Jewish shoppers were generous tippers.

He walked on.

He saw the two young men waiting at the corner.

"Is everything according to plan?'" He asked in a whisper without stopping.

The tall one nodded his head. "Get out fast. You have ten minutes to return to the old city."

Ibn Najad increased his pace followed by his two friends.

Ten minutes later, the bomb exploded. The blast killed twenty-seven Jewish shoppers and injured forty-two.

Ibn Najad agreed to build the non-violent Bismillah as Haj Amin instructed, but he did not feel obligated to abandon his old followers from the days of the Hebron riots.

* * *

1939

"What news do you bring, Ibn Najad?"

"Nine years have past since I accepted your appointment to establish Bismillah," Ibn Najad confronted Haj Amin.

"You have done a good job. You built a vast organization that gathered important information for our cause."

"I don't know if it was important. I *do* know that nine years have past and we have not succeeded in our struggle against the Jews. The riots of 1929 were repeated and intensified in 1936 and this year, but I was not called to organize them. After nine years the Jews are getting stronger every day,"

"I have a great plan to change the situation."

"Maybe you do, but I am not part of it. I was an action man and you converted me to a manager of an espionage network and an administrator of a non-violent organization. I built a large network of spies but nothing is done with the information that they gather. Hitler is talking about solving the Jewish problem in Europe. We should join forces with him and ask him to help us solve the Jewish problem in Palestine. Bismillah can spy for him and build a fifth column here to supply military information to the Germans. My spies are very good and I am sure that the Germans will appreciate our cooperation."

"I am pleased to hear your frustration."

Ibn Najad was stunned.

I came to complain and Haj Amin is pleased?

"I invited you to talk about the future of Bismillah, but you already defined it today. I like your ideas, they coincide with mine."

Ibn Najad could not understand the Mufti's statement.

"I am going to Berlin to meet with Adolf Himmler to implement my plan. If he will accept my proposal, I will not return to Jerusalem. You will fight here and I will fight there."

*   *   *

1940

"Thank you for inviting me to Berlin," Haj Amin expressed his gratitude.

"I was very pleased with your riots against the Jews in Palestine, in 1936 and 1939," Adolf Eichman was delighted. "You are a true friend of the Third Reich. The Fuhrer is pleased."

"Your financial support is greatly appreciated," Haj Amin reacted. "But now I need different assistance. I need your advice on how to settle the Jewish problem in Palestine."

"Your request is music to my ears."

"I want to visit a Jewish concentration camp. I want to learn how you deal with the Jewish problem in Germany."

"It will be easy to arrange, but one visit will not provide you with a solution."

"It will provide me with a lesson."

"I'll let you in on a secret. A few of the concentration camps will be extermination camps. After we complete our campaign, we'll help you build a similar concentration and extermination camp in Palestine."

Haj Amin could not believe Eichman's offer.

"Meanwhile, we invite you to stay in Berlin until our victory will be achieved."

Haj Amin spent the rest of World War II as Hitler's special guest in Berlin.

CHAPTER 6

1946-1950

1946

"I SAW YOUR high school teacher in the market today," Sima said to her son Avner. "She told me about your essay on the Maccabees."

"What did she tell you?" Avner's heart beat faster.

"She thinks you're an excellent student. She loves your imaginary dialogue between Judah the Maccabee, and you."

"Did she say anything about the literary competition? I entered the story for the contest."

"Don't you know?"

"What should I know?"

"They will announce tomorrow that you are the first prize winner of the competition."

"Hooray!" shouted Avner with delight. "This land of Judea inspires me, Ima. I guess this showed in my essay. It's exciting to imagine the ingenuity of Judah and his Maccabee followers."

Avner's mother's eyes turned to heaven as he continued. It was a story she had heard all too often in the last few weeks. His eyes sparkled when he talked about the Maccabees.

"I admire them, not only for their bravery in battle. Their clever strategies made their success possible. They inspired the nation. I have been reading about them, Ima, did you know? They were masters of planning and implementing battle tactics that enabled their small number of volunteers to overcome a much larger Seleucid Greek army. They remind me of the young shepherd David who faced the enormous Goliath, and won."

Avner's voice trailed off when he saw his mother divert her attention from him and start reading a newspaper. His fascination was obviously not shared by everyone. But for him, the Maccabees represented the greatness of his country. He would draw strength from these ancient heroes in the days to come.

They did not possess the weapons, the supplies, the chariots and the battering rams like the Greeks, but they succeeded in expelling their oppressors and in starting the Hashmonean era of independence that lasted more than a century. How did they do it?

While his classmates played games, Avner read books. He preferred to quench his thirst for knowledge rather than waste time in trivial entertainments. He was an avid reader of history. His favorites included *The War of the Jews against the Romans* by Josephus Flavius, *The Rise and Fall of the Roman Empire, Samson* by Ze'ev Jabotinsky, *The Kuzari* by Yehudah Halevi and similar philosophy and adventure books.

Avner also read about the Jewish partisans who fought against the Nazis in Europe. He learned the Hebrew translation of their song:

> *Do not say that this is my last road*
> *That a cloud blocked the light of the day*

The day we have longed for will come
And our marching will thunder—we are here.

The words of the song lit a spark in Avner's heart. He admired the Jewish partisans, viewing them as heirs of the Maccabees who fought the Seleucid Greeks over twenty centuries earlier.

After the war, the refusal of the British authorities to allow holocaust survivors from entering Palestine had an intense impact on Avner. He witnessed a confrontation between a British naval destroyer and a ship of these Jewish refugees who tried to land near a Haifa beach. He later read a report written by the captain of the ship known as "The Chaim Arlozorov". As it approached the shores of Haifa with 1346 immigrants in February, 1947, it was surrounded by four British naval destroyers.

The Arlozorov ship captain's report included a dialogue on a loudspeaker between the captain and the British Navy commander:

British navy destroyer:

"Jewish refugees, you are entering the territorial waters of Palestine illegally. His Majesty's destroyers will escort you to the island of Cyprus, where you will be placed in a camp until your fate is determined."

The Arlozorov Captain:

"British sailors, we are Jewish refugees returning to our homeland after a long exile and the extermination of millions of Jews by the Nazis. You are breaking human laws by preventing us from entering our homeland. This is our land. It will be ours. No one will stop us."

British navy destroyer:

"When you cross the territorial boundary of Palestine, we shall fire at you."

Arlozorov captain: (To the refugees on his ship)

"Brothers and sisters, in a few minutes we shall enter the waters of our homeland. You all know your duties. If we are brave, this land will be ours. No one will be able to stop us. Let us sing our national anthem, Hatikva."

British navy destroyer:

"Who is the captain of your ship, who endangers your lives?"

Arlozorov captain record:

(A ten year old boy was standing near me. I called him over, took him to my room, gave him my gold-decorated captain's hat and my binoculars. I took him to the captain's bridge. The boy stood there all alone facing the British ship)

Arlozorov captain:

"British sailors, look at our young captain. Because of him, and in his name, we will fight you if you fire at us."

Arlozorov captain record:

The destroyer backed 100 meters and fired a warning shot. We ordered the women and the children to the bottom of the ship, and 700 men remained on the deck. The British sailors tried to board the ship under fire, but they were held back by our fire. There were many casualties on both sides, and our ship managed to pull away from the destroyers only to hit a rock and run aground outside the Bat-Galim shore of Haifa. All the immigrants were eventually taken to a concentration camp in Cyprus.

Avner admired the brave refugees and their leaders. They were in a crowded passenger ship facing a Royal British navy destroyer, inspired just like his heroes of old. But were they the last Maccabees?

He tried to imagine the joy and anger of the ship's refugees.

They survived concentration camps and crematoriums, dreaming of a new life in Palestine. They could see Mount Carmel from the deck. They thought they had arrived to safety and a new beginning. So close, but yet so far—blocked by British destroyers.

This episode, though it ended with the apprehension of the refugees, generated a wave of pride among the Jewish youth of the country. It inspired many young men and women to join one of the three underground organizations to fight the British so that refugees could enter the country. Avner was invited to join the Etzel "National Military Organization", which was known as the "Irgun". Avner was also invited to join the Haganah, but the Irgun most matched his vision of the Maccabees. Others joined Lechi, a smaller underground force.

The Irgun was an underground military organization created by the followers of Ze'ev Jabotinsky for the purpose of training Jewish youth in Palestine to defend the homeland from Arab attacks and to prepare them for the upcoming revolt to establish a Jewish state in Palestine. The British government referred to Irgun members as terrorists, while the Irgun youth considered themselves freedom fighters dedicated to provide a safe home for the holocaust survivors.

When Jewish partisans killed Nazis, would anybody describe them as terrorists? The fight against the British, then, was justified for its purpose was saving lives of holocaust survivors.

Individuals could join the Irgun only after a careful investigation of their dedication to the cause, their ability to maintain the strict secrecy required and their willingness to sacrifice their life, if necessary.

The Irgun had strict rules of secrecy in its operations. Avner did not know the real names of any members outside his cell. It was a measure taken to insure that he would not be able, even under torture by the British, to reveal the names of more than few members. He acquired an underground code name. He did not know the real name of his commander. He learned the use of revolvers, rifles, sub-machine guns, light-machine guns and hand grenades. The basic training was conducted in secret locations—either in the heavily wooded hills of Mount Carmel or in different Haifa buildings at night.

He read many of Jabotinsky's lectures on the fate of the Jewish people and on his warnings in the thirties about the coming Holocaust in Europe. Irgun ideological lectures emphasized the need to fight the British Mandate in Palestine to achieve the Zionist goal of establishing a free Jewish state in Palestine.

*   *   *

"Sorry to see you here, Bashir," Kassem Ibn Masood welcomed the elder son of Ibn Najad at the courtyard of the prison compound.

"My father told me that you were arrested by the British police after the attack on the farmers market, but I didn't expect to see you in Acre Prison."

"What happened?"

"Two policemen came to our house and said I had to go with them to the police station to answer a few questions."

"What did they want to know?"

"Nothing, the whole arrest was a ruse. My father, Ibn Najad, was at the office of the British detective when they brought me to the station."

"Was he arrested too?"

"No, he was there to tell me that my arrest was a ploy and that he was working with the British against the Jews."

"A ploy? What do you mean?"

"The British want to calm the Jewish leaders in Palestine. They want to demonstrate that they do not favor the Arabs. Jewish underground fighters are imprisoned here and eight Irgun fighters were sent to the gallows here. There are sixty Irgun members and eleven Lechi members, but only six Arab political prisoners. There are 400 Arab criminals and the British want to increase the number of political Arabs."

"But why did they include you? You are the son of a prominent leader and a close friend of the British High Commissioner."

"My father suggested it to show that even prominent Arab families can be included."

"Did he say anything about me?"

"Yes, Kassem. He gave me a message for you. He wants you to organize the imprisoned Bismillah members."

A loud explosion and a machine-gun fire shattered the silence of the afternoon. The three-dozen Arab prisoners in the courtyard panicked. They ran into the prison building and away from the location of the explosion.

Once inside, they saw a group of Jewish prisoners running in the opposite direction shouting in Arabic:

"The prison compound is now under control of the Irgun. Get out of the way. Go to your cells and wait there. You will not be harmed if you don't interfere with us. We placed all the British prison guards in locked cells."

Two groups of Irgun members, dressed in British soldiers' uniforms, gave instructions in Hebrew to their fellow imprisoned fighters, guiding them to the large hole formed by the exploding bomb on the external prison wall. One by one, more than thirty Jewish fighters went quickly through the breach and jumped from the second floor into an army truck parked outside. When the first truck was full and drove away, another vehicle pulled in to take the remaining Irgun and Lechi escapees.

"This is your opportunity to get out of jail, Kassem." Bashir knew how to take advantage of opportunities.

"Will you come with me, Bashir?"

"No, I will stay and help other imprisoned Bismillah members to escape. I will be set free in a few days."

"Where is the British Army? How can this great escape be possible?"

"The Irgun chose a convenient time. I saw the whole regiment of the British Acre command on the beach. They are swimming. It will take them some time before they return to Acre."

Twenty Irgun and seven Lechi fighters escaped. Nine were killed in clashes with the British Army. Eight escapees were caught and returned to prison. 180 Arab prisoners escaped as well, including Kassem.

*   *   *

Following the Irgun officers training course, Avner attained the rank of lieutenant and assumed command of a platoon. Several weeks later, the British police surprised another group of Irgun trainees, arrested them and spent them for an extended stay in prison. Some were sent to the British concentration camp in Asmara, Eritrea, where 251 members of the Irgun and Lechi underground members were jailed until the State of Israel was established in 1948.

In contrast to the ideology of the Irgun, the Haganah organization chose to wait for the British to implement the Balfour Declaration plan of establishing a Jewish homeland in Palestine. Its members were ordered to stop the Irgun fighting against the British. A conflict of policies developed, causing friction between the two groups. This was especially true in Haifa where the Haganah was very strong. When the British police discovered that Avner was a member of the Irgun, he had to leave Haifa and move to Tel-Aviv where he trained fighters and worked in manufacturing Irgun-designed sub-machine guns at daytime.

1947

Tel-Aviv became one of the central front lines between the Jewish and the Arab sides in Palestine.

"This is not Hebron. This is our stronghold Jaffa."

"I know, my friend and teacher," Ibn Najad responded to his village Mukhtar. "You left the village to guide the battle of Jaffa, and I gathered eighty young men who volunteered to spread fear among the Jews in Tel Aviv."

"Your mission is important. Tel Aviv is the main reservoir of Jewish fighting personnel. The more havoc you cause, the more Jewish young men will be needed to defend Tel-Aviv until the Egyptian navy arrives."

"Last week my men threw hand grenades into three stores and two schools. My snipers shot seven Jews in Tel Aviv's Allenby Street. Now that the British have left Tel Aviv, we operate there freely."

"You are too confident. You should remember that Tel Aviv is the stronghold of the Irgun."

"I am aware of their fighters, but they cannot stop my snipers who are on the top of the highest minaret of the Jaffa Mosque, unless they capture Jaffa."

"Don't worry. The British army will defend Jaffa. The British are on our side. They hate the Jews more than we do. The Irgun will never be able to capture Jaffa."

1948

The Irgun launched the attack on Jaffa in April of 1948. Its major objective was to prevent the Egyptian navy from landing large Arab forces there. Such an Egyptian beachhead could have spelled the end of Tel Aviv and, probably the end of the Jewish hopes to survive the Arab onslaught of May. Two attacking Irgun companies faced several British army units whose task was to defend the Arab forces and prevent the Jewish forces from overtaking Arab positions.

"Station 18 calling! Station 18 calling!—Send a medic and three stretchers immediately," Avner heard the SOS call from the front line. "A British tank shell hit our position and we are left with only three fighters manning it."

"A medic and two stretchers are on the way." Avner responded from his Irgun command post. "A third one will follow."

"Gideon!" Avner told his company commander. "I must rush to help station 18 with the only five fighters that I kept on reserve. We must stop the advance of the British tank."

"Go ahead. I'll assign someone to replace you at the command center," Gideon gave his consent.

"To reach station 18, we'll have to cross the street under the tank fire." Avner explained to his five fighters. "But we will pass behind a wall of sandbags that were placed across the street last night. They will protect us from being seen by the tank."

When Avner noticed a lull in the tank shelling, he led his five fighters as they crawled behind the sandbags barricade. When they were half way across the street, a British tank shell hit their cover. Two of Avner's fighters were killed instantly, but Avner and his remaining three fighters managed to reach the desired building on the other side of the street.

Avner took command of the building. He assigned two fighters to the first floor and climbed to the roof to inspect the injured Irgun fighters. Within a few minutes, a brave nurse arrived with four other young teenage boys who volunteered as stretcher carriers.

"Who sent young teenagers to the front line?" asked one of his fighters with anger.

"Age does not count in our fight for survival." Avner informed the fighter. "We need everyone who is able. Even fourteen year old boys, if they are able and willing to volunteer. If we lose this battle, the Egyptian army will be here next week, and our dream of an independent Jewish state will be gone forever."

Avner replaced the machine gunner who was injured. He instructed the second machine gunner to prepare the rifle-propelled Molotov cocktails for use against the tank.

The tank slowly advanced toward their position while both machine guns showered it with bullets. The tank driver rotated its canon to face the roof. Not knowing if he should wait until the tank came closer, Avner made the decision of his life.

If I fire the Molotov cocktails now, they may not reach the tank. If I wait until the tank is closer, it may be too late. We may not survive the next shell.

He gave the order. The first Molotov fired by his companion reached far enough, but missed the tank. He fired his Molotov at the same time that the next shell was fired. The tank was on fire and the shell hit the first floor of his building. A second shell followed and the tank driver jumped out of the tank. The second shell hit the roof position.

"I did not know I was injured and I did not feel any pain," Avner told the second Irgun nurse who arrived after his injury. "I was too pre-occupied attempting to help my fellow Irgun fighter. A large shell fragment hit him in his stomach and I could see his exposed intestines. When I tried to move toward him, I could not move my foot. I also felt blood running down my left cheek."

"I can see it well," said the nurse. "One shell fragment hit your skull and another entered your left foot."

Two stretcher-bearers carried Avner downstairs to wait for the battlefront ambulance. The ambulance, with two other Irgun nurses, took him and another injured fighter to the Irgun field hospital inside Tel Aviv. Other Irgun fighters came to replace him and to hold station 18.

Next day, Avner learned that Menachem Begin gave the British Army an ultimatum: if the shelling did not stop by 12:00 noon, the Irgun would start shelling the British headquarters in Jaffa, where 4500 British soldiers were preparing an attack on Tel Aviv. The ultimatum worked. The British stopped their attack, and station 18 never fell.

Two days later, the Arab forces in Jaffa surrendered and the Egyptian navy never arrived.

When Menachem Begin dissolved the Irgun, Avner joined the Army of the new State of Israel. As a lieutenant in the Armored Corps, Avner participated in many battles during Israel's War of Independence.

CHAPTER 7

1950-1959

1950

"WHAT ARE YOUR plans, now that our War of Independence is over?" Benjamin asked his son Avner.

"First I want to document my battle experiences and the heroic cases of Israeli soldiers who fought against seven invading armies when the State of Israel faced a looming destruction."

"But what's your plan for your future?"

"Oh! I am philosophical. I'm influenced by my love of history and philosophy. I compare my life to a wanderer arriving at an intersection on the road, not knowing if he should turn right or left or just move forward. Life presents many conflicting choices. It offers too many beguiling doors through which a person can walk in search of his destiny. If I choose the wrong door, my destiny may bring me to music while my passion should guide me through the door of engineering or history or archaeology. How can a young man know which door to choose when he faces three or five or seventeen doors? Fortunate are those who walk through the door of their passion. I struggle with selecting the right door. Wherever you dig in Israel, your shovel will find history. But the sciences fascinate me. I think that I'll choose the engineering door, which may not be an easy door to enter, but I'll try.

"If I don't aim high, I will not accomplish anything meaningful in my life. I applied to the Sorbonne and Harvard, knowing I may not be accepted by either. I want to be an engineer, but maybe one day I'll also be an archaeologist. Time will tell."

*   *   *

1952

At Harvard, Avner's life was a continuous series of lectures and laboratory projects in weird combinations of physics and English, chemistry and American history, calculus and psychology, electronics and political science. He was surrounded by American students who had just returned from fighting during the Korean War, and whose college tuition was paid by the United States GI Bill of Rights. His world was a room of solitude and loneliness. He had no family in America and he longed for the moment when he would complete his studies and return to the land that he loved—the land of Israel.

1953

Avner met Elaine. She was a beautiful, petite student with brown hair and bright, hazel eyes that fascinated him. They met when she attended an archaeology lecture he gave at a local synagogue.

Avner, in contrast to Elaine, was quite tall, with dark hair that made him feel clumsy when he faced one of his short professors who had blond hair. Although motivated in his studies and self-confident, he became downright bashful in the presence of Elaine.

People talk of love at first sight, but for Avner, meeting Elaine was more like being hit by lightning; like a sudden guiding light in the somber tunnel of loneliness. She opened his eyes with her beauty, her charm, her humility and her wisdom. She revealed to him the meaning of joy. She transformed his loneliness into excitement. He found in her the motivation to look at life with a new light, a light that brought an end to his dark solitude. From the moment that he met her he knew that he wanted her to be his partner in life and share with him the rest of his days on earth, if she would have him.

1955

Avner and Elaine were married in Boston.

Elaine had exceptional artistic talent. Her love for art was encompassing. Knowing that she could not afford to own oil paintings of French impressionists like Renoir or Sisley, she settled for her own oil canvasses. Avner praised her for her home—created art. He slowly added serigraphs and a few oil paintings by painters that she liked. The collection grew steadily to include works of Marc Chagall, Picasso, David Sharir, Igor Galanin, Samuel Bak and others. Elaine's paintings were proudly displayed in their home along with the expensive works of art, a private gallery that was much admired by visiting friends and relatives.

Being a great admirer of Persian rugs that she could not afford, Elaine learned how to weave her own versions of famous Persian and Chinese rugs. She later started to organize evening classes for teaching Persian and Chinese rug making. She was an accomplished artist in the eyes of her friends, and especially in the eyes of Avner.

Elaine was also a talented piano player. Avner loved listening to her favorite Chopin etudes and preludes. She provided background music when he was reading a book or sitting at his desk engaged in an engineering design task or in creating a new scientific project. He loved the interludes that her music offered, causing him to stop reading, close his eyes and enjoy the music. *"It's impossible to concentrate on reading while listening to Elaine's rendition of Chopin."*

1958

Elaine earned her Bachelor degree in History of Art from Radcliff and Avner earned his PhD in engineering from Harvard University. They lived in Boston, Massachusetts until 1959 when Avner was offered a position as an electronic engineer in Israel. They moved to Haifa, the beautiful city in northern Israel, with their six month old son, who was named Benjamin in honor of Avner's father.

* * *

Twelve members of the newly-formed Tibetan Advisory Council, seven monks and five laymen, accompanied by three secretarial aides; gathered in their meeting hall. Small talk and a few shouting matches filled the room until the young Dalai Lama entered, walking slowly. He wore a stained and slightly torn copper-colored robe.

The fourteenth Dalai Lama was only twenty-four years old. He had just arrived in the city of Dharamsala, India, together with 100,000 Tibetan refugees seeking safety following their failed uprising against the Chinese.

"This is our first meeting outside Tibet," the Dalai Lama addressed his compatriots. "I am the youngest man in this room surrounded by wise and experienced men. We are gathered here to informally discuss our new situation in a foreign land."

"What do you mean when you say informal?" Chakradar, the eldest council member asked.

"My teacher, Chakradar. I would like you and everyone in this room to participate in an open discussion to address our new situation after our flight from Tibet, just like you would in your own home."

"But this is our formal Council-in-Exile meeting and we are ready to follow your instructions," said another young council member.

"I am the Dalai Lama, but in these extra-ordinary circumstances, I want to hear the opinions of everyone on what should be our next course. During the last three days, I was in complete seclusion in my new chambers. I reflected on our options in exile. I want to discuss them with you, but I first want to hear your opinions.

"You are members of the new council. Some of you are elder statesmen with considerable experience and loyalty. A few served in the council during my regency when I was a child. Some of you are young and new cabinet members who fought with me against the Communist Chinese and have demonstrated special skills of leadership. I need your assistance and your advice, without which I'll fail in fulfilling my duties as a Dalai Lama."

He paused and looked around the group for a reaction. The few seconds of silence puzzled him.

"You are the re-incarnation of Buddha," Chakradar broke the silence. "You are our leader and will always be. I speak in the name of all council members. We will provide you with our advice and assistance with unquestioned loyalty."

"Thank you, my friend, Chakradar," continued the Dalai Lama. "The flight from Tibet is a pivotal event in my life, in the lives of all the Tibetan refugees who came with us and in the unfolding history of Tibet. Being in exile, we must search for wisdom on how to lead our people."

The Dalai Lama stopped again and scanned the room looking into the eyes of every silent man facing him.

"In our search for wisdom, we should first seek it in the archival writings of Thubten Gyatso," Chakradar again was the first to break the silence.

"In our search for truth, we should rely heavily on the teachings of Buddha," seconded a young warrior who seemed to be only a few years older than the Dalai Lama.

"However, in my search for advice, I will rely on you and your experience."

An air of renewed confidence appeared among the council members.

"I cherish the writings of my predecessor Thubten Gyatso and I consider him to be a wise leader. He highlighted the importance of learning from the history of the Jewish people. He wanted to be prepared if Tibet would ever be overrun by a foreign power.

"Now that we are in exile, I realize how prophetic he was. I am now a powerless leader and a guest in a foreign land. I am determined to learn how to better lead our compatriots who were left behind under Chinese occupation."

The tension among the council members subsided. A raucous free-for-all discussion ensued. The Dalai Lama relaxed and started to think about his options.

I must follow in the footsteps of Thubten Gyatso. The position of the Tibetan people is similar to that of the Jewish people. The Jews were forced out from their homeland, certainly under worse conditions than us. The Jews did not leave their land as refugees. They fought until they were overwhelmed. They were taken out of their land as slaves. They were not honored guests in their lands of exile.

They were two thousand years in exile, yet they survived. How did they do this? How did they keep their religion, their culture and their language?

Fifty years ago, the returning Jews built a small two-street suburb of Jaffa. Now it is a metropolis, and Jaffa is its suburb. The Jews not only kept their faith while in exile, they thrived upon their return. We must find a way to learn from them.

The Dalai Lama faced a dilemma.

I am in an arena with high-stakes players where I clearly hold the weakest hand compared to the leaders of the powerful Peoples Republic of China. If I was born to be the leader of the Tibetan people, I have to find realistic answers to my many questions. How can I know if I am capable to be their leader? I am young and inexperienced, how could I lead the experienced and wise men who followed me to exile? If I am capable, I have to define major strategic objectives with realistic and achievable action plans. How can I inspire in my people the belief that there could be a better future? How can I lead the Tibetans who were left behind while I am in exile? I have to redefine myself. I have to be a different Dalai Lama with different objectives compared to my predecessors.

He interrupted the disputations of the council and addressed its members again:

"I have listened to your discussions and I heard the different points of view. Going back to fight the Chinese is not an option. China has a large and powerful army and we were defeated. We must find a way to regroup and to analyze all the options carefully. The most important lesson which I learned from Thubten Gyatso's writings is not to make impulsive decisions, and not to make any decision without carefully studying their consequences.

"I have decided. I would like a report from each one of you detailing your recommendations concerning two questions:

1. How do we deal with the people who were left behind in Tibet?
2. What should be our plan of action if we remain in exile many years?

"Each of these subjects includes many others that have to be addressed in detail, prioritized and carefully analyzed. I am leaving the challenge of defining them in your hands."

The Dalai Lama did not ask the council the more important questions:

> *Will the Tibetan people survive as a nation? Or will*
> *they be assimilated and become Chinese or Indians?*
> *Will their children and their descendents manage*
> *to retain the Tibetan Culture? Or will their culture*
> *disappear after three or four generations?*
>
> *With the potential of eventual assimilation outside*
> *Tibet, the Dalai Lama considered this matter as*

having the highest importance. His mission would be to place it on the top of his own list of priorities.

The Jewish people long ago faced what we Tibetans face today. Knowing how they managed to preserve their culture might be the answer to our survival.

CHAPTER 8

1964 The Six Monks

"ALBERTO! HOW IS your Mandarin?" Ricardo asked with great laughter.

"Mandarin?—I never had the pleasure of visiting China. If your Chinese tourists cannot understand English, or French, or German, or Italian, or Spanish, you will need another tour guide, unless they know Hebrew. How about Yiddish?"

"I didn't know you speak Yiddish. What other languages you know?"

"What is the chance that your Chinese guests know Ladino?"

Ricardo, the manager of the Grand Hotel Olympia in Rome hesitated before answering the question of his friend, Alberto Maimon.

"A group of six Tibetan monks are looking for a tour guide. They arrived last night from Paris and they'll be in Rome only two days."

"I don't know Sanskrit, or Sino-Tibetan, or whatever language they speak in Tibet."

"Don't worry, Alberto. They speak French and English. They want to visit the Vatican and to see the ancient historical sights of Rome. They want a guide who could tell them about the history of Rome. You are the ideal guide for this group. Can you schedule them for tomorrow morning? They will leave Rome the next day".

Alberto was a very popular tour guide. His fluency in several languages was his asset in conducting tours for foreign visitors. He was born in Rome where he had acquired a vast knowledge of its history and the history of the Roman Empire. He conducted tours delivering historical lectures to foreign tourists from many countries. Local hotel managers and travel agencies in several European cities sought him for his talent, which was not common among Roman tour guides. Alberto especially liked the Grand Hotel Olympia because it was centrally located, with easy access to the Vatican and to the Plaza del Popolo. It was favored by several foreign travel agencies.

Ricardo was right. The six monks spoke English and French, but with a strange accent. Alberto could not identify it.

"You were recommended as the best tour guide in Rome." The dark-skinned monk with brown eyes introduced himself in English. "My name is Tziangu. My friends chose me as their leader."

"I understand that you know both English and French," Alberto responded. "I assume that you prefer to use English today."

"Actually, two monks in our group prefer French. Our hotel manager informed us that you can conduct the tour in French."

"Where did you learn English and French?" Alberto asked.

"We were selected by the Dalai Lama. He assigned two private tutors, one was an Indian Professor who earned his Doctoral Degree at the University of London, and the other was a Chinese teacher who learned his French when he studied at the University of Geneva."

"Are you vacationing? Or are you attending a conference?"

"Business with pleasure is our motto. We are on a special mission to purchase books on 20th century Europe and the Middle-East for the Dalai Lama's library in Dharamsala. We have already been in Athens, where we purchased books on modern Greece."

"Did you visit London or Madrid?" Alberto asked.

"We did not visit Madrid, but we spent some time in the libraries of Oxford University and last week we spent three days at the Sorbonne library. We also visited the Louvre, the *Palais de L'Orangerie* Museum and the *Arc de Triomphe,* the Napoleon Triumphal Arch. In Rome we want to see the Vatican City, the Roman Forum and the Titus Triumphal Arch. We are scheduled to go next to Turkey to visit the vast library of the Great Mosque of Istanbul before returning to India."

Alberto was surprised. "Why is the Dalai Lama interested in the Titus Triumphal Arch?"

"It is on the list given to us by his deputy. He is interested in the Middle East, and Jewish history is an important part of the Middle East. The Dalai Lama has a small collection of books on the history of the Jewish People."

The group of monks with their copper-colored robes attracted the attention of local residents and tourists alike. Such a parade of monks was not a common sight in Rome. The tour included the standard route which Alberto used often.

Tziangu was taller than his companions. He did most of the talking while his five friends kept silent most of the time. He carried a small notepad and a pen attached to it with a string. He asked many questions and showed special interest in the history of the Roman underground catacombs and in the Triumphal Arch of Titus. He constantly wrote in his notepad during the historical talks of the tour guide. Alberto observed Tziangu and wondered about his note taking.

He is writing in French and not in Sanskrit. It just
does not make sense. Is Sanskrit or Tibetan his
mother's tongue or is it French? He probably writes in
French because I am talking in French? Is he really a
monk?

When Alberto returned the monks to the hotel, Tziangu asked him if he was willing to deliver a small gift to a friend he met in Paris.

"My friend will arrive in Rome with his wife tomorrow," said the Tziangu. "They have never been to Rome and they asked me to find a tour guide who would show them Rome and the Vatican. Judging from our observation today, you are the perfect guide for them. Will you be free tomorrow to be their tour guide?"

"My schedule is completely filled for the rest of the week," said Alberto. "But I will find time to meet them and to deliver your gift. Where will I find your friend? How will I recognize him?"

"Mr. Angelo and his wife plan to stay at the Hotel de Roma," said the monk. "Just ask for him at the hotel reception desk. We will leave Rome today, and I will not be here to meet them. My gift to them is an oil painting that I purchased yesterday from a street vendor in Rome. I will be grateful if you will deliver it to him. I don't trust the clerk at the hotel. You are the only person I can trust."

Tziangu went to his room and returned with a small package wrapped in colorful paper.

"This is the painting."

"How will I know he is the right person?"

"That will be easy. Just ask him if he is Angelo from the Arch. He will tell you that he met us in Paris."

"It was a pleasure being your guide. I hope we can meet again. Call me if you return for another visit."

"I don't know if we'll ever be back in Rome. We'll leave tomorrow to Istanbul on our way home. Although I wish we could visit the Isle of Capri too. I hear that it is a very nice place, but I prefer Monte Carlo. I once tried my luck in gambling and lost a bundle, money that I could not afford to lose."

Alberto wondered about Tziangu. *Are monks allowed to gamble?*

* * *

Tziangu entered the hotel lobby to face his five companions.

"Tonight we'll need both our French and Turkish passports."

He went to his room, changed his name to Francois and replaced his copper-colored robe with a modern, two-piece suit. He and his companions drove from Rome to Monaco in their rented Peugeot.

"How can you trust the tour guide with the important painting?" asked one of his assistants. "Ibn Najad will kill us if it will be lost."

"Don't worry," Francois responded. "I placed one of our men in the hotel to make sure that the painting and its contents will be safe until Angelo arrives from Paris."

They entered the Monte Carlo casino looking for a table to try their luck. The tables in the gambling hall were surrounded by men and women who were watching the games and guarding their piles of casino chips. Most of the gamblers were at dice tables or roulette tables. The six gamblers chose the roulette table at the far corner of the hall.

"*Rien ne va plus,*" announced the roulette croupier as Francois and three of his five companions approached the side of his table. He spun the roulette. The ball bounced several times and landed on number 12. Francois opened his wallet and placed a pile of

US Dollar bills on the table. The croupier counted the money and gave him a pile of chips. He placed several chips on number 12, and the ball landed on number 12. His pile of chips increased considerably. He placed the pile on *red*, and the ball landed on *red*. He placed all the chips of his new pile on number 8, and the ball landed on number 8. The crowd around the table shouted with amazement, attracting other gamblers who enjoyed cheering a winner. Francois withdrew half the pile of chips and placed them in his pockets. As he repeated alternating his bets from a number and a color, he won six times and his pile of chips increased to a level that attracted many more observers around the table.

Francois pulled his pile of chips and placed them out of play. The next six times, the ball did not land on numbers 12 or on his lucky 8. Francois smiled and most of the crowd moved to other tables. He tapped on the table lightly. The croupier got the hint and immediately signaled to a waitress to offer him another drink. With a glass of whiskey in one hand, he placed half his pile on number 12 with his other hand. The ball landed on number 13. He hesitated while continuing to drink and missed the next croupier call of *"Rien ne va plus"*. The ball landed on number 12. Feeling cheated for missing the call, he complained to the croupier for not allowing him to place his bet before the call. The hall supervisor was called in to settle the complaint, but to no avail. With anger in his eyes, Francois placed the second half of his pile *red*, the ball landed on *black*. He placed all the chips that were in his pockets on number 12. The ball landed on 13. He was left with only a few chips. He ordered another drink.

The six-foot-two Francois wore an expensive pin-striped, charcoal grey Armani suit sporting a white silk handkerchief and a silver silk tie. Bringing his companions to the casino was originally for pleasure, but having lost most of his money, he was determined to get it back. He called the casino supervisor and gave him a marker for 5,000 US Dollars. Looking at him with examining eyes, the supervisor hesitated, asked for his French passport, placed the passport in his vest pocket and approved the marker.

Lady luck played tricks with Francois and his silent companions. The pile increased ten-fold and decreased back to less than $100. He wrote a second marker of another $5,000. It was approved, and within ten minutes he lost all his money. The supervisor refused to accept a third marker. Francois did not seem to be worried. He turned to the supervisor, informed him that he expected a wire transfer of $50,000 from Paris, and assured him the markers would be honored on the next day. The inspector smiled and walked to the door marked "Casino Management". He returned informing Francois that his manager also refused to honor more markers, but agreed to wait another day until the $50,000 would arrive. Naturally, the manager kept Francois' French passport pending resolution of the markers.

Francois and his five companions left the casino, entered their rented Peugeot and drove away followed by a black Citroen driven by a Monte Carlo security officer and his companion.

"A black Citroen is following us," Francois heard a warning from behind his driver seat.

"Don't worry," he replied. "Once we cross into France proper, they will leave us."

He was wrong. The Citroen followed them as if they did not cross the border.

Francois entered the town of Villefranche and stopped in front of a small hotel. They walked to the lobby presenting their Turkish passports. The concierge checked their reservations and gave them keys for three rooms. Two were shared by the five companions and one was a private room for Francois who has already changed his name to Kamal.

Kamal woke up at sunrise. Looking out his window, he enjoyed the beautiful view of the Mediterranean shore. After shaving and showering, the breakfast he had ordered was brought in by a young waitress who placed it on the round table and left. As soon as he finished his breakfast, there was another knock on the door. *She must have forgotten something. And I forgot to tip her.*

He opened the door to find himself facing a tall and husky man who entered briskly into the room closing the door behind him. Kamal knew that he was in trouble. The intruder pushed him and pressed him to the wall:

"You left Monaco without settling your markers," the intruder was adamant. "How are you going to settle this debt?"

"I will simply pay you in cash from my suitcase if you return my passport."

"I have your passport with me. Go get the money."

Kamal walked to his suitcase, opened it and pulled out his favorite switch-blade knife. He turned around swinging the knife trying to strike the intruder when a left hook hit him in the face. He was blinded momentarily and lost the grip of his knife. The intruder tried to strike him with a right hook just as Kamal's brass knuckle hit him in the face. The intruder bent forward with agonizing pain from his bleeding nose. Kamal tied him to a chair and placed a tape across his mouth. He closed his suitcase and left.

The six Peugeot passengers left the hotel followed by the Black Citroen. They were headed to Nice to board the Turkish Airline flight to Istanbul. They never reached Nice.

CHAPTER 9

1964 The Shlom-Zion Scroll

A VNER BECAME ADDICTED to Jewish history, especially Jewish heroes who fought against foreign occupiers of the Promised Land. He was enchanted by archaeology books and excavation sites. When Elaine suggested a vacation in Rome to visit Italian art museums, he jumped on the opportunity to see ancient Greek and Roman sites. It was the summer of 1964, when they departed on the Greek ship Olympia sailing from the port of Haifa to Greece.

"This is where the statue of Zeus came from," Elaine declared in Hebrew on the observation deck as the ship approached the port of Piraeus.

"Yes, this is the place," responded a stranger behind Avner, also in Hebrew. "Allow me to introduce myself. My name is Aaron Bar David and my wife is Dalia. I am also interested in the statue of Zeus."

"Allow me to return the honor by introducing my husband, Avner Amram."

"Are you the archaeologist Bar David?" Avner asked.

"Yes I am. How do you know my name?"

"I read several of your recent articles on archaeological findings at the Mount Ararat excavation site in Turkey. It is very informative."

"Are you an archaeologist?"

"I wish it. I am an electronics engineer, but one day I'll be an archaeologist."

"In that case, you must be the engineer who lives in the realm of electrons and holes computing their semiconductor mobility."

Avner was stunned. "How does an archaeologist know about electron mobility? It surely is not taught in archaeology lectures."

"I am a post-doctoral archeology researcher at the Hebrew University, but my hobby is physics. Mobility is the action of electrons inside atoms and molecules."

"I am in trouble," interrupted Elaine. "I am listening to gibberish that is the secret language of scientists."

She turned around and started a conversation with Dalia, while Avner and Aaron continued their gibberish dialogue.

After disembarking at the port of Piraeus, the foursome shared a taxi to Athens and checked into the same hotel.

While Elaine and Dalia were shopping the next day in Athens, Avner and Aaron spent several hours discussing recent archaeological excavation projects in Israel and Turkey. Avner expressed his plan to go back to Harvard and earn a second doctoral degree, this time in the Anthropology department. He wanted to concentrate on archaeological research in Israel with special emphasis on ancient manuscripts and documents of the Hashmonean era.

"You should concentrate on the field of your specialty," Bar David said to Avner. "I read that your dissertation was on transistors technology. It's an exciting field. You published papers on electron mobility in semiconductors. Those complex equations dealing with the micro world of electrons are beyond my comprehension."

"You are right," responded Avner. "I love my profession, but I also love history. I always wanted to learn more about our history as a Jewish nation. Ten of our twelve tribes were exiled by the Assyrians and were lost. We were expelled three times from our land, first in 586 BCE by the Babylonians and again in 70 CE by the Romans. Our history is everywhere in Israel. The information must be somewhere in Israel, in neighboring countries, in Italy and in Spain. Why can't I work in electronics and at the same time search our history?"

"You probably could," said Aaron. "However, if you do, you will dilute your achievements in both fields. Your results will not be as spectacular as your thesis. Remember the old Talmudic saying that if you tackle too much you tackle nothing. You should dedicate your career to engineering. The new electronics technology is in its infancy. It will revolutionize the world of communications, trade, manufacturing, medical research, sub-molecular research and even space research. You can be a successful international participant in this revolution."

"I agree with everything you say," was Avner's reaction. "The transistor, invented in 1951, was just a forerunner of a new world of semiconductors that one day will result in microcomputers the size of a hand-watch—just like the one in the Dick Tracy movies."

"You talk with great passion about the electronic revolution. You wear your passion on the outside."

"I love my work, but one day I'll take the time to seek the answers to questions that have always been burning in me. I want to know what happened to the Jerusalem Menorah during the destruction of the second Temple. Did the Romans take it with them to be displayed during the Titus victory march in Rome? Or did they carry a fake replica? I want to answer many questions about our history, but I don't want to limit myself to reading history books. I want to experience the actual finding of relics and documents that belonged to the people who lived in the land of Israel. That can only be accomplished with archaeology."

"Now I understand your passion," said Dr. Bar David. "I may be able to help you if you decide to go back to Cambridge. Harvard just offered me a position as an Associate Professor of Archaeology, and I am going to accept it. If you ever decide to pursue your idea, contact me. Working on archaeology research with a PhD in electronics will still require an archaeology professor as your mentor. I would be delighted to be that person. Maybe we can work together and initiate a project to discover the secret of the Menorah."

"Thank you. I may take advantage of your offer, especially if you'll help me in raising the money for a new archaeological excavation project or to team up with another research team."

"We could start our research immediately. The next port of our ship will be Rome where we can see the triumphal arch built to commemorate the victory of Titus over Judea. Dalia and I have planned to see the Roman sites, and we'll be happy if you and Elaine decide to join us."

*   *   *

"Our visit in Rome will include museums," said Elaine to Dalia when the two vacationing couples disembarked in Italy. "Avner loves art, engineering and archaeology. I tolerate archaeology and I know nothing about engineering. As a compromise, we always plan our trips to include museums."

"Your passion for art makes me envious," Dalia responded. "Aaron's archaeology is not my cup of tea. I tolerate it because I love history. I teach it in high school."

"I've been waiting a long time for the opportunity to see the works of the great Italian masters," said Elaine. "I especially want to see the paintings of MichaelAngelo and Rafael."

While Avner and Elaine stood at the reception counter of the Hotel de Roma, Elaine noticed a man walking toward them. He seemed to be about thirty or forty years old. Except for their new Bar David friends, they did not know anyone in Rome and she did not know what to expect. The stranger approached Avner and asked in English with a heavy Italian accent:

"Are you Angelo from the Arch?"

"I don't know anyone by the name of Angelo." Avner looked with suspicion at the stranger.

"Please forgive me," said the stranger. "My name is Alberto Maimon. I am a tour guide and I am waiting for a couple to show them the sights of Rome."

"What a coincidence?" Elaine was excited. "We are looking for a guide to show us the Roman Forum and the Triumphal Arch of Titus."

"It's an interesting coincidence," said Alberto. "I was booked for the rest of the week, but there was a cancellation, and I'll be free tomorrow."

"Are you familiar with the Jewish history from the time of the Romans?" asked Elaine. "We are from Israel."

"I certainly am," was his response. "I am Jewish myself. I was born in Rome and I promote Jewish-Catholic dialogues in Rome, especially in holocaust education. I send Catholic teachers to spend summers in Jerusalem. I send Italian teachers to visit Jewish leaders in America to learn about plans for establishing a national Holocaust Museum in Washington, DC. The teachers return to

Italy to teach the children about the holocaust. I conduct tours for groups of Catholic priests that include the Titus Triumphal Aarch where I tell them about Jewish history."

They agreed to retain Alberto as a tour guide for the following day. When they met their new friends for dinner at the hotel restaurant, Aaron and Dalia were delighted to hear about the next day's plan.

On the next morning, the two couples met Alberto at the hotel lobby. He took them to the Roman Forum, to the gladiators' arena and to the Titus Triumphal Arch. Standing before the Arch; Avner's mind transported him to a Jewish history lecture he once heard at the Hebrew University. While Alberto was talking about the Titus Arch, Avner closed his eyes and felt that he was at the university listening again to the history professor.

Alberto recited his lecture:

> *"The destruction of the Jerusalem Temple in 70 CE is one of the pivotal events in Jewish History. The Jewish revolt against the Greeks was very successful resulting in a century of independence. Their revolt against Rome was crushed brutally and their Temple was destroyed. The Romans built the Triumphal Arch of Titus to commemorate the fall of Jerusalem. It depicts a victory march showing Roman soldiers carrying the Golden Jewish Candelabra—the Menorah, presumably taken from Jerusalem."*

Avner returned to reality. He was obsessed by a central question.

"Why don't we have any information on the fate of the original Menorah?" He asked the guide. "What happened to it? How could it disappear without any trace?"

"I have always asked myself the same question." Alberto seemed pleased to hear the question. "Why the Jewish people had not actively searched for information on the fate of the golden Ark of the Covenant and the golden Menorah? The mighty Roman Empire rose, fell and disappeared, but the Jewish people survived in spite of their defeat two thousand years ago."

"Are there any theories about the possible location of the Menorah?" asked Elaine.

"There are many legends on the Menorah," answered Alberto. "But there is only one truth."

"Can you tell us some of the legends?" Avner reacted swiftly.

Smiling, Alberto stared at the two couples. He often expected to hear this question from Jewish tourists.

"I can tell you about speculations on the location of the original Menorah. I recently overheard a conversation between two priests in Saint Peter's Basilica at the Vatican City. When the first priest said that he saw an ancient golden relic hidden in the catacombs of Rome, the second priest asked if it was the golden Judean Candelabra. The first priest responded by whispering that they should not talk about it at all."

"That is an outstanding discovery,' shouted Elaine.

"It was not a discovery," Alberto reacted. "It was just a conversation."

"Did he say that it was a Vatican secret?"

"He certainly implied it." Alberto responded with a facial expression of regret for having used the word "truth."

He did not know what the truth was, and he did not know much about the four Israelis.

"Could you tell us about the Menorah legends?" Elaine asked.

"There are several legends," started Alberto. "Some people say that the Menorah was never brought to Rome and that Titus made one up just to demonstrate the might of his army in conquering the brave fighters of Judea.

"There is also a legend claiming that the Menorah is now in the basement of the Great Mosque of Istanbul. There are other legends, but the most popular one may already be known to you. It is that the Menorah and the Ark of the Covenant are both hidden in the catacombs under the Vatican City and that the Vatican will not allow anyone to see them. Who knows which story is right?

"The legend that the Menorah and the Ark are in Ethiopia makes no sense. The Queen of Sheba visited King Solomon, who built the first temple of Jerusalem. The two relics were still in Jerusalem in the second temple centuries later. If you have the time and patience, I will tell you my favorite legend now."

"Please tell us," reacted Elaine with enthusiasm.

Alberto smiled and started his favorite legend:

> Queen Shlom-Zion, also known as Salome Alexandra,
> was the Hashmonean ruler in Judea before the arrival
> of the Romans. She is the central figure in this legend.
> She became queen in 75 BCE after the death of her
> ruthless husband, Alexander Yanai. She presented
> her series of reforms to the leaders of the Sanhedrin.
> According to this legend, this is what she told them:

> "Judea has always been surrounded by enemies
> who tried to conquer our land. The Romans
> have a powerful army which could threaten our
> independence. Our ancestors, Judah the Maccabee
> and his four brothers, fought with ingenious tactics
> and bravery against the Greek domination. Now we
> have a powerful army capable of defending us, but we

must be prepared for a potential war with the mighty Romans.

"I have in my possession a secret sheepskin scroll written by the scribe of Judah the Maccabee a century ago. It includes a plan for hiding the Menorah and the Ark of the Covenant in time of an invasion by a foreign army. The document instructs us to hide the Menorah in one location and the Ark of the Covenant in another. It is a precautionary plan so that if an enemy discovers one, the other could be saved for future generations.

"I have decided that hiding the Menorah and the Ark is important, but it is not enough. I have instructed my son Horcanus to construct replicas of both the Menorah and the Ark. I left instructions to have the replicas replace the original ones if the walls surrounding Jerusalem are ever breached by an invading army."

Alberto stopped talking. He looked at his audience of four tourists with a smile. He had told that story before to other tourists, but he never experienced such a great interest in its details. Avner took out a small notepad and wrote in it a reminder. He named the Queen document as the "Shlom-Zion Scroll", concluding that it had to be the original Judah the Maccabee scroll, if the legend was not a legend.

"If this legend is the true one," interjected Elaine, "it means that both the originals and the replicas disappeared. If one of them is ever found, it would be hard to determine if it is an original or a replica."

"That would be an interesting problem that the finders will face," Alberto responded.

"Can you tell us about the other legends, and which one is the true one?" asked Elaine.

"Not today," answered Alberto to the first question. Avoiding the second one, he added: "I must leave you now."

Alberto left. Elaine was not satisfied to have her question ignored.

"Why did he avoid my question about the truth? Does he know something he is afraid to reveal?"

There was no response.

"These legends strengthen my resolve about archaeology." Avner was pleased. "The importance of the Menorah is underscored by its symbolic value to the Jewish people. Clearly, the Menorah inspired the ancient Judeans in both the first and the second temples' periods. Clearly, it inspired the modern Jewish leaders to place a replica of the Menorah at the Knesset Parliament building."

Looking at Dr. Bar David he added, "You asked me where I got my passion for archaeology. Today you heard the answer to your question. The information on the Shlom-Zion scroll should be sufficient to ignite the imagination of any researcher. If this scroll was important to Judah the Maccabee and to Queen Shlom-Zion, it is important to me. It is an example of what my passion is all about."

In 1966, Elaine was delighted when Avner decided to return to Cambridge and work on his doctoral degree in archaeology. Without telling Avner and without thinking of the consequences, she submitted an application to Harvard to earn a second degree in history of art. She never expected to be accepted six years after earning her first degree, but when the letter of acceptance arrived, it presented her with a dilemma on how she could be a full time student and a mother of her six-year old son, Benjamin, at the same time. Avner was pleased and assured her that they were able to afford a caretaker during her studies.

While Avner worked on his doctoral degree in Cambridge, Elaine took the required courses and tackled a research project on Impressionism. She even found time to weave two Persian and one Chinese rug.

CHAPTER 10

1967 The Monastery Parchment

JUNE 6, 1967 was a beautiful summer day in Cambridge, Massachusetts when Avner heard the news of the war that erupted in the Middle East. He could not concentrate on his thesis at Harvard. The Israel Air Force had destroyed the Egyptian Air Force in a pre-emptive strike and heavy tank battles were throughout the Sinai Desert. The next morning, he received a telephone call from the Israeli embassy in Washington, informing him that all Israeli officers in the United States were called back to join their reserve battalions in Israel. Avner reported to the designated place in New York on the next day, where he waited to board an El-Al flight to Israel. That flight was delayed.

On the third day of the war, Avner was on the El-Al flight together with other Israelis; some were called by the army, and others just volunteered. The flight arrived in Tel Aviv when the Israeli Army cancelled the call. The collapse of the Egyptian defenses was so complete that the Israeli forces reached the Suez

Canal in five days. There was no need to send additional reserve units to the frontlines. On the sixth day the war was over.

*   *   *

June 20 was a hot day in Haifa.

"So you missed the war," Colonel Menachem Amram said to his brother Avner when they met in Haifa.

"I had full confidence in your ability to defend Israel." Avner embraced his brother. "Tell me about the battles you were in."

"I was the Operations Officer of my armored division on the Egyptian front."

"Are you on leave now?"

"Only for three days. After our tank division reached the Suez Canal, I was released from my operational duties. I have to prepare a special report to the Division General."

"Can you tell me about it? Or is it a military secret?"

"It is a military secret, but I can tell it to you."

"I am all ears."

"I have a better idea. How would you like to join me in visiting the battle sites? My assignment is to analyze the division's tank battles and to make recommendations on the lessons that could be learned from them."

"I wish I could join you. I heard that the Sinai Peninsula had been declared a military zone, with no civilians allowed in. I am still a civilian. The army does not need me."

"Don't worry. I can get you a permit to join me if you are interested."

"I am interested and excited."

Avner, Menachem, his assisting lieutenant and a driver, departed in an army jeep from the southern city of Ashkelon. They drove through the city of Gaza and into the Sinai desert. They stopped at several battle sites where Menachem dictated his observations while his lieutenant took notes. They passed hundreds of Egyptian tanks, munitions supply trains, trucks, jeeps and many other vehicles. Many were destroyed by the Israeli air force and others destroyed by Menachem's armored division tanks.

When they reached the eastern bank of the Suez Canal, the driver stopped at the water's edge facing the Egyptian city of Ismailia on the western bank. The driver climbed on the jeep's hood waving a large Israeli flag. Looking across the canal, Avner saw an Egyptian soldier standing on the hood of his Egyptian jeep and waving an Egyptian flag.

"Is the Egyptian soldier signaling a message of peace? Or is he sending a message that revenge will come?" Avner thought without revealing his question to his brother.

*　　*　　*

Following the excitement at the shores of the Suez Canal, Avner had an idea.

"Menachem, as long as we are here, can we visit Mount Sinai?"

"That area had no involvement in the war, Avner. It's not part of my mission of analyzing the battles and recommending lessons from them."

"Have you ever been there?"

"No, but one day I will find the time for it. Besides . . ."

"Come on, Menachem. This is a perfect opportunity. You can scout out the mountain to evaluate it as a possible observation post. Remember the South Pacific musical. Such a post was extremely valuable in the war with Japan. What do you say?"

Menachem smiled at his brother. "I am a sucker for Jewish history, just like you. I always wanted to see the site of the biblical burning bush. I will just have to find an excuse for not meeting my deadline."

Avner smiled back. "You know, of course, there's no proof that the mountain they call Mount Sinai is the one where Moses received the Ten Commandments."

"And no proof it's not, either. Okay, you talked me into it. I'll investigate the strategic value of the site." Menachem winked at his brother.

They stood at the base of the mountain and looked at the beginning of the four—thousand steps "Path of Moses" that wound toward the summit.

"Who knows?" Menachem said. "This could be the route Moses took."

"And Moses was eighty years old. If he could do it, we certainly can."

"There's nothing to see at the mountain, except an old 4th century monastery. That's 7500 feet in elevation, Avner. It's quite a climb, even for us."

"You are an army colonel. Would you have an eighty-year old man put you to shame? Besides, how can you assess the military potential from here? Let's do it."

They encountered several small structures along the four thousand steps. Some were marked as chapels in English, French and Arabic. Some were inscribed in Greek. Along the route they saw several signs in Arabic which named the route "The Path of Moses." They reached a small plateau.

"Maybe this is where Aaron was left behind when Moses continued the climb." exclaimed Menachem.

"I am not Moses," Avner was adamant. "I am not going to continue the climb alone. You will have to come with me."

"I never thought of staying behind." Colonel Menachem was authoritative. "Let me remind you that I am the one who has the army permit to be here in the first place. Without it, you would not be allowed into the Sinai desert today."

They were near the walls of the Katrina monastery when two black-robed monks walked toward them.

"Welcome to the Santa Katrina Monastery," said one of them. "I am Father Neophytos. I am one of the few monks in this monastery who have been here more than ten years. I have been assigned to greet all visitors."

"*Salam Aleikom*," Menachem returned a greeting of peace in Arabic. "We hope that you will allow us to visit inside the walls of the monastery."

"*Shalom Aleichem*," responded the monk with the Hebrew greeting of peace. "I will be pleased to escort you during the visit. You are tired, hungry and thirsty after the long climb. You should first eat the food and drink the water that we can offer you."

When they entered the monastery compound, they were surprised to see an orchard of almond, pomegranate and olive trees. The latter ones were probably planted several hundred years earlier. They expected to see an arid mountain, but found a pleasant climate with relative abundance of water. They accepted the monk's offer of food and water, but they were more interested in looking at the bell tower of the church and in visiting its library.

"Can we visit your library?" Avner asked.

"We have the second largest collection of ancient manuscripts in the world after the one at the Vatican Library."

"We are very interested in ancient documents." Avner was excited.

The library was very large with many wooden tables in its central hall. Three monks were at a table sitting on two wooden benches inspecting a large rolled scroll on which were written words in Latin.

"They are making preparations for copying the text of this document on several parchment pages which will be used to create a replica of the original scroll," remarked Father Neophytos. "The original is very old and it will soon be placed in our protected archives to prevent its further deterioration and to preserve it for future generations."

"What is the nature of this document? Why is it so precious?" asked Avner.

"It is part of the Latin version of the Book of the Maccabees," answered the monk. "The original was written in ancient Hebrew. It was translated into Greek in the first century and later it was translated from Greek to Latin. The Saint James English version of the Bible is a translation from the Latin version."

"Why are you interested in the Book of the Maccabees?" Menachem asked. "It is a book about Jewish history, not about Christian events or prophesies. It is not part of the Bible."

"It certainly is part of the Greek Orthodox and the Catholic Bibles. It is a sacred book," responded the monk. "I know that it is not part of the Old Testament, which you call the Jewish Bible. The Jews celebrate the festival of the Maccabees, the festival of Chanukah, but we do not. This is an issue that puzzles us Christians, but I am sure that there is an explanation."

"Do you have many ancient documents in your library?"

"It all depends what you mean by ancient. Our archives include a large collection of documents in Hebrew, Greek, Latin, Coptic, Armenian, Arabic, Georgian and Syrian. Most of them are less than 500 years old. We do have many older ones. They are available for review, except one parchment page that is in a sealed vault. The vault can only be opened by a special written permit issued by the Orthodox Patriarch in Cairo."

"What secrets does the sealed document have that it is so important?"

"I don't know. I never saw it. The vault was never opened since I arrived ten years ago. Maybe it will never be known."

"Do you know what type of a document it is?"

"I don't know much about it," responded Father Neophytos. "I do know that it is written in ancient Hebrew. Our record shows that it was brought to the Monastery by a Roman soldier and that the vault was opened only three times since then."

Avner made another note in his notebook. He named the hidden document "the Katrina Monastery parchment" to differentiate it from the Shlom-Zion scroll. Its existence triggered his inquisitive mind.

"Could it provide any clues on the location of the original Judah Maccabee scroll or the golden Menorah?"

CHAPTER 11

1970 The Tel-Dor Parchments

A VNER RETURNED TO Cambridge to earn a second doctoral degree at the Harvard Department of Anthropology. In the summer of 1970, he volunteered to work at the Tel-Dor excavation site on the Mediterranean shore south of Haifa, Israel. His tall figure and his dark and deep brown eyes conveyed an image of an intelligent young man. In the eyes of his friends and colleagues, he was a gifted scholar, always considerate of others and humble in his actions.

Archaeology Professor Emeritus Yigal Yadin, who had been a General in the Israeli Army during the 1948 Israel War of Independence, stood at the site observing young volunteers and excavation workers. Five young men and two young women were in an area ten to twelve feet below the surrounding land. They were sifting sand from a mound of rubble, sand and broken clay artifacts. Five Arab day laborers, wearing white Kefyahs to protect themselves from the heat of the high-noon sun, were digging along the southern edge of the site.

Shimon Mizrachi, Professor of Archaeology at the Hebrew University in Jerusalem, had invited General Yadin to see the site and talk to the volunteers about two parchments discovered by Dr. Amram earlier that week.

"Have you had any problems with your Arab workers?" Yadin asked the Professor.

"They are good workers and I have full confidence in them."

At the request of Professor Mizrachi, Avner described his finding to General Yadin:

"The two discoveries are puzzling. They were found at two different depths about twenty feet apart from each other. One of the young volunteers called me saying that he found a few broken pieces of clay. I noticed that they were no different from hundreds of clay pieces I had seen before. When I lifted a large one, I found a rolled cylinder in a torn fabric. I lifted it and saw a small parchment falling to the ground. I was excited. Here was my first archaeological discovery."

Avner paused.

"I can't claim credit for finding the parchment. The credit belongs to the young volunteer who dug in that shallow pit."

"His name is Gedalia from Tel Aviv University," Professor Mizrachi noted.

"The second find was in a much deeper pit," Avner continued. "I cleared the sand around a stone nine feet deeper than the first find. Noticing that the stone was cylindrical, I replaced my shovel with a brush and cleared the sand with my bare hands until I identified the object as a clay jar of approximately twenty centimeters in diameter. I retrieved it from the sand. It contained a rolled copper sheet wrapped around another object and several coins. Suspecting that removing the copper sheet at the site might result in damaging its content, I followed Professor Mizrachi's suggestion and took it to the Chemical Engineering laboratory at the Technion Institute of

Technology in Haifa. I removed the copper sheet. It was wrapped around another small jar, approximately six centimeters in diameter. The jar included a rolled fragment of a parchment page, apparently part of a larger scroll."

"I am very interested in the coins you found", General Yadin noted. "Coins are generally good sources of information in any archaeological find. How many coins were there? Did you try to determine when they were minted?"

"I found twenty-six coins. We think they were minted before the reign of Shlom-Zion, the Hashmonean Queen. However, we haven't run any scanning tests to date them. I would appreciate your evaluation and your recommendations."

"When can I see the coins and the jars?" asked General Yadin.

"If you have the time, we can go to the Technion today," said Avner, looking at Professor Mizrachi for consent. He was puzzled by General Yadin's interest in the coins and the jar rather than the two parchments.

"Yigal", said Professor Mizrachi, "if you have the time, I'll join you. The volunteers can continue working at the excavation site without our supervision."

The driver assigned to the excavation crew was summoned and drove the two archaeologists and Avner to the Technion on Mount Carmel. On one side of the hallway leading to the Chemical Engineering laboratory, Avner saw large and well decorated offices. *Probably assigned to the senior professors of the faculty,* he thought. When he looked out of their windows he saw the beauty of Haifa Bay.

> *What historical and archaeological secrets are*
> *hidden in the shores of the bay? Secrets from the*
> *ancient Kingdom of Israel, from the Greeks, from the*

Maccabees, from the Romans, from the revolt against
the Romans, from the Crusaders, from Napoleon
Bonaparte and whoever else walked this land."

Signs of anxiety appeared on the faces of the two laboratory technicians as they waited for the expected visitors. Waiting with them was a group which the Chemical Engineering faculty dean called "functional elements". They were the laboratory manager, a laboratory photographer and a stenographer. They were always summoned whenever important guests visited the laboratory.

The visitors entered the laboratory. Following introductory remarks by Professor Mizrachi, they gathered around the centrally located workbench to see the Tel-Dor artifacts placed on it, each with its own marking.

Avner distributed a printed page to each visitor and read its content:

THE 1970 TEL-DOR LIST OF ARTIFACTS

Parchment with an Arabic Inscription	Marked	TDP-AR-1970
Parchment with a Hebrew Inscription	Marked	TDP-HE-1970
20 Centimeters Clay Jar	Marked	TDJ-20-1970
6 Centimeters Clay Jar	Marked	TDJ-6-1970
Copper sheet	Marked	TDS-CU-1970
26 Coins, each	Marked	TDC-X-1970
		(X is from 1 through 26)

"This is the Arabic parchment," Avner pointed at the first artifact. It was found alone, approximately three feet below the surface. All the other artifacts were found about 20 feet south of this one."

"Receiving archaeological artifacts has never occurred at the Technion," remarked the Dean.

"I have always argued that the Technion should add an Archaeology faculty," commented General Yadin. "Engineering technology is often needed to evaluate ancient artifacts."

"What do you think?" asked Avner, addressing the faculty dean.

"It is a good idea," replied the dean. "I'll present this question to the President of the Technion in our next weekly meeting. Maybe he knows a rich American friend of the Technion who would be willing to write a check for two million Dollars. I wonder how high on his priority list it will be placed. I'll keep you informed, General Yadin."

Everyone smiled at the response, but kept silent when Avner started to talk of what he called "Primary Initial Information" concerning the Tel-Dor findings. He talked humbly but still with a sense of pride. He was careful not to break the spell of the moment in the presence of the two great archaeology giants, General Yadin and Professor Mizrachi.

Someone knocked on the door. The laboratory manager, who was the formal host, opened the door and the Technion President entered. Professor Mizrachi addressed him as though he was still the Israeli Ambassador to Italy. The President reacted with a wide smile.

"You are just the man we need," said General Yigal Yadin. "It has been suggested that the Technion should consider adding an Archaeology faculty. Are there any new plans for such an addition?"

"General Yadin! You were the initiator of this idea," the President responded.

"And I will continue to push for it."

"Do you know a rich American who would be willing to write a check for three million dollars? If you do, we can start such a faculty next week."

"The price has gone up," shouted the lab photographer.

The room was filled with laughter.

"I heard about the new discoveries," the President ignored the laughter. "I came to meet Dr. Amram and to hear from him the details of his findings."

Professor Mizrachi stepped forward and invited the President to look at the Tel-Dor parchments, jars and coins.

The humility and the politeness of Professor Mizrachi impressed Avner, especially as Mizrachi expressed his appreciation for having access to the Laboratory at the Technion.

General Yadin paid little attention to the two parchments. He was more interested in the coins. A black coating covered them, indicating centuries of deterioration. He carefully cleaned the surface of one coin with a soft brush, revealing an image of the Temple. He promptly confirmed that it was minted during the Hashmonean era—most probably by Judah the Maccabee after the re-consecration of the Jerusalem Temple. He highlighted the need to clear coins with great care to avoid scratching their surfaces or damaging them in any way. Avner took the six coins marked 21 through 26, cleaned them and inspected them with the shiny magnifying glass he always carried in his bag whenever he was on an archaeology project. He placed the six coins in a small transparent plastic bag and put the bag in his pocket.

"Taking a few coins from this treasure is against all rules of operation of any dig," protested General Yadin. "All the coins should be kept together for a group evaluation".

"I know the logic and the value of a group evaluation," responded Avner. "I already discussed it with Professor Mizrachi and he consented. The Hebrew University will still have twenty coins to evaluate. I want to have the six coins evaluated by Professor Le Corbellier at the Sorbonne. If his finding coincides with the evaluation results at the Hebrew University, it will be a confirmation by another prominent archaeology laboratory."

General Yadin agreed reluctantly and the matter was forgotten.

Finally, Yadin looked at the flat Arabic parchment. Its edges were apparently damaged by fire, and parts of its inscription were not readable. The ancient Hebrew parchment was in worse condition. It was fragmented with several sections missing. He doubted if anyone could decipher it. He expressed some doubt about the authenticity of both parchments. He had seen fraudulent parchments before. He was also experienced with stolen artifacts found in excavation sites. On many occasions he had to deal with the theft of important artifacts, sometimes stolen by prominent political individuals.

"Let me tell you about my experience with stolen artifacts," he addressed Avner. "It is not a secret that our famous General Moshe Dayan is a collector of archaeological artifacts. In one famous instance of parchment theft which was widely thought to be contracted by our one-eyed General Dayan, I gave a lecture on the subject in which I said, 'I know who did it. I am not going to name him, but if I ever catch him, I will poke out his other eye'."

Avner found it hard to suppress a smile.

He asked the laboratory director to provide him with copies of the photographs and promised Professor Mizrachi to send him the results of his investigation.

Two weeks later, a letter from General Yadin arrived.

"Dear Professor Mizrachi and Dr. Avner Amram,

"Thank you for inviting me to see the clay jars, the coins and the parchments that your team

found at the Tel-Dor excavation site. I studied the photographs of the two sheepskin inscriptions. Both parchments seem to be authentic but I am waiting to receive your carbon-dating test results on both.

"The Hebrew parchment was not preserved well. Several sections are lost and other sections are hard to read with a naked eye. It is still remarkable that the parchment survived at all, considering that it was found so close to the salty waters of the Mediterranean Sea. Several sentences are hard to decipher because many words are missing. The inscription is in ancient Hebrew script. I include in this letter—in modern Hebrew script—the sections that I could read. I left spaces for the missing words and clauses. I am interested in receiving your opinion on the chances of filling the missing parts. Please send me a report on the carbon-dating tests. You should give this document a name.

"The Arabic parchment is in a much better condition, but it apparently survived a fire, because its edges are badly charred. I am attaching the text of both inscriptions to this letter.

Best Regards,
Yigal Yadin

The following is the text of the "Hebrew Tel-Dor Manuscript"
that I could read:

> *"When our father initiated the revolt against*
> *the Greeks in the village of Modi'in, his main*
> *objective was to fight the imposition of the Hellenic*
> *idol—worshiping in the country. Now that we have*
> *liberated Jerusalem and re-consecrated the Temple,*
> *I, Judah the son of Matityahu, am proposing*
> *to . . . . et . . . lan . . . .*
> *for . . . . By this I mean the very long . . . . .*
> *. . . . .*

> *"We have succeeded in our revolt because we*
> *gathered men who are dedicated to our cause. Men*
> *who fought not only with great bravery, but also*
> *with their belief in our G-d and the belief that . . . .*
> *. . . . . must always*
> *be . . . . The . . . .*
> *. . . . . exceptional significance"*

> *"The First Temple built by King Solomon was*
> *desecrated by King Nebuchadnetzar and its treasures*
> *were taken away to Babylon. The second Temple was*
> *desecrated by the Greeks and some of its treasures*
> *were taken from Jerusalem to Athens. . . . .*
> *. . . . .*
> *. o guard the . . . . from any . . . . . .*
> *in . . . . . .*

*"We have underestimated the importance of
the . . . . ms . . . d by the . . . .
. . . . their . . . .
. . . . duties. The . . . .
t, the Menorah and all the ceremonial items used by
the Priests have a monumental . . . . lue
that . . . . not only our soldiers but also every
Judean man, woman and child. We must . . . .
. . . . plan to . . . . these sacr
ed . . . . preparation for future possible
wars when the Temple may again be threatened by
an invading foreign army.*

*The plan must have the highest level of secrecy.
Its existence and its details will be revealed to onl
y . . . .
. . . .
The . . . . will be a future . . . . of
Judea, a future . . . ., inted by
. . . . and . . . .
appo . . . by . . . . as well as . . . .
. . . . . At the death of any of the . . . . . . an, the . . . . .
. . . . will appoint another . . . .
. . . . man within . . . . days. Each . . . .
. . . . ill appear before . . . .
. . . . to take a vow, to . .
. . . .
. . . . . . declaring that he . . . . the secret
to any person and . . . .
. . . to sacrifice his life rather than reveal the secret.
The group of . . . . men will be called "The
. . . ."*

The following is the text of the "Tel-Dor Arabic Manuscript" that I could read:

> Bism-Il-Allah Al-Rachman Ul-Rachim. In the name
> of Allah, the Beneficent and Merciful. I, Ibn Arabi,
> the philosopher of Islam in the great Mosque of
> Cordova, have seen the letter written by our prophet
> Mohammad.

In the letter, Mohammad wrote:

> **Allah is the unity of love, the lover and the**
> **beloved. Every love is a wish for union. Every love,**
> **consciously and unconsciously, is a love of Allah.**
> **Learn to discover in each man the seed of a desire**
> **for Allah. I received this second revelation on**
> **the Holy Mountain of Yerushalem Al Kuds after**
> **crossing the Jordan River on my Al Burak horse.**

> *In the name of Allah,*
> *I am Ibn Arabi"*

Professor Mizrachi summoned Dr. Avner Amram to see the letter. The Professor knew that it would not be a simple task to fill in the missing sections of the Hebrew parchment. The text was in ancient Hebrew script not known to readers of 20th century Hebrew script.

Professor Mizrachi looked at the short list of candidates who could be considered for the appointment as project researcher to evaluate the Tel-Dor findings. His "short list" consisted of only one candidate. He faced a dilemma and called the Tel Aviv office of General Yadin to ask for his advice.

"Hello Yigal," the Professor said. "I want to thank you for your assistance. I received your letter with the text of the two parchment inscriptions."

"I am the one who should thank you," responded Yigal Yadin. "You honored me by inviting me to see the Tel-Dor coins and parchments."

"I need your assistance again."

"I will be happy to offer my assistance in any way. How can I help you?"

"You know that I run a tight ship with my group of researchers and doctoral students. They demonstrate special interest in the subject matter of any project. We have dedicated and talented staff. When they receive a challenge, they face it with resolve and go to bat. They concentrate on issues directly related to the goal of the research project.

"For the evaluation of the Tel-Dor findings, I am considering Dr. Daphna Ben Horin as the project research manager. She is the only researcher I can trust, and she certainly has the credentials and the experience to tackle the problem. She is a post-doctoral archaeology researcher in our department. She received her PhD from the Sorbonne. Her doctoral dissertation was on the reliability and accuracy of carbon-14 dating technology used in evaluating ancient artifacts. However . . ."

"She seems to be the ideal candidate," interrupted Yigal Yadin.

"I agree with you, if it was not for a small problem. She minored in ancient Hebrew, but she may not know enough to reconstruct the inscription of the Hebrew parchment. Many fragments are missing and we'll need a researcher who specialized, not only in the ancient Hebrew scripts, but who is also well-versed with the sentence structures and idioms used in ancient Hebrew at the time of Judah the Maccabee. Besides . . ."

"Speak no more," General Yadin interrupted him. "I have the right man for the job. He was a student of Professor Le Corbellier at the Sorbonne. His name is Dr. Solomon Buzaglo. I don't know where he is now, but he is the man you are looking for. I am sure that Le Corbellier will be able to find him. Call Paris. He'll help you to locate Dr. Buzaglo."

Professor Mizrachi took the advice of General Yadin and called Paris.

The next day, Professor Mizrachi, Dr. Daphna Ben-Horin and Dr. Amram met to inspect the jars, the coins and the parchment. Avner added two new entries to his list of documents. He wrote "Tel-Dor Hebrew Parchment" and "Tel-Dor Arabic Parchment", again wondering if they were authentic or copies of original documents. He wished he could gather a team of Jewish researchers whose mission would be to locate the original "Judah Maccabee Scroll", which might have been in the hands of Queen Shlom-Zion. He concluded that such a group would require considerable funding. It would be extremely difficult, and maybe impossible, to convince any Jewish philanthropist to finance such a project.

Or would it?

Avner tried to understand the operation of the Archaeology faculty at the Hebrew University. From the twelve doctoral students at the faculty who were engaged in research, only five were assistant lecturers. They worked on different aspects of archaeology and in projects requiring cooperation with other faculties or other universities. All twelve students knew that only one has a future career at the Hebrew University. They were encouraged to start working on a career either in another university or in an organization that could benefit from their training in archaeology. The senior lecturers looked at them as potential followers who might contribute to their own careers. Having heard of fierce competition and even cases of active interference and sabotage of research projects by fellow student lecturers at MIT, Avner was intrigued by the lack of competition between the assistant lecturers at the Hebrew University.

Am I missing something? Is one of the scholars so careful that he can hide his efforts to undermine the research of his colleagues? Are the Tel-Dor findings safe at the open campus? Can an Arab student have access to our parchments? Can the Arab workers at the site interfere with the search by stealing artifacts for profit?

*   *   *

"I completed the Tel-Dor carbon-dating tests," Dr. Daphna Ben-Horin informed Professor Mizrachi as she entered his laboratory without knocking on the door.

"I hope that all your results are conclusive without any reservations or doubts," was his response as he lifted his head from a microscope. "I don't want to repeat the Massada case when we had to perform a secondary evaluation in Paris."

"Well, here is the story," Dr. Ben-Horin continued. "I can definitely confirm that the coins and the jars are authentic. The coins bear their minting date, which was just after the temple of Jerusalem re-consecration by Judah the Maccabee. This places them at ninety years before the reign of Shlom-Zion, the Hashmonean Queen."

Daphna hesitated a moment prompting the Professor to turn his head with impatient eyes.

"I can also confirm that the Arabic parchment is from the 6th century. Carbon tests cannot be used to date the ink. One method of dating ink is by using spectrographic methods to determine its composition and comparing the result to tables showing what inks were used in what historical periods. The spectrographic scanning test shows that it is ink from the 18th century. Naturally, the 12th century Ibn Arabi philosopher could not have written this inscription using 18th century ink. There is only one conclusion. It's either a copy of an original one written by Ibn Arabi, or it is fraudulent. General Yadin warned us about fraudulent artifacts."

"What about the Hebrew parchment?"

"I am afraid that the carbon-dating tests of the Hebrew parchment provided us with two different dates. One indicates that it is from the second century BCE and two other tests indicate that it is from first century BCE. I want to obtain the opinion of two different experts."

"This means that there will be another delay."

"Yes. I'll need more time."

CHAPTER 12

1970 Fathers and Sons

B ASHIR, THE ELDER son of Ahmad Ibn Najad, entered his father's office with a smile.

"They found it," he announced without enthusiasm.

"I know. I already received a report from Suleiman," replied Ibn Najad. "He is very valuable. When he volunteered to work last summer at the Tel-Dor excavation site, Professor Mizrachi was delighted. He issued a news release announcing the addition of an Arab student to the team of volunteers."

"Was it your idea to plant the parchment at Tel-Dor?"

"I considered it as an option, but without one of our man on the digging team, it was pointless. I had already planted it in a Jerusalem cave."

"So you changed your mind after Suleiman's application was approved?"

"Yes, when he started working there as our spy, I reconsidered. He found an ideal place for the parchment. I approved it and he placed the parchment on a Saturday, when the Jewish volunteers did not work."

"Were you at the site last week?" Ibn Najad asked.

"I was there yesterday," Bashir was not excited about his father's schemes of planting fake parchments, but he knew how to follow orders.

*   *   *

Reaching the age of seventy has always been considered a special gift from Allah. It was an occasion to celebrate in every city, town and village—in palaces, mansions and in Bedouin tents.

In 1970, Bashir invited the village Mukhtar, the village Imam and several distinguished guests from Jerusalem, to celebrate the seventieth birthday of his father, Ahmad Ibn-Najad. Not wanting to distract from his father's birthday, he did not inform any of his guests that he himself was celebrating his own fiftieth birthday.

*   *   *

Bashir was a gifted manager. After completing his studies at the American University in Beirut, he managed his father's farm and the selling of its fruits, olives, olive oil and other farm produce to the Jerusalem farmers market. He became his father's trusted advisor on many Bismillah activities. A few of his subordinates at Bismillah called him "the Dinosaur". They had heard a legend that dinosaurs were peaceful creatures, but they considered him an exception. They were constantly afraid of him. His bulging eyes, his sharp tongue, his uncontrolled temper and his demand for perfection, installed in them an image of a despot. His shadow was always in the air even when he was not in their presence. They feared his unpredictable temperament when he returned, always asking the same question: "What did you accomplish when I was not here?"

While waiting for his guests to arrive, Bashir reflected about his gradual ascent on the echelon of Bismillah.

*　　*　　*

Although Bashir did not live on a farm, his home was no mere farmhouse, but a mansion of magnificent design. It was located at the outskirts of the village. It had eight large guest rooms and a beautiful garden known in the village as "Bashir's Bustan". Colorful rose bushes decorated the flowerbeds with several orange and grapefruit trees planted along the Bustan fences. Bashir personally took special care of the one sweet lemon tree near the house gate. He took pride in offering his guests homegrown sweet lemons not found in most villages. A grove of forty olive trees spanned from outside the eastern fence of the Bustan to the edge of his farmland. When he had purchased the farm, its previous owner informed him that the olive trees were planted there four hundred years earlier. He had five sons and three daughters. Because he spent most of his time assisting his father at Bismillah, he delegated the managing of his farm to his elder son Farid.

Farid and his four brothers led the invited guests to the circular garden with a large water fountain at its center surrounded by blooming rose bushes. They escorted each guest to a garden armchair with a small table next to it. The three daughters brought plates of food and drinks, and placed them on the tables of the guests.

Following an hour of socializing, Bashir stood at the center of his garden to welcome his guests:

"*Bism-Allah Al Rahman Ul-Rahim*. In the name of Allah the Beneficent and the Merciful, I welcome all of our guests to my home. I thank you all for coming here today to honor my father Ahmad Ibn Najad on his seventieth birthday.

"You all know my father's dedication in creating and operating the Bismillah organization and for advancing our cause in undermining the Jewish claim to Jerusalem. He has accomplished much in helping the poor and in performing important research in the service of the Arab people. He has been a model father to his children and a good provider to our family. I must admit that I am prejudiced about my father. Instead of my praising him, I invited our most honored Mukhtar to say a few words in his honor."

The Mukhtar, the leading figure in the village and a member of the Muslim High Council of Palestine, walked to the center of the garden and addressed the guests:

"I cannot say anything about our friend Ibn Najad without reminding you that the Bismillah organization was the creation of our great leader Haj Amin Al-Husseini, the former Grand Mufti of Jerusalem. His successes in the 1920 and the 1929 riots are noteworthy. His call to arms resulted in the killing and expulsion of all the Jews of Hebron. He organized the 1929 and 1936 riots, calling us to kill Jews anywhere in Palestine. Our enemies call him radical, but we all call him the true hero who started our jihad against the Jews. He is the man who declared that the Arabs will definitely drive the Jews out of Palestine, even if it takes a thousand years to do it.

"When you selected me to be your representative in the Muslim Council, I took an oath to work for the success of the Grand Mufti plan. I promise you that soon we will accomplish his goal of throwing the Jews of Palestine into the sea. It will not be a thousand years from now.

"Haj Amin deserves the credit for creating Bismillah, but Ahmad Ibn Najad gets the credit for making it happen, for managing it and for making it grow to the formidable organization it is today."

Five other guests followed the Mukhtar in praising Ibn Najad. Bashir invited his father to respond.

Ibn Najad stood up, walked to the center of the garden, looked around and invited his son to stand next to him.

"I thank you all for coming here today. I especially want to honor all of you who have helped me in raising the money to make Bismillah successful.

"Instead of delivering a speech about me, I want to say a few words about my son, your host today.

"Bashir deserves a great deal of credit for all the work he has done as my deputy at Bismillah. When I sent him to Istanbul to explore the possibility of creating a chapter there, he created the most important chapter in our network. I was especially impressed when the Great Imam of Istanbul invited Bashir to his home and provided a sizable donation to the original welfare center for poor Muslims in the suburbs. In less than three years, the Istanbul branch became the jewel of Bismillah. Bashir organized chapters of our organizations in several Islamic centers in the Middle East. Now he plans to open new chapters in other countries.

"During the last ten years, I have monitored my son's work and I groomed him for the day when he would be ready to replace me. Today is the day. It is my pleasure to announce my decision to retire and to appoint my son as the next Director of Bismillah."

The guests stood up clapping their hands with a bursting applause to congratulate Bashir on his new promotion. The Mukhtar called for a village festival to honor the new director. Praising him for his dedication to the Arab cause, he invited him to say a few words.

"I am honored and privileged," said Bashir. "I stand here before you and pledge to continue expanding the operations of Bismillah. I'll follow my father's example to groom my son, Farid, to take over from me when the time arrives."

Farid celebrated his twentieth birthday.

CHAPTER 13

1970 The New Direction

B ASHIR NEVER LIKED the Bismillah charter's directive of limiting it to non-violent operations. He knew about his father's schemes of creating fraudulent ancient parchments and using them to deceive Jewish researchers, but he considered such schemes too tame in fighting the Jews. As the new director of the organization, he wanted to be more like Haj Amin Al-Husseini. He wanted to be aggressive in undermining the Jewish claim to any part of what he still considered Arab Palestine, from the Jordan River to the sea.

"Congratulations are in order," Farid greeted his father as he entered his office. "Did you prepare an agenda for today's meeting?"

"We don't need an agenda, and we don't need a meeting. I have a mission for you, if you think you can handle it."

"What type of a mission?"

"The Jews discovered an ancient parchment at an excavation site in Tel-Dor. I want you to find where the parchment is kept.

You are a student at the University. You can ask someone in the archaeology department."

"Why does it interest you?"

"You already know that your grandfather had prepared fake parchments and planted them in various places to mislead the Jewish researchers. I want to own the Tel-Dor authentic ancient parchment. I want to be more active in placing obstacles and in interfering with the archaeological research of Professor Mizrachi."

"How can we do anything?" Farid asked. "What do we know about archaeology or about deciphering parchments?"

"I'll find someone who can help us. I'll recruit an Arab scholar at the Hebrew University who is specializing in archaeology. I may even recruit a scholar in Middle East studies at Oxford or at the Sorbonne."

"Forget the Hebrew University. There are only ten archaeology scholars at the Hebrew University, and they are all Jewish."

"Farid. If I have to, I'll even recruit one of them."

Bashir's declaration amazed Farid.

*   *   *

Mahmood Azkari was an excellent student at the Hebrew University under a full scholarship awarded by the Section of Arab Affairs in the Israeli Ministry of Education. After he earned his first degree majoring in political science, the ministry offered him an additional stipend to pursue an advanced degree in Middle Eastern studies. On the advice of his mother, he went to meet Bashir.

"I hear nothing but praises about your success at the university," Bashir welcomed Mahmood in his large village home.

"Don't believe these praises," Mahmood was humble about his studies. "They are exaggerated. I worked hard to earn my degree."

"I also heard that you've been offered a new stipend for continuing your studies."

"I am not sure I want to accept it."

"Why would you refuse to accept a stipend?"

"I have to go back to the farm to support my mother and three brothers," Mahmood explained. "My father died last year, and the stipend will not feed my family."

"So it's a financial decision. If your family had adequate income, would you want to continue your studies and earn an advanced degree?"

"Certainly I would. I love political science, and I would want to specialize in Middle Eastern Studies. Before my father's death, my goal was to work for the Israeli Ministry of Foreign Affairs. I had visions of being appointed the first Arab Ambassador of Israel in a foreign country. Now I'll have to become a farmer with a college degree."

Bashir did not respond. He examined Mahmood as if he wanted to penetrate his brain and read his thoughts.

Mahmood waited in silence trying to understand the purpose of the meeting.

"Instead of becoming a farmer," Bashir broke the silence, "you could work for me. Bismillah can use your abilities and I can pay you more than the stipend."

"I am interested," Mahmood had at last figured out the purpose of the meeting. "I'll agree only if you'll cover my family's expenses and help me and my brothers to run the farm."

"What will I do in Bismillah?" He added.

"Let me worry about that. For a start, I want you to accept the stipend."

Mahmood was shocked.

It makes no sense. First he offers me a job instead of
the stipend and then he tells me to accept the stipend.
What does he really want me to do?

He decided to remain cool and collected.

"You'll have to pay me a very good salary, to support my family and to hire another man to help my young brothers manage the farm."

"Naturally," Bashir reacted reassuringly. "I'll cover your family's expenses. I want to invest in you for the future. I may ask you to help Bismillah in some of our activities."

"It sounds good to me." Mahmood could not believe his luck.

Two weeks later, Mahmood came out from his mother's house in the village to see Bashir approaching.

"Mahmood," the visitor addressed his new recruit. "I have an important job for you."

"Welcome to our home. May I offer you some coffee? We could have it on the porch."

"I prefer to talk to you outside. Let's take a walk."

Mahmood followed him.

"Have you heard of the Tel-Dor excavation project?" Bashir asked.

"I have heard that ancient coins and an old parchment were discovered there."

"That is the story. However, we found that it's not the truth. It's a ploy spread by the Jews." Bashir stated. "We found an envelope marked "Tel-Dor—Confidential" in the office of Professor Mizrachi. We photographed it and its content. We found that it included *only* six old coins and a note written in Hebrew. There was no parchment in the envelope."

"What was written in the note?" Mahmood asked.

"It included a secret message:

> 'To protect the valuable coins, we must release a
> news item telling the media that we found an old
> parchment. It will help our status in archaeological
> circles and will divert the public's interest from the
> coins'."

"How did you manage to find the envelope?" Mahmood asked.

"One of our members walked into the office of Professor Mizrachi at night and searched his desk."

> *I won't tell Bashir that I know the answer to my*
> *question. I helped Farid to look for the parchment.*
> *Farid has been my friend since childhood. I don't*
> *want to get him in trouble with his father.*

"Can I see the picture of the coins?" Mahmood asked curiously.

Bashir was pleased to see the interest his recent recruit showed. "I brought it with me to show you."

"I am not an archaeologist, but I think that they are fake coins," Mahmood declared after inspecting the photograph.

"Are you sure?"

"As sure as 'today is Sunday'. Your operative was tricked. I bet the envelope was left purposely on the professor's desk. Bismillah knows nothing about archaeology. You need an expert."

"That is the reason for my bringing you into Bismillah." Bashir declared with a smile. "You are not an archaeologist, but you can find the parchment and bring it to me."

"How will I do that? I don't know where to look for it."

"You must find a way," Bashir was adamant, "unless you want me to stop paying for your mother's surgery."

Mahmood's face froze. He had not expected such blatant blackmail, especially after being such a dedicated supporter of Bashir and after successfully recruiting three new Arab students. *Bashir is still 'Bashir the Dinosaur'.*

"This is a new Bismillah. We are going to be more like Haj Amin and like my father, Ibn Najad, used to be. We are going to kill Jews, just like my father did in Hebron."

"Those days are gone. There are no British soldiers. We succeeded because the British did not protect the Hebron Jews. The Israeli army knows how to protect every Jewish town and village."

"I have a plan, and I want you to be in charge of this operation."

*   *   *

Mahmood and his six Bismillah cell members gathered at the Village of Kafr-El-Araby. It was only six kilometers from the Egyptian border and five kilometers from the Jewish Kibbutz of Ein-Darom. They were armed with AK-47 assault rifles.

"Today is the day when you will show your dedication to Bismillah's Jihad," Mahmood enjoyed his new authority over his younger recruits.

As they approached the Kibbutz dunes after sunset, Mahmood heard a warning.

"I hear people approaching."

"Lie down. It could be an Israeli army patrol."

In the shadow of the moon, they saw a group of soldiers passing quietly twenty meters away and disappearing into the night. They hid until midnight in the shallow valley east of the Kibbutz.

They infiltrated one by one through the Kibbutz barbed wire fence. The Ein-Darom children's dormitory was a one story building located near the fence. The Bismillah militants entered the building before dawn, finding all the children asleep.

"The western fence has been breached," the Kibbutz night watchman informed his security officer. "I saw footsteps in the sand. Several men entered the Kibbutz compound. Sound the alarm. We are under attack by Intifada Jihadists."

The army patrol entered through the main gate when the siren woke everyone in the Kibbutz.

"They are in the children's dormitory," shouted a young woman dressed in pajamas. "I ran out when I heard the children crying."

"I speak in the name of Allah and our leader Arafat," Mahmood announced on the Kibbutz loudspeakers. "All your children and three adults are in the dormitory hallway. They will be our hostages until our demands are met."

After several hours of assessing the situation by the Israeli army general staff, an elite Sayeret Matkal special force unit arrived in the Kibbutz. The Prime Minister decided to negotiate with the Jihadists. Their demand was the release of 400 Arab terrorists.

Before any negotiation started, Mahmood decided that his demand would be more credible if he demonstrated that he meant business. Three shots were heard, and three dead children were thrown out of a dormitory window. They were all under the age of five.

The Sayeret Matkal unit commander was given the green light to attack the dormitory. His squads broke through the building from three different directions. The commander shot at Mahmood while he was firing at the children with his sub-machine gun.

*　　*　　*

Bashir read the news about Ein-Darom. His Bismillah fighters killed eighteen pre-school children. He was pleased. *Mahmood's six recruits sacrificed their lives for our cause. They are our newest martyrs.*

CHAPTER 14

1970 Parchments at Sea

A VNER WAS BACK at Harvard preparing a research program for his doctorate thesis. The Tel-Dor excavation project was a central component of the research needed to obtain his degree in archaeology. He struggled with the way he would present the subject to make it unique and different from other dissertations. He prepared a synopsis of his proposed thesis for submittal to several notable archaeologists with a request for their reviews and opinions. He selected three from a list proposed to him by Professor Mizrachi.

He wanted to start with his friend, the Israeli born Professor Bar David of Harvard, but Bar David had departed to spend the following three months in Turkey. He tried Professor Thomas King, the Dean of Archaeology at Oxford, only to learn that he was on a two-month project in India. When he contacted Professor Armand Le Corbellier's office at the Sorbonne, he learned that the professor planned to conduct a Biblical seminar on a Caribbean cruise.

Being an engineer, Avner tried to calculate the probability of having all three professors unavailable at the same time. According to his calculation, if no external factors are considered, the probability was not very high, unless all three professors were attending an archaeology conference. Because this was not the case, he gave up on the idea of solving the problem using a mathematical tool. He started to identify less notable academic archaeologists to be his advisors.

On the following day, Avner received a telephone call from Paris.

"My office informed me that you requested a meeting with me," Professor Le Corbellier was on the phone. "I left instructions not to make any new appointments for me during the next three months. I will be on a seminar at sea and on another project away from Paris during the following two months."

"Thank you for responding to my request. I had hoped that we could meet sometime next week. I want to obtain your advice on a special project that I plan for my dissertation at Harvard. Will you make an exception and see me this week? I can be in Paris tomorrow if you could find the time."

"I had planned not to make any exceptions, but a telephone call from Professor Mizrachi changed my mind. He told me about your Tel-Dor discoveries and suggested that I invite you and Dr. Daphna Ben-Horin to join me in the seminar at sea. Next week I'll conduct a seminar on a Caribbean cruise ship sponsored by the American Biblical Archaeology Society. I am very interested in hearing about the Tel-Dor discoveries. I am extending an invitation for you and your wife to attend the seminar. If you accept my invitation, I'll invite Dr. Ben-Horin and her husband."

Avner was excited about the invitation but responded politely.

"I accept your invitation and I am sure that my wife will be delighted."

Avner admired Le Corbellier. He was an international giant in his field. Everyone agreed that if Le Corbellier labeled an archaeologist as being "adequate", that individual should immediately look for another profession.

Avner and Elaine had never been on a cruise ship before. While Elaine was excited about visiting the Caribbean Islands, for Avner, it was an opportunity he could not miss. He had hoped to spend half an hour with Professor Le Corbellier in his office in Paris to discuss his doctoral thesis. Instead, he had the opportunity to spend ten days with him on a cruise ship. Combining business and pleasure is always nice when you can plan it, but he never expected Divine intervention in this unexpected plan.

Professor Le Corbellier scheduled a meeting with Avner for the day before the embarkation of the Norwegian cruise ship at Fort Lauderdale. However, the flight from Boston to Fort Lauderdale was delayed before take off after all the passengers boarded. Waiting for the mechanical problem to be resolved, the flight captain instructed the crew to entertain the passengers.

"Unfortunately, we have a small mechanical problem," the Captain announced over the loudspeakers. "We are forced to wait on the tarmac for a replacement part. The delay should be less than an hour."

Such delays were common, but this one was unique.

"To entertain you, I have instructed our crew to announce a game at the end of which the winner will receive a bottle of Champagne. Look in your pockets or purses and find a coin with the oldest minting date. The winner will be the person who can produce the oldest coin, maybe a penny from the First World War or an old buffalo nickel, a Canadian Maple Leaf, A French Louis from the time of Napoleon, a Mexican Peso or any coin minted by any country. Members of our crew will stop at your seat if you have a coin they can inspect. Good luck."

The passengers were busy inspecting coins found in their pockets and purses. Two airline attendants moved from row to row announcing the dates of the coins presented to them.

"1948 US penny, 1892 US buffalo nickel, 1790 British shilling, 1895 French Louis," the dates were announced by passengers, repeated by an attending stewardess and repeated again by an announcer on the loudspeakers. Avner stood up and announced,

"Six coins minted by Judah the Maccabee in 160 BCE."

All announcements stopped. The Captain came out of the cockpit heading to Avner's seat. He looked at the six coins in amazement.

"Are they really that old?" He asked.

"They were discovered in an Israeli excavation site this summer. My wife and I are on our way to show them in an archaeology seminar".

"There is no doubt that you are the winner," announced the captain, "unless someone else has a coin from the time of Moses."

Everyone laughed at the captain's remark. When no one answered his Moses challenge, the captain walked back to the cockpit and returned with two bottles in his hands. He took the microphone from the flight attendant and announced.

"For six coins from the time of the Maccabees, you deserve six bottles of champagne, but I only have two," announced the captain. "I am pleased to award you with two champagne bottles. They are not 800-dollar bottles of 1964 Dom Perignon, but they are French, and reasonably good, I'm told. Congratulations! A flight attendant will see that you get them when we reach our destination. Speaking of which, we have just been cleared for takeoff. Please fasten your seatbelts, everyone."

"Why did you have the old coins in your pocket?" Elaine asked. "I thought that you packed them in your suitcase."

"They are too valuable to take a chance. My suitcase could be lost," replied Avner. "Besides, last night I had a dream that I would be rewarded for finding the Maccabee coins. I am starting to believe in dreams. My coins have proven to be worth something. They are worth at least two bottles of Champagne, and you thought that archaeology does not pay."

*   *   *

Avner and Elaine arrived at the Fort Lauderdale port just in time for the cruise embarkation. The first meeting of the Biblical Archaeology Society group on the ship was held on the following afternoon when the ship was already at sea heading to the Caribbean islands. Most of the seminar attendees were members of the Archaeology Society, including one rabbi, two priests, two ministers and three professors. The Biblical Society cruise director conducted the first meeting without the presence of Professor Le Corbellier.

On the following day, Le Corbellier opened the seminar by giving a lecture he called "Hebrew Archaeology and Document Research 101."

> "The search for lost Hebrew parchments from the time of the Temple has fascinated and captivated generations of archaeologists, historians and researchers in many universities and research centers. Many Hebrew manuscripts and documents have been found, but only a few are from the time of the Temple.

"Digging in excavation sites is aimed primarily in searches for towns, buildings, clay jars, coins, ancient tools, ancient weapons and other artifacts which can shed light on a specific period of interest. Documents are rarely found, nor are they expected to be found in excavation digs, especially if they are written on biodegradable paper. Paper decomposes in the presence of the lightest humidity. Sheepskin parchments do not decompose but they do deteriorate in different environments.

"Manuscripts less than five hundred years old have survived relatively well when compared to older ones, especially Roman-era documents. The manuscripts found in the Cairo *Genizah* in the 19th century by Solomon Schechter, were stored inside a synagogue in the dry weather of Egypt. The 2000 years old Dead Sea Scrolls, survived primarily because they were in the Qumran caves of the dry Judean desert. In contrast, most manuscripts in the humid European climate have severely decomposed. The many Hebrew parchments found in Europe are mostly less than 500 years old. The only manuscripts found in Europe have been kept inside dry buildings.

"The Italian *Genizah* at the University of Bologna includes thousands of manuscripts that survived because they were kept in dry storage rooms of monasteries, convents and book binders. During the 15th and 16th centuries, the Spanish and Portuguese Inquisitions confiscated and burned Jewish books in the Iberian Peninsula. In 1553, Pope Julius III issued a decree to burn all the Talmud books which could be found. In 1614, another Pope confiscated all Hebrew books written on parchments. Hundreds of Church notary books were found with bindings made of Torah scroll pages glued together. Many Torah scroll pages were used in church financial and deed records written on the clear back side of scroll pages. Archival restorers and researchers painstakingly managed to separate the glued pages and catalog them as Torah pages from the Iberian Peninsula or from Germany, a few dating as far back as the 9th century."

Following the first lecture, Avner introduced himself to the professor and Dr. Ben-Horin introduced her husband.

"My dear Daphna," announced Professor Le Corbellier with delight. "It's nice to see you again. When Professor Mizrachi called me, I told him that he was fortunate to have you on his team of researchers."

"It's good to see you again," Daphna responded repeating the same greeting. "You have always been my inspiration at the Sorbonne. You are the leader of young archeologists who dream about emulating you. You are our role model."

"Camille would love to see you," added Le Corbellier. "I reserved a table for six for dinner tonight hoping that you and your husband would accept my invitation. I also invited Dr. Amram and his wife to join us."

As the ship was cruising toward the Caribbean Island of Aruba, the three couples were socializing at the dinner table in the ship's large dining hall. Professor Le Corbellier introduced his wife Camille to the two couples.

"It is a pleasure to welcome archaeologists to our seminar," opened the professor in his heavy French accent. "However, this evening I prefer to avoid talking about any topic that is related to the seminar. Leave such topics for the lecture hall."

"I love this opportunity to avoid archaeology for one evening," reacted Elaine joyfully. "How about art? Does anyone know anything about the collection of paintings that are shown on the main deck of the ship?"

"Paintings are not my specialty," said Camille. "However, I read that there will be several art auctions of serigraphs, prints and even a few original paintings by Picasso, Salvador Dali, Delacroix, Velasquez, David Sharir and many others."

"Originals by Picasso, Dali, Delacroix and Velasquez would require astronomical insurance premiums," Elaine reacted.

"Maybe they are all copies by students like your copies," Camille responded.

Elaine smiled.

Hearing no other comments about paintings, Avner took the initiative to start another topic.

"I must tell you a little episode that entertained Elaine and me on our flight from Boston."

"You cannot tell them about it," reacted Elaine. "It's an entertaining episode, but it includes an archaeology element."

"Well," said Le Corbellier, "If the episode is entertaining, it won't break my rule. I will allow it to bend it a little."

"Elaine is right," said Avner. "I'll accept her opinion and tell the episode during the seminar."

"Let me tell you about my love of the sea," Le Corbellier started another topic. "I spent two years in underwater research under the supervision of Jacques Cousteau, the French marine researcher. I observed, assisted and participated in lowering his mini-submarine down the northern shores of the Mediterranean Sea at Monte Carlo."

"Did you ever go down in the submarine?" Elaine asked.

"I certainly did. I have a collection of photographs that I personally took from inside the research submarine. I photographed the underwater cave with prehistoric art near Marseilles. I also photographed the multitude of fish that chose to live in Mediterranean waters. Many of the photographs are decorating our home. I consider them just as beautiful as the paintings that you admire, Mrs. Amram."

The professor kept everyone in a daze. He succeeded in presenting himself as a remarkable individual who took his research work seriously, but who also knew how to enjoy life by finding non-scholarly activities outside the world of research. At the end of the evening, Le Corbellier invited both Dr. Avner Amram and Dr. Daphna Ben-Horin to participate in the seminar and talk about the discoveries at the Tel-Dor excavation site.

"There will be a change in the seminar plan," Le Corbellier announced at the second meeting. "We'll have three lectures on artifacts and documents related to the book of the Maccabees. Two archaeology researchers will tell us about their recent discoveries in an excavation site in Israel and their research on artifacts and parchments from the time of the Maccabees."

Avner invited questions after his lecture on Tel-Dor,

"Dr. Amram! Are there other scrolls that have such a significant impact on Jewish history?" Asked one of the priests.

"The Dead Sea scrolls are just an example of how much we learned about our ancient history. Any scrolls or parchments from the time of the First Temple of Jerusalem would present dramatic new information. There is a significant document written in the second century CE and discovered in the 13th century."

"Is it related to your search for the lost scroll?"

"Yes. It was hidden together with our scroll."

"Can you tell us about it?"

Avner looked at Le Corbellier as though he pleaded for permission. The Professor did not nod back with his consent.

"It is not part of my lecture today."

After the following lecture, Le Corbellier met with Avner to hear his dissertation plan. Avner had prepared a detailed presentation for Le Corbellier. He showed the professor a photograph of the Tel-Dor parchment and the partially deciphered inscription by General Yadin.

"We cannot complete the deciphering. We need the assistance of a scholar who specialized in the ancient Hebrew spoken at the time of the Maccabees. Deciphering the Tel-Dor inscription is central to my plan. I don't know if the fragment is part of the real Judah Maccabee scroll. We also need your advice on how to deal with the uncertainty of the parchment carbon dating results."

Le Corbellier listened patiently without interrupting Avner's presentation.

"The Tel-Dor project might not represent the end of my research. It could be just the beginning of a bigger project which I plan to implement. I need your assistance. I also hope to find some clues on the location of the hidden Menorah."

Avner stopped his presentation, waiting to hear if Le Corbellier would ask any questions, but he heard none.

"This is a good opportunity to tell you about my plan to launch a project by archaeologists and other scientists to search for the missing Judah Maccabee scroll. It will be an interesting project requiring considerable funding. I hope that you will agree to advise us or even join the Board of Directors of the project, when it is ready for launching."

The Professor listened patiently while making notes on issues that seemed important to him.

"I took notes on every detail that you described," Le Corbellier said after Avner's presentation. "I'll hold my comments until after the next seminar lecture."

"We have a few minutes left," Le Corbellier added after the next lecture. "I can tell you a little about the second century document.

"One of my teachers at the Sorbonne was Dr. Sukenic, the father of General Yadin. He gave a lecture on this manuscript at the university and later gave me a copy of his notes. It was about the second century manuscript.

"The very long manuscript was written by the prominent Talmudic Rabbi Shimon Bar Yochai who was sentenced to death by the Romans. Together with his son and eight other rabbis, he hid in a cave from 162 CE to 175 CE when he wrote the manuscript. After his death, his companions hid all his writings together with the scroll of Rabbi Akiva. The manuscript was lost until the 13th century when a prominent rabbi in Spain discovered it and published it as the most important Kabala document. The scroll was never found."

CHAPTER 15

1970 The Curaçao Parchment

"IT IS A great puzzle," Avner interrupted Le Corbellier's lecture. "We know so much about Bar Yochai, and yet we know so little. He is mentioned four thousand times in the Talmud. His hiding in a cave has been documented over centuries, but nobody knows what happened to the secret scroll given to him by Rabbi Akiva."

"Historical researchers suggest that the Bar Yochai manuscripts and the scroll were taken to Spain by Jewish refugees." Le Corbellier continued. "After the Bar-Kochva revolt, the Romans expelled all the Jews from Jerusalem, punishing them brutally. They resettled the royal families and the nobility as far away from Jerusalem as possible. The farthest territory at that time was Spain.

"Spanish and Portuguese Inquisition archives from the fifteenth and sixteenth centuries include lists of families who were descendants of Judean royal families. We know that Don Yitzchak Abravanel, the financial advisor of King Ferdinand and Queen Isabella of Castile, was a direct descendant of King David.

It is, therefore, reasonable to assume that Judean state secrets and religious documents were taken to the Iberian Peninsula and hidden there.

"Most researchers agree that philosophical and mystical parts of the Bar Yochai manuscripts were discovered in Spain in the 13th century. They were published as 'The Book of the Zohar' by the Kabbalist Rabbi Moshe De Leon."

"This should raise an important question," interrupted one of the seminar participants. "What prevented Rabbi Moshe De Leon from publishing the content of the scroll?"

"You raised a reasonable question," Le Corbellier responded. "One possibility is that the Akiva scroll was not found with the Bar Yochai manuscripts. The other is that the scroll may have included information considered by Rabbi De Leon as secret and should be hidden from the public, especially if it identified the hidden locations of the Menorah and the Ark of the Covenant. Let us speculate on what could have happened to Rabbi Akiva's scroll.

"If the Akiva scroll was taken to Spain by refugees from Jerusalem, it could have been lost or destroyed at the time of the expulsion of Jews from Spain in 1492. In that case, it may never be found, because Torquemada, Queen Isabella's confessor, instructed the Spanish Inquisition to burn all Hebrew books and manuscripts left behind by the expelled Jews.

"It is possible, and even probable, that one of the expelled Jews took the scroll with him to Constantinople, or Amsterdam, or any Mediterranean country where the Jews refugees settled after the expulsion.

"It could also be in Curaçao, where refugees settled in the 16th century. Who knows? Maybe we can find someone who could provide us with some information tomorrow."

"Tomorrow?" a participant inquired with amazement.

"Yes. Tomorrow, after our ship docks in Curaçao, we'll visit the Willemstad synagogue which was built in 1651."

Avner added the scroll to his list. He gave it two names; one was the "Bar Yochai Scroll" and the other was the "Rabbi Akiva Scroll". He added a note: "It was probably the original "Judah the Maccabee Scroll."

*   *   *

On the next day, the cruise ship docked at the harbor of Willemstad. The Biblical Archaeology seminar group chartered a guided tour that included a visit to the Mikve-Yisrael Synagogue, whose director was also the curator of the adjacent Jewish Museum.

"It is my pleasure to introduce to you my friend, Dr. Solomon Buzaglo," Le Corbellier addressed the seminar group at the museum. "He was one of my star students at the Sorbonne. I asked him to tell us about the museum and about his family history."

"Yes, Dr. Amram," he added joyfully while looking at Avner with a big smile. "Dr. Buzaglo is the most competent researcher who could help your project."

Addressing the curator, he added:

"Dear Solomon. One of the central subjects of our seminar is his recent discovery of an ancient parchment in Israel. It was analyzed and determined to be from the time of the Maccabees. You told me about an old family parchment inherited from one of your ancestors. Please tell our group of visitors about your family and anything you may know about this parchment."

"I am honored to be asked to say a few words," opened the curator, "especially because of the ancient parchment."

"During the expulsion from Spain, some of my family members moved from Toledo, Spain to Portugal seeking refuge there, only to be expelled again five years later. Some moved to Amsterdam, while others sailed to the new world and settled in Recife, a small harbor town in Brazil, where they enjoyed religious freedom under the Dutch. After the 1654 defeat by the Portuguese, the Jewish community disintegrated and its members left with the Dutch to escape from the Portuguese Inquisition. My family moved to the Curaçao Island where they again found religious freedom under the Dutch. Two members of my family were among the twenty three Recife refugees who sought refuge in New Amsterdam, and who founded the first Jewish community in the town which later became the city of New York.

"There is a family story about an ancient parchment which was in the possession of an ancestor refugee from Spain, Don Miguel de Leon. He apparently took the parchment to Amsterdam and gave it to its Chief Rabbi. We were told that it had a Hebrew inscription that only Don Miguel was able to read. I don't know what happened to it, but I imagine that its secret may be found in the Amsterdam Jewish community archives."

Avner added another entry to his list. He named the Curaçao document "The Miguel de Leon parchment".

When Dr. Buzaglo continued his other family stories, Avner did not pay any attention to the speaker. His mind created new questions and speculations on his growing list of the scrolls and parchments.

> "How is each parchment or scroll connected to another on my list? Which one is the most probable to be the same as another? Which one is authentic and real, if any? Which one is a fake parchment, if any? Would I ever find the answer? Am I on a wild goose chase? It could take me years or decades to find the answer, or never. Maybe I have bitten off more than I can chew."

Before leaving the Curaçao museum, Le Corbellier and Dr. Buzaglo met privately in the curator's office.

"I received a request from Professor Mizrachi," started Le Corbellier. "He needs your assistance on the Tel-Dor project. He asked me to intervene on his behalf."

"Professor Mizrachi is a prominent archaeology scholar," responded Dr. Buzaglo. "I am just a dwarf without any understanding in archaeology. I don't know how I could help him."

"He needs your knowledge and experience in his effort to decipher the inscription of the Tel-Dor parchment. Many fragments are missing from it and some sections are unreadable. He plans to assign the project to Dr. Daphna Ben-Horin, whose expertise is carbon-dating. The only hope to reconstruct the complete inscription of the Tel-Dor parchment lies in your field of expertise. You are the only scholar that I know who understands the sentence structures and the idioms used in the time of the Maccabees. That was the central subject of your dissertation. You are the one who could reconstruct the inscription text by adding the missing words and sentences."

"It will be a very exciting opportunity for me," said Dr. Buzaglo. "I'll be happy to participate in Professor Mizrachi's project."

Avner was eager to visit the Jewish Community in Amsterdam, where he hoped to find information on the Don Miguel parchment.

"Avner," Elaine said after they returned from Curacao, "the cruise sparked my interest in the paintings of the Dutch and Flemish masters." She smiled mischievously.

"I know. You always liked Vermeer. Didn't you copy one of his paintings at the Boston Museum of Art?"

"Yes, I did. I gave it as a gift to a high school friend."

"Since you would like to go to Amsterdam in your scroll search," she added, "how about we schedule a trip there? You can do your research, and I can see those famous paintings in person."

Avner smiled back at his wife. "Now, why didn't I think of that?"

CHAPTER 16

1972 The Amsterdam Letter

IN 1970, AVNER had incorporated the ideas of Professor LeCorbellier in his dissertation, highlighting the relation between the Tel Dor findings and other Hasmonaean era artifacts found in Israel.

"The Israel Antiquities Authority rejected my proposal," Avner informed Professor Mizrachi.

"Was it a matter of money?"

"They liked the article published by the Biblical Society. They also liked my proposal, but they rejected it for lack of funds."

"I rather suspected it would turn out that way," said Mizrachi. "Searching for information on the two-thousand-year-old Maccabee scroll will never be supported by public money. There would be an outcry in the Knesset."

"I didn't ask for a million dollars. It was only two-hundred thousand Shekels and the cost of using your laboratories and office space."

"I can help. I'll offer you access to our laboratory and part-time assistance from my research staff."

"That is very generous. But I'll need additional funding."

"After the publication of your article, a large donation was made from an anonymous source to the universities of Oxford and Princeton. I'll try to find the name of the donor."

Oxford was interested only in the Ark, while Princeton defended Avner's choice of including the Menorah as well. In his thesis, Avner argued that although the Ark of the Covenant was certainly of great religious importance because it contained the original Ten Commandments tablets, the Menorah, on the other hand, was of higher importance: not only was it a religious symbol, but also a national one.

*　　*　　*

"Our visit to Amsterdam should be very exciting." Elaine smiled at Avner during their KLM flight to the Amsterdam Schiphol airport.

"I am looking forward to meeting the rabbi of the great Portuguese Synagogue there," Avner said and smiled back.

"Your agenda is not my agenda. I want to see the paintings of the great masters. I mean, like Rembrandt, Rubens, Vermeer, and others. I have read about them, and I have seen many prints and sketches of their work, but I have never seen their original paintings."

Being a painter herself, Elaine's love of art placed museums at a higher priority than Avner's research on parchments and scrolls. Avner yielded. They spent their first two days in Holland enjoying the paintings at the Rembrandt House Museum, the Van Gogh Museum, the Amsterdam Historic Museum, and the Jewish Historical Museum. They also visited Anne Frank's house. Elaine wanted to visit the Rubens House Museum in Antwerp, but their time was limited.

On Saturday morning, they walked from their hotel to the Portuguese Synagogue. Following the Sabbath morning service, the rabbi met Avner and Elaine and invited them for lunch. At the rabbi's house, Avner expressed his interest in the Amsterdam's Jewish community and asked if any synagogue members had traced their family ancestors to Toledo, in Spain.

"Many Jewish tourists who visit our synagogue ask about the origin of our congregation and the family trees of our members," the rabbi said. "Why are you interested in Toledo?"

"I was born in Israel, and my family was originally from Toledo," Avner answered. "Naturally, I am looking for anyone who may be a distant relative. From your name, Rabbi Toledano, it is logical to assume that your ancestors also came from Toledo."

"Your guess is correct. Some of my Toledo ancestors followed Don Yitzchak Abravanel to Italy in 1492 after their expulsion from Spain. Others went to North Africa, and yet others went to Portugal. The Lisbon branch moved to Amsterdam in 1495 before the forced conversion of Jews by the Portuguese Inquisition."

"Wherever I meet persons who can trace their origin to Toledo, I feel that I am with members of my own family," Avner added. "My family history is filled with memories, trials, tribulations, and achievements. Who knows, Rabbi? Maybe you and I are related."

"All Jews are one family."

"My family arrived at the Ottoman territory of Palestine in 1804, but we have a more important issue to discuss, Rabbi."

"I know about the parchment you discovered at Tel Dor."

"In seeking assistance to decipher its inscription, we went to Curaçao to meet with Dr. Solomon Buzaglo."

"I know Dr. Buzaglo personally," the rabbi answered. "We have close contacts with Curaçao. I interviewed him before his appointment as the Curaçao Museum curator."

"He told us a legend of a parchment owned by his ancestor Don Miguel de Leon. Is there a legend about a parchment in Amsterdam? Is there someone in your congregation who may know of it?"

"He once told me about the legend of his family parchment. If it ever existed and was not lost after his family's arrival in Amsterdam, it is unlikely to have survived the Second World War, when Holland was under occupation by the Nazis."

"We heard about the archive of old documents in your synagogue. Can we look there?"

"We have many old documents, manuscripts, and books. Many are from the libraries of three Sephardic synagogues established in the seventeenth century. If you are interested, I can show you the room tomorrow. If you have the time, you can search the collection. Maybe you will find some reference to such a parchment."

The rabbi continued talking about the history of the Jewish community in Amsterdam. When the descendants of Jews who'd fled to Portugal from Spain later emigrated to Amsterdam, they presented themselves as Portuguese rather than Spanish—a prudent move, since the Dutch at that time were at war with Spain.

During the following two days, Avner and Elaine searched for clues in the synagogue archive. They read many documents and letters without finding any information related to their search.

"It is a waste of time," Elaine complained. "I would rather go to a museum."

"You have seen enough art." Avner became impatient. "It is not a waste of time. We are looking for important information."

This time, it was Elaine's turn to yield.

Avner was ready to give up the search just as Elaine called him.

"Avner! Look, I found an old yellowish letter. Is it of any value? I think it is written in Spanish."

Avner took the letter and read it. Written in Castilian Spanish, it was a letter from a person by the name of Yaacov Tagger to his daughter.

Avner's knowledge of modern Spanish was limited, but his grandmother taught him Ladino, a Sephardic language derived from fifteenth-century Castilian Spanish. The expelled Spanish Jews continued using fifteenth-century Castilian Spanish and passed it on from generation to generation over a period of five centuries. Before immigrating to Jerusalem, Avner's grandmother grew up in Sarajevo, Bosnia. She was the daughter of the chief rabbi there, where Ladino was the spoken language. As a child, he talked with his grandmother in dual-language conversations. He talked to her in Hebrew, and she answered him in Ladino.

Avner read the letter translating each sentence for Elaine.

My Dear Allegra,

I am writing this letter to congratulate you on your
wedding to Senior Emanuel Angel. You are joining
a very distinguished family with several generations
of Talmudic scholars. May G-d bless you with many
years of happiness and health to see children and
grandchildren growing up and learning the Torah.

I am pleased to learn that the ancient parchment,
which I gave you when you left Curaçao, arrived
safely in Amsterdam. It is important that you give
the parchment to my brother Daniel together with

the chart that includes its history. Do not provide any
information on it to anyone, including the chief rabbi
of Amsterdam. My ancestors who brought it from
Brazil to Curaçao left specific instructions to keep its
existence confidential.

I send you all my love.
Your father, Yaacov

Avner photographed the letter and returned the original to its
folder. He considered the letter as another fragment of the large
puzzle of documents, a puzzle that had become more complex.
*Will I ever gather sufficient clues to reconstruct the mystery of the
Maccabee scroll?*

*   *   *

"My high school French lessons will pay off today," Elaine
declared after their Air France flight landed at the Charles de Gaulle
International Airport in Paris. "It will be a continuing saga of an
art appreciation visit after our exciting viewing of Dutch masters'
paintings in Amsterdam."

Avner sighed. "We won't have time for any museum, Elaine.
I have a very tight schedule today meeting with professors
LeCorbellier and Bar David at the Sorbonne."

"You may want to reschedule your meeting after you read this
article." Elaine handed him the French newspaper she purchased
at the Paris airport. "I know that you remember your high school
French."

Avner did not respond until they were in a taxi on the way from
the airport to their hotel.

"What is the French article about?"

"It tells us not to miss the opportunity of a lifetime. It is about an exceptional exhibit at the *Petit Palais* museum."

"In Paris, everything about art is claimed to be exceptional. It is a known scheme aimed at gullible American tourists."

"It may be a scheme, but this time it is not a lie, Avner. It is a collection of 120 paintings by Renoir, my favorite impressionist."

Hearing no response, she added, "Archaeology is your passion, but mine is French impressionism. I must find time to see this Renoir exhibit."

"Didn't you have enough art in Amsterdam? Honey, can't you visit the *Petit Palais some* other time?"

"Your attitude toward art qualifies you to be labeled a *square engineer*. Are you familiar with the term *square engineer*?"

"Yes, but how does it apply to art?"

"Well, well. This requires a special explanation."

"Do I have to listen to another lecture?"

"Not another lecture, Avner, but you deserve an answer. Engineers think in square terms, like those used in designing classical buildings built with square boxes. They have sharp right angle corners. Think of the Eiffel Tower. It is constructed on a square base. The Empire State Building is a gigantic block of squares. Everything in such buildings is either a flat horizontal square or a flat vertical square. If you ask an engineer to draw something, the first thing that he draws is a square, which he later develops into a house with symmetrical square windows, rectangular doors, and a rectangular chimney. Engineers think in symmetrical square terms. They don't think of curved surfaces or nonsymmetrical designs. Think of the Guggenheim Museum in New York. It certainly is not square. It was designed by artists and not by engineers or, should I say, by traditional engineers. Modern architects have recognized that their 'square' history is outdated, and they have become 'rounded' artistic architects. Yes, they are hybrid professionals who combined traditional engineering with contemporary art. They have created the 'round engineering' profession to distance themselves from 'square engineers.'"

"You have a good point. I am a traditional engineer, but not as square as the ones you described. I also love French impressionists like Renoir. Unfortunately, I will not have time for impressionism. We'll be in Paris only two days. You'll have other opportunities."

"It is the opportunity of a lifetime," Elaine insisted. "This is the last day of the one-month exhibition. There has never been an exhibition with so many Renoir paintings. They were brought from French museums, several international museums and private art collections. It may never be done again, at least not in my lifetime. I will not give up. If you do not have the time, I'll go alone. If you really love Renoir, how can you pass up this opportunity?"

Avner yielded again. He admired Elaine for her persistence on issues that were important to her. She had been, and still was, instrumental in helping him to find the golden path between being a "square engineer" and a nontechnical researcher who loved music and art. She offered a way for him to look at archaeology and engineering with a different perspective. Elaine never complained about joining him on archaeology meetings. He called Professor LeCorbellier to reschedule the meeting for the following day.

Elaine and Avner stood in line over four hours at the *Petit Palais*. The museum management allowed only one hundred visitors to enter the museum every ten minutes. The waiting line advanced slowly. Elaine and Avner stood in line over four hours before they could enjoy viewing the most impressive collection of impressionism, 120 works of art by Renoir all gathered in one place.

Elaine came out exhilarated, but Avner's mind was on the excitement he expected during his next day's meeting at Professor LeCorbellier's office.

CHAPTER 17

1972 The São Paulo Parchment

"IT IS TIME to implement our project," LeCorbellier said to Avner and Bar David when they met to explore ideas on how to advance the search for the Maccabee scroll.

"Any new ideas?"

"We still don't have a name for our proposed society," Avner responded.

"I thought we had already agreed on the name," was Bar David's comment. "Didn't we decide that it should be the *Maccabee Society*?"

"That name was proposed, but not chosen," Avner said. "We need a name that will appeal to potential donors. People associate the name *Maccabee* with the Maccabia Games held in Israel every four years."

"Has anyone thought of another name?" LeCorbellier asked.

"I have," Elaine, who was just a guest, interrupted the discussion.

Silence followed. Avner smiled at Elaine with pleasure. *She is a smart girl.* Elaine appeared to be embarrassed. He winked at her to express his support.

The silence lasted a few seconds, but it seemed like eternity to Elaine.

"Painters have imagination and creativity," LeCorbellier said, sensing the awkward situation she was in. "What is the name you propose?"

"*The Society of the Ark,*" Elaine responded, feeling a release of tension in the room.

LeCorbellier smiled at her and looked inquisitively at Avner before reacting to the proposed name.

"I like it. It is a name with a double meaning. When spelled a-r-k, it indicates that our central '*raison d'être*' is the research and the search for information related to the Ark of the Covenant and the Menorah. When spelled a-r-c, the name indicates that archaeology is the principal tool of our research."

Avner smiled with pride. He had asked Elaine to propose a name, but she had not discussed her idea with him prior to the meeting. He was pleased LeCorbellier liked the name.

They agreed on the name and *then* founded the new society.

*   *   *

"Elaine found a sixteenth-century letter in the Amsterdam Portuguese Synagogue archive," Avner addressed LeCorbellier on the following day's meeting with several members of his research team.

"Was it written in Portuguese?" the professor asked.

"It's in Castilian Spanish. I photographed it."

"You are a magician with many talents." LeCorbellier wanted to talk about languages. "Not only are you an archaeologist, but a multilingual at that—fluent in modern Hebrew and ancient Hebrew, ancient Greek, Aramaic, Arabic, French, Italian, English, Ladino, and now, sixteenth-century Castilian Spanish."

Avner was embarrassed. "Thank you for remembering my languages. Oddly enough, I do all my arithmetic in French, but I dream in Hebrew. I always wondered how the brain of a multilingual person selects the language of its dreams. Perhaps Sigmund Freud knew the answer to that. One day I'll ask my shrink."

Noticing Avner's embarrassment, LeCorbellier changed the subject. "Who wrote the Castilian Spanish letter?"

"It was written by a person named Yaacov Tagger in Curaçao to his daughter Allegra prior to her marriage to a person named Emanuel Angel—"

"Emanuel Angel? This is a remarkable coincidence." LeCorbellier pressed the intercom button on his desk telling his secretary, Jeanette, to locate Dr. Angel and invite him to join the meeting.

Turning back to Avner and Elaine, he continued, "A sixteenth-century letter? Emanuel Angel is a postdoctoral history researcher at the Sorbonne. He was born in Brazil, and his thesis was on the history of Jews and Crypto-Jews who lived in Recife before the reconquest of Brazil by Portugal in the seventeenth century."

"Let me guess," commented Elaine, looking at Avner and then addressing LeCorbellier. "Avner is trying to determine the probability of your twentieth-century Emanuel Angel being a direct descendant of our sixteenth-century Emanuel Angel. As far as I am concerned, it is a waste of time."

"Elaine knows my interest in the theory of probability. Life is a series of chances we face. When we purchase something, we end up either being satisfied with our decision or regretting the purchase. When we decide on the food we eat, we play the probability game of indigestion or increased cholesterol or endangering our blood sugar balance. The theory of probability is a way to understand the random factors that lurk behind every decision we make in life."

Avner stopped, realizing that he was lecturing. He continued by using his marriage as an example.

"Look at my own life. When I chose Elaine to be my life partner, and when she chose me, we gambled on having a successful marriage. We are fortunate that we were right, but we both gambled, and we both won in the game of chance. In any case, Elaine is right. Spending time on probabilities of every aspect of life is often a waste of time."

They heard the voice of Jeanette over the intercom announcing the arrival of Dr. Angel. She entered the room followed by a young man in his late twenties, his long shining black hair tied in a ponytail with a black ribbon.

"Dr. Angel," LeCorbellier greeted him, "meet Dr. Avner Amram and his wife, Elaine. They have brought a photograph of a letter that may interest you."

"It is a pleasure meeting you. Being summoned by Professor LeCorbellier assures me that your photograph must be very interesting."

Dr. Angel looked at the photograph. "It is a letter written in Spanish."

"Can you read it?" LeCorbellier asked.

"The photograph is small and hard to read."

Jeanette retrieved a large magnifying glass from a desk drawer and handed it to Dr. Angel. He used it and read the letter aloud. When he reached his own name, he stopped abruptly.

"This is very exciting," he said, looking at Avner. "My name is also Emanuel. I have the same name as my grandfather. Our family follows the Sephardic tradition of naming the first son after his paternal grandfather, whether he is still alive or deceased. I am the sixth generation in a series of Emanuel-the-son-of-Solomon and Solomon-the-son-of-Emanuel. With that tradition, the probability is high that your sixteenth-century Emanuel Angel may be my direct ancestor. I'd love to hear more about him."

The use of the word *probability* by Dr. Angel caused LeCorbellier to smile. Avner smiled and winked at Elaine. She winked back.

Dr. Angel continued reading the letter and stopped abruptly.

"Wow!" he shouted with excitement. "Where did you get this photograph? My father will jump with joy if he sees this letter with its reference to a parchment. In his will, my grandfather left us a sheepskin parchment written in Hebrew."

The excitement in the office was explosive, as if Dr. Angel had thrown a metaphorical hand grenade on LeCorbellier's desk. Everyone started speaking simultaneously. Dr. Angel was the only one who did not say a word, appearing to be overwhelmed and dumbfounded.

When the wave of excitement subsided, he continued, "Our family parchment was wrapped in a dry fabric inside a jar to protect it from humidity. My father considered it the most important family possession. I looked at it several times, but I could not read it. I have been planning to ask Professor LeCorbellier if he could decipher it."

LeCorbellier explained the reason for the excitement and asked, "When was the last time you saw the family parchment?"

"That was a long time ago. I heard of its existence when I was a teenager. My father had shown it to a relative who came to visit us from Holland."

"I would like to see the parchment. Do you think that your father will agree to have us inspect it?" asked the professor.

"You mean in São Paulo?"

"No. Would he agree to send it to us for evaluation?"

"I will call tomorrow and ask him. I am sure that he will be happy to hear of your interest in deciphering the inscription."

* * *

Bashir was unhappy about the slow progress of his plan to establish Bismillah chapters in Buenos Aires and São Paulo, where there were large Jewish communities. Occupied with Middle Eastern operations, he delegated the task to Haroun-ibn-Hussein, his senior manager in charge of European operations stationed in Paris. Haroun sent two senior deputies to scout the two South American cities and to prepare plans for opening branches there, so far without success. The Buenos Aires case was completely hopeless. After three months spent in Argentina without any results, he considered recalling his Buenos Aires deputy back to Europe. There was some hope for Rio de Janeiro, so he gave Fauzi, his man in Rio, another month. Fauzi tried to recruit two former German Nazi officers who had sought refuge in Argentina and then moved to Rio. When he approached them with an offer of recruitment, they demanded unreasonable financial rewards.

"We have just received a coded message from Brazil," announced Haroun's secretarial aide upon entering without knocking on the office door. "Fauzi intercepted a telephone call from Paris to one of the leading members of the Jewish community in São Paulo."

"I hope it is not a foolish, mundane message to convince me that something is happening in Brazil. Is it any different from the three messages we received last week?"

"This one seems important. The son of a Jewish community leader in São Paulo is a history lecturer at the Sorbonne. He asked his father to send to Paris an old parchment with a Hebrew inscription, and he—"

"Did you say a parchment?" Haroun interrupted him with excitement.

"Yes. He said that he wants to show a sheepskin document to Dr. LeCorbellier at the Sorbonne."

"This may be the opportunity for which Bashir is waiting," was Haroun's reaction. "His father has been searching for an ancient Hebrew parchment during the last thirty years. I must inform him about it. Get me Jerusalem on the secure telephone immediately."

When Bashir heard the news, his reaction was the same. He repeated the same question: "Did you say parchment? What do you know about it? How old is it? Send me all the details you have on it."

Instructions followed the questions: "Send a coded message immediately to Fauzi. Compliment him for intercepting the telephone call, but tell him that intercepting the parchment is a thousand times more important."

"Fauzi is a one-man operation in Brazil," said Haroun. "There is not much he can do alone."

"I have heard a lot about his two Nazi friends. Surely he could get help from them. Tell Fauzi to contact them and try again to make a deal."

"Fauzi has already tried three times, Bashir. They turned him down three times. You've refused to meet their demands every time."

"They are out of their minds asking $100,000 for just agreeing to cooperate with us and another $50,000 for each mission."

"They may be out of their minds, but if we don't have the money, we must find another way of getting the parchment."

"Did we ever make a counteroffer?"

"No, we did not."

"Then it is time to do it now." Bashir was authoritative. "Offer each one of them $25,000 now and $20,000 for each mission to be paid in two installments—$10,000 immediately and the remainder after each mission is completed successfully. They may not be interested in advancing our Arab cause. However, as former SS officers, they may be interested in undermining the Jewish cause."

Two days later, Haroun received a coded message from São Paulo.

"I received your request. My two friends have agreed to help us, Fauzi."

Haroun relayed the information to Bashir in Jerusalem. Several hours later, another message arrived.

"Our two friends have a friend in Paris. He'll solve the problem." Haroun relayed the second message to Bashir.

Bashir sent his own message directly to São Paulo.

"Don't fail me, Fauzi."

CHAPTER 18

1972 The Stolen Parchment

WHEN ISRA FLIGHT 1218 from Tel Aviv to Paris started toward the take-off runway, there was no reason to foresee the events that occurred when the plane reached the skies over Greece. The passengers sat comfortably and talked about their plans to vacation in Paris or their business associates.

Colonel Menachem Amram was not traveling in uniform. Wearing a gray suit with a light blue shirt and a fashionable tie, he sat next to his wife, Rivik. He finished his kosher chicken sautéed in wine and sipped his favorite coffee-flavored Sabra liqueur while Rivik ate her dessert. He glanced at the latest headlines on the Israeli-Egyptian front line at the Suez Canal, but decided instead to talk about food.

"I love these special missions that take me to Europe, Rivik. I can order kosher meals on almost any airline, but I have to become a vegetarian on land. Can you imagine ordering a kosher meal in Germany?"

"You'd probably have the same problem in Spain, Menachem."

"I once asked a waiter in Madrid for anything '*sin carne*.' He looked at me as if I was a lunatic. Meat is the standard staple in Madrid. I settled for a salad."

"Don't talk about food. I'm looking forward to this Paris visit," Rivik said. "I hope we'll have time to go to the opera or a concert."

They were passionate about the highly acclaimed Israel Philharmonic, but Israeli operas were second or third-rate productions. They longed for opportunities to see the extravagant productions at the *Opéra National de Paris*, at La Scala, at the *Teatro dell'Opera di Roma*, and at the Met in New York.

"This visit is not for pleasure, Rivik. I didn't purchase any tickets this time. I am on a special mission for my favorite person—my brother, Avner. I love and enjoy special missions that take me away from my daily duties in the Armored Corps. You could visit the Louvre again or shop at one of the Printemps department stores while I do my job."

Menachem's assignments on special missions in security operations outside the corps were infrequent, but he liked them. The army headquarters issued such assignments, and his divisional commander always complained when he was obliged to send Menachem on missions on which he had no control. General Moshe Dayan himself had complained about them before the 1956 war with Egypt.

A few minutes after the meal, the situation changed fast. When a flight attendant started to close the access to the cockpit, with the intention of serving dinner to the pilots, one of the passengers ran into the business class section. When he was almost at the cockpit door, he found himself pushed down flat on the floor with a husky man sitting on his back, pressing a Beretta to his skull.

"Don't shoot!" the business class passengers screamed.

"Airline security!" the husky man shouted. "Someone get me a rope, a belt, anything to tie his legs together."

A young man dressed in slacks and a golf shirt came up the isle, taking off his belt.

"Thanks," the security guard said. "Could you fasten it tight around his legs?"

The young man nodded and bent down to his task while the guard pulled handcuffs from his own belt and secured the tackled man's hands behind his back.

"I only wanted to go to the bathroom," protested the man, still lying and feeling the gun threatening to blow his brains out.

"And this is why you have a switchblade in your pocket?" The guard said, pulling a knife from the right rear pocket of the man's pants. From the other rear pocket, he retrieved a wallet. He stood up, put his gun back into its holster concealed beneath his sport coat, and examined the wallet's contents.

A driver's license revealed the man to be an Israeli Arab from one of the villages in Western Galilee. A Haifa University student ID card and a membership card in an Arab welfare organization called Bismillah were also found.

Avner met Menachem and Rivik at Charles de Gaulle International Airport and took them to the Sorbonne. Professor LeCorbellier and Dr. Angel were waiting for them. LeCorbellier introduced Dr. Angel to his guests.

"I am pleased to meet you," Dr. Angel addressed Colonel Menachem. "I thank you for offering your assistance to protect my family parchment."

"I need to know more about it."

"My father sent it from São Paulo by registered mail. It arrived at the central mailroom of our department. The post office record shows that someone tried to sign for the envelope when I was out of the office. As my personal signature was required, nobody else could take delivery. It is now safe in Professor LeCorbellier's desk. Someone has learned about the parchment and tried to steal it. Professor LeCorbellier has already seen it."

"Can I see it now?" Avner asked.

LeCorbellier opened his desk drawer, pulled out a large fragment of a sheepskin parchment in a transparent sheet protector, and placed it flat on his conference table. Without saying a single word, Avner pulled out a camera and photographed the document several times. He was amazed at its good condition. He made a mental note to add it to his list. He would enter it as the Angel parchment with a note that it could also be the Don Miguel de Leon parchment.

They met again on the next day.

"I have bad news," said LeCorbellier. "The parchment has disappeared."

Dr. Angel's face changed color abruptly. He was visibly upset.

"We must inform the police," Dr. Angel spluttered his agitation and distress. "My father will never forgive me."

"Informing the police isn't a good idea," Menachem disagreed. "I suggest that we start investigating the matter ourselves. I'd like to interview a few people."

"Who will you start with?"

"With everyone in this department. There must be—"

"We should start with the communications and media department," interrupted Dr. Angel.

"Why them?"

"One of their lecturers held a video-cinematography demonstration for his students in the main hall of this department yesterday. Maybe they saw something."

"Do you know the lecturer?"

"Yes. He invited me to see the video recordings taken during his demonstration."

In the third clip of the screening, the camera had captured the figure of a blond-haired young man walking toward the exit of the hall, carrying a cylindrical tube in one hand and a leather briefcase in the other.

"Stop!" Menachem shouted. "The camera zoomed in on the student. Can you enlarge this frame? I want to read the word on the briefcase."

The lecturer enlarged the image showing a label on which was printed the word DÜSSELDORF.

"Look at the cylinder he is carrying!" Menachem added. "Dr. Angel, was the family document packed in a cylinder like this one?"

"No. It arrived from São Paulo in an envelope, but I placed it in a cylinder yesterday, and this one looks just like it."

"Does anyone recognize this young man?"

"I know him. It's Denis," said Dr. Angel. "He is a doctoral history student who was born in France. His German parents moved to Paris from Düsseldorf."

"Get me his address immediately," Menachem instructed with his usual military determination.

"What made you zoom in on this man?" he asked the lecturer.

"I demonstrated the technique to my students. Zooming a camera on a moving object is not easy, but it is very effective in capturing and presenting interesting video scenes. Students must learn the use of the zooming technique and must practice it well to avoid losing moving objects."

The next day, Menachem walked along the street leading to Denis's address. Students and tourists walked in both directions carrying books or knapsacks. It was easy to identify the tourists since most of them carried cameras. As he approached the designated street, pedestrian traffic thinned significantly. When he turned right at the next corner, he saw only one person. A young woman stood at the entrance to Denis's building. He continued walking past her, looking as if he was searching for the right address. At the next corner, he turned around, looking back, and saw that she was still there. He walked back toward her.

"Do you happen to know where Denis lives?" he asked.

"He lives in this building, but he is not in his apartment. He's away visiting his brother in Germany."

"Do you know when he'll be back?"

"He'll be there two days."

"I am on a short visit from Quebec. He invited me to see his apartment and his collection of history books."

"You are out of luck. Who are you?"

"My name is Maurice. I am a history professor from the University of Quebec. If you know Denis, please tell him that I came to see him."

Menachem started to walk away, hoping that she would stop him.

"Wait a minute," she called out. "My name is Gretchen. Maybe I can help you. I have a key to his apartment, and I am sure that he would not mind if I show you his library."

"That would be great. I was hoping to see his book on the 1871 French-Prussian war."

They walked up to the third floor. She opened the door, and they entered the spacious apartment. The two bookcases on both sides of the living room, filled with many books, did not attract Menachem's attention. He was more interested in the large photographs hung along the long central wall.

"Are these photographs of Düsseldorf?" he asked her.

"Yes. Have you ever been there?"

"I've never had the pleasure. I've heard it's a very nice city."

"It is my hometown. Denis and I are childhood friends."

The telephone rang. Gretchen picked it up. After carrying on a short conversation in German, she looked disturbed.

"I must leave now," she said. "My brother called, asking me to obtain some information that he needs tonight."

"Can I look at Denis's books for a few minutes?"

"I don't have the time."

"Maybe I'll call Denis on my next visit."

"I'll be happy to let you in tomorrow if you postpone your departure another day."

"No, I must leave Paris tomorrow. *C'est la vie ou c'est la guerre.*"

They left. Gretchen locked the apartment and left in a hurry.

Menachem walked to his hotel and returned at midnight with improvised B & E Tools. He broke into Denis's apartment. Behind one of the pictures, he discovered an old primitive safe hidden in the wall. Having worked as an apprentice to a locksmith in his youth, he was familiar with various cheap safes and managed to open it without any difficulty. He found a large envelope marked in Spanish: Angel Family Archive. He opened the envelope. It was empty except for a small slip of paper. *Another failure*, he thought. He tucked the paper in his pocket and left the apartment.

*   *   *

In Jerusalem, Bashir received a coded message from Paris.

"The document is in the hands of our friend in Paris. He wants $100,000 for it. I am waiting for your instructions, Haroun."

Bashir was furious. He sent back a response.

"We had a deal. We have already given them $10,000. I won't pay a penny until this mission is completed."

"Yes, we had a deal with them." Haroun was frustrated. "However, we are not in any position to bargain. We aren't dealing with honorable men. They have the parchment and we want it. Either we meet their price, or we forget about the parchment. They will gladly destroy it. It all depends on how valuable the parchment is to us."

"We don't even know if the parchment is worth anything." Bashir was also frustrated. "But it's a gamble we must take—like a crapshoot. Win or lose. Offer them $50,000."

An hour later, a new message arrived from Paris: "Our friend accepted our offer. He will send the document to you tomorrow."

The next day, Bashir received another message from Paris: "Our friend took the money, but the document disappeared."

Bashir's anger resulted in a two-word message: "Kill him."

CHAPTER 19

1972 Düsseldorf

M ENACHEM, WEARING THE same gray business suit on the Air France flight to Düsseldorf, sipped his favorite coffee-flavored Sabra liqueur. He always carried a small bottle of the Sabra liqueur when he was on a non-Israeli airline. He read a critique of Hoffman's operetta *La Pericole* staged at the *Opera Comique* in Paris. He loved the opera, but he had never seen *La Pericole*. He hoped to see it later that week before returning to Israel, knowing well that his chances of finding time to see it were poor, but reading about it distracted him from the more important mission of locating the Angel parchment.

He tried to analyze the events that led him to be on this flight to Düsseldorf:

> *The German student managed to steal the Angel*
> *parchment, but his mistake was leaving the envelope*
> *in the safe with what he thought was a useless piece of*

paper. He'll be surprised when I trace him using the
receipt from a bookstore in Düsseldorf.

From the Düsseldorf airport, Menachem took a taxi to his hotel, two blocks from the bookstore. He checked in and immediately walked to the store. Behind the cash register sat a young man reading a French magazine while nervously tapping his fingers on the table. He was the German student in the Paris video clip, unless he was his direct clone or his identical twin brother. Although fluent in German, Menachem decided that using German with his foreign accent might reveal his Israeli identity.

"My name is Maurice," Menachem introduced himself in French. "Do you speak French? I am a visitor from Canada."

"Welcome to Düsseldorf," responded the young man in perfect French. "My name is Denis. Yes, I can tell that you are not Parisian. The Canadians who live in Quebec speak French with an accent that is influenced by English."

"You are absolutely right. Where did *you* learn to speak such perfect French? Are you a Frenchman living in Düsseldorf? You have no accent at all. You sound like one."

"Actually, I am German, born and brought up in Paris, and am currently a student at the Sorbonne. I still have family living in Düsseldorf."

Menachem and the student continued their friendly dialogue when a customer entered the bookstore. The man who entered was the spitting image of Denis.

The situation is more complex than I expected. How
will I recognize one brother from his identical twin?

"Meet my brother Wolfgang," Denis said in German.
Menachem looked at him blankly.

Denis switched to French. "My brother Wolfgang lives in Düsseldorf. He manages our family bookstore. We have several bookstores in Germany and two in South America. My uncle manages the stores in Rio and São Paulo. As I mentioned earlier, I am here on a visit."

"Do you have any French books?" Menachem addressed Wolfgang.

"We certainly do," Wolfgang replied in slightly broken French.

Menachem was relieved. The two brothers were identical twins in appearance, but not in their French accent. *Wolfgang must have spent many years in Düsseldorf.*

"Only half of our books are in German," continued Wolfgang. "We try to serve the tourists who come to Düsseldorf. We have sections in French, in English, in Italian, and in Dutch. I also have one section with books in other languages, mostly for European tourists."

"I am looking for a book in French on the Franco-Prussian war. Can you recommend one?"

"I don't have one here, but I can get you one later today," said Wolfgang. "Can you come back after lunch?"

"That would be nice. My hotel is within walking distance from here."

Menachem left the bookstore and returned after lunch to pick up the book.

"Are you Denis or Wolfgang?"

"I am Wolfgang. Can't you tell from my accent?"

There were no customers in the store. Menachem and Wolfgang exchanged information on Quebec and Düsseldorf. When Menachem learned that Wolfgang seemed to be very familiar with Quebec City, he changed the subject.

"Is Denis going back to Paris?"

"He is leaving tonight."

"If you are free, maybe you can show me Düsseldorf tomorrow."

"Actually, I am joining him. We are both flying to Paris later this evening. If you come back to Düsseldorf, call me. I'll be happy to show you the city."

At midnight, knowing that the twins had already left for Paris, Menachem went to Wolfgang's apartment. With his B & E Tools, he entered the apartment to see a display of nine pictures hung along three walls of the central room and a large red swastika painted on the ceiling. The pictures dated from the Third Reich. The one in the center was a large picture of Adolf Hitler with his hand lifted in response to hundreds of SS officers saluting him. Four words were painted in red under Hitler's photograph.

DEUTSCHLAND—DEUTSCHLAND—UBER—ALLES

Menachem looked behind several pictures hoping to find a safe. He removed Hitler's picture and placed it on the floor after seeing a wall safe behind it. It was a combination-type safe with a solid steel door and alphanumeric keys. He did not know the combination nor did he have tools to drill through the door. He cursed the moment at which he turned down Avner's suggestion to carry a drill with him.

What shall I do now? his standard question surfaced again.

He searched the apartment hoping to find an electric drill or a clue for the keyboard code. He found neither.

What would Avner do? he asked himself.

He looked at the keyboard and decided to try his luck. He looked at Hitler's picture and typed HITLER without luck.

He tried DEUTSCHLAND without luck.

He tried DEUTSCHLAND-DEUTSCHLAND without luck.

This is silly. They would never use the whole sentence.

He tried typing DEUTSCHLAND-DEUTSCHLAND-UBER-ALLES, again without luck.

He gave up and decided to leave. He walked to the door, stopped, returned to the keyboard, and retyped the four words without hyphens and with one small letter. dEUTSCHLANDDEUTSCHLANDUBERALLES

The safe door clicked open.

He saw the cylinder, retrieved the stolen parchment, checked it, and placed it back in the cylinder.

He pulled out a small blue-and-white Israeli flag from his pocket, placed it inside the safe, and locked it. He hung the Hitler photograph back and left the apartment carrying the cylinder.

*   *   *

Menachem again enjoyed his favorite Sabra liqueur on the next Lufthansa flight from Düsseldorf to Paris.

The next day, he was on an EL AL flight from Paris to Tel Aviv, sitting next to his wife, Rivik.

"That was a *superb* production of *La Pericole* operetta," he said to his wife. "I am glad I could accomplish the mission and see an operetta during this trip."

"I told you it would be possible," responded Rivik. "If you try hard enough, you can succeed in fitting in work and pleasure over a weekend. You just have to be determined enough and believe that you can do it."

CHAPTER 20

1973 Jerusalem

THE LIGHT OF the partial moon was hazy at that late hour of the night. The blanket of sand formed by desert winds on both sides of the deserted road in the Sinai desert reduced the visibility considerably. Lieutenant Dromi and his twelve Israeli soldiers were on patrol along the Suez Canal, looking for infiltrators from Egypt. They walked in a single column in complete silence, all wearing wraparound army goggles to protect their eyes from the blowing sand.

"Have you heard about the Egyptian Army's maneuvers across the canal?" a soldier whispered to his friend.

"Stop talking," the lieutenant whispered back. "You are on patrol. I want complete silence."

The patrol kept moving.

"I hear something on our right," a corporal whispered. "It could be an animal, maybe a cat."

The patrol stopped.

A shadowy figure approached the side of the road, gradually revealing itself as human. The absolute silence was disturbed by the sound of steps that grew louder as the approaching figure materialized as a young man.

"Halt!" the lieutenant addressed the stranger in Arabic. "Don't move and raise your hands."

"Don't shoot," the man stopped. Shaking with fear, he raised his hands. He wore a lightweight jacket with a kaffiyeh wrapped around his face and covering his head. The weight of his backpack caused him to stoop forward.

Lieutenant Dromi disarmed him, tied his hands, and instructed Corporal Daniel to take two soldiers to escort the prisoner back to base for interrogation.

*   *   *

"Halt!" the three soldiers heard a cry in the dark.

All four stopped and dropped to the ground. The three soldiers aimed their guns in the direction of the caller.

"Don't move!" they heard a call from behind them. It was in Hebrew with a heavy Arabic flavor.

"Don't shoot!" cried the prisoner in Arabic. I am an Arab.

"I know, we followed you when you were arrested."

The prisoner was shaking with fear. He got up and walked toward the second caller who untied his hands, instructing him to collect the rifles.

In the dark of night, the desert wind continued to howl.

"Come closer," their leader called to the soldiers. Two soldiers advanced.

"Where is the third one?" asked the Arab prisoner.

There was no answer.

The corporal retrieved his .45. With two consecutive shots, he killed the two Arabs and called on the prisoner to lie down.

"Your friends are formidable, but they are no match to Israeli soldiers."

"One is the Bismillah guy who hired me," he said, still shaking.

The corporal and two soldiers escorted the prisoner to base.

The prisoner was a drug smuggler—just like the other three the patrol had caught in the previous week. This one was different. He was more than a smuggler. The interrogators discovered a document hidden in the lining of his jacket.

The Yom Kippur War erupted two weeks later.

*   *   *

During the war, Menachem was on active duty as a divisional operations officer in the Israeli armored corps under the command of General Sharon. He was injured in a tank battle, but he remained at the front line to oversee the division's tank battles. His spearheading unit repelled the Egyptian Army and crossed the Suez Canal heading to Cairo.

*   *   *

"Avner, it's a pleasure seeing you again!" Professor Mizrachi greeted the two men as they entered his Jerusalem office. "I am happy to meet you, Menachem. I was told about your injury and wish you a complete and speedy recovery. I've heard so much about you from Avner and from your divisional commander, a family friend."

"Thank you for your good wishes," Menachem responded. "I hope this will be our last war. Maybe it will finally bring us peace with our neighbors."

"Amen," the professor agreed.

"Thank you for taking the time from your busy schedule to see us. I don't know if Avner has already told you all the details about our visit to the Santa Katrina Monastery in 1967."

"Avner told me about your interesting climb to the monastery, but I'd love to hear more about your conversation with Father Neophytos."

"He showed us the vast library and a few ancient documents at the monastery and told us about the parchment in a sealed vault."

"Avner gave me a lot of information on your visit. I tried to see the parchment personally to determine if it has any Jewish connection, but I was not successful. I sent a message to the monastery, offering to come in person, but they referred me to the Greek Orthodox patriarch in Cairo who referred me to Istanbul. The patriarch's office in Istanbul referred me to the Israeli army. The army referred me to the Israeli Antiquities Administration. The director of the Antiquity office in Jerusalem referred me back to the patriarch.

"I tried to obtain information on other ancient documents in the monastery," continued Mizrachi, "but I only succeeded in receiving suggestions that I should contact the Israeli Government or the Egyptian patriarch in Cairo."

"Maybe we could appeal to the patriarch personally," interjected Menachem. "Maybe the chief rabbi of Israel could intercede on our behalf."

"That won't be necessary," Professor Mizrachi replied. "The Mossad tried to obtain information on the monastery parchment but found that it has disappeared. During an investigation, they learned that an operative of Bismillah stole the parchment from the monastery. Their operative claimed to be a personal messenger from the patriarch's office in Istanbul by presenting a false document with authorization to inspect the vault. He managed to remove the document and take it out of the monastery."

"Does anyone know what happened to it?"

"A monastery spokesman claimed that several documents were misplaced and not removed from the compound."

"Is it a lost case?"

"No, Menachem. It's not lost. Before the war, an Israeli army patrol apprehended a Bedouin drug smuggler and found the stolen parchment sewn into the lining of his jacket. During his interrogation, he provided interesting details. He was a new worker at the monastery when Bismillah recruited him by offering a reward of five hundred dollars if he would smuggle drugs from Egypt."

"Where is the parchment now?"

"It's in our laboratory, Menachem. It wasn't easy to get it from the army. The red tape bureaucracy of the Mossad and objections from our own archaeological authorities presented obstacles that were not easy to overcome. It required some arm-twisting and intervention by the minister of defense before I obtained authorization to have the parchment consigned to us."

"Is it of any value?"

"It is valuable as a general archaeological treasure. But its inscription is of special relevance to our research in trying to fill in the missing information from another parchment, the one discovered at Tel Dor in 1970. I wondered if the monastery parchment holds information which could help us solve the mystery of the Tel Dor parchment."

"Can you tell us about its content?" Avner asked.

"Avner," responded the professor, "you will be surprised, even stunned, when you read the inscription."

Avner listened impatiently.

"The inscription is in ancient Hebrew script. It seems to be almost the same as the text given to me by General Yadin after his initial evaluation of the Tel Dor parchment in 1970. However, it includes an additional paragraph at the beginning that I could not immediately decipher. On the back of the parchment, we found another paragraph, which has not yet been deciphered. It is a fragment of a larger sheepskin scroll. We are now trying to determine the connection between the two parchments. Naturally, nothing can be concluded until Dr. Ben-Horin provides her carbon dating report."

Avner reflected on what he should write in his notepad.

They found the missing Katrina Monastery parchment.
Could it be part of the Judah Maccabee scroll?
Something is very strange. It is very unusual to have
any writing on the back of an ancient parchment.

The added inscription on the back of the parchment
could be the key to understanding this parchment.

I'll have to solve this puzzle.

CHAPTER 21

1982 The Rome Kidnap

I T WAS THREE o'clock on an ill-fated morning in Rome when a soft knock on the door of the apartment woke up Mrs. Maimon from her sleep. Her husband was not disturbed. She got out of bed and came quietly to the door.

"Who are you? Why are you disturbing us at this hour?" she asked.

"Please forgive me," pleaded softly the man outside the apartment door. "I am a friend of your husband, Alberto. I need his help."

"What is your name?"

"My name is Alessandro."

"What kind of trouble are you in at this hour?"

"I was robbed, and I need a few liras to get home."

"How do you know my husband?"

"I am a tour guide like him, and I work at the Olympia Hotel."

"Do you know Ricardo?"

"Ricardo is my manager."

"Alberto is asleep. I'll get you the money."

She unlocked the security latch and opened the door; four masked men rushed in, pushed her aside, and went directly to the bedroom, finding Alberto seated on the bed and rubbing his eyes.

"Mr. Maimon, you have in your possession a painting that belongs to us," one of the intruders announced. "In 1964, six members of our organization visited Rome and then they disappeared. We have been looking for them since then, and we finally learned that you had conducted a tour of Rome for them. You were the last person who saw them. They carried a painting that belongs to us. We want to know what happened to it."

"I remember conducting a guided tour for six men. I'll take your word that it was in 1964, but they did not look like monks to me."

"Yes, they were Tibetan monks."

"I have no idea what happened to them. I never saw them again."

"One of the monks gave you a painting."

"I don't know anything about a painting."

"The painting was given to you for delivery to a friend of ours who arrived the next day, but he did not find you."

"It makes no sense. How would your friend find me? If your six monks disappeared, how do you know that one of them gave me anything?"

"We know that he gave it to a tour guide, and now we know that you are the one."

"You still didn't explain to me how he would find me."

"We have our ways of finding anyone," replied the leader of the intruders.

"This also makes no sense. You just told me that you looked for me for eighteen years. Now you tell me that your friend could find me in one day."

Alberto was amazed at his own courage for confronting the four uninvited men at 3:00 AM.

"If your painting is lost, why don't you report it to the police in Rome?"

"We don't believe you. You received the painting and never delivered it to our friend. We know how to make you tell the truth. We are experienced in obtaining information from people. If you insist in telling us lies, we'll use methods you won't like at all to extract the information from you."

The leader stepped back, and two of the four men moved forward. One hit Alberto with a club and the other with two brass knuckles until he was bleeding from his head, shoulders, hands, and chest. His wife started screaming, trying to wake up their neighbors. Fearing the possible arrival of police officers, the intruders stopped their violent assault, and their leader signaled them to leave the apartment.

"Our visit this morning is only a warning," said the leader. "I'll give you two days to think about revealing the information that we want. We will contact you. If you refuse to cooperate with us, we will have to resort to harsher methods."

After the intruders left, Mrs. Maimon washed her husband's head and dressed his wounds. He comforted her, trying to assure her that they will overcome this episode.

Alberto faced a dilemma.

I am in great danger. It is too dangerous to stay in my apartment another day. I hid the painting in a safe place, but I will not give it to criminals. I should have given it to the police in 1964. It would not be wise to give it to them now, after hiding it for eighteen years. I must act immediately. Who can help me?

He suddenly remembered Avner.

At sunrise, he walked out of the apartment house wearing a pair of wraparound sunglasses. He scanned the street. Confident that the street was clear, he returned to get his two-cylinder Vespa motorbike. He put on his helmet and drove along the street, checking again to make sure that no one followed him. After turning right at the next corner, he spotted two men standing across the boulevard. Assuming they were Italian plainclothes security men, he continued toward his destination, a hotel on the outskirts of Rome. It was the only way to avoid the criminals.

When he left the hotel on the next day, Alberto saw a minivan parked across the street. Two young men came out, grabbed him, and forced him into the vehicle in which two other young men waited. He recognized them. They were the ones who had assaulted him in his apartment. They blindfolded him, placed handcuffs on his hands and a tape on his mouth to ensure his silence. The minivan driver drove away slowly and reached the main road that led to an unknown location outside Rome. One of the captors unlocked his handcuffs, removed his blindfold, and left.

Alberto found himself in a small room that seemed to be in a farmhouse basement. It had no windows and a single lightbulb hung down from its ceiling. A rusted faucet above a sink was at the far corner of the room. An old wobbly table and two creaky metal chairs were at its center. A mattress was on the floor with a blanket, two pillows, and two towels. On the table, he saw half a baguette, a small block of cheese, and a glass pitcher of water.

He thought about his fate. His kidnappers were clever, and he had to find a way to outsmart them. Sitting at the table, he pretended to be free.

Free people don't value their freedom until they lose it.

He thought of all the events that had led to his kidnapping. He was tired and fell asleep.

Several scenes from his recent experiences appeared in his imagination one after the other like a series of slides projected on a screen. The quiet life as a tour guide, the six monks, the painting,

Mr. Angelo who never showed up, his first meeting with Avner and his wife in 1964, the hiding of the painting, the intruders into his apartment, the beating, the search for a hiding place from the mafia gang, and the kidnapping, with the loss of his freedom.

His uncle's loss of freedom was the next scene that played in his mind, the uncle he had never met. In 1937, the University of Hamburg had awarded his uncle a full scholarship. He saw a slide of the Hamburg University campus. The next slide was an image of his uncle as a young smartly dressed student standing with other students next to a large university library. In the next slide, his uncle wore a striped outfit, identical to those worn by all who were around him in a concentration camp—that image was in Treblinka. His uncle never returned to Rome. He tried to imagine how his uncle felt when his life took a sudden turn from being a university student to becoming a prisoner in an SS interrogation chamber with no hope of escaping.

His mind transported him to his childhood, to the stories his grandmother had told him, stories passed on to her from generation to generation about her ancestors imprisoned and tortured in the dungeons of the Spanish Inquisition. She herself was a Holocaust survivor. She repeatedly reminded him that freedom is not free. It can only exist by fighting evil and can be easily lost without the will to defend it. He grew up as a free man who did not experience the suffering of those sent to concentration camps or Inquisition dungeons.

His grandmother had told him about one of her ancestors who had suffered and died on a torture wheel at the time of the Spanish Inquisition. Alberto found himself tied in chains to such a giant spiked torture wheel. A hooded man strapped his two hands to the wheel above his head and then shackled his two feet to the ground below the wheel. A brown-eyed man faced him with a whip in his hand, while another told him that he could escape the pain of torture and certain death by dismemberment. All he had to do was denounce his family as conspiring against the church. The hooded man pushed the handle at the center of the wheel, pulling his hands upward and stretching his body to the limit of tolerance. His arms were close to be torn from his body. The pain was unbearable.

Alberto started screaming with agony when he suddenly opened his eyes to find one of his captors standing near the table.

The man introduced himself as the interrogator of an international intelligence service, which he did not identify.

"I want to tell you the reason for your being here," the interrogator said. "I'll ask you a few questions. If you provide us with the information we want, we'll set you free. I'll start by asking you about the guided tour you conducted for the six monks in 1964."

"I remember them, but I don't remember the detailed route. I probably took them on my standard tour of Rome."

"You were the last person to have seen them. Tell me all you can remember about them and what questions they asked you."

"How can you expect me to remember details? It was eighteen years ago. They arrived from Paris after visiting Napoleon's *Arc de Triomphe*, where they had met a man named Mr. Angelo."

"Now we are getting somewhere. I am especially interested in what they said about their travel plans after the tour."

"They said they were headed to Istanbul."

"Istanbul? Did they mention any other place?"

"I think they mentioned Athens, but I am not sure. They planned to return to India after Istanbul."

"I am pleased that you decided to cooperate with us, Mr. Maimon."

"I have no reason to keep any information from you. You apparently mistake me for someone else."

"Did they mention any other cities?"

"I don't think they did."

"Wait a minute," Alberto recalled. "One of the monks said that he would love to visit the Isle of Capri. Maybe he wanted to gamble in the casino at the Isle of Capri. Are monks allowed to gamble? I don't know if he ever did."

"You sound like a very intelligent man." The interrogator offered him a cigarette. "You must understand that we are determined to find the painting."

"What painting?"

"The one they gave to you in 1964. It's a very valuable piece of art by your compatriot Botticelli. Our organization will take whatever steps it deems necessary to find it."

"I don't know anything about a painting."

"We know that you are not telling the truth," insisted the interrogator before leaving the room.

The captors gave Alberto a sandwich and a bottle of water. He was amazed how he kept his cool on the outside, while he was terrified inside, shaking as a kidnapped prisoner by an international mafia—a group apparently involved in the theft of a very valuable painting.

When the interrogator returned, his facial expression changed. He has adopted a different tone.

"We have decided to offer you a reward for the information," said the interrogator. "If you continue to cooperate with us, we'll invite you to become a member of the organization, and you'll report directly to me. I offer you an opportunity to earn a considerable amount of money, much more than you earn as a tour guide. The alternative is not a pleasant one. I remind you of the beating that our associates gave to you. They are rough men who obtain information from their prisoners using methods of torture that never fail. I don't want to hand you over to them. I'll give you two hours to think about my proposal and to reflect on what would happen to you if you refuse."

Alberto was alone again.

At the end of the day, the interrogator entered the room without saying a word. The silence was frightening.

"I have been thinking about your offer," Alberto wanted to break the silence. "It is very interesting, but I want more details."

Figuring that he had managed to crack the resistance of his prisoner, the interrogator added intriguing details.

"Your life will be considerably better with a large increase in your income. Three recent new members of our organization have seen a dramatic increase in their standard of living. Two have moved their families to the most prestigious neighborhoods in Rome."

"It does sound very attractive," responded the prisoner. "However, it is hard for me to think clearly when I am under duress as a prisoner against my will. My wife is very sick, and I have to help her. I want to see her."

"It sounds reasonable," answered the interrogator. "I agree to wait forty-eight hours so you can think about my proposal. My friends will take you to another building where you will stay two days while you think about my offer."

It was late evening when two masked captors walked into the interrogation room. They blindfolded Alberto again, guided him to a minivan, and locked him in the rear section of the vehicle. He could not understand why they did not shackle his hands. He sat in the vehicle until he heard someone opening the driver's door and, soon after, starting the engine. Not hearing the passenger door or any conversation inside the minivan, he concluded that the driver was alone.

"Where are you taking me?" he asked the driver.

"Not far, only three kilometers from here—on a forsaken farm road."

After the minivan reached its destination, the driver got out, opened the rear door, and reached for Alberto.

"We have arrived."

Alberto came out and nonchalantly removed the blindfold himself.

The driver smiled while grabbing his prisoner's hand. "There's nothing else around us, and it's pitch-dark."

This is my chance.

Alberto pulled his hand, swiftly wrapped the blindfolding cloth around the driver's neck, and stuffed his mouth with a handkerchief.

Reaching for the driver's pocket, he retrieved a pair of handcuffs and placed them on the driver's hands. He tied his legs together with a rope he found in the van.

"I have to leave you here. You are not good enough for this job. Find another profession."

The car key was still in the ignition, making it easy for Alberto to drive away free.

He did not go back to the hotel. He had to decide fast what his next step should be. He called his friend Avner, asking for help and urging him to come immediately. It was a matter of life and death.

They agreed to meet the next day in Paris.

CHAPTER 22

1982 Botticelli's Painting

AVNER RANG HIS brother.

"Menachem, Alberto just called from Rome. He is in trouble and wants to meet me tomorrow in Paris. Can you join me? We may need your expertise."

"Did he say why?"

"He only said that it was a matter of life and death. He sounded panicked. Ever since that guided tour in 1964, I felt that he knew more than he was willing to reveal to us. When Elaine asked him to recount a legend, he avoided the subject. I had the same feeling again in 1979 when we met during a two-hour stopover at the Fiumicino Airport, where we exchanged memories. He is afraid of something or of someone."

*   *   *

At the Charles de Gaulle International Airport in Paris, Avner and Menachem rented a car and drove to meet Alberto at Hotel

Moliere. He was not at the hotel. He left a sealed message at the concierge desk with directions to a small café on the outskirts of Paris. They arrived at the roadside café to find Alberto waiting for them impatiently. After a short exchange of greetings, he started to talk without prompting.

"Thank you for responding so promptly to my call for help. Meeting here is safer than at the hotel. I am in danger, and you are the only ones I could turn to with confidence.

"Yesterday, I was kidnapped in Rome. Before I tell you about it, you should know more about me, my family, and recent information concerning your search for the hidden scroll."

"We are very interested in you and your family," Avner commented, not knowing what else to say.

"My family is originally from Toledo," Alberto started. "They came to Italy as Jewish refugees during the expulsion of 1492. I was born in Rome, and I became a tour guide, though not by choice.

"My grandfather was the chief rabbi of Rome. My father sent me to learn at the Porat-Yoseph Sephardic Yeshivah in Jerusalem. I returned to Rome when my father died several months prior to my ordination. I remained in Rome to support my mother and my brother. They call me the Touring Guide Rabbi."

"You already told us you are Jewish," Avner commented. "But after our 1964 visit, I could not understand how a tour guide in Rome could be a walking encyclopedia on Jewish history. Now I do."

Alberto continued.

"It is time to warn you of the danger you are in because of your search for the hidden scroll. Eighteen years ago, you asked me about the legends of the Menorah and I told you a few. Interested groups and organizations fabricated some legends. A few thought that they knew the truth about the Menorah, others thought that its discovery could help their causes, and yet others believed that its discovery could hurt their causes.

"I know of two organizations actively looking for important relics related to their causes." he continued. "You probably know of the Bismillah society, a group of fundamentalist Muslims who are looking for the lost portions of the Koran. A Muslim cleric once said, 'Those who claim that they know all the Koran are greatly mistaken. A large part of the Koran was lost, and nobody knows its content. Muhammad had a second revelation that his followers documented before his ascent to heaven on the *Al Burak* white horse. The documents were lost. Every Muslim should follow the laws of the Koran they know, praying to Allah that the missing documents on the second revelation will be found one day.'

"I also know of the Novotemplars Society. It was recently established by a group of European anti-Semites and followers of the Ordo Novi Templi Society created by the Austrian occultist and excommunicated Benedictine monk Jorg Lanz von Liebenfels in 1907. The ONT had a large following of Germans and Austrians. Heinrich Himmler adopted its racial text when he created the SS Order of German Manhood.

"The Novotemplars Society adopted the ONT system of qualifying its members for advancements according to the candidate's percentage of Aryan blood as determined by a special test devised by Lanz. Candidates with less than 50 percent Aryan blood can become entry templars but can never be elevated to a higher rank. Candidates tested between 50 percent and 70 percent Aryan blood can start with the rank of entry templar and eventually can reach the novice-templar rank. The next rank of novo templar is for members who test over 70 percent. The master-templar rank is for the very few who can test at over 90 percent.

"After Lanz died in 1954, the details of his test formula were lost, and the new organization has no way of testing new candidates. It has established a group of operatives who are searching for the documents that Jorg Lanz hid somewhere in Europe.

"Some of the Novotemplars are descendants of the German Templars who settled in Haifa in the nineteenth century and who were expelled by the British during the Second World War. They may be dangerous because they are anti-Semites. They are actively looking for the Lanz documents in the Haifa area, where their ancestors had built a new neighborhood calling it the German Colony.

"Recently, I discovered a new group that is interested in the Menorah parchment. First, I thought that it was a secret society of Buddhist monks from Tibet. I had no idea why Buddhists would be interested in any Jewish relics. Being interested in the history of Tibet, I did some research and gathered information on its background. This is what I concluded:

Ever since 1959, the fourteenth Dalai Lama has been seeking advice from several world leaders on how to maintain the unity of the Tibetan people after their land was annexed by the People's Republic of China. Greatly impressed by the victory of the Israeli army in the 1956 Sinai Campaign and in the 1967 Six-Day War, he decided that the best advice could be from the Jewish people. He requested a meeting with Rabbi Nissim, the chief Sephardic rabbi of Israel at that time.

The rabbi was delighted to hear from the Dalai Lama, but he was concerned about the value of such a meeting, considering that the Dalai Lama was only thirty-four years old at that time. He responded politely and positively to the request.

The Dalai Lama had never been to Israel and looked forward to the visit. For unknown reasons, he was not able to travel at that time, and he sent his deputy Ishimar instead. The deputy, who also had never been to Israel, expected to see a third world country struggling to provide its people with minimum necessities of life and spending all its resources to combat its surrounding enemies. Instead, he saw a modern society with bustling cities and hardworking people.

Ishimar presented to the rabbi a gift from the Dalai Lama. It was an ancient shofar, a Jewish ceremonial musical trumpet made of a ram's horn. It is blown by Jews on High Holidays. A shepherd found it in a Tibet mountain cave. It was placed in a vault and forgotten."

Avner already knew about the shofar, which he had seen on display at the Sephardic Rabbinical archive.

Alberto continued, "After the rabbi and Ishimar exchanged information on their respective religions and cultures, Ishimar delivered the message from the Dalai Lama, who wanted to learn the secret of success of the Jews, the secret that enabled the Jewish people to survive after losing their land and after being scattered in many countries over a span of twenty centuries. Ishimar expected a very long reply with detailed analysis of Jewish survival schemes and actions, but he received a very simple explanation from Rabbi Nissim:

The secret is not a secret. It is just two words—*faith* and *tradition*. The Jewish people have always had faith in what we call **Netzach Ysrael** in Hebrew, the Eternity of Israel. With faith in our eternity, the teaching of our tradition is our highest priority. Our Torah and our Menorah, the seven-branch candelabra,

have been with us over three thousand years. The
Menorah is described in detail in our Bible. It was
in the Temple of Jerusalem, and its image is now the
emblem of the State of Israel. A twenty-foot steel
version was constructed and placed in front of the
Knesset building, the Israeli Parliament. If you want
to keep the Tibetans a united people, teach them faith
and tradition and give them a national emblem that is
unique to your tradition.

"After Ishimar's return to India, the Dalai Lama pondered on
Rabbi Nissim's advice. He decided to study and decipher the ancient
parchment found in Tibet with the hope of learning how to build
the faith of the Tibetan people in their eternity, just like the Jews
believe in theirs."

"Your lecture is very interesting," interrupted Avner. "I am sure
that you did not send an SOS message to give us a lecture. Why
the secrecy?"

"Eighteen years ago, I conducted a tour for a group of six
Tibetan monks. Their leader had purchased an oil painting from
a street vendor. He asked me to deliver it as a gift to his friend, a
Mr. Angelo he had met in Paris. I tried to meet Mr. Angelo the next
day, but he did not show up.

"When I first met you that year, I asked you if you were Angelo
from the Arch, the code words given to me by the monk. When
you responded differently, I knew that you were not the friend
from Paris. I went back to the hotel several times trying to find
Mr. Angelo, but I was not successful."

"What happened to the painting?" Avner asked.

"Not knowing what to do, I placed it in a safe and waited for
one of the six monks to come back looking for it. It has been there
eighteen years."

"Did the monks come back for the painting?"

"No. A few months later, I became suspicious about the monks and the package. Their leader did not give me the full name of his friend. He gave me a good description, but I asked myself a few questions: Why was I to use a coded question? How would his friend know the exact words of a coded response? I became suspicious and scared. How could I be so gullible? Maybe the package contained illegal drugs or stolen jewelry. If that was the case, I might have endangered myself. Not knowing what to do at that time, I hid the package and tried to forget it. I concluded that the monks were not real monks and that their friends are the ones who are now looking for me and the package."

Avner interrupted him again, "Is your package in Rome?"

"No, I brought it with me, Avner. I'm afraid to have it in my possession any longer. I am even afraid to open it. I had to leave Rome to escape from a murderous organization.

"Before overpowering one of my captors yesterday, I learned that the men who kidnapped me are looking for a very valuable painting. In exchange for the information, their leader offered me the chance to join his organization and gave me forty-eight hours to think about the offer. I suspect that it could be an international mafia dealing with drug trafficking."

"Why don't we open the package now?" said Avner. "Maybe it does not contain drugs. Maybe it really contains a painting."

Alberto handed the package to Avner, who removed the wrapping paper carefully to reveal a frame covered by a white cardboard with two strings around it. He removed the cardboard and saw the famous *Birth of Venus* painting by Sandro Botticelli.

"A Botticelli?" Avner jumped from his chair. "I know this painting well."

"It was probably stolen from the Uffizi Museum in Florence," Alberto declared with fear. "There is a rumor that the one in the museum is a fake, but it was denied by the curator. Maybe they used me as a courier of a stolen painting. I have hidden this package and endured many sleepless nights worrying about what I should do with it, fearing that it might contain illegal drugs. I did not report it to the police."

"The painting is not an original. It is probably a copy by a good artist," said Avner. "There are many copies of famous paintings. Art students are encouraged to sit at museums and learn the art by copying paintings of the great masters. My wife, Elaine, copied several paintings of famous painters including Renoir, Fragonard, and even a Botticelli."

"She copied a Botticelli painting? Which one?"

"*The Birth of Venus*." Avner was perplexed. "She donated it to the Jerusalem School of Art."

Alberto gave the Botticelli copy to Avner.

"There is another possibility," continued Alberto. "A breakaway group of Tibetan monks, dissatisfied with the peaceful policy of the Dalai Lama, may have reason to publicize their cause and embarrass him. Given the interest of the Dalai Lama in the Jewish people, they may want to decipher the inscription of the Tibetan parchment. They may have established a clandestine group to undermine the policies of the Dalai Lama. In that case, the six tourists may have been real monks.

"My greatest fear, however, is another possibility. Bismillah knows about the Society of the Ark and its objective of locating the hidden Judah Maccabee scroll. If they find it before you, it would deprive the Jewish people of an important document that can be strong evidence that the present Muslim Dome of the Rock building is located on the same site as the Jewish Temple destroyed by the Romans."

"You asked us to meet you in Paris urgently to help you in a matter of life and death," said Avner. "However, you still haven't told us how we can help you."

"My SOS message was only a ruse to ensure that you would come," responded Alberto. "I asked you to meet me in Paris because I could not come to meet you in Israel or Rome. The information I gave to you today is important for your safety and for your research program."

"What are your plans now?" Menachem asked.

"Don't be concerned about my safety or my family's safety," added Alberto. "I just want to warn you of the danger you may be facing in your search. As far as my safety is concerned, I'll deal with it myself from now on. My life is in danger, and I must not stay in Paris or return to Rome. I managed to get my wife and son out of Rome so that they will not become hostages. I will leave for South America where they will join me. You will not be able to contact me. I'll contact you if I have additional information."

Menachem looked at his brother with a slight smile. "Do you think what I think?" he asked.

"Of course I do," was Avner's response.

"In that case, do you agree that we should convince Alberto to think about it too?"

"I certainly do."

"Avner and I are asking you to return to Rome and wait for your interrogator's contact."

"I just ran away from them, and you want me to go back to Rome?"

"If you join their organization, we will learn if they are affiliated with a mafia group or with Bismillah. It is important for us to know more about the Bismillah operations in Rome. I'll make arrangements to assign two men to protect you while you are in Rome, and I will appoint someone as your contact man."

"If I accept your suggestion, I'll endanger you as well as myself. I am not sure I have the courage to face them again."

"Yesterday you had a lot of courage when you tied one of the captors and drove away in his minivan. You can join our cause."

Alberto hesitated but accepted.

"What shall I tell them about the painting?"

"That is an important question," replied Menachem. "If you tell them you sold it to an American art collector in 1964, it would be very hard to trace, and they may believe you."

Alberto hesitated again but agreed to return to Rome on the next day.

*   *   *

Back in his hotel room, Alberto questioned the wisdom of returning to Rome from the safety of Paris, even after he had already given his word to Menachem. However, staying another day in Paris was out of the question. It would mean that the forty-eight hours granted by the interrogator would expire the next day. He started packing his clothes and called a taxi to take him to the airport.

The room telephone rang.

"My name is Suzanne, may I talk to M. Monclairon?" was the voice that he heard when he answered telephone. The calling woman spoke French with a German accent and a touch of Middle Eastern flavor.

"You have the wrong room," he answered. "There is nobody here named Monclairon."

"M. Maimon. I know you registered as Monclair, and not Monclairon, but I want to see you."

"Who are you?" asked Alberto.

"I have a message for you," was her response. "It is from your friend in Italy. He wants to know if you are planning to return to

Rome today. He wants to meet you and to know if you decided to accept his offer. I am in the lobby now. Can you come to the lobby? Or do you want me to come to your room?"

"I don't know who you are," responded Alberto, "and I don't want to meet you."

"You sound upset, Mr. Maimon," said the woman. "I'll call you again in fifteen minutes."

Alberto panicked. Five minutes later, the telephone rang again. He panicked again. Naturally, he had only one option left. If he tried to leave the hotel, they would see him as they were probably waiting for him in the lobby. If he managed to leave by a back door, they would still find him. He called Menachem, but his phone was busy. The room telephone rang again, but he did not answer it. A few minutes later, he heard a knock on the door. He did not open it and kept quiet. The person outside the door opened it with a key. He hid in the closet. A maid entered the room and placed two clean towels in the bathroom. After she left, he continued packing his clothes.

He heard another knock on the door. He kept his silence. The person outside the door opened it with a key. This time it was an attractive young brown-haired woman accompanied by a dark-haired and dark-skinned man sporting a leather jacket. Alberto came out of his hiding, informing the couple that they were in the wrong room.

"I am Suzanne, Mr. Maimon," said the young woman. "My companion is Robert, my assistant. We only want to know if you are planning to return to Rome today."

"I will return tomorrow," replied Alberto. "I already have the return ticket on Air France. I came to Paris to visit my cousin who will be undergoing open heart surgery tomorrow morning."

He heard three knocks on the door followed by two knocks. Alberto panicked again. Suzanne's friend Robert opened the door.

A blond-haired man walked in wearing a leather jacket and high black leather boots. Suzanne introduced him to Alberto.

"Mr. Maimon," she said, "our driver came to take us to the airport. Your friend wants to see you today in Rome. I see that you are packing your clothes. I will be happy to help you with it. We have to leave now. Our van is waiting in front of the hotel."

"I cannot return today," said Alberto. "I have to see my cousin tomorrow before returning to Rome."

"That won't be a problem. We can take you to the hospital on the way to the airport. You will have time to visit your cousin before our departure for Rome."

The driver approached Suzanne and whispered something to her in German. Alberto heard it and realized that his uninvited guests consisted of a young Middle Eastern couple and a blond-haired German. *Possibly a neo-Nazi, to judge from his style of dress.*

In an attempt of last resort, he spoke to Suzanne in German. Suzanne and the blond-haired driver looked at each other, and both reacted simultaneously with threats in German, telling him that the time for cordiality was over.

"Your threats—"

Two men burst into the room. The first was Menachem aiming his Beretta at Robert. His companion, also holding a Beretta, tackled the driver. Suzanne froze at this unexpected interruption and cursed the moment in which she had instructed the driver to leave his van and come to the room. She reached for her purse when Avner hit her hand with the butt of his gun. The purse dropped, and another Beretta slipped out of it, landing with clatter on the floor. Menachem's companion tied the driver and Suzanne to two chairs with ropes. Menachem tied Robert to a third chair after taking his gun.

"Menachem, where have you been?" asked Alberto.

Without answering him, Menachem walked to the center of the room, picked up Suzanne's Beretta from the floor, inspected it, and put it in his pocket.

"A very nice Beretta," he said approvingly. "Thank you, Suzanne, for donating it to Israel."

Leaving Suzanne and her two companions tied and blindfolded in the room, Menachem, his assistant, and Alberto left the hotel, entered the rented car, and headed for Charles de Gaulle International Airport.

CHAPTER 23

1982 Elaine

A VNER RETURNED TO Haifa with *The Birth of Venus* painting to have it examined by Elaine. She was a successful artist. Her oils were on display in several exhibitions in Boston and Jerusalem. Two were at the New York Metropolitan Museum of Art.

"Where did you find this painting?" Elaine exclaimed as soon as she looked at it. "It is the one I copied in the Uffizi Museum on my first visit to Florence."

"It couldn't be yours, Elaine. Yours is in the Jerusalem School for Arts."

"This is *my* copy of the original Botticelli," Elaine insisted. "But something is odd about it."

"What can be odd about a copy?" Avner asked. "It's either a good copy or a bad one."

"Avner, it's a good copy, and I know it's mine, but it has been reframed, and it seems to be thicker. It's much thicker than any painting I have ever seen."

Elaine inspected it closely.

"This is *my* painting." Her excitement was evident.

Passing her fingers along the edge of the canvas, she remarked, "The edges of the canvas are thinner than its center. I suspect that another painting is hidden behind it."

Dr. Bar David reached for the canvas with enthusiasm. With great care, Avner removed it from its frame.

"This is remarkable. If it's a double canvas, maybe the front copy hides a very valuable original behind it."

Elaine reached for the canvas and touched its edges.

"I am not interested in the financial value of the hidden canvas. I just want to see the back of the visible one."

After working on the painting carefully inch by inch, she separated the two canvases. The rear canvas was blank, but a parchment lodged between the two canvases fell out onto the floor. She picked it up and looked at it.

"It's in Aramaic!" she shouted.

She looked at the back of the painting. "Look at the back of the canvas. You won't need a magnifying glass, Avner?"

Avner picked up the painting. At the back of the canvas he saw a signature ELAINE HORENSTEIN—BOSTON—1954.

*   *   *

Avner, Bar David, and Elaine sat at the conference table each holding a large magnifying glass as if they were holding their swords ready for battle. A secretary wrote in Modern Hebrew script the words that Avner read from the Botticelli parchment. Avner photographed the inscription on the parchment and sent it to Professor LeCorbellier at the Sorbonne.

*   *   *

"Did you go for your annual checkup today?" Avner asked Elaine three months later.

"I've just returned from my appointment with Dr. Cohen," answered Elaine. "He wants me to see a cardiologist today."

"What are we waiting for?" said Avner with a stunned expression. "I'll call Dr. Tratner to ask him if he can see you immediately."

"It has already been scheduled. He will see me this afternoon."

Their lives took a dramatic turn when Elaine was diagnosed with a rare type of cancer that damaged the mitral valve in her heart. Elaine's health was deteriorating rapidly. The cardiologist contacted the Mayo Clinic in Rochester, Minnesota, for an opinion. Dr. Levine, the clinic's head of open-heart surgery, recommended immediate replacement of the mitral valve with an artificial one.

During Elaine's surgery at the Mayo Clinic, Avner sat in the cardiology waiting room. Dozens of men and women filled the room waiting for news of family members who were in surgery. He saw bearded Pakistanis with turbans, Indian women with spots on their foreheads, kaffiyeh-wearing Saudis, a Texan with a cowboy hat, and numerous people of other nationalities. He was overwhelmed by the flood of foreign languages and decided to close his eyes and let his mind wander.

Medical technology has not advanced much since 1965, when I designed a heart pump at the Tufts Medical Center in Boston, at least not enough to help my Elaine. Can an artificial valve really replace her failed heart valve? Could it bring her back to normal health?

In 1965, Avner had been the engineering member attached to a team of cardiologists, surgeons, and nurses at the Tufts Medical Center. Their research objective was the evaluation of a prototype artificial heart-assist pump manufactured to his design. Surgeons used it during open-heart operations on hundreds of laboratory dogs.

Avner remembered Dr. Cliff Maxwell, the Tufts Research Center director of cardiology, who was very optimistic about the heart-assist project. He claimed that it could become a forerunner of an implantable heart pump, which would replace defective hearts in humans. That was seventeen years ago, yet medical technology had not advanced much toward the design of an implantable heart pump.

He closed his eyes. In his mind, he saw circles of many colors. He found himself in a large ballroom.

> *He stood alone near the pale green wall of a large ballroom; at the center of its ceiling hung a large crystal chandelier. Forty or fifty couples were dancing on the dance floor to the music of a ten-piece band and a female singer. All the men were in white surgical robes with white surgical caps and white rubber gloves. All the women were in green robes with green caps and green rubber gloves. The music was cheerful, and everyone joined the singer in "Happy days are here again."*

> *Dressed exactly like all the other men, a stranger walked toward him.*

> *"Hello, Avner," the stranger greeted him.*

Avner looked at him but didn't recognize him.

"Have we met before?"

"We certainly have, Avner," the stranger replied. "I am Cliff Maxwell, the director of Research at the Tufts Medical Research Center. You designed the heart-assist pump for us. Don't you remember me?"

"Oh, now I do, Dr. Maxwell. You look like all the other clones who are dancing in this ballroom."

"Why don't you join the celebration? Why don't you dance?"

"What is the reason for this celebration?"

"Don't you know? I can't believe nobody told you. We are celebrating the success of Elaine's operation," the director said.

"Wow!" he exclaimed, "My prayers have been answered."

"Your design was the pioneering project that triggered many other heart pump programs. Its success convinced the United States National Institute of Health to fund similar programs in other universities."

"I never dreamt that it would be so successful," Avner reacted with surprise.

"If it is adopted as a standard by NIH, I'll nominate you for the Nobel Prize in medicine," Dr. Maxwell declared.

"Oh! No!" Avner reacted. "If the success of the heart pump ever results in a Nobel Prize for medicine, the credit should belong to you, not to me. You are the one who made the heart pump successful."

"If you insist, but I would be ready to share it with you." Dr. Maxwell smiled and danced away.

Suddenly the music stopped, the singing stopped, Dr. Maxwell disappeared, and the ballroom was empty.

"Wake up! Wake up!" was all he heard.

The call disturbed him. "Why am I told to wake up? I am not asleep. This is not a dream. Or is it?"

Avner opened his eyes and saw the heart surgeon Dr. Levine standing beside him.

"Dr. Amram," the surgeon said, "your wife is now in the recovery room. The open-heart surgery was successful."

"When can I see Elaine?" he asked, unable to contain his joy.

"A nurse will inform you when she wakes up, which should be in about two hours. She'll be up and walking tomorrow."

Avner was stunned.

How is it possible to walk only twenty-four hours after open-heart surgery? Has the medical technology advanced so much that replacing a human heart valve with a mechanical one has become routine? I may have been wrong about the progress of medical engineering. Maybe the day is not far when an artificial heart will replace a faulty original.

I can't imagine any man or any woman living without a human heart. All societies on earth have been claiming that emotions, passion, compassion, love, and even hate, come from the human heart. They certainly could not come from a mechanical heart. It's impossible to predict the future progress of medical science. The next development might be a noninvasive human heart repair pill to heal any scar tissue caused by heart attacks. That is unimaginable or just science fiction.

The operation was successful. The discovery of Elaine's defective heart valve had been a wake-up call. Now hope replaced despair—hope that the artificial valve would bring her back to her previous health.

It was a false hope.

The operation was successful, but Elaine continued to suffer from the cancer that had spread to her liver. In 1983, she lost her battle at the age of forty-seven.

When Elaine was diagnosed with terminal cancer, she had insisted that they purchase burial plots in a cemetery near Haifa. She wanted them to be in the land that she had fallen in love with. Avner purchased two plots near the Tel Dor excavation site on the shores of the Mediterranean Sea.

At her funeral, in the presence of family and friends, Avner delivered a eulogy in which he described her work and her love of Israel. At the end of the eulogy, he quoted the words about death written by his late father, Benjamin. He had read these words at his father's funeral a year earlier. He wanted to read them again.

Nothing is as bitter as the bitterness of death.
Nothing is harder to accept than the hardness of death.

Steel is hard, but fire can melt it.
Fire is hard, but water can extinguish it.
Water is hard, but the clouds can carry it,
Clouds are hard, but the wind can disperse them.
But death,
Death is harder than all of G-d's creations,
And there is no cure or wisdom against death.

There is only the memory of my beloved Elaine,
who has been called to return her soul to G-d who loaned it to her.

During twenty-seven years of living with Elaine, Avner felt fortunate to be blessed with a jewel of a wife who gave him joy and gladness. He admired her soul, her love, and her compassion. Above all, he valued her clear thinking, and he relied heavily on her understanding and advice. When he faced a serious problem in life, she helped him see what he could not see without her. He mourned deeply when he lost her. Her departure from his life was the arrival of inconsolable emptiness. The following three years were devastating. He had lost the most precious person he had in life. His sole comfort was their only son, Benjamin, who had earned his medical degree specializing in orthopedic surgery. Avner's passion for archaeology and engineering kept him going. Unable to concentrate on his work, he took three months off from his research.

*   *   *

Avner turned to his other passion of researching his family history. He had managed to gather considerable information on the Amram family after its arrival from Algeria to Jerusalem in the late eighteenth century. However, his goal was to obtain information about his family prior to its arrival to Israel. He hoped to find evidence confirming his father's orally transmitted information that the Amram family lived in Toledo prior to the 1492 expulsion of the Jews.

He visited France searching the archives of the Jewish community in Paris. He consulted the Aix-en-Provence University archives, where he learned that the French government had awarded French citizenship to the Jews of Algeria at the beginning of the nineteenth century. He found records of voters from Oran, Algeria, whose name was Amram, but none earlier than 1830.

He visited the city of Toledo, an hour's drive south of Madrid. It had been a center of Jewish scholarship and Hebrew literature. It is one of the very few towns in Spain where remnants of Jewish buildings have been preserved.

CHAPTER 24

1983 The Wild-Goose Chase

"THERE'S A CODED message from the Rome office sent by Hassan himself," Bashir's secretarial aide said.

"Read it."

"With your permission:

> Good news and bad news. We have located the Jewish
> tour guide and interrogated him. The bad news is that
> he escaped."

"Another botched operation by that incompetent Rome manager." Bashir's face was red with fury. "Send an alert to all European chapter managers to find him."

The aide left the room and immediately returned.

"There is another coded message," the aide announced. "This one is from Yusuf in Paris:

We spotted Alberto meeting two Israeli men in Paris.
We await your instructions.

Yusuf."

Bashir weighed his options. This could be the right opportunity for his son Farid. During the last ten years, he had closely observed his son's work as he was being groomed for higher responsibilities in Bismillah. Farid managed the family farm meeting customers, hiring farm labor, contracting with suppliers, and managing the household operation. However, Bashir was not pleased with his performance at Bismillah.

> *Farid is not taking his Bismillah work seriously*
> *enough. His obsessive love for his mother*
> *distracts him from his duties. He is intelligent,*
> *and his managing skills impress everyone,*
> *but he is very soft-hearted. He loves singing.*
> *He always hums melodies he learned from his*
> *mother when he was a child. I must take him*
> *away from her.*

"Farid," Bashir called when his son entered the office, "there is an important matter in Europe that we must deal with as soon as possible. It requires a senior operative, but I want to choose an individual whom I can trust, and who will not fail me."

"What makes this matter so special?" Farid asked.

"It is very special. I want you to undertake this mission."

"Tell me about it."

"There is a man in Paris who has some important information. We tried to get it from him in Rome, but we failed. He managed to escape, and he has been spotted in Paris. You will go to supervise the search for this man. Yusuf will brief you about him in Paris."

"What information are we looking for?" asked Farid.

"Alberto Maimon was a tour guide in Rome. Eighteen years ago, we sent six operatives to Rome on a mission. They carried a painting by the famous Italian painter Botticelli. We sent it to Europe with the six men. They never accomplished their mission. The men and the painting disappeared in 1964, and we have been looking for them ever since—without success. We believe that they gave the painting to Mr. Maimon. He may lead us to the painting, and he may know what happened to the six missing men."

"Why did we wait eighteen years to look for the painting?" asked Farid.

"I asked myself the same question many times. It happened when my father, Ibn Najad, was the director of Bismillah, and I don't want to ask him. We recently learned about a guided tour held in 1964. I now want to investigate the matter not only to learn about the missing men, but also because a considerable amount of money is involved."

"Who will interrogate Alberto?" Farid asked.

"We have to bring him to Istanbul, where I'll interrogate him personally."

"How will I do that?"

"Yusuf will make those arrangements, Farid."

"When do I leave for Paris and for how long? This is the time of year to deliver truck loads of olives and olive oil to our customers."

"Don't worry about olives or olive oil. Your brothers can handle that. This mission is much more important than the olives."

"So when do I leave?"

"Immediately," said Bashir. "I want you to be there within the next two days."

Before leaving on his mission, Farid and his mother spent the last evening alone. She retold him stories of her childhood in Jerusalem and about her parents whom he had never met.

*   *   *

Carrying a fake French passport, Farid passed the control gate at the Charles de Gaulle International Airport without any difficulty. Yusuf met him near the Europcar rental counter.

"Welcome to *La Belle Paris*, Farid," Yusuf greeted him. "It is a pleasure to meet you after hearing so much about you."

Farid knew his type well.

> *Yusuf knows how to identify an opportunity when he sees one. This one is special. He knows that I could be his boss one day.*

"Thank you for coming out to meet me at the airport. I hope you've got some details about Mr. Maimon."

"I've prepared a written report with all the information we have on him."

"Good. My time is limited. When can I meet the two operatives assigned to me?"

"They'll be ready to meet you any time after you check in at the hotel. However, I want to talk to you about the mission before you meet them. Two days ago, we located Maimon's hiding place. I have three men following him day and night. Now I need your instructions. He is staying at the *Hotel Toulouse* in Montparnasse. I reserved a room for you at the Randis hotel nearby."

Two hours later, Farid, Yusuf, and the two operatives met in an isolated corner of the lobby of Farid's hotel.

"My plan for kidnapping Mr. Maimon is completed," started Yusuf. "We pick him up, transfer him by train to Marseilles, and smuggle him into a Turkish ship scheduled to sail to Istanbul."

Farid asked many questions on the plan. He interrogated the two men to determine their competence and their readiness to follow his instructions.

"We could do it tomorrow. Everything is in place, and we just need your approval."

"It would be wise to wait another day," Farid asserted his authority. "I want to review the details of the plan, scout the area, inspect the hotel, and visit the train station."

"It is agreed."

Two days later, Farid and Yusuf went to the *Toulouse* hotel. While Yusuf waited outside, Farid entered the lobby and walked to the *concierge* desk.

"*Bonjour, madame*," he addressed the woman behind the counter, "I am a friend of your guest Mr. Maimon. Please inform him that I am here to see him with a message from his wife."

"We don't have a guest by the name of Maimon," the concierge responded.

"My cousin always plays tricks on us," Farid said with a smile. "He uses different names when he does not want us to know where he is."

He pulled out a photograph of Alberto and showed it to the concierge.

"*Ah oui*," reacted the concierge, "M. Manuel de Silva. He checked out of the hotel this morning."

"Did he leave any forwarding address?"

"He did not leave any information."

Farid reacted calmly. He thought about the kidnapping plan. The day's delay had given Mr. Maimon an opportunity to give them the slip. This would not have happened if he had not given the instruction to wait an extra day. He was determined to blame Yusuf, who had assured him that Alberto was under constant surveillance. He walked out from the hotel and poured out his anger on Yusuf.

"Your rooster fled the coop again, Yusuf. What kind of an operation do you run here? I thought your men were on the job day and night. They must have fallen asleep last night. You'd better come up with a good idea now," Farid said impatiently.

"Don't be angry and don't worry. I can assure you that we'll find him within a day or two."

Farid listened without losing his temper.

"While you were inside the hotel, a taxi driver informed me that Mr. Maimon was sighted boarding an Air France flight to Madrid. We have informed our office there to place him under immediate surveillance upon his arrival in Spain."

Farid was on the next flight to Madrid.

After passing through passport control at the Madrid airport, he went to the Europcar counter. Bismillah had strict travel procedures for every traveling member. Operatives arriving at any airport were instructed to go to a car rental counter where a local contact met them. It was a precautionary measure to ensure that the arriving person was not followed. Approaching the car rental desk, a young woman introduced herself to Farid.

"You must be Farid Ibn Bashir," said the young woman. "I am Margot, Shukri's assistant."

"It's a pleasure to be met by a beautiful young woman," responded Farid. "I wish I had time to spend an evening with you, but my visit to Madrid will be short. I have to see Shukri as soon as possible. Please arrange it."

"Already done. Shukri asked me to apologize for not coming to meet you personally. He was detained by an urgent matter, but he will be waiting to meet you at your hotel."

Margot drove him to a small hotel on the outskirts of Madrid where Shukri was waiting.

"Farid Ibn Bashir." Shukri welcomed him at the hotel with a great smile. "Welcome to Madrid."

Farid expected to hear this greeting. He knew Shukri well.

Shukri and Yusuf grew up together in the same neighborhood. As teenagers, they played soccer on the same team. Just like Yusuf, Shukri knows how to recognize an opportunity that could advance his career. He knows that one day I may be his boss.

"Two agents carrying a photograph of Alberto waited for him at the arrival gate," continued Shukri. "We also checked the Air France flight manifest. There was nobody by the name of Alberto or Maimon. We believe that he is not in Madrid."

"Did you really expect Alberto to use his real name?" Farid asked with a touch of sarcasm. "He is running away from us, so you expect him to travel as himself? Golda Meir went to meet King Abdullah in Amman disguised as a Bedouin woman. General Ehud Barak visited Damascus disguised as a woman. Think, man!"

Farid dismissed Shukri and told him to wait for further instructions. He felt like a fool.

These Bismillah branch managers are incompetent. Alberto succeeded in evading them in Rome, in Paris, and now in Madrid—a proverbial moving target. Now

I understand the meaning of the farmer who runs
around in circles on a wild-goose chase.

What do I do now?

If I return to Jerusalem empty-handed, my father will
laugh at me.

He dismissed Margot with instructions to pick him up the next day. He called Shukri, who informed him that Alberto did not fly to Madrid. He boarded an Air France flight to Buenos Aires.

This is becoming ridiculous, but it could be an
interesting challenge.

He was amazed at Alberto's ability to improvise an escape, elude his followers, and then vanish completely—quite resourceful for a tour guide. He wondered if it was the ingenuity of the fugitive or the bumbling incompetence of the Bismillah operatives.

Farid considered calling Bashir for advice but reconsidered and decided it was an occasion for independent action. He sent a coded message to his father, updating him on the evolving saga of the wild-goose chase and informing him that he planned to be on the next flight to Buenos Aires.

CHAPTER 25

1983 The Buenos Aires Kidnap

THE BUENOS AIRES Bismillah branch was relatively new. Bachtiar had been its manager for only three months. Receiving a double-coded message directly from Bashir in Jerusalem indicated that it was important and urgent. Double coding required the message to be deciphered in two consecutive stages. He read the first message:

> "You personally will be at the Buenos Aires airport
> to identify the man in the photograph. He will be on
> the Air France flight 728 from Paris. You will assign
> a surveillance team whose only task will be to follow
> the man while waiting for new instructions on the
> following day. Look at the second message."

The second message was a color photograph of a man under which was the name Alberto Maimon.

Bachtiar checked the Air France flight schedule and called two of his operatives to accompany him to the airport. An hour later, he received another message from Jerusalem, again in double-coded format. The instructions were very specific:

> You will arrange to kidnap Alberto as soon as
> possible, take him to a secure location in the vicinity
> of Buenos Aires, and keep him there until Bashir's
> arrival.

Bachtiar was shocked.

> *Not kidnapping! In the name of Allah! I am still*
> *learning the territory. That's insane. I knew that*
> *accepting this appointment required a high level of*
> *responsibility, and I expected surprises, but not this,*
> *only three months after my appointment. Bashir should*
> *have given this task to a person with appropriate*
> *experience and who is familiar with Buenos Aires. I've*
> *never kidnapped anyone, and I have no idea how to do*
> *it.*

He summoned the most experienced man on his staff, his security officer Taleb, and assigned him the responsibility of planning the kidnapping.

Bachtiar, Taleb, and two operatives arrived at Buenos Aires airport an hour before the midnight landing of the Air France flight from Paris. They scouted the airport's security arrangements to ensure that their presence would not attract the attention of airport security personnel. Having studied the color photograph of Alberto, they had no trouble identifying him. The fake moustache did not hide his other facial features.

Alberto picked up his suitcase and walked toward the line of cabs waiting for customers. A stranger carrying a suitcase approached him.

"Do you need a ride to town?" asked the stranger.

"Yes, I am going to the city."

"I just arrived from Rio de Janeiro," said the stranger. "I am looking for someone to share a taxi with me."

"I am interested. We could split the cost."

"Naturally," said the Rio traveler.

They flagged down a small minivan taxi that was parked at the curb and retained him for the ride. As soon as they left the airport, the stranger pulled out a gun aiming it at Alberto, who reacted swiftly, knocking the gun out of the stranger's hand.

The stranger grabbed his arm screaming with pain.

Alberto reached for the gun on the floor.

The driver stopped the van abruptly, causing the gun to fly forward under the driver's seat.

The stranger recovered and struck Alberto's chest with a brass knuckle.

Alberto grabbed his chest still struggling with pain.

The stranger pulled a rope from his vest and managed to place it around Alberto's neck.

"Move and you are dead," threatened the traveler from Rio. "All I have to do is pull."

Alberto stopped struggling.

The stranger loosened the rope, tied Alberto's hands, and blindfolded him.

Alberto tried to stay calm, but he remembered his two previous kidnappings and wondered if Menachem had received his message and if help was on the way.

The minivan driver headed to the secure house four miles from the airport followed by Bachtiar's car.

Bachtiar was pleased. The kidnapping was accomplished. His security officer demonstrated his skills as an accomplished and seasoned operative.

*   *   *

At the Madrid airport, Farid boarded an Iberia flight to JFK.

At the Ben Gurion Airport, Bashir boarded a Continental flight to JFK.

At the Ben Gurion Airport, Avner boarded an El-Al Airlines flight to JFK.

At the JFK Terminal, Bashir and Farid boarded an American Airlines flight to Buenos Aires. So did Avner.

At the Buenos Aires Airport, Bashir and Farid disembarked. A man met Bashir, walked with him to his car and drove away. Another man met Farid, walked with him to his car and drove away.

Avner disembarked with apprehension at Buenos Aires, where Menachem met him. They embraced and walked to Menachem's rented car. He followed Bachtiar's car, keeping a safe distance but not letting it get out of sight.

"Thank you for saving Alberto in Paris," Avner said to his brother.

"I received a message from the airport while Alberto was already on the Air France airplane," was Menachem's reply. "He informed me that he was on his way to Buenos Aires. He suspected that the men who kidnapped him in Paris could be waiting for him on his arrival. He wrote that he would send another message after disembarking in Argentina, and if such a message did not arrive within the next twenty-four hours, it would mean that Bismillah kidnapped or killed him. I immediately boarded the next plane to Buenos Aires."

"I know all about it," said Avner. "He sent me the same message. I waited impatiently to receive another message from him, but it never arrived. Now you know the reason for my request to meet me here. I must try to help Alberto."

"What are brothers for?" asked Menachem. "We were taught by our parents to help each other all our lives at any cost. If Alberto is important to you, he is also important to me. He is like our brother. We saved him in Paris, and we will save him again here."

"If he is still alive," added Avner.

"He is alive. Bashir bought a ticket to come here. He wouldn't come chasing after a dead man all the way from Jerusalem to Argentina."

Avner noticed that the car they were following led them away from downtown Buenos Aires, several miles from the airport. It stopped in front of a house surrounded by a garden with bushes and trees. He saw Bashir and two other men getting out of their car and entering the house. The car drove away.

"We now know where to find Bashir," said Avner. "But how do we find Alberto?"

"We have two options," responded Menachem. "We could go to our hotel and analyze the situation, in which case, we will surely lose the opportunity to get any information on Alberto from Bashir. We will probably lose Bashir as well. Or we could act right now by testing our ingenuity on how to find Alberto."

"You are not only a good brother," said Avner, "you are also a good analyst. Let us look around."

When Menachem drove the car past the house, he noticed a small van parked across the street where a man was talking on his car phone.

"He may be a Bismillah man guarding the safe house," he said to Avner.

"It could also be an Argentine security agent watching the house," responded Avner. "We have to be careful not to engage in anything that would alert the Argentine Security Agency."

Menachem drove past the van and parked his car on the next street.

They walked slowly back toward the house, scouting the area for possible guards. Satisfying themselves that there were no guards outside the house, they approached the van from behind, attempting to hear its driver talking on his car telephone.

"*Bism-Allah Al Rachman Ul-Rahim. La Allah Illa Allah WaMuhammad Rassul Allah,*" they heard the driver reciting his prayers in Arabic.

"It is a strange world," said Menachem. "Imagine the Argentine Security Agency teaching their agents to pray, 'In the name of Allah, the beneficent and the merciful, there is no G-d but Allah, and Muhammad is his messenger.'"

"Now we know that the van belongs to Bismillah," he added.

Hearing the sound of an approaching car, Avner and Menachem retreated fast to hide behind a row of bushes. The car stopped next to the van. Two men got out. One man talked to the driver of the van and went into the house while the other returned to the car and drove away followed by the van.

With the area clear, Avner and Menachem quietly entered the yard of the house. They tiptoed toward the first-floor windows and looked at the room inside. It appeared to be a library. They saw Bashir lounging in a comfortable chair, laughing and drinking with another man.

Menachem gave the signal. They walked to the backyard looking for a way to enter the building. Between two trees in the yard, a man sat on a bench, smoking a pipe. Menachem pulled a large scarf and quietly approached the bench behind the man. With swift action, he wrapped the scarf around the man's head, timing it to the moment when the pipe was not in his mouth. The man almost choked, but the sound of his scream was muffled by the scarf. Avner pulled a rope from Menachem's coat, tied the man's hands behind him, and tied him to the bench. Menachem placed a handkerchief in his mouth and tightened the scarf around his head.

They entered the house using the back door, which was left open, and tiptoed to a hallway that led them to the library. They heard Bashir's voice.

"Did you place a guard outside?" Bashir asked.

"Why do you ask?" Bachtiar responded with another question.

"I heard some footsteps from the hallway."

"It must be the guard or Farid. Don't worry. This is a safe house. There are no Israelis here."

Menachem pulled out his Beretta and burst into the library.

Taken by surprise, Bashir reached for his vest and pulled out a gun, but not fast enough. Menachem shot first hitting Bashir's gun out of his hand.

The brothers tied the two men to their chairs.

"We know why you are in Buenos Aires," Avner addressed Bashir. "And you know why we are here. We don't care about you. We have only one question: where is Alberto?"

"Who is Alberto?" Bashir asked.

"Don't take us for fools," said Menachem. "I am a colonel in the Israeli army, and I am not an idiot. Your men forced themselves into Alberto's house in Rome and assaulted him. They kidnapped him in Rome, and others tried to kidnap him in Paris. Now you've kidnapped him again in Buenos Aires. I advise you to cooperate with us and tell us where he is. We don't torture our prisoners, but we'll be happy to turn you over to the Argentina Security."

"Don't bother with them until we've searched the house," Avner interrupted the interrogation. "He may be in the basement or in the attic. I'll search the house while you continue your friendly chat with our hosts."

Avner started his search. Hearing footsteps in the basement, he cautiously went downstairs to find Alberto lying down, bound with a rope to a bed, a handkerchief stuffed in his mouth. Avner hugged him and softly whispered, "Alberto, we came as soon as we could." He removed the handkerchief and freed him.

"I thought I would never see you again." Alberto was still shaking with fear. "But I knew that you would find a way to help me. Be careful. One of my captors ran off when he heard your footsteps. He started to untie my hands and told me that he would help me to escape. Who is that man? Is he an Israeli agent?"

Alberto's question was not answered. Avner ran out of the room looking for the third man. A thought struck him; he returned and hurriedly brought Alberto up the stairs to the main floor, where Menachem was still carrying on his friendly chat with Bashir and his friend. When they walked into the library, Menachem hugged Alberto. The two Israelis escorted Alberto out of the house and drove away, leaving their hosts tied to their chairs.

They checked into a small hotel. Avner whispered his standard question to his brother, "What do we do now?"

"I know what we should do now," said Menachem. "How about taking Alberto to a good restaurant? He deserves a good dinner. It will be on me."

"I don't know who tried to help you in the basement," said Avner at the restaurant. "It is a puzzle. When he heard my footsteps, he probably thought that I was Bashir coming down to check on him."

Alberto expressed his gratitude to Avner and Menachem for risking their lives to save him. He reminded Avner of his visit at the triumphal Arch of Titus in Rome and added, "Your courage and ingenuity qualify both of you to be named the modern followers of the Maccabees."

"Our ingenuity and courage are dwarfed by those of the Israelis who brought Adolph Eichman to justice in 1960," Avner responded. "They surely needed both to succeed in capturing Eichman in a suburb of Buenos Aires and then secretly transporting him to Jerusalem to face trial. Most of those modern Maccabees had lost family members in Auschwitz."

"They had imagination, creativity, and determination, Avner."

"We should learn from them, Menachem. And now we must think of a creative way to smuggle Alberto out of Buenos Aires. Don't forget that he entered this country illegally under a false name and passport."

"OK," responded Menachem with a big smile. "We'll have to use our great Israeli army creativity. He will just have to leave Argentina using the same false identity and the same fake passport."

"This is what I call great thinking. You are a real genius. What would I do without your advice, my little brother?" Avner laughed and clapped Menachem on the back.

They left the restaurant and drove to meet Alberto's wife and son who had fled from Rome.

*   *   *

Tied to his chair in the library, Bashir looked at Bachtiar trying to figure out how they were going to free themselves. He regretted allowing Farid to leave the house earlier. Had Farid been with them, they could have overpowered the two Israelis. Bringing his son with him was part of his plan to train him for the day when he would take over the Bismillah operation. He started wondering about the competence of Bachtiar, who had left the house unguarded.

Walking toward the safe house, Farid dropped his cigarette on the sidewalk, opened the front door, and entered the library. He appeared to be disturbed to see his father and Bachtiar tied to their chairs. He rushed to remove the handkerchief from his father's mouth and untie him. Together they freed Bachtiar.

"Where have you been?" asked Bashir.

"I was outside waiting for the van to return with a guard," answered Farid. "I saw three men walking on the street, but the van did not arrive."

Bashir knew that the two Israelis had outsmarted him, but he was determined to use this operation as a lesson to his son. During the flight from Buenos Aires to JFK, he gave a lecture to Farid on the importance of learning from failed operations as well as from successful ones.

Farid has to learn how to avoid repeating the same mistakes in future operations. It is a good lesson to prepare him for the Istanbul project.

CHAPTER 26

1985 Istanbul Parchments

"THANK YOU FOR sending me the tournament schedule," Bashir said when he entered Mansoor's home in Istanbul. "I played soccer in my youth and hope to see at least two games during this visit."

"It is my favorite sport." Mansoor was enthusiastic about the game. "Stay three days, and you'll see three games. Why not bring along Farid?"

"Establishing the sports league for poor Muslim teenagers demonstrates one of the ways that makes you a great Bismillah branch manager. You invest in today's youth to prepare them for the future."

"It's a great game, but today we have a more important matter to discuss."

"I'm listening."

"Two days ago," started Mansoor, "I visited the library of the Great Mosque looking for an eighteenth-century book. I saw a group of students sitting at one of the tables. One student held a magnifying glass, inspecting an old document that was covered by a transparent sheet. I approached him and asked in Turkish to tell me what he was looking at. He said that he was inspecting the inscription on an ancient sheepskin parchment but he could not read it. I borrowed his magnifying glass and looked at the parchment, but I also could not read it."

"What were the other students doing?"

"Some stood next to me. Others stood next to a second student who was inspecting another document with a magnifying glass. A middle-aged man, apparently their professor or lecturer, stood behind them smiling. I approached the second student and asked the same question. Turning his head toward me, he said that it was another parchment which he could not read."

"Is this why you insisted on having our meeting in Istanbul this month and not in Jerusalem?" Bashir asked.

"Yes, it is. But that's not all. The professor told the students that one parchment had an ancient Hebrew inscription and the other had one in Arabic. He had taken photographs of the parchments and planned to discuss them back at the university."

"This is interesting," said Bashir. "I am neither an archaeologist nor a historian, but the matter requires further investigation. Many years ago, one of our spies reported that a synagogue rabbi in Algeria found two ancient Hebrew parchments. My father never told me what he did with that information."

"We could try to have them deciphered before the professor does," said Mansoor.

"You are naive. If the professor lets the students look at the parchments, he most probably knows what is written in them."

"Even so, Bashir, we still should try to decipher them. We could use the information in one of the schemes that your father started."

"I am not a great believer in my father's schemes, but it would be interesting to know more about these parchments. Keep it confidential. Did you try to remove the parchments from the mosque?"

"I didn't want to do it without your consent. It should be easy."

"Good. Do it and deliver them to me as soon as possible. I have a friend with a PhD in ancient Middle Eastern languages from Oxford. He is now a professor of archaeology at Cairo University."

*   *   *

"Do you remember me?" Mansoor asked the student at the archives library. "Last week you showed me a page from an old parchment."

"How can I forget?" said the student. "You couldn't read it either."

"Has your professor read it to you?"

"Not yet. He'll discuss it in class next week."

"Can I see it again?"

"It is locked in a sealed safe. The two parchments were returned to the safe, and they cannot be taken out without the curator's permission."

"You can still see the inscriptions," the student added, "if you can get the professor to show you the photographs he took. If he is not at the university, he may be in his other office at the mosque archive."

Mansoor walked away thinking, *Removing the parchments from the mosque will not be as easy as I expected. I must find the photographs.*

He went to the archive building during the lunch hour hoping to find it empty. A young woman sat at the reception desk in front of the office reserved for use by university professors. He kept walking along the hallway. Looking around to ensure that nobody followed him, he entered a conference room. It was empty. He waited until he heard footsteps in the hallway. He opened the door slightly and saw the secretary walking away from her desk.

He walked back to her desk and knocked on the professor's door when the secretary reappeared.

"May I help you?" she asked.

"I must be in the wrong office," he said nervously. "I am looking for Professor Kirklereli."

"This is his office," she said. "Do you have an appointment?"

"No, I don't, but I wanted to know if he can help my son."

"Maybe I can help you. He is not in the office today."

"When will he be back?"

"He is not in town. He'll return on Tuesday."

"Thank you. I'll call on Tuesday to schedule an appointment."

Mansoor walked away.

Lunchtime is not the time. I'll have to try again at midnight.

He was surprised to find the professor's office unlocked at midnight. He did not need his B & E Tools. Using his flashlight, he tried the drawers of the professor's desk, which were all locked. On a small conference table, he saw several envelopes, one from the photo lab was marked For Professor Kirklereli. He removed the twenty-two photographs from the envelope and found the two that he wanted. He placed the others back in the envelope and left.

The two photographs arrived in the Jerusalem office of Bashir.

*   *   *

Three months later, Bashir received a letter from Mansoor. It included a reference to his deteriorating health.

Is Mansoor asking me to relieve him from his responsibilities at Bismillah?

I have to review my file of potential candidates for promotion. Farid is the only one on my list for branch manager candidates. It is time to advance him on the Bismillah ladder to prepare him for the eventual directorship.

"Farid," Bashir said as his son entered the office, "when was the last time you came with me to Istanbul?"

"Two years ago," replied Farid. "It was during the youth soccer league tournament."

"Would you like to join me next week? It's soccer league time again."

"I'd love it. I know most of the branch members. It will be nice to reconnect with them and to see Istanbul again."

"The tournament is not the only reason for inviting you. Mansoor wants to see you. He wants to show you the operation of the Istanbul branch. It's our center of interrogations and a convenient place to keep confidential records. Close enough to Jerusalem and away from the inquisitive agents of the Israeli Mossad. Your grandfather established it away from the eyes of the British intelligence service in Palestine."

Looking forward to the Istanbul trip, Farid went to see his mother before his departing.

"Farid, my dear son," said his mother, "your father has confided in me. He told me the reason for your upcoming visit to Istanbul." Farid and his mother spent that evening alone.

*   *   *

"This is the first time you'll attend a monthly meeting here," Bashir told his son at Mansoor's office. "Nobody has ever been present at my previous meetings with Mansoor. Your presence today is important."

"Mansoor," he addressed the branch manager, "before presenting your monthly report, please tell Farid about your plans."

Farid had been anticipating that moment. *My mother was right.*

"Farid," Mansoor said, "soon I'll be assigned to another city in our organization. I've requested your father to appoint you as my senior advisor until I leave. I can train you and prepare you to take over as my successor here. Congratulations, Farid."

Farid acted surprised, not wanting to reveal that he knew about the promotion. He had to protect his mother, with whom he had a very close relationship. She was exceptional when compared to mothers of his friends in the village.

"I am pleased and fortunate to have you as my tutor," responded Farid.

"Your training will be my priority. I received glowing reports of your ability to manage your family farm. I am confident you'll be a successful branch manager."

*   *   *

Farid settled with ease into his new environment. He concentrated on familiarizing himself with his new responsibilities in the short time left before Mansoor's departure. He met regularly with staff members and their assistants to evaluate their capabilities and learn their strengths and shortcomings. In his spare time, he read the books he had brought with him, and he wrote regularly to his mother. Every Friday he went to the Great Mosque of Istanbul to the imam's sermons.

He became a regular visitor at the Great Mosque. He admired the extravagance of its architecture. He was especially interested in the library with its vast collection of books written by great Arabic philosophers of the tenth and eleventh centuries. He read about Süleyman the Magnificent and about the modern Kemal Atatürk who replaced the Arabic alphabet with the Latin alphabet.

The mosque is an ideal place for historical research. Great historical secrets must be hidden within its walls.

Farid visited the library two or three times each week. On one of those visits, he saw a group of students sitting around a table with their professor photographing several documents.

Could these documents help me in my dilemma?

CHAPTER 27

1985 Farid's Dilemma

IT WAS FRIDAY evening when Farid went for a walk that led him to the street of the Great Istanbul Synagogue. He heard singing. It was a familiar melody, though he could not remember when or where he had heard it. He had never been to a synagogue, although he often thought about visiting one in Jerusalem. He forgot about it as he continued his walk.

A week later, humming the melody that he had heard near the synagogue, he took the same walk again. This time, it was Jewish New Year's eve, and he walked into the sanctuary. Standing near the wall, he looked at the congregants sitting and chanting in unison several prayers with melodies that he had never heard before. Suddenly he heard one melody that he did remember from his childhood. When the singing stopped, the rabbi stood up and delivered a sermon in French about the Jewish High Holidays. Farid listened, pleased that it was not in Ladino, which he would not have understood. After making the hardest decision of his life, he walked out of the sanctuary and waited at the entrance. When most of the men and women left, the rabbi approached him.

"I havn't seen you here before," said the rabbi. "What is your name? Where do you come from?"

"I live in Jerusalem. I am visiting Istanbul, and I enjoyed the services tonight."

"A visitor from Jerusalem?" said Rabbi Sasson. "Would you like to join our family for the Shabbat dinner?"

"Thank you. I'd love to," responded Farid.

Together they walked to the rabbi's house. Rabbi Sasson introduced the guest to his wife, his three children, and two other invited guests. The rabbi's wife asked several questions, and her guest responded with one-word answers. She concluded that he was shy.

Following the Shabbat dinner, Farid looked at the Shabbat song booklet, humming Hebrew words, when the rabbi asked him which song he would like to sing to honor the Shabbat. Farid pointed at one song.

"We sang that one in the synagogue, and we already sang it here," said the rabbi. "How about choosing another one?"

"I'd like to hear this song again."

"You must love it very much," said the rabbi's wife. "It was always sung in my father's home on Friday nights when I grew up. It is the poem of Bar Yochai about the miracles of the great Talmud rabbi who wrote *The Book of the Zohar*."

They sang the Bar Yochai song again, and Farid hummed it with a happy smile.

Before leaving the house, he approached the rabbi and whispered, "Rabbi, would you have a few minutes to talk to me privately? I need your help."

Rabbi Sasson escorted the guest to his private study and locked the door behind him.

"You still have not answered my question," said the rabbi. "I asked you to tell me your name, what is it? Where are you from?"

"My name is Farid Ibn Bashir," he responded. "I am a Muslim from Jerusalem, and I may want to convert. I may want to become a Jew. Can you help me? Can you teach me how to become a Jew?"

The rabbi was dumbfounded.

How could I have been so wrong? I thought he was Jewish.

"Why do you want to be a Jew? It's not easy to be a Jew. Why do you want to suffer?"

"I am the grandson of Ahmad Ibn Najad. I am from a Muslim village near Jerusalem. My mother is ailing, and recently she told me that she was born Jewish. My being the son of a Jewish mother was kept a secret from me all my life. My father wanted to raise me as a dedicated Muslim. My mother was afraid to tell me that she was born Jewish. She must have been ashamed all these years. Recently, she confided in me that she regrets marrying a Muslim, but she prayed that her transgression would be forgiven on this year's Yom Kippur. She gave me a few old documents. They included my birth certificate and her birth certificate proving that she was born Jewish. I keep them in a safe place in Jerusalem."

Farid stopped talking to gaze at the rabbi's beard as though it was a dream.

"Did you go to the mosque every Friday?"

"Yes, I learned the Koran and became a fundamental Muslim. But I have always questioned such extreme interpretation of the Koran."

"In what way do you question it?"

"Knowing now that my mother was born Jewish, I wonder why the Koran teaches us to kill Jews when it teaches us to love everyone. I was taught that I'll be greatly rewarded if I kill Jews. Is radical Islam interpreting the Koran this way for political reasons? I could never understand why killing old Jewish men, women, and children would make me a hero. Are the Jews not human? Don't they have the right to live? I understand that killing enemy soldiers may be heroic, but I don't understand why we should kill innocent Jewish children. The Jews should have the right to live just like anyone else."

"Did you ever discuss these questions with your imam?"

"I never did."

"What else can you tell me?"

"I remember my mother humming melodies in my childhood. Last week I was here, and I heard all of you singing one. Today I heard another one that I remember. My mother always sang songs without words."

"What about your mother's parents?"

"I've never even seen them. I want to meet them and learn about her family background. If my mother was born Jewish, I may want to convert to Judaism, but I am not sure. Can you help me, Rabbi?"

Rabbi Sasson never expected to be approached by a Muslim who wanted to become Jewish, especially not in a Muslim country like Turkey.

He quickly responded, "You don't have to convert. According to Jewish law, if your mother is Jewish, you are already a Jew. If you decide to live as one, let us pray that your decision will provide comfort to your mother."

"How can I decide?"

"To learn about how to live as a Jew, you will have to learn Jewish laws, tradition, history, and customs. You grew up in Jerusalem. You probably have some knowledge of Hebrew."

THE HIDDEN SCROLL

"I have. I managed my father's farm, and many of our customers are Jewish. I am fluent in Hebrew."

"In that case, when you make your decision, you will be able to learn the Torah in Hebrew. I recommend that you consult with a rabbi in Jerusalem who can help you more than I can. I will give you a letter to introduce you to my friend Rabbi Shlomo Ohayon. It would be unwise for you to come to this synagogue again. You can call me if you have any questions. To protect your mother, you should keep your intention secret until you are certain about your decision."

"I'll follow your instructions and your advice," said Farid. "However, I am requesting your permission to come here again in ten days. I want to attend the prayers on Yom Kippur. I know it is a day on which Jews repent their sins. Maybe I'll find a way to repent my sins of not keeping Jewish laws."

"You don't have to repent for not knowing Jewish laws," commented the rabbi. "You are welcome to visit us on Yom Kippur if you feel that it will clarify your thoughts and help you in making your decision."

*   *   *

Farid spent three weeks of every month in Istanbul and one week in his village to help with the management of the family farm. On his next visit to Jerusalem, he called on Rabbi Ohayon and presented him with the rabbi Sasson's letter of introduction.

After reading the letter, Rabbi Ohayon wanted to know more about Farid.

"If you decide to live as a Jew, I will help you," said the rabbi. "However, you must first weigh all the consequences."

"I struggle with two conflicting ideas." Farid became emotional. "My father claims that Palestine belongs to the Arabs.

Arabs have been here before the many Jewish immigrants arrived at the turn of the last century and after the Holocaust. His claim always seemed reasonable to me. I grew up ready to fight for the rights of Arabs to this land."

"Your father is right," the rabbi was patient. "You must take his claim seriously."

"Do you agree with my father's claim?" Farid was surprised.

"I certainly do not. I only agree that many Jews started to return to Palestine at the end of the nineteenth century, after being in exile two thousand years. Until the beginning of the nineteenth century, there were very few Arabs in Palestine. However, before I continue, I think that you should discuss this matter with your mother."

Farid returned to Istanbul to continue his training and to think about the decision he had to make.

> *I have three weeks before my next visit to Jerusalem.*
> *I can't postpone my decision anymore. Do I want*
> *to remain a Muslim Arab and fight for my father's*
> *cause? Or do I want to be a Jew and fight for my*
> *mother's cause?*

I have to talk to my mother before I see Rabbi Ohayon.

"How can you help me?" Farid asked Rabbi Ohayon in Jerusalem after consulting with his mother.

"I don't know." Rabbi Ohayon had been waiting to hear from Farid. "What did your mother say?"

"She completely contradicted my father's claim. She talked about the Jewish forefathers and the long history of the Jewish people who lived here for centuries from the time of Moses until today. She also said that Arabs only started to come to Palestine in the eighteenth century."

"Has that cleared your thinking?"

"It certainly has," was Farid's quick reply. "I want to learn more about Jewish history and about King David who chose Jerusalem for his capital more than a thousand years before Islam was established in Saudi Arabia and not in Jerusalem. It seems to me that my mother's claim to this land is much more convincing than my father's claim."

"Did you make your decision already?"

"Yes, Rabbi, I want to live as a Jew, and I want to learn about my mother's family tradition."

"Now that you think you have convinced yourself and made your decision, you will have to convince me," was the rabbi's reaction. "You will write me a letter in which you will describe in detail why you want to lead a life of a Jew. You may change your mind after putting all your emotions on paper."

Agreeing to the rabbi's request, Farid left the office, found a quiet corner in the library, and spent the next two hours writing a six-page letter in which he explained his desire to lead a Jewish life. He included all the information he had been able to gather about the Jews. He placed his letter in an envelope and delivered it in person to the rabbi's secretarial assistant.

On the next day, a sealed letter was hand delivered to Farid. He opened the letter, read it, and immediately went to see his mother.

"Mother, Rabbi Ohayon wants me to come to his office. I told you about my decision."

"Go with my blessings, and may G-d be with you." She placed her two hands on his head and gave him the Hebrew blessing she remembered from her youth.

At the rabbi's office, the secretarial aide greeted Farid with warmth, presenting him with another letter. He opened it and read,

"I am impressed by the sincerity of your long letter. You've succeeded in convincing me. If you decide to go ahead, you will need a Hebrew name. I propose the Jewish name of Shmuel ben Avraham, Samuel the son of Abraham, in honor of the prophet Samuel and our ancestor Abraham. I will be happy to see you when you next visit Jerusalem."

* * *

Back in Istanbul, Farid was excited about the new double life he would be leading. For three weeks of every month, he would be a Muslim in Istanbul, training to become Bismillah's branch manager while learning in secrecy how to lead a life of a Jew. For one week of every month, he would live in his village helping to manage his father's farm and meeting Rabbi Ohayon.

Farid's life became a complicated logistical operation. He risked discovery by his father, but he considered it a challenge worth facing. Four months later, Bashir officially named him branch manager.

Farid met with Rabbi Ohayon every month in Jerusalem. In one of these meetings, he brought up a recent concern.

"I need your advice on how to deal with a security problem in Istanbul," he told the rabbi.

"I am not an authority on security matters." The rabbi was unprepared for such a request. "I can only advise you on spiritual matters, or on historical matters, but not on security."

"Who should I talk to about it?"

"My advice is to take your problem to my friend Colonel Menachem Amram. Just tell him that I sent you and that you are my student."

CHAPTER 28

1990 The Reluctant Shahid

T HE HOT DAYS of summer were relentless. The sun fried the desert dunes and rocks throughout the Israeli Negev. The *Chamsin* sirocco that settled on the Negev was bone-dry and tiring as it is in the Sahara desert, but it did not prevent Bashir from wearing, as always, his white suit with a white tie and a red rose on his lapel. This he would not relinquish even in the heat of the desert. It was his way of showing his authority whenever he left his village.

The skies were clear without a sign of a single cloud. Bashir drove his new air-conditioned Mercedes Benz sedan on Route 25 south of Beersheba heading toward Dimona and stopped near a group of Bedouin tents at the village of Abu Jamda. Teenage boys were playing soccer in the open field under the scorching sun. Bashir felt a momentary pang of guilt for being in an air-conditioned luxury sedan his position provided him.

He could easily identify the Bismillah tent. It was the only tent with two flags—one was the tricolored Palestinian flag and the other was the blue-and-white Star of David flag of Israel. He smiled at the tolerance of the Jews. There was no chance of seeing the same tolerance displayed in the Palestinian territory or in any Arab country.

Bashir entered the tent to find his friend Samir talking to two young Bedouins who stood at the center of the tent.

"Mr. Bashir Ibn Ahmad, welcome to our humble tent in the name of Allah," Samir greeted him, demonstrating his respect for authority and introduced his two companions, Abdullah and Ali. "These are the two young men who volunteered for the mission."

"I am pleased to meet you," Bashir addressed the volunteers. "Your dedication to our cause was brought to my attention. Samir informed me that you have already participated in several missions in Pakistan and Turkey. I am here to present you with the Bismillah award for acting beyond the call of duty. The certificate of award states that you have worked to advance the mission of our organization in our effort to help the poor and provide assistance to sick and old men and women in Arab villages. Naturally, there is no reference to your military missions, and you can show the certificates to anyone. Each award also includes one thousand shekels in cash."

"Your mission in Turkey is important to Bismillah. Your passports will have other names, just like the ones you used in your last mission. You will depart on a Turkish Airlines flight from Tel Aviv, and our man will meet you at the Istanbul airport. You will carry a sealed envelope, which you will deliver to him personally. He will provide you with detailed instructions on the mission."

*   *   *

At the Europcar counter of Istanbul's International Airport, Farid's deputy met the two dark-eyed passengers and drove them to their hotel on the shores of the Dardanelles.

When Farid read the coded message from his father, his heart started pounding like a jackhammer. He actually heard the thumping of his heart.

The day of judgment has arrived.

When he accepted the position as Istanbul branch manager, he knew that he was expected to plan and execute acts of violence, but he had hoped that his father would spare him that honor. The instructions in the sealed envelope proved him wrong. They were clear. He had to plan the details for the two volunteers to enter the Great Synagogue of Istanbul disguised as Jews. They were to become simultaneous suicide bombers during the ninth day of the month of Av memorial service, which commemorates the destruction of the First Temple by the Babylonians. Such an operation, if carried out, would surely kill dozens of Jews.

Farid locked himself in his office, sat at his desk, and closed his eyes.

What is the purpose of killing so many innocent Jews?

What will Bismillah gain from the publicity that will follow?

How will the operation serve the cause of Islam?

How is such an operation justified in the Koran?

Why was the Ninth of Av chosen?

He had other questions, but all remained unanswered. He could not find a single justification even as a Muslim, certainly not as the Jew that he was. It was an example of irrational radicalization of the Koran.

Farid opened his eyes and started listing his options:

> *I could resign my position as branch manager and return to Jerusalem. In that case, I would not be able to sleep at night for not acting to save lives.*

> *I can assign the responsibility of planning and implementing the operation to my security officer. That would leave me without involvement in the killing, but it would still leave me with blood on my hands.*

> *I can delay the operation until after the Ninth of Av memorial service with the hope that I can convince my father to change his mind. That is a reasonable action, but he may not stand for it, no matter how many excuses I could think of.*

> *My only option is the most logical one. I must talk to Colonel Amram.*

A knock on his office door interrupted his thought. He walked to the door and found a sealed envelope had been slipped under it. He opened the door, but there was no one in sight. He closed the door, took the envelope, and walked back to his desk. The envelope was addressed to him and marked Private and Confidential. He opened it and read the short note:

I must meet you tonight at 8:00 PM in the Turkiyeh restaurant. Ali.

Farid was alarmed. This could be a dangerous ruse by someone in Bismillah. He summoned his deputy.

"I want to interrogate Abdullah and Ali separately. I want to evaluate them and determine their competence."

"I have already evaluated them." The deputy felt slighted for having his competence called into question. "They are competent and trustworthy."

"They've volunteered for a very important mission. I want to do my own evaluation."

When Abdullah entered, Farid inquired about his childhood and his family. He praised him for his participation in previous Bismillah operations. After Abdullah left, Ali was sent in. As it was near dinnertime, Farid invited Ali to join him for dinner in his favorite restaurant.

"Did you receive the note I left for you today?" Ali asked at the restaurant.

"Yes, I did. First, I would like to hear about your childhood and your family. Then you can tell me the rest."

"I am Ali Ibn Mussa," started Ali. "I was born in Abu Jamda village."

"Why did you join Bismillah?" asked Farid.

"That is an unreasonable question. You don't want to hear what I have to tell you, and you ask questions about information that you already have. I was one of the many Bedouins from the Negev who volunteered to serve in the border guard battalions of the Israeli army. It is not a secret. I used to visit my family in my Israeli army uniform. I held the rank of corporal, and I participated in many border patrols."

"Yes," commented Farid, "I know all about your service, and I also know that you provided information about the army to Bismillah."

"If you think you know all about me," continued Ali, "I have a surprise for you. I wanted to see you privately to give you a special message from my former commander in the border patrol battalion. He contacted me before I left Ben Gurion Airport and told me that there is a plan to kill many Jews in the Great Synagogue of Istanbul. He did not know much more than that, but he did find out that someone purchased an airline ticket from Tel Aviv to Istanbul using my name. He just wanted to warn me that someone has stolen my identity."

"Is that the truth?" asked Farid. "Or is it a story that you made up?"

"Why would I make up such a story? Why would I endanger myself by writing you a note? I thought you should know that another organization plans to kill Jews. I will never understand the logic of killing Jews just because they are Jews. It is written in the Koran that if a person takes the life of one soul for no reason, it is the same as if he took the life of all mankind."

"Thank you for the information," said Farid with a decisive look. "We can now have our dinner, and we shall discuss our plan tomorrow."

Farid's driver took them back to the Bismillah office, and thirty minutes later, he took Farid to catch the next plane to Tel Aviv.

* * *

"What brings you to Jerusalem, Farid?" Bashir was surprised to see his son.

"I came to clarify the instructions I received on the Istanbul mission."

"They are simple and clear," Bashir reacted with anger. "There is nothing to clarify. Kill as many Jews as you can, but no less than fifty."

"This is in complete contradiction to the Bismillah charter. My grandfather Ibn Najad prepared the charter according to instructions from Haj Amin al-Husseini. The Bismillah charter, approved and signed by the Grand Mufti, specifically states that no actions of violence will be taken by its members and that it should concentrate only on providing assistance to poor Arabs and on gathering information about Jewish communities to undermine the Jewish claim to Palestine."

"The Bismillah charter was written in 1930, sixty years ago," Bashir was emphatic and angrier. "It is out of date."

"Remember 1929," he continued. "Haj Amin was the leader who planned the 1929 riots with great success. It ended in the killing of all the Jews in Hebron, a classic example of ethnic cleansing. From 1940 until the end of the Second World War, he was in Berlin. He planned to build crematoriums in Palestine to solve the Jewish problem, just like the ones built by Heinrich Himmler and Adolf Eichmann in Europe. He even gave instructions to his cousin Yasser Arafat to build the terrorist organization that killed Jewish women and children. Haj Amin was not a pacifist."

"If that is the case, then why was the Bismillah charter not changed?"

"I'll change it now." Bashir hit his desk with a fist. "You must return immediately to Istanbul and carry out your orders."

Before going to bed, Farid went to see his mother. Her face turned as white as fresh snow when he recited to her the details of the instructions given to him by his father. Observing that she was on the verge of fainting, he ran to get her a glass of water. He returned to find his father at her bedside.

The next morning, Farid stopped at the office of Rabbi Ohayon and found him occupied in a meeting with a few other men.

Noticing Farid at the door, Rabbi Ohayon dismissed his companions and invited Farid in.

"What brings you to Jerusalem?" asked the rabbi.

"I need your urgent help and advice," answered Farid. "I need it immediately before I leave for Istanbul."

He told the rabbi about his predicament.

"I am willing to live a double life as a Jew and a Muslim Arab, but not with blood on my hands, not by killing dozens of Jews." Observing the rabbi's reaction, he continued, "I would rather die . . ."

"You came for advice, but you've already found your own answer," interrupted Rabbi Ohayon. "Our Talmud teaches us that he who saves one life is like one who saved the whole world. You have the opportunity to save many lives. As a matter of fact, the Koran adopted the same concept centuries later. My advice to you is to talk to my friend Colonel Menachem Amram before you return to Istanbul. You have already seen him several times. He will help you."

Back in his Istanbul office, Farid met with his deputy and the two volunteers to discuss the details of Bashir's orders in preparation for the attack on the synagogue.

On the evening before the Ninth of Av, the doors of the Great Istanbul Synagogue were opened prior to sunset. As is done on all Jewish holidays, the Turkish police assigned a larger contingency of officers to guard the synagogue from terrorists. Police officers and security personnel opened all bags and purses to inspect them. This routine was effective and successful in preventing anyone from bringing weapons into the synagogue. Six unarmed police officers were standing along the walls inside the sanctuary during the service.

By nightfall, men, women, and children filled the sanctuary. They sat on low benches and on the floor with prayer books on their laps. The rabbi started the service by reading the biblical Book of Lamentation in memory of the destruction of its First Temple by the Babylonians. The sad melody of the reading increased the spiritual emotions of the people who were mourning the brutal massacre of Jews over twenty-five centuries earlier.

After the completion of the service, as the congregants started to walk to the main door of the synagogue, the rabbi noticed a young man pushing his way toward the exit and causing men and women to scream. Shouting and pushing spread throughout the sanctuary. Pointing to the stranger, the rabbi signaled to the police officer near one wall, who signaled to a second officer by the opposite wall. Two young congregants took the initiative. They tripped the running young man who fell down, his face hitting the floor of the central isle, but managed to get up to punch one of his two assailants and ran faster toward the exit.

A police officer closed in on the stranger, signaling to two other officers to join him. They approached the man from different directions, causing the crowd to shout and further push each other with confusion and screams. The agile young man reached the exit before the officer and burst through, running so fast that he knocked over an officer who was standing just outside the door.

The young man kept running from one officer in pursuit, ordering him to stop. The young man ignored him and continued running. An officer fired a shot in the air. It did not stop the fugitive who accelerated his flight. Another shot pierced his spinal cord. He fell down across the street.

The incident made the headline news on the following morning in Istanbul and Tel Aviv. Associated Press issued a report detailing the Turkish police report. It included amazing details on a failed attempt to kill Jews during the Ninth of Av memorial service. The man shot by the police was Abdullah Ibn Taleb, a Palestinian suicide bomber who wore a belt loaded with explosives. The police report stated that the suicide bomber did not succeed because someone had removed the detonator from his belt.

The next day, Farid entered the library of the Great Mosque, obtained permission to see some documents that were in the locked vault. He located the two parchment pages that were described to him by Menachem, photographed them, returned them to the vault, and left the mosque with the photographs.

Farid returned to Jerusalem to celebrate his fortieth birthday.

*　　*　　*

"I have a present for you," said Menachem to his brother. "I know you'll love to add two more parchment pages to your list. Well, they are not real parchments, but their photographs just arrived from Istanbul."

*　　*　　*

After the death of Elaine in 1983, Avner dedicated most of his time enjoying his four grandchildren and working as the director of the Society of the Ark and as a professor of archaeology.

Avner's life changed when he heard that Dr. Daphna Ben-Horin, the carbon dating researcher at the Hebrew University, had become a widow. He decided to renew their acquaintance and went to express his sympathy for the loss of her husband.

With Daphna, he found a common chemistry of soul and purpose. In addition to their passion for their work in archaeology, they shared other interests. They both loved classical music, operas, and contemporary theater. They were both active in the local community. Daphna was a great supporter of the center for abused women—an admirable, charitable cause. He considered this match as a second one made in heaven. Daphna gave Avner the will to continue living. She had two daughters and one son who was a professor of cardiology. Daphna and Avner were married in 1990.

CHAPTER 29

2008 Scrolls And Parchments

WHILE PREPARING A presentation for a scheduled research meeting, Avner was perplexed about the lack of information on the Tibetan parchment, which nobody had seen. He wondered if it could provide any information to help his search for the hidden scroll. He wanted to learn more on the struggle of the Tibetan people under the recent Chinese rule.

He put down the Tibetan history book when Daphna began to play "Appalachian Spring."

"How can anyone concentrate on reading when you're playing Aaron Copeland?" He smiled at her.

He closed his eyes.

> *This reminds me of the music that Elaine used to*
> *play on the piano, especially melodies from my*
> *favorite Romanceros, the Ladino love songs that my*
> *grandmother used to sing.*

I used to ask her the same question, how can anyone concentrate on a book while listening to such beautiful melodies from the Jewish golden age in Spain?

He opened his eyes, smiled at Daphna, and enjoyed the music.

*   *   *

Avner convened a meeting with his archaeology research staff to review reports on his scrolls and the parchments. He invited Professor Bar David, his brother Menachem, his friend Alberto and his wife, Dr. Daphna Amram.

He entered the conference room, still an impressive figure in spite of the nagging discomfort from deteriorating disks in his spinal cord. An occasional twinge of pain flickered across his face, but he was still imposing after losing four inches in height. He had once worried about his hair turning gray, but the thick mane only made him look more commanding, at least in the eyes of Daphna.

Prior to the meeting, Avner wrote four names on the wallboard:

1. The MACCABEE scroll
2. The SHLOM-ZION scroll
3. The RABBI AKIVA scroll
4. The BAR YOCHAI scroll

"We have read reports on the existence of these four scrolls," he opened the meeting. "We are engaged in archaeological research on something that none of us has ever seen."

"I saw the Shlom-Zion scroll in my dream," interrupted Daphna with a smile.

"Me too," added Professor Bar David.

Avner smiled at them and responded, "Such evidence is not acceptable in this court without signed confirmations from your guardian angels. It would be more convincing if you could bring them to the hearing. In our next meeting, we'll discuss these four scrolls in detail, but without the aid of guardian angels."

Avner turned to the wallboard and wrote his second list:

1. The KATERINA MONASTERY parchment
2. The DON MIGUEL parchment
3. The ANGEL parchment
4. The BOTTICELLI parchment
5. The Hebrew TEL DOR parchment
6. The Aramaic TEL DOR parchment
7. The Hebrew ISTANBUL parchment
8. The Arabic ISTANBUL parchment

"These are the parchments which we know do exist. With the exception of one, we have seen them or their photographed inscriptions." He tapped the whiteboard with his marker.

Avner invited questions and comments on each parchment on the list.

"My carbon dating tests place the monastery parchment in the sixth century CE," Daphna reported. "It could have been copied from an earlier parchment."

"It could have been written by a descendant of a Judean refugee who was exiled from Judea by the Romans," Menachem remarked.

"Or by a sixth-century monk who was assigned the task of copying important documents," added Avner. "Copying originals was common before the invention of the printing press. It was the only way to send information to faraway readers."

"We must note that it includes an introductory statement which is not in the Hebrew Tel Dor parchment," intervened Dr. Bar David.

"Now is the time to release new information on the monastery parchment," Avner announced. "You all know that another inscription was added on its back surface."

"Was that one ever deciphered?" Alberto asked.

"Yes, it yielded some unexpected information. I will read it to you now."

> The golden Menorah is hidden in a cave in the Hordon Mountain. I placed it there at the order of our Queen Shlom-Zion.
>
> Penuel ben Shimon

Avner was surprised at the silence that followed. He waited for a flood of questions and speculations, but none came. Breaking the silence, he continued.

"We've determined that the message is a very recent addition by a person who is well trained in the latest techniques of archaeological forgeries."

"You mean the parchment is fraudulent?"

"No, the parchment is authentic and confirmed by carbon 14 dating tests to be from the sixth century. The added message is fraudulent."

"Do you know who wrote the added message?" Alberto asked again.

"It is a puzzle. The penmanship is superb. Whoever wrote it knew ancient Hebrew very well. However, the ink used, while being at most five hundred years old, is not from the sixth century like the parchment itself."

A heated discussion followed. Every participant pressed for a quick answer to the puzzle, but nobody knew how to find it. Avner elected to investigate the matter, emphasizing his belief that the monastery parchment was a copy of an original page from the hidden Maccabee scroll.

He went on to discuss the next two named on the list.

"Now, the Angel parchment. We believe that it is the actual Don Miguel document. It is a treasured family heirloom, probably from a larger unknown scroll written at the end of the twelfth century. It includes a family tree and refers to an ancestor who was known to be a direct descendant of King David. The family kept the parchment confidential to avoid being discovered by the Inquisition."

"How is the Angel parchment related to the search for the hidden Maccabee scroll?" Menachem asked.

"It is not related," responded Avner. "It is just a collateral discovery during our search, but it does provide information on life in Spain during the Golden Era. It has already been returned to the Angel family in São Paulo."

The discussion on the Botticelli parchment held unanswered questions, but Avner decided to cut it short while waiting for new information.

"It is named the Botticelli parchment because it was hidden behind a copy of a famous painting by Botticelli. The carbon dating tests place it also in the sixth century. Its inscription is in Aramaic and not in ancient Hebrew."

The two Tel Dor parchments were next.

"You already know about the Hebrew Tel Dor parchment," opened Avner. "The carbon dating tests were inconclusive when they were first done in 1970. We took the parchment to the Sorbonne for evaluation. Professor LeCorbellier determined that it was from the Maccabean era. The inscription was in ancient Hebrew, and the ink is from the same period. The quality of the parchment is poor, with many missing sections. Only a part of the text could be deciphered.

"The Arabic Tel Dor parchment was dated to the thirteenth century, presumably written by the Arab philosopher Ibn Arabi. We concluded that it was fraudulent. Its inscription was written using ink that is only one hundred years old, over seven hundred years after the Ibn Arabi died. We have concluded that it was one of six fraudulent parchments written by Ahmad Ibn Najad between 1930 and 1935.

"The two Istanbul parchments were also found to be relatively recent," continued Avner on the next topic. "We only have photographs. The originals are still in the archives of the Great Mosque there. One is in Hebrew, and the other is in Arabic. The archive's record shows that they are both from the thirteenth century.

"The Hebrew Istanbul parchment includes a long inscription stating that Mohammad arrived in Bethlehem on a white horse with ten disciples to visit the tomb of Abraham before his travel to Jerusalem. The inscription has a signature of a rabbi who was one of the disciples. We concluded that it is another one of Ibn Najad's fraudulent parchments created between 1930 and 1935 and planted in Istanbul.

"The same conclusion applies to the Arabic Istanbul parchment. It includes a claim that Muhammad planted an olive tree at the site of the present Al-Aqsa Mosque before ascending to heaven on Al

Burak, his white horse. Ibn Najad apparently owned six blank old parchments on which he wrote his forgeries to undermine our claim to the present Jerusalem."

"The last subject is the Tibetan parchment," announced Avner. "Although I have never seen it, I know that it exists. The chief rabbinate's archives in Jerusalem had on display an ancient shofar sent as a gift from the Dalai Lama to the former chief Rabbi Nissim in 1969. According to the Tibetan delegation, it was found together with other artifacts. Mr. Maimon conducted extensive research on Tibet. He reported that the shofar was found with a parchment that includes some mysterious information. The Dalai Lama's staff was supposed to locate someone to decipher the inscription."

"We can only speculate on how the shofar and the parchment reached the high mountains of Tibet," explained Avner. "Any suggestion that they were carried by the lost tribes must be discarded at this time. The ten tribes of the northern Kingdom of Israel were exiled by the Assyrians. It was a century before the destruction of the First Temple built by King Solomon. That occurred about eight hundred years before the destruction of the Second Temple by the Romans."

"Are there any other theories?" Menachem asked.

"No theories. But there are speculations. We can hypothesize that these artifacts were carried by Judean refugees who fled eastward in the time of the Roman Empire or possibly after the conquest of the Khazar Kingdom by the invading northern tribes to the northern shores of the Caspian Sea. The theory that Alexander the Great took them to India is baseless because he lived before the Maccabean revolt. Maybe it reached Tibet with Marco Polo on his journey along the Silk Route. We may never know. These are no more than guesses. I hope that one day we'll be able to see the Tibetan parchment."

"Why don't we ask the Dalai Lama directly?" asked Menachem.

"I already sent a message asking him to confirm its existence and to consign it to the Hebrew University for study."

*   *   *

Professor Elda, the chairman of plastic surgery at the Hadassah University Hospital, was a friend of Avner. They had been students at Harvard. They were both members of the Hebrew University Board of Directors. Outside the field of medicine, Elda's passion was Jewish history. He often walked into Avner's office with questions on the progress of the search for the hidden scroll.

"An Associated Press reporter called me from New York yesterday," he told Avner.

"What did he want?" Avner asked.

"He wanted to ask about our skin bank at the university hospital."

"Did you talk to him?"

"I met him when I lectured at the last conference on plastic surgery in Cambridge. He'd heard about my interview in London."

"Did he want to interview you for an article?"

"His editor wants him to write a report on a Bismillah woman."

"Bismillah? Did I hear you right?"

"Yes, I came here to tell you about it."

"Who is this woman? What is her story?" Avner asked.

"Avner! This is not a story." Professor Elda was upset. "It really happened."

"OK, give me the details."

"You already know that I was instrumental in establishing the Israeli National Skin Bank, the largest one in the world. The skin bank stores skin for everyday burn patients and for wartime or mass casualty situations."

"But that is not news." Avner was impatient.

"True, but the recent case of the Gaza woman brought its existence to the limelight. Last year, I was asked to supply skin for an Arab woman from Gaza. She was a patient in a hospital in Beersheba after her brother in Gaza burned her hair and face to protect the family's honor. It's outrageous that such atrocities still occur in radical Arab families when their women are suspected of having an affair. Anyway, we supplied all the skin grafts for her treatment and saved her life. She was discharged and sent home to Gaza."

"Have you seen her since then?"

"She was invited to come for regular follow-up visits as an outpatient, but she did not come until last summer when she came to the outpatient clinic wearing a heavy coat. An alert guard was suspicious and asked her to remove it. When she refused, he threatened to shoot her unless she complied. She panicked and started to cry. She finally took off the coat, revealing a suicide bomber belt strapped to her waist."

"Why did she do it?"

"During her interrogation, she broke down and revealed the facts. Her brother, who is a member of Bismillah, received an order from Bashir to send her on a suicide mission to clear the name of the family. She planned to explode herself in the outpatient clinic of the hospital where we saved her life."

"This is not the Bismillah which you described to me," he added. "It is not a nonviolent organization."

"The new Bismillah operates with violence now that Bashir is its director," Avner commented.

Professor Elda added, "This is only one example of the war between Jews and the radical Muslims in the land of Israel. It is not a territorial conflict. It is a conflict of civilizations."

CHAPTER 30

2008 The Dalai Lama Visit

"WELCOME TO DHARAMSALA," the Dalai Lama welcomed his guest Omar Al-Sharif, the secretary general of the Tibetan Muslim Assembly in Lhasa. "I am pleased that you accepted my invitation."

"It's a great pleasure to be here," answered the imam. "I look forward to find enlightenment and seek a meeting of minds on our different religions."

"Seeking to understand the universe, I have some small knowledge of Jewish philosophy, but not of Islam. I hope that your visit will remedy that."

"Where did you acquire your understanding of the Jewish philosophy?"

"In 1969, I sent a delegation to meet with Rabbi Nissim in Israel. In 1989, I met with a group of Jewish rabbinical scholars in New York. I also read the whole Jewish Bible. You already know that the president of the Islamic School of Venice has recommended you as the imam who can expound on Islamic philosophy."

Omar Al-Sharif was born in Lhasa to a Saudi Arabian father and a Tibetan mother who converted to Islam. He earned his first degree in Islamic history at Oxford University and a second degree in philosophy and religion from Cairo University. He received the title of imam from the Islamic School of Venice.

In Dharamsala, the Dalai Lama and the imam conducted seven sessions exchanging philosophical disputations on their respective religions. During one of the dialogues, the Dalai Lama was surprised to hear his guest's comments on Judaism.

"I have studied some of the Jewish philosophies," the imam stated. "They were written in Arabic by the Jewish philosopher Maimonides, who lived in Cordova and Egypt. The Jewish religion and philosophy have merits that could add to the understanding of both Islam and Tibetan Buddhism."

"When did Maimonides write his philosophical ideas?" the Dalai Lama asked.

"He lived in the thirteenth century, during the reign of King Alfonso III, who considered Maimonides a great philosopher. This is what the king wrote:

> Here is the most glorious accomplishment of my reign. I have created at Murcia, with a Muslim philosopher, Muhammad Al Riquti, the first school in the world where Christians, Jews and Muslims teach together under the Christian philosopher Averoes, the Muslim philosopher Ibn Arabi and the Jewish philosopher Maimonides. Under my reign, thanks to the efforts of wise men of the three religions, 13th century Spain could awaken in all of Europe a true Renaissance: that which would take place not against God, but with God.

"King Alfonso's quotation became a topic of discussion.

"We know that Judaism is the foundation of both Christianity and Islam," Al-Sharif reminded the Dalai Lama. "A prominent Jewish theologian could enlighten both of us."

Wanting to experience a direct and immediate exchange of ideas with a Jewish theologian, the Dalai Lama accepted the imam's suggestion. He contacted the American rabbi Joseph Goldberg, whom he had met during his 1989 visit to New York, inviting him to join the imam in a three-way conference on their respective philosophies. Rabbi Goldberg accepted the invitation and came to Dharamsala.

During their first joint meeting, the rabbi was amazed to hear the imam's greeting.

"I am overjoyed at your willingness to join us," said Imam Al-Sharif to the rabbi. "I want to be known as a self-proclaimed Muslim Zionist. I have very strong views concerning the security of Israel."

"Did I hear security?" Rabbi Goldberg asked. "I came here to learn about the theologies and philosophies of Islam and Buddhism. I did not expect to carry a discussion on Israel's security. I am not a security expert. However, it pleases me to meet a Muslim Zionist. I'd love to hear your views on Zionism."

"Islam is a peaceful religion," continued the imam. "The word *Islam* is derived from the word *salam*, which means "peace" in Arabic. However, Islam has built an extremely radical movement that encourages young Muslims to sacrifice their lives as suicide bombers in missions that result in killing innocent Jews in restaurants, schools, and shopping centers. After every such incident, the media demands condemnation from moderate Muslims, and especially from imams who claim to be moderate. Some religious and political Muslim leaders do condemn the attacks, but nothing is being done to isolate the terrorists, to excommunicate them, and to prevent them from teaching the next generation of Muslims to act against the laws of the Koran, which favor peaceful coexistence with other religions. It is not enough to condemn atrocities. Action is required to stop them."

"Your opinion on suicide bombers is interesting, but what security solution do you propose for Israel?"

"The existence of the State of Israel is a fact, and suicide bombers will not destroy it. The Muslim world must learn to accept it and to make peace with it. I have a vision of a future in which imams will start teaching their followers that peace is not only right, but it is also in the interest of Islam. This vision makes me a Muslim Zionist."

The imam elaborated on his proposal for a bilateral agreement between Israel and Jordan and his plan to teach Muslim children peace instead of suicide bombing.

On his return to New York, Rabbi Goldberg stopped in Jerusalem to visit his friend, the prominent Rabbi Lauberg. His visit resulted in considerable excitement after the rabbi informed a television reporter that he brought news about a Tibetan Muslim Zionist imam. He urged the president of Israel to invite Imam Omar Al-Sharif on an official visit to Israel.

*   *   *

The seventy-three-year-old Dalai Lama summoned his leading researcher to a private meeting.

"Did you obtain the information that I requested?" asked the Dalai Lama.

"Your Holiness, I have very little information," answered the director of research.

"Well, tell me whatever you do know about the discovery in 1931."

"Our records show that a parchment was found with a shofar," continued the research director. "We sent the shofar as a gift to a rabbi in Jerusalem. The parchment was placed in a sealed vault in 1969 and forgotten there. It is still in the vault."

The Dalai Lama was irked, but he did not show his displeasure. He instructed the director to prepare a report that would include all the information that was available about the parchment.

Following two weeks of turmoil between members of the research team, a report was presented to the Dalai Lama. It was very short. It provided no new information. It included a proposal to invite a Jewish scholar who could assist in reading and deciphering the ancient inscription of the parchment.

The Dalai Lama decided to travel personally to Jerusalem and meet with Rabbi Ysrael Lauberg who survived the Holocaust, arrived in Israel as an eight-year-old orphan, and had grown up in Jerusalem to become one of the more respected chief rabbis of Israel. The Dalai Lama sent his request to the rabbi, explaining that he wished to discuss a confidential matter concerning an archaeological artifact found in Tibet. No mention was made of the ancient parchment.

The semiretired Rabbi Lauberg responded favorably. He informed the president of Israel about the Dalai Lama's request, suggesting that a formal presidential letter be sent to him, inviting him to Jerusalem for the May celebration of Israel's sixtieth anniversary.

The Dalai Lama and his delegation of Tibetan monks arrived two days before Israel's Independence Day. Rabbi Lauberg received them at Ben Gurion Airport.

The Ministry of Foreign Affairs reserved the VIP suite at the King David Hotel for the Dalai Lama and four other rooms for his delegation. The motorcade of limousines left the airport escorted by a group of police motorcycles. As it approached the hotel, the Dalai Lama noticed that King David Street included the prestigious King David Citadel Hotel and the new Waldorf=Astoria Hotel, which was still under construction.

"This is a royal welcome," he said to Rabbi Lauberg. "Everything that I see reminds me of King David himself who established this city as the capital of your people."

"This is just the beginning," the rabbi responded. "If time will allow, I'll be happy to escort you to king David's tomb."

Jerusalem was decorated with thousands of flags and large signs depicting two large numbers, 40 and 60. The number 40 designated the fortieth anniversary of the unification of Jerusalem, and the number 60 designated the sixtieth anniversary of Israel's independence. He was amazed at the modern city before him, quite different from the Jerusalem that had been described to him in 1969 by his delegates. The two-lane road leading to the city was widened to become a four-lane superhighway. Many of the two-story buildings were dwarfed by high-rise buildings. This modern city represented creativity and vibrancy of its inhabitants.

After greetings had been exchanged the next morning in Rabbi Lauberg's office, the Dalai Lama began, "I have with me an important document."

He retrieved a cylindrical tube from his briefcase. He removed a parchment in a large transparent sheet protector from the tube, unrolled it, and placed it on the rabbi's desk. Lying in its sealed envelope, it was the only object on the desk. He reached again inside his briefcase, took out another cylindrical tube, and removed from it two transparent sheet protectors. Each contained a fabric.

He related the details of how the parchment was found by a sheep farmer in a Tibet mountain cave together with the ancient shofar that he had sent to Rabbi Nissim in 1969. Each of the two artifacts was wrapped by one of the flaxseed fabrics.

"I requested this audience to ask for your assistance in evaluating the parchment, determining its age and deciphering its inscription."

"This is a miracle, a real story of a dream come true," Rabbi Lauberg reacted by invoking divine intervention. "Our Professor Amram will be the happiest man alive. He has just given a seminar on ancient parchments in which he expressed the wish that one day he would see the Tibetan parchment. Earlier this week, he sent a letter to Dharamsala, requesting your permission to consign to him the parchment for evaluation."

Rabbi Lauberg invited Professor Amram to join the meeting and introduced him to the Dalai Lama.

"I have a surprise for you, Avner. The Dalai Lama has asked us to evaluate an ancient parchment found in Tibet."

"Where was it found?" Avner's curiosity was evident.

"In a cave near an isolated monastery in the Himalayan foothills," the Dalai Lama informed Avner.

"Oh! It must have been in a Jewish Shangri-la," Avner reacted with delight. "It will be a great honor and a great pleasure to evaluate the parchment. When can I see it?"

"It's on the table. You can see it now. It was found with the shofar that you have already seen."

Avner approached the desk and looked at the three items. The document was only a fragment. He reached for his camera and photographed the fragment and the two pieces of fabric before inspecting them.

"This cloth seems to be made out of *pishtan*—that is Hebrew for *flaxseed*. It seems to have a density of fifty-by-fifty threads per square inch, very similar to fabric woven to wrap the Torah scrolls at the time of the Temple. The two fabrics will be of special interest to us because they provide a more accurate determination of their age. The carbon 14 dating test can determine when the flaxseed plant ceased to grow as a living plant."

When he inspected the inscription on the fragment, he declared, "This may be the most significant parchment in our research. It may be as important as the one we have been looking for. With your permission, I would like to start working on it immediately."

Receiving the consent of the Dalai Lama, Avner rolled the three transparent sheet protectors, placed them in their cylinders, and departed.

*   *   *

With the cylinders under his arm, Avner walked into his private office and locked the door behind him. Reading the inscription of the fragmented Tibetan parchment was more important to him than performing the carbon 14 dating tests. He had only scanned the fragment inscription before leaving Rabbi Lauberg's office, but it left him with a hunch that he could find some indication on how the parchment reached Tibet.

Avner started reading the ancient Hebrew inscription, carefully searching for clues on its origin:

The Ark of the Covenant with its contents and the
Menorah are the most important treasures of the
Temple of Jerusalem. They must be protected at all
cost from being removed from Judea by our enemies.
The Assyrian army of King Shalmaneser had exiled
the ten tribes of the northern Kingdom of Israel, and

our treasures are at risk. In the name of Hezekiah,
king of Judea, it is therefore decided that . . .

Avner was troubled. Could it really be a fragment of a message
from King Hezekiah before the destruction of the First Temple? Or
was this another fraudulent parchment? If it was not fraudulent,
it would be the oldest fragment of a parchment ever discovered.
It would stun the world of biblical archaeology. King Hezekiah
reigned in the southern kingdom of Judea about eight hundred
years before the destruction of the Second Temple by the Romans
and about one hundred years before the destruction of the First
Temple by the Babylonians.

Avner searched his soul about what he should tell the Dalai
Lama before his departure to India. It would be premature to
express an opinion on the authenticity of the fragment. He passed
his hand over the parchment, causing it to fall to the floor. Picking
it up, he noticed a few miniscule words written on the back of the
fragment. He retrieved a magnifying glass from his desk and read
the small Hebrew letters:

. . . A-M-N . . . D-R-M . . .

CHAPTER 31

2008 The Gift

T HE DALAI LAMA heard a continuous wail of a siren as
he stepped out of the presidential limousine at the entrance
of the Great Synagogue of Jerusalem.

"It must be a security warning," he told Rabbi Lauberg who
escorted him. "What is happening?"

"Today is Israel's Memorial Day," responded the rabbi. "It is
just a two-minute siren heard all over the country. It is done every
year on this day to honor and remember the fallen soldiers and
those who fought before Israel achieved statehood, those who gave
up their lives in the wars of Israel."

Every vehicle on the street stopped. Their occupants stepped out
and stood silently beside their vehicles. The sidewalks were filled
with pedestrians who also stopped all activity—men, women, and
children of all ages. The Dalai Lama joined them with admiration,
signaling to his delegation members to do the same. He was
impressed by this memorial event. He later told Rabbi Lauberg that

he considered this national silence to be a great honor to the modern followers of the Maccabees.

They entered the synagogue where Rabbi Lauberg introduced the Dalai Lama to the Sephardic and the Ashkenazy chief rabbis of Israel.

The next day was Israel's sixtieth Independence Day. At the request of the president of Israel, Avner convened a closed session to present a preliminary report on the Tibetan parchment evaluation to the Dalai Lama. He invited the Dalai Lama's delegation, Rabbi Lauberg, the two chief rabbis, the mayor of Jerusalem, his wife, Daphna, his brother Menachem, Dr. Aharon Bar David and a few dignitaries.

"Honorable Dalai Lama," Avner started his report, "our research team has conducted preliminary tests on the Tibet parchment consigned to us. Before my report on its content, I want to tell you about our speculation concerning the parchment.

"We have no idea how it reached Tibet. But our curiosity was hard to ignore. It fed our imaginations, and we decided to speculate.

"Earlier this year, Professor Theodor Prattford of the School of Oriental and African Languages at the University of London published details about his research on the lost Ark of the Covenant. For his work, he earned the title of the British Indiana Jones. He theorizes that many Judeans found refuge in Yemen after the destruction of the First Temple of Jerusalem by the Babylonians. Another wave of Jewish refugees followed them after the destruction of the Second Temple by the Romans. It is credible to assume a refugee brought the parchment to Yemen. During the rise of Islam in the sixth century, many Jews left Yemen, seeking refuge in the East—some might have reached Tibet.

"It may be the oldest ancient Hebrew parchment ever discovered, antedating some of the Dead Sea Scrolls. We are puzzled by the results of its sheepskin carbon dating test, which placed it at the time of the First Temple. We are not certain about the accuracy of this dating test because it was performed hastily to provide initial information for today's meeting."

After delivering his report, Avner invited comments from the Dalai Lama.

"First, I want to thank the president of Israel for inviting me to Jerusalem. It is a great honor to be here in King David's city, the capital of Israel and of the Jewish people. I also want to thank the two chief rabbis who greatly increased my knowledge of the Jewish faith and traditions.

"I am grateful to Rabbi Lauberg who took me to visit the tomb of King David, to the Western Wall of the Temple, and to the Yad Vashem Holocaust Memorial Museum.

"Many of you know of my continued interest in the fate of the Jewish people. It mirrors the fate of my own countrymen. Actually, the opposite would be more accurate to say. Our fate mirrors the fate of the Jewish people.

"I stand in awe at the resiliency and courage of the Jews after hearing about the evaluation of the Tibet parchment. I had planned to take it with me back to Dharamsala after the Hebrew University had studied it. I consider it to be of great value to the Tibetan people. However, after hearing today's report by Professor Amram, and after seeing with my own eyes the reestablished Jewish state after two thousand years of exile, I have concluded that its value to the Jewish people exceeds its value to my people. I am, therefore, presenting the Tibetan parchment as a gift from the Tibetan people to the city of Jerusalem as a token of our friendship."

*　　*　　*

"What is the meaning of the letters written on the back of the Tibetan parchment?" Daphna asked Avner after the Dalai Lama's visit. "The Hebrew letters *ayin, mem,* and *nun* followed by a space and the letters *dalet, reish,* and *mem* don't mean much to me."

"I asked myself the same question." Avner wore a frustrated look. "It's not a sentence. It's only part of a sentence."

"Could it be the name of the scribe who wrote it?" she asked.

"This is a new idea which I did not consider." Avner perked up. "But I can't think of any man's name which fits these letters."

"In that case, could the sentence refer to a place?" Daphna asked.

"Originally, I thought the letters *A-M-N* may refer to Amman, the capital of Jordan. It was known as Rabat Amon in biblical time," Avner elaborated on his own speculation. "But I can't figure out how that idea can help us."

"It is probably an unimportant sentence," Daphna concluded.

"Don't be so quick to dismiss the letters. We must keep looking for their significance." Avner turned to his brother. "What is your view, Menachem?"

"Well, I am not an archaeologist, but I was thinking about the Hebrew alphabet. It does not have any vowels. If we read the three Hebrew letters *D-R-M* as *darom,* it means 'south.' Maybe the sentence is an instruction to hide the parchment in a place south of Rabat Amon."

"Good thinking, Menachem. If you imply that we should start an excavation site south of Amman, I will draft you to become its project manager."

"I am too old for that." Menachem laughed at the suggestion. "I am retired, and I want to enjoy the life of a retiree."

"Let's be serious." Avner was serious. "I like your way of thinking and analyzing situations. Can you think of another interpretation of the letters?"

"Let me see." Menachem looked serious again. "Suppose that there is a missing letter and the first three letters read *atzmon*, then the sentence may refer to Mount Aztmon—a few kilometers south of Yodfat, the fortress fortified by Josephus Flavius."

"Bingo!" Avner's excitement was evident. "Maybe we could find the answer at Yodfat."

CHAPTER 32

2008 The Cave

"MENACHEM, OUR SEARCH for the hidden scroll cannot be complete without learning more about Rabbi Akiva's scroll."

"Do you have new information, Avner?"

"Professor Halevy at the Sorbonne located a short summary of a lecture given once by Professor Sukenic, the father of General Yadin. It is about that scroll. Would you like to hear it?"

"I am all ears."

"It is entitled 'The Cave.'"

* * *

Elazar walked slowly along a path leading to his father's house. He had just learned that the Roman governor of Judea had sentenced his father to death for preaching in public against the Romans. His father, Rabbi Shimon Bar Yochai, was a devoted and dedicated follower of the revolutionary Rabbi Akiva, the spiritual leader of the Bar-Kochva revolt against the Romans. In his youth, Bar Yochai was the most outstanding student of Rabbi Akiva.

Young Rabbi Elazar was a Talmudic scholar with an exceptional talent and a rare analytical mind. He spent most of his time on legal Torah issues dealing with ethical decisions of judges imposing fines on defendants found guilty in rabbinical courts. He loved to dissect and analyze cases brought to court by two disputing individuals. Analyzing complex cases was the pepper of his life. His guide was the biblical command instructing judges to pursue justice. He was especially concerned about the temptation of judges to deal lightly with rich defendants and harshly with poor defendants. He never missed an opportunity to express his opinion on specific cases to his fellow scholars. Ethical issues were constantly on his mind. However, on this fateful evening, bringing bad news of a Roman legal decision, he was engrossed in thoughts about his father with great anxiety and fear.

> How can I face my father? How can I tell him the bad
> news? What will be his reaction? What advice can I
> give him?

He considered various ideas and used his analytical experience to predict their consequences. He chose one plan, dissected it, and discarded it in favor of another. He thought again and replaced the new one with a third one, but none of them presented the hope of saving his father from execution. He stopped walking and looked at the full moon that had appeared from behind the clouds. A beam of moonlight on his face hypnotized him.

He closed his eyes and still saw the moonlight penetrating through his eyelids. He saw a man walking in a large orchard gathering apples on the ground. The man took a few apples and placed them in his basket. He walked on finding better apples.

He threw away the first batch and replaced them with the new ones. He continued walking, found yet better apples, discarded the previous ones, and replaced them with yet another group of nicer-looking apples. Finally, the man found a pearl. He threw away his basket with all the apples, took the pearl, examined it carefully, and disappeared.

Elazar opened his eyes with amazement. The vision of the apple orchard might have been a way of predicting that he could find a plan for saving his father.

> *Giving up is not an option. Was divine intervention involved in clearing my mind? I have to find a place where my father could hide from the Romans without interfering with his passion for teaching his disciples and unraveling the secrets of the Torah.*

He had a solution.

> *The only way to save my father is to find a hiding place away from any town or village, a place where he and his nine followers can continue their disputation on the Torah. Young David found a safe refuge in a cave at Adulam to escape King Saul's attempts to kill him. David survived to become the greatest king that Israel has ever had. If young King David could find safety in caves, then so can my father.*

Elazar was also worried about the fate of Rabbi Yehudah and the seven other rabbis who met regularly with his father. The Romans knew that the rabbis met in his father's house, and they probably knew that they also had preached against Rome. They were all in danger.

He saw his father standing outside his house with eyes fixed on a point at the top of an olive tree with his hands raised toward heaven. His father often walked alone in the fields or among the olive trees, always returning in haste to his dark room with increased passion to write. Bar Yochai spent the great majority of his time writing. Elazar discarded all his plans and walked toward his father to confront him with the bad news.

"Good day to you, Father," he said.

"Good day to you, my son," responded Bar Yochai after lowering his hands from heaven and his eyes from the olive tree. "I know you came to tell me about the governor's decision. I also know that the sentence is death."

"Who came here before me to tell you the news?"

"I received the message through my prayers. I just returned from a long walk in the olive grove seeking divine instructions on what I must do next."

"I also received a message through my prayers." Elazar was excited. "It opened my eyes to realize that the only solution is to find a cave somewhere to hide in—like King David. But it must be a large one, much larger than the one you saw near the village of Peki'in."

"I have been inside that cave several times. I know it well. It is hard to find because it has a very narrow opening, but it is very large inside. Now is the time to hide from the Romans, and the Peki'in cave is an ideal choice.

"Go to inform Rabbi Yehudah and our group of seven rabbis about the verdict. Tell them to join us at sunrise in the olive grove at the same site where we met last week."

Understanding the urgency of his father's request, Elazar left with great haste.

The ten rabbis met at the designated grove before sunrise of the following morning.

"We gathered here to decide about our next action," started Bar Yochai. "My death sentence is of no concern to me, and it should not be of concern to you. My only desire is to keep my promise to Rabbi Akiva before I die, a promise and a vow that I must keep for the sake of future generations."

"What is that promise?" asked Rabbi Yehudah.

"We must hurry now. I will reveal the message to you in our next meeting. The Romans know all of us. We have to leave our homes and our families immediately and go into hiding. You will be away from your families and friends over a long period. We shall meet in two days at the secluded cave that my son will show you."

The eight rabbis joined Bar Yochai and his son at the foot of a hill near the village of Peki'in, previously known as Lud. They stood under a carob tree next to a small stream of water flowing to a brook nearby. While everyone was scanning the hill looking for a cave, Bar Yochai looked up toward the slope of the hill. Elazar wondered if his father made a mistake or if he did not know the exact location of the cave, again seeking divine guidance. He looked at the direction at which his father's eyes aimed. He noticed a very thin crack between two large rocks on the hillside several feet above the carob tree. Looking back at his father's face, he noticed a miniscule smile accompanied by a shining gleam in his eyes. Without hesitation, Elazar climbed on the side of the rock toward the crack where he found a narrow opening between two rocks. Estimating that he could squeeze through the opening, he shouted, "I found it! Here it is! Here is the cave!"

Walking through the very narrow entrance of the cave, the ten men entered into its dark and low pathway in a single line. Each rabbi carried an oil lamp in one hand and his belongings in the other. Soon they entered a large bell-shaped limestone chamber whose size was overwhelming. Nature created the cave with stalactites and stalagmites reaching up and down to touch each other like fingers reaching up from the ground to fingers hanging down from heaven.

Sunlight entered the cave through an almost circular opening at the center of the cave ceiling. It gave a yellowish tint to the curved walls. Smaller alcoves along the walls varied in size, some as large as a small room and others as large as a small house.

"This cave is ideal for our purpose," Bar Yochai explained. "I chose it not only for its relative safety from the Romans, but also for its unique configuration to accommodate our livelihood and our continuing studies. We will use the central chamber for our group study sessions, and the side alcoves will be used for sleeping, individual studies, and storage of our personal belongings."

Bar Yochai started to reveal his information to his companions, "We all know that my teacher, Rabbi Akiva, was one of the ten rabbis who were brutally executed in public by the Romans. Before his arrest, he gave me a secret sheepskin scroll with an important inscription. It is of great importance to us and to future generations of the Judean people. The scribe of Judah the Maccabee wrote it following the victory over the Seleucid Greeks and after the reconsecration of the Temple in Jerusalem. Judah and his brothers hid the scroll in Jerusalem. The secret passed on to the Hasmonaean Dynasty kings and to the high priests over the following century until it reached Queen Shlom-Zion and eventually to Rabbi Akiva before the Roman siege of Jerusalem.

"The inscription on the scroll includes instructions for hiding the Temple Menorah and the Ark of the Covenant in a safe place to prevent their capture by an invading foreign army. It does not include information on the hiding site. However, prior to the Roman siege, Rabbi Akiva managed to take the Menorah out of the city walls and place it in a secret location outside Jerusalem.

"Before his execution, when he gave me the scroll, he revealed to me the site where the Menorah and the Ark of the Covenant were hidden. He made me take an oath not to reveal the locations to anyone except to nine rabbis that I would select and who are willing to take the same oath. They must also be dedicated Torah scholars and willing to study the Torah with the purpose of unraveling its secrets. Now the time has arrived to comply with the wishes of Rabbi Akiva. I have chosen you as the most qualified Torah scholars. You accepted the Maccabee conditions, you took the oath, and you agreed to join me in searching for the secrets of the Torah. We will stay in the cave as long as the Romans will be looking for us and as long as it will take to understand the secrets of the Torah. We will sustain ourselves by eating from the carob tree and drinking water from its adjacent spring.

"We will continue to document our Talmudic disputations. Writing the details of our studies is important to better understand them and to have our conclusions available to future generations of rabbinical scholars."

The ten rabbis spent the first three days clearing the cave and the alcoves in preparation for their long stay.

At the end of the first day of deliberations, Bar Yochai entered his private alcove carrying his oil lamp and sat on its floor. He stared at the wooden box in which he kept his writings. He opened the box and looked at the layers of pages scattered in a pile like a group of wheat stalks in a field after the harvest. Great silence surrounded him while all his nine colleagues were asleep. He gathered the bundle of empty white sheets and placed them aside. He removed the numerous sheets of his writings and placed them near the empty sheets. The cylindrical tube at the bottom of the box was wrapped with a deep purple cotton fabric and bound with a golden thread. Without touching it, he stared at the cylinder with great fear in his eyes.

The historical value of this cylinder is frightening. I have in my possession a message that I must pass on

to future generations at any cost. It is frightening to
have such a responsibility. Am I worthy of it?

Bar Yochai untied the binding and opened the package from which he removed a sheepskin scroll. Carefully placing it flat on the clear floor, his hand trembled as he ran his shaking fingers along the surface of the scroll.

> *I am touching the surface that had once been touched*
> *by Judah the Maccabee, by each of the Hasmonaean*
> *kings and high priests, by Queen Shlom-Zion, and by*
> *Rabbi Akiva. I took an oath to provide a safe hiding*
> *place for this scroll for future generations. Will I be*
> *able to accomplish the task assigned to me? Maybe I*
> *was born for this destiny.*

Bar Yochai's mind compared his destiny of leading his nine companions to a captain of a ship in troubled waters.

> *This ship that I am on, what kind is it? Will I be able*
> *to guide my nine passengers to safety? Will I know*
> *how? Will I be able to guide them in learning the*
> *secrets of the Torah, of creation, of living souls that*
> *G-d gives to all humans when they are born? Maybe*
> *I will err and I'll guide my disciples to death in this*
> *cave. What should I do with the scroll? Am I worthy*
> *of keeping its secret with me? When should I reveal its*
> *content to my son Elazar and to the nine rabbis?*

As he struggled with these questions, he fell asleep.

In his dream, he walked along the stream of water near the cave to explore its source and reached a small pond. Its surface was calm, its water transparent. Its surface revealed a light. He did not know if the water was the source of the light or the light was at the bottom of the pond. He moved closer and saw a reflection of his face in the water, but he did not recognize himself. Instead, a strange face was staring at him. He retreated a few steps thinking that it might be the reflection of another man standing at the edge of the pond. He looked at both sides, but there was no one beside him. He looked at the pond, and again, it was not his own face that reflected back at him. He rubbed his eyes and looked again. He now recognized the face—it was the face of his deceased teacher, Rabbi Akiva. Large black clouds appeared on the horizon; the sunlight was covered, and he found himself on a ship. With the black clouds came high winds and powerful waves pounding on the sides of the ship.

I am in the middle of an ocean. How did I get here?
Who appointed me the captain of this ship?

It was a very powerful storm. The man at the wheel fell sick, and he personally had to control the wheel. The ship swayed from side to side as if it was a ball kicked back and forth by playing children. The strong waves reached the top of the mast. While his nine passengers were in their chambers, he lost control of the ship's steering wheel several times.

This is my last day on earth. My passengers will
surely die with me if I leave the helm. Maybe I am
being punished like Jonah was punished at sea.

Suddenly the storm subsided. It was replaced by a soft wind that guided the ship to a safe harbor. He saw a light that was brighter then the sun, forcing him to look away. He woke up. Bar Yochai understood the meaning of his dream. He knew that he was able to guide his ship to safety.

He lit a new candle, wrapped and bound the scroll. He placed it back at the bottom of his box. He took an empty sheet of paper and started writing his interpretation of the dream. This mission was not a punishment like Jonah's. It was like Abraham's test. It was a test of his determination to unravel the secrets of the Torah and to accomplish his mission.

He took another sheet and started to record the details of the opinions expressed by his nine companions during the study sessions of that day. He added his own opinions and conclusions on each subject. He continued writing until he fell asleep.

On the next day, Bar Yochai informed his group of rabbis that the golden Ark of the Covenant was placed in a cave under the city of Jerusalem just prior to the Roman siege. He secretly informed his son that Rabbi Akiva managed to move the Menorah out of the besieged city and to hide it in the very same cave where they were hiding. It was in an inner small alcove inside the Peki'in cave, well concealed and was not to be removed at that time.

Every day, Bar Yochai added new pages of his writings. There were weeks during which he was so engrossed in this task that he hardly came out of his alcove to study with his companions while his son brought him carobs and water from the spring outside the cave. Elazar and his colleagues continued their Talmudic disputations and the recording of their studies without him, but they waited for him to settle issues that they could not agree on. When such periods of isolation ended, Bar Yochai came out from his alcove with a great smile, indicating that he had seen the light and had discovered an answer to a question that dealt with creation.

Bar Yochai and his companions stayed in the cave for thirteen years. He revealed to them the location of the Ark and the Menorah, but he never revealed the secret of Rabbi Akiva's scroll. He decided that it had to be a secret until the time when he would tell it to his son Elazar. He kept the scroll in his box with all his writings.

Knowing that the golden Menorah was hidden in the same cave where he was with his companions inspired Bar Yochai to expound on his deliberations and disputations during thirteen years. He wrote all his notes in Aramaic except when he included Hebrew quotations from the Torah. Parts of his writings became central to the mystical Kabbalah tradition. After his death, his son Elazar and his disciples hid all his writings and the Maccabee scroll to conceal them from the Romans.

CHAPTER 33

2008 The Deciphering

F OUR MONTHS LATER, Professor Amram and his research team gathered at the faculty's conference room. He invited Rabbi Lauberg, Dr. Buzaglo, and Dr. Angel to attend the deciphering meeting. Four parchments were at the center of the conference table under a large protective transparent sheet. They were the Botticelli parchment, the Monastery parchment, and the two Tel Dor parchments. The newly acquired Tibetan fragment was not included.

Prior to the meeting, Avner again wrote the names of four scrolls on the conference room wallboard:

1. The MACCABEE scroll
2. The SHLOM-ZION scroll
3. The RABBI AKIVA scroll
4. The BAR YOCHAI scroll

He opened the meeting.

"I will start by repeating some information that I have already discussed with my colleagues.

"Although we have not seen any of these scrolls, we reached the following conclusions:

1. Judah created the Maccabee scroll after the success of the revolt against the Greeks.
2. It passed in succession to the Hasmonaean kings and high priests.
3. A century later, it reached Queen Shlom-Zion.
4. She hid it in a safe location in Jerusalem.
5. It was taken out of Jerusalem during the Roman siege, probably by Rabbi Yochanan ben-Zakai.
6. Rabbi Akiva had possession of the scroll after the destruction of the Second Temple.
7. He gave it to his disciple Bar Yochai.
8. Bar Yochai hid it in the Peki'in cave.

"In other words, the consensus of our research team is that the four scrolls are one. It is a remarkable research conclusion without any evidence and based only on plain hearsay.

"So, no proofs, but the answer may be in one of the parchment pages or fragments or scrolls that we did discover.

"The information that you will hear today is confidential. The president of Israel requested not to make it public until a formal announcement by his office.

"The first slide is a photograph of what we call the Botticelli parchment. It is an old one, as indicated by yellowish and blackish tints. Carbon 14 dating tests confirm that it is from the sixth century of the common era. However, its inscription is recent.

"The scribe who wrote this inscription used several Aramaic words not known in Babylonian and Roman times. That person probably learned Aramaic in a modern university, possibly a scholar who studied ancient Middle East languages and did not know the Aramaic of the Talmud. This suspicion led us to doubt its authenticity, and on further investigation, we conclude that it is definitely a forgery.

"What happened to this parchment is a saga of larceny, theft, smuggling, kidnappings, forgery, and events too elaborate to be part of our research. I'll try to summarize.

"It was hidden in Baghdad between 1930 and 1935. In 1959, a copy of Botticelli's famous *Birth of Venus* painting disappeared from the Jerusalem School of Art. Ironically, it was donated to the school by my late wife, Elaine. The parchment was placed between the stolen copy and another blank canvas.

"Several years later, the double canvas with the parchment was sent by Bismillah to an operative in Paris with instructions to plant the parchment in the Oran Synagogue archive, but the painting was lost until it appeared in the gallery of a French art dealer. In 1964, the art dealer sold it to a visiting Saudi tourist, passing it off as an original Botticelli. The tourist was a Bismillah agent whose instructions were to deliver it to a contact man in Rome. Six operatives, disguised as Tibetan monks, took it to Rome. When they learned that the Italian police were looking for the painting, they decided that it was too dangerous to have it in their possession, and they gave it to a tour guide in Rome to hold for a day. The six monks disappeared, and recently, we learned that they owed money to a casino in Monte Carlo. We don't know what happened to them.

"Believing that it was an original Botticelli worth two million dollars, Bismillah sent several operatives to locate it in 1982. They found the tour guide and kidnapped him twice, once in Rome and again in Buenos Aires, where Menachem rescued him and brought him to Israel. With assistance and information from Mr. Maimon, we were able to deduce that Ahmad Ibn Najad, the first director of the Bismillah organization, was the scribe of this and five other fraudulent parchments."

Avner paused waiting for questions.

"The second slide is the Monastery parchment. It is from the sixth century CE, possibly written by a monk who copied it from another document. In 1967, Menachem and I visited the Santa Katrina Monastery in the Sinai Peninsula where a Greek Orthodox monk informed us that there was an ancient Hebrew document in a sealed vault of the monastery.

"This parchment is in our possession after a Bismillah agent managed to steal it from the monastery. It is of great interest because it includes an inscription very similar to the one on the Tel Dor parchment with three short additions. The first addition, an introductory statement, apparently prepared by Queen Shlom-Zion after her ascent to the throne, has only two sentences. We successfully deciphered them, as I will now read to you:

> After removal of the statue of Zeus from the Temple
> of Jerusalem and the consecration of the Temple,
> Judah the Maccabee proposed a plan to safeguard the
> Temple treasures from future foreign invaders. This
> is what he said to his brothers and a small group of
> elderly leaders of Jerusalem.

"The remainder of the inscription is very close to the Tel Dor inscription, which I will detail later.

"The Monastery parchment includes an additional section which we have not completely deciphered. It states that the Menorah was hidden in a canal under the city of Jerusalem, apparently meaning the water canal constructed by King Hezekiah before the Assyrian siege of Jerusalem around 700 BCE. This was very similar to the legend about the Queen Shlom-Zion parchment recounted by Mr. Maimon in 1964.

"Another inscription is on the back of the parchment. It states that the Menorah was hidden in a cave on the Hordon Mountain. We determined that it was a spurious addition created by Ibn Najad. Its purpose was to mislead Jewish researchers and the media into concentrating their efforts on Mount Herodion, seven miles south of Jerusalem. Now my brother, Menachem, will elaborate on it."

Menachem walked to the podium.

"It became clear to us that Bismillah had possession of the Monastery parchment from the day it was stolen until it was recovered by an army patrol. During that period, Bismillah secretly recruited two experts to add the inscription. One is a Tunisian researcher at the Sorbonne. The other is a retired professor of archaeology from the University of Hamburg, known expert in the latest techniques in the creation of fraudulent documents. During the Second World War, he was a young officer serving in the forged document section of the SS. After the inscription was completed, Bismillah purposely sent a smuggler with the parchment on a route where an army patrol would catch him, thus hoping it would be handed to the scholars of the Hebrew University, who would report its discovery to the media.

"Bismillah's intention in this regard is not clear. We do not understand the purpose of the added inscription."

Avner returned to the podium and resumed his discourse.

"We can now conclude that the Monastery parchment is a copy of a section from the Shlom-Zion scroll.

"The third slide shows the Angel parchment.

"The Angel family of São Paulo consigned it to us for evaluation. The family's story is that an ancestor carried it from Spain to Portugal sometime around 1492. Later, it was carried to

Amsterdam and then to Recife in Brazil. Carbon dating tests place it at the end of the twelfth century, which leads us to believe that this parchment was originally owned by the family's ancestor Don Miguel de Leon.

"The inscription is written in both Hebrew and old Castilian Spanish. Dr. Buzaglo identified minute variations between fifteenth-century Castilian Spanish and the twelfth-century Spanish that was spoken in the region of Leon, a region that later became part of the Kingdom of Castile. This implies that the parchment came originally from the city of Leon at the time of Rabbi Moshe de Leon, who compiled the writings of Bar Yochai and published the Kabbalah book *The Zohar*. The inscription includes a few interpretations of some Kabbalistic concepts, apparently for someone who could not understand the original Aramaic language of *The Zohar*.

"The fourth slide shows the Tel Dor Hebrew parchment.

"The biblical archaeology community has conducted extensive research on the Hebrew parchment and has confirmed its authenticity. There is no need to repeat that information. We believe that it is an authentic page of the scroll written by a scribe for Judah the Maccabee.

"Today we can announce that we succeeded in reconstructing its deciphered text. Only 30 percent of the words were readable by the naked eye. Forty percent of the words could be read using the latest technology for script enhancements such as infrared scanners, image-enhancing cameras, and other techniques. The remaining 30 percent of the words have been added thanks to the knowledge and dedication of Dr. Solomon Buzaglo. I will now read to you the almost complete inscription of the original page from Judah the Maccabee message to his brothers:

**When our father initiated the revolt against the
Greeks in the village of Modi'in, his main objective**

was to fight the imposition of Hellenic idol worshiping in the country. Now that we have liberated Jerusalem and consecrated the Temple, I am proposing a secret plan to protect the Temple's treasures in the future. I mean the very long future for generations to come. We have succeeded in our revolt because we gathered men who are dedicated to our cause. They fought not only with great bravery, but also with their belief in our G-d and the belief that Jerusalem must always be free of invaders. The Temple treasures and especially the ceremonial items used by the priests are of exceptional significance.

We have underestimated the importance of the Temple's items used by the priests in performing their ceremonial duties. The Ark of the Covenant, the Menorah and all the ceremonial items have monumental spiritual and symbolic value that inspired not only our soldiers but also every Judean man, woman and child. We must plan to hide these sacred items in preparation for a possible future war with an invading foreign army. The plan must have the highest level of secrecy. Its existence and its details will be confidential and revealed to only ten trusted men at any time. The ten men will be a future King of Judea, a future High Priest of Jerusalem, four men appointed by the king and four men appointed by the High Priest. Upon the death of any of the eight appointed men, the King or the High Priest will appoint another trusted man within thirty days. Each appointed man will appear before the King and the High Priest to swear allegiance to G-d, to the King and to the High Priest declaring that he will not reveal the secret to any person and that he

is willing to sacrifice his life rather than reveal the secret. The group of ten men will be called the Society of the Ark.

General excitement filled the conference room. Rabbi Lauberg was especially jubilant but was disappointed that there was no mention of the hiding places of the Menorah and the Ark of the Covenant.

Dr. Amram continued.

"We constructed a chart listing our guesses on the Hebrew Tel Dor parchment from the village of the Maccabees at Modi'in to the Tel Dor site at the shores of the Mediterranean Sea. It is based on a combination of factors ranging from scientific research to mere speculations. We call it the Maccabee Scroll Road Map. It is a time traveler's tale of the Maccabee scroll. Here is its magical journey over time, station by station:

- Judah Maccabee's hidden scroll was written by his scribe during the revolt against the Seleucid Greeks, probably in the year 165 BCE.
- A century later, the Hasmonaean Queen Shlom-Zion hid the scroll in the Hezekiah water tunnel under the city of Jerusalem. She also added instructions on building replicas of the Menorah and the Ark of the Covenant.
- During the siege of Jerusalem by the Romans in the year 69 or 70 CE, Rabbi Yochanan Ben Zakai retrieved the scroll from its hiding site and placed it in his coat when he was smuggled out of the city in a coffin. He subsequently hid it in a cave.
- During the Bar-Kochva revolt in 69 or 70 CE, before his execution by the Romans, Rabbi Akiva informed his most

trusted disciple, Rabbi Shimon Bar Yochai, about the location of the scroll.

- Bar Yochai found the scroll in the Peki'in cave and kept it there during his thirteen years of hiding from the Romans.

- From that time on, our theory is less credible, but we decided to continue our speculation.

- After the unsuccessful revolt against the Romans, an unidentified refugee carried the scroll with him to Spain. Somehow, it turned up on the shores of the Caspian Sea during the rule of the Khazars in the eighth century.

- In the twelfth century, Rabbi Yehudah Halevy in Spain wrote his famous book on the king of the Khazars who had adopted Judaism as the religion for his kingdom in the eighth century. We speculate that the scroll was carried by a refugee who moved there and was later carried away by another person during the influx of Jews to Spain during the time of Chasdai Ibn Shaprut or when the Khazar kingdom was overrun by the Kievan Rus in the tenth century.

- In the thirteenth century, Rabbi Moshe de Leon, who lived in the city of Leon in Spain, discovered the parchment together with the Bar Yochai lengthy manuscript. He published the manuscript as *The Book of the Zohar*, but he hid the scroll.

- We speculate that before 1492, Don Ytzchak Abravanel sent the scroll to the chief rabbi of Amsterdam for safekeeping.

- In 1501, Dona Gracia Mendes Nassi, a member of a prominent Marrano family in Amsterdam, could have taken the scroll with her to the Holy Land after receiving authorization from the son of Süleyman the Magnificent, the sultan in Constantinople, to establish a Jewish community in Tiberias. We do not have evidence that she brought the parchment with her.

- Our speculation ends here, but we decided to imagine on. It is possible that a parchment, a part of the Judah Maccabee scroll, found its way from Tiberias to Tel Dor in the sixteenth century. This theory, if found to be true, could explain how the parchment survived and was returned to Israel. Maybe someone in the future will find the answer to this speculation.

"The next slide shows the Arabic Tel Dor parchment.

"This one is of interest especially because we determined that it was fraudulent. We concluded that it was one of the six parchments created by Ibn Najad and placed in the Tel Dor excavation site intentionally to be discovered by our team. The purpose was to sow doubt in the international community on the credibility of our reports. Its inscription claiming that Mohammad visited Jerusalem is known to be false, as it contradicts the writings of the Koran in which there is not a single mention of the city.

"The last slide is on the Tibet parchment.

"It is a blank slide. The unexpected information it contains is of special value and great interest to the Jewish people. The president of Israel has instructed us to keep it confidential until further investigations are completed, and the information has been studied and assessed by several scholars.

"I regret that I am unable to show it to you today. There will be a formal announcement on this parchment at a later date."

CHAPTER 34

2010 The Haifa Treasure

HAIFA WAS BLESSED with natural beauty and a panoramic view that many cities in the world would envy. It is located on the slopes of a mountain covered in evergreens, looking out toward the shores of the Mediterranean Sea to the north and west up to the top of Mount Carmel of biblical repute.

Avner considered it incomparable and, by far, his favorite among all cities. It remained in his thoughts, soothing him through the demands and discouragements of his various projects, his mind's eye able to conjure up a sight he cherished—Haifa Bay and the mountains of Western Galilee as seen from the top of his mountain.

Avner sat on the balcony of his condominium, enjoying a quiet spring afternoon as he looked down at the bay and its harbor. The air was clear, and he observed six cargo ships waiting to dock. Looking farther, he saw the city of Acre at the far northern end of the bay. Farther yet, twenty kilometers beyond the bay, were peaks of the Western Galilee mountain range along the Lebanese border.

The view from his porch was so spectacular that the adjacent street was called Panorama Street.

His three-room apartment was relatively small, but the spacious balcony made up for it. Looking down at the streets by the harbor, he sometimes felt like Gulliver in the land of Lilliput. The people were like dwarves in toy vehicles. A brown sofa and two blue armchairs furnished his living room, contrasting with the profusion of books that covered almost every square inch of three walls. Near one of the armchairs was a floor lamp under which was a blue-and-white Chinese-patterned rug, which had been woven by Elaine. The archaeology and history books were mixed with biblical and Talmudic books, works of philosophy by Aristotle and Saadia Gaon, *Guide for the Perplexed* by Maimonides, a complete set of twenty-three volumes of *The Zohar* in Hebrew. There were also contemporary books like *The Spy Who Came in from the Cold* by John Le Carré—both in Hebrew and English, *Samson* by Vladimir Jabotinsky, *Madame Bovary* by Gustave Flaubert, and plays by Molière.

Avner had already retired from his work in electronics. His semiconductor expertise had become outdated. It was replaced by the faster-than-lightning revolution of microcomputers, nanotechnology, and complex software algorithms that were light-years ahead of the electronics that he had published in his Harvard thesis. While he followed his work in archaeology with passion, he barely kept up with the advances in electronics.

Reaching the ripe age of eighty did not prevent him from continuing his work in the field he loved the most—archaeology. He prepared two lectures for the annual Haifa Archaeology Conference. He thought about the recent discovery at the Shikmona Marine Research Center south of Haifa. He wanted to include a lecture on that project in the conference, wondering why he never considered underwater archaeology research. He opened his laptop computer and started typing a letter in French to his friend in Paris, Professor Alphonse Halevy.

Cher Professeur Halevy,

From the day you replaced Professor LeCorbellier as the dean of archaeology at the Sorbonne, I have admired your work and have read with enthusiasm your publications. You are a true follower of the great LeCorbellier, who was my lifetime idol.

I congratulate you on the new discovery by your team at the Shikmona shores. Jacques Cousteau would have given his right arm, not to mention his most cherished minisubmarine, just to be present at the site of your underwater discovery.

I offer you the opportunity to deliver the keynote address at the upcoming Haifa Archaeology Conference and to shed some light on the underwater discovery in the sands of the Shikmona's waters. Your consent will be greatly appreciated. I am aware of the Israel Antiquities Authority decision not to reveal details at this time. However, any information that will not contradict the authority's restrictions would be of great interest to the scientists at the conference.

Please inform me if you can join our conference.

Best regards from your friend and colleague,
Avner Amram.

Satisfied with his draft, Avner clicked the SEND button on his laptop computer. He was confident that Professor Halevy would not pass up the opportunity of this nature. As he expected, that evening, he received an e-mail response from Halevy informing him that he accepted the invitation.

*   *   *

The 2010 Archaeology Conference was held in Haifa at the Dan Carmel Hotel on the summit of Mount Carmel. Avner introduced Professor Halevy, thanking him for being present.

Professor Halevy's presentation included slides and photographs never shown before due to restrictions imposed by the Israel Antiquities Authority. He opened his address with an announcement:

> I am delighted to report to you that I received a telephone call yesterday after my arrival from Paris. The restrictions on the Shikmona discovery have been removed with the consent of the director of the Israel National Institute of Oceanography. I am free to make public the information on our project. I am fortunate to do it here in Haifa—just three kilometers from the Shikmona Marine Center.

> Three years ago, the Sorbonne sent two students and a professor to visit the Shikmona research facility to establish joint research programs in oceanography. The two students were marine researchers with experience at the Woods Hole Oceanographic Institution laboratories in Massachusetts. The professor had several years of experience working at the Jacques Cousteau Marine Research Center in Monte Carlo. They submitted a proposal prepared jointly with Shikmona research staff. The Israel National Institute of Oceanography approved the project.

> The proposal cited previous discoveries of numerous ancient marine items found on the seabed of the Mediterranean shores south of Haifa. Many were proven to be items thrown overboard from ships

during storms in the time of Herod when Caesarea
was the main port of Roman trade with Judea. Based
on these historical findings, the two teams suggested
that there are still many items buried under the sand in
that area.

The project was approved by the Sorbonne, and a
joint program was initiated three years ago. Using the
state-of-the-art technology in marine research, we did
find many items discarded by ancient Roman sailors
and some that were below the surface of the seabed.
Only a few held any historical significance. Many
of them are either at the Shikmona archives or at the
Israel Antiquities archives in Jerusalem.

This year, we hit the jackpot—actually, a double
jackpot. One is of a significant archaeological value,
and the other is of a most significant financial value.

At this time, I ask Dr. Baruch Savion, the director
general of the Israel Oceanographic Research
Authority, to join me at the podium for answering
questions on the slides that I will now show.

Ladies and gentlemen, the first slide on the screen
is a photograph of the sealed cast-iron box we found
buried deep in the sand underwater between Caesarea
and the Shikmona Marine Center. It has not been
found before because it was twenty feet below the
seabed.

Marine researchers use a side-scan sonar instrument to generate excellent mapping records of the seafloor by transmitting sonar pulses and recording their reflected echoes. It is a very effective technique for locating items that are on the surface of the seabed. It was developed for the U.S. Navy by the American company EG&G in conjunction with the Woods Hole Oceanographic Institution and MIT.

However, side-scanning sonar instruments do not provide any information on items that are below the seabed surface. To search for items below such surface, we used a device called a Marine Boomer, which was also developed for the U.S. Navy by the engineers of EG&G. The boomer sends high-energy sonar pulses deep below the sea bottom, and the reflected pulse echoes enable the researchers on a boat to locate and map items that are deep below the sea bottom.

The next slide is the photograph of the same box after we opened it. It is very exciting. The box was full of gold coins. It is estimated that today's value of this gold—and I mean just gold by weight and not by its archaeological value—is over four million euros.

Excitement and applause filled the conference room.

The impact of this finding is now being investigated.

Where did the coins come from?

Did the cast-iron box sink twenty feet under the seabed?

Or was it placed there intentionally as a hidden treasure?

There are many other questions that we hope to answer. With the assistance of the archaeology staff at the Hebrew University, we expect to have answers to most of these questions next year. Meanwhile, the box and the coins are now in the custody of the Israeli government.

CHAPTER 35

2012 The Yodfat Proposal

REMEMBERING THE EXCITEMENT that followed his discovery at the Tel Dor excavation site in 1970, Avner stood on the balcony of his Haifa apartment and wondered if he would ever experience a similar excitement in his remaining days on earth.

Almost eighty-two now, he searched his memory for an event in his career that could compare to the one at Tel Dor. There had been many professional successes in both his chosen fields of archaeology and electronic engineering. He had published seven books on archaeology, one book on history, two books on electronics, and numerous articles. He owned eight patents on electronic engineering technologies. He especially cherished the patent related to the detection of a rare gas, which was the principal cause of pancreatic cancer. His professional achievements were important to him, but none had brought the elation he felt at the time of the Tel Dor discovery.

He looked at the panorama view from his balcony. This time his eyes turned to the eastern mountain range beyond which was the city of Nazareth, the Valley of Jezreel and the ancient fortress of Yodfat.

That is the region where events took place that changed history for Jews, Christians, and Muslims.

He was excited about the potential of an extraordinary new discovery from the moment when he first saw the Tibetan parchment. Based on Menachem's guess concerning Mount Atzmon, he had proposed a new excavation site near the ancient fortress of Yodfat. Archaeological discoveries often began with educated guesswork and inspired hunches, followed by hard work, sometimes rewarded with success.

While researching the history of Mount Atzmon, he discovered that Josephus Flavius had visited the northern slope of the mountain while planning the surrounding defenses of the Yodfat fortress. Avner had walked up and down the northern slope of the mountain looking for clues. When he found two Judean coins on a small plateau, he made his decision. It would be the site of the new excavation.

In his proposal, he highlighted the historical importance of the Yodfat fortress, especially its success in holding out for forty-seven days when besieged by the Romans during the Bar-Kochva revolt. In previous excavations at the fortress, arrows and stones used by the Roman ballistae had been found on the fortifications. Originally, he named the project the Atzmon Excavation, but later changed it to the Yodfat Project to stress its connection with Josephus.

The proposal faced competition for state funding with another site in the region. Excavations in ancient Zipori had yielded impressive results. Exploration there since 1985 had revealed the deep ruts made by Roman chariots on the cobblestone surface of the main street of ancient Zipori. Several large mosaic floors were uncovered depicting both Roman and Jewish symbols.

Avner's proposal received the necessary approval, but a year had passed without a decision on funding. He suspected his age was a factor that influenced that decision and that a younger researcher might face less-dilatory tactics. But he worried nonetheless. Had Professor LeCorbellier still been alive, he would have found the money, even if it came from the Sorbonne's own budget. Avner started to consider other sources of funding. Suddenly a new idea surfaced. He ran back into his study, brought his laptop to the porch, and started drafting a letter to the Dalai Lama.

Honorable Dalai Lama,

I am writing this letter to request your help. I am extremely indebted to you and the Tibetan people.

When you donated the Tibetan parchment to the City of Jerusalem, you told me that if I ever needed your help, I should not hesitate to contact you. I do need your help now, and I did hesitate, but I have gathered sufficient courage to request your assistance today.

I spent considerable time in evaluating the inscription on Tibet parchment. I found sufficient information in it to justify the initiation of a new excavation site. The inscription suggests that important items might have been hidden near the ancient Yodfat fortress during the war with the Romans.

I hope that Your Honor will respond to my request with a formal letter to the President of Israel asking him to intervene on my behalf to accelerate the funding decision on my proposal. I am attaching a copy of the proposal for your information.

Your humble friend and admirer,
Avner Amram

He read the draft and modified it seven times, fearing that it might not be respectful enough. He attached the proposal to the e-mail and pressed the SEND button on his laptop.

Avner waited four days before receiving a response, which presented more questions than answers. The Dalai Lama informed him that he should start the Yodfat project immediately without worrying about its funding.

The money will be available within thirty days?

The response did not state the source of the funds. It would seem that the Dalai Lama appeal had been successful. Avner did not have the courage to bother the Dalai Lama with another letter, nor did he have the courage to contact the office of the president of Israel. He decided to wait and see.

Three days later, he received an e-mail from Professor Alphonse Halevy at the Sorbonne.

Dear Professor Amram,

I am writing this letter at the request of the Dalai Lama. He sent me a copy of your proposal for the Yodfat excavation site and informed me that you cannot obtain the required funding. I read the proposal and it has great merit with a potential discovery that would be of importance to the world of Biblical archaeology.

With your permission, I want to present your proposal to the University Budgetary Committee with a request to approve a joint project to be performed by our two teams of researchers and financed by the University and another institute. Please let me know if I have your consent to present the proposal.

Best Regards,
Alphonse Halevy

Without hesitation, Avner picked up the telephone and dialed Paris, giving his consent. A week later, he received a special delivery DHL envelope from Paris. It included a formal letter on a Sorbonne letterhead.

Dear Professor Amram,

Your proposal for initiating a new excavation site near the ancient fortress of Yodfat in Israel has been approved by the Sorbonne Budgetary Committee. According to the university regulations, the university allows only fifty percent funding from its budget. Another source is required to fund the remainder.

I took the liberty of contacting the Abravanel Foundation in Paris, and I am pleased to inform you that the foundation has agreed to fund the remaining fifty percent. I am grateful for providing me with the opportunity to participate in this joint project. I will be happy to come to Haifa in order that we may meet and start its planning.

Your friend,
Alphonse Halevy

CHAPTER 36

2012 The Yodfat Excavation

E VERY SUMMER, WHEN most students in academic institutions are on vacation, many prefer to spend their free time working on archaeological excavation sites. Some are interested in archaeology and others in history. Some want to feel the excitement of connecting with the past in a desperate search for artifacts and specks of history. Others want to meet new friends or just follow friends who convinced them that it is a cool thing to excavate while baking in the hot summer sun of Israel.

They gathered in mid-May at the Atzmon plateau, standing in a semicircle, facing professors Amram and Halevy.

"You are standing on the ground on which the Yodfat defenders stood," Avner addressed the team. "We are launching today a new excavation site that may result in a great discovery or great disappointment. I want to warn you about the probability of success. I am an engineer, and I love the theory of probability. Before I tackle any engineering problem, I try to predict the chances of finding a solution to the problem. In electronics, I have been successful in

80 percent of my predictions. However, in excavations, my success rate has been between 10 and 15 percent. In other words, there may be only one chance in ten to find what we are looking for. It sounds very discouraging, but we also expect to find here general information that will be valuable in learning about life at Yodfat under the siege of the Romans."

The group included a young professor from the Hebrew University, a postdoctoral researcher from the Sorbonne, one doctoral student from each of the two universities, ten student volunteers on vacation, and support personnel. Professor Amram was delighted to add his grandson to the group of volunteers. His name was also Avner. Having passed the Israel bar examinations, young Avner wanted to spend the summer with his grandfather before starting a legal career in a prestigious Tel Aviv law firm.

"At the end of this summer, we'll evaluate our progress and determine if there is justification to continue next summer. If we are successful, this site may be active for years to come. If we fail to find anything of significance, this project will not continue next year."

"Professor Halevy"—Avner faced his companion—"please start this dig with my inaugural shovel. I used it in my first dig over fifty years ago."

"Thank you for the honor," Halevy replied, taking the shovel.

He walked toward the flagged post and started the dig.

"It's time to start working," Avner announced. "Enjoy your summer, and pray for success."

*   *   *

The summer at the excavation site was hard on the workers. Avner compressed the schedule with the hope of showing some signs of progress before his volunteers left the site for the following academic year. The digging progressed slowly until the discovery of an ancient wall. As the end of September approached, he doubted if the progress justified funding to continue the project on the following summer. He released all the volunteers but kept the site active with four students and the two hired workers. Avner wanted to push forward before the rainy season.

"Professor Amram," he heard someone call him. "Your grandson discovered a stone gate along the wall at the mountain."

He looked at the announcing student when he saw young Avner running to meet him.

"You must come and see the opening at the gate, Saba," young Avner addressed his grandfather.

"Look who is behind you. It's your father."

Young Avner turned to meet Benjamin and gave him a big hug.

"What are you doing here?" he asked.

"I came to see my father, my son, and the progress of your project. I was looking for you when I heard the excitement."

"Let's go to see the gate in the mountain," Grandpa Avner suggested.

Everyone on the site ran to see the gate, except the eighty-two-year-old Avner who walked slowly, following the medical advice of his son the surgeon.

"It must lead to a cave," young Avner announced.

"That makes sense," Benjamin said. "I don't think that Josephus Flavius built a gate that leads nowhere."

The next day, young Avner discovered a cave behind the stone gate.

Avner, Benjamin, young Avner, and the Arab student Omar walked to the cave and entered through the narrow entrance, each one carrying a flashlight. The beams of light scanned the walls of the cave, revealing a few stone-carved letters and symbols on the eastern wall.

"Can you read these letters?" young Avner asked his father. "I am a surgeon and not a scholar in ancient wall carvings. They all look like hieroglyphic script."

"This is what happens when a father is an archaeologist and his son is a surgeon," noted Professor Avner. "I can only read two words. The rest is not readable."

"What are the words?"

"You know that the Hebrew alphabet does not include vowels. The two words can be sounded as *shalom Zion*, which means "peace to Zion," or *Shlom-Zion*, which is the name of the Hasmonaean queen."

"Is this a clue of some sort?" Benjamin asked.

"If it is 'peace to Zion,' it is probably a greeting for anyone who enters the cave or a prayer for peace in Israel," Avner replied. "But if it is the name of Queen Shlom-Zion, it may be the most important clue of our project. It may indicate that this cave holds some object or manuscript originated by the queen and hidden here by Josephus Flavius before the Roman siege on the Yodfat fortress. Maybe that *something* is the golden Menorah, but it is just a wish, not an observation. We must keep searching for that *something* in the cave."

Young Avner and Omar entered the cave with Professor Amram. Benjamin, who joined them later, wandered deeper into the cave along the eastern wall, while the professor and the two students stayed near the wall carving discussing the possibility of a parchment find.

"Help! Help! I need your help now," they heard Benjamin shouting from deep in the cave.

They ran along the eastern wall to find Benjamin lying on the floor trapped under a large stone.

"I shouldn't have tried to remove this stone without help," whispered Benjamin. "I am not hurt. I am just trapped."

Young Avner and Omar lifted the stone, enabling Benjamin to withdraw his leg safely. He got up and started limping to the cave's entrance, assuring everyone that he was not injured. The professor escorted him.

The two students remained in the cave to explore the new area found by Benjamin.

"Look at the hole in this wall," young Avner said to his friend. "I see a clay jar and a few rectangular stones."

He passed his flashlight to his friend and reached with both hands to retrieve the found items.

"This may be a significant discovery." Omar aimed his flashlight to the artifacts. "Is the jar empty?"

"I don't know. Let's check it."

It was not empty.

"It's a parchment. My grandfather will be excited. Thanks for your help. You are an Arab helping a Jew. Together we can demonstrate that Jews and Arabs can live peacefully in this land."

The two archaeology amateurs walked together out of the cave carrying the new parchment and the jar.

Young Avner was right. His grandfather was excited. The professor unrolled the small parchment, looked at it, and declared, "We'll be back here next summer."

He hugged his grandson, shook the hand of Omar, and thanked them both.

Carrying the jar and the parchment, he walked to his car and drove away.

"Let's look at the stones," young Avner said to Omar.

They walked back into the cave and brought out the two stones.

"We forgot to tell my grandfather about the stones."

"We can keep them here. He'll see them tomorrow."

*   *   *

"Omar wants to see you," Bashir's aide informed his boss. "He has an urgent message."

"Let him in."

"Bashir—"

"Omar, you have strict instructions never to come to my office."

"I had no choice. This is urgent."

"I'll skin you alive if you don't have a good excuse."

"I am following your instructions to come directly to you if I have news of a new parchment discovery."

"Did you say a new parchment?"

"Yes, they discovered it at the Yodfat site."

"Where is it now?"

"I don't know. Professor Amram took it with him. We also found two engraved stones."

"Was he able to read the engravings?"

"He did not know about the stones. He was in a hurry."

"Why didn't you bring the stones?

"I brought one of them. I went back to the cave after everyone left the site at dusk."

Omar walked out of the office, returned with the stone and placed it on the desk with the engraving facing up. Bashir looked at it with evident pleasure.

"You were right to come directly to me."

Bashir dismissed Omar. *It is time to call Mahmood again.*

*   *   *

Mahmood had no trouble finding the Yodfat parchment. He had returned to Jerusalem after completing his postdoctoral research at Oxford. Disguised as an Orthodox rabbi, he entered the tall office building on the outskirts of Haifa and took the elevator to the sixteenth floor. Only a few secretaries walked in the hallway. He reached a door with a sign: Professor Emeritus A. Amram. He found the office empty. He scanned the room and saw a mountain of books, files, and documents strewn all over the room. He walked to the large desk. The locked drawers presented no obstacles. He opened a cabinet and saw a pile of colored envelopes.

Hearing footsteps approaching the office, he grabbed a large red envelope marked Yodfat, put it in his briefcase, and walked out.

The secretary called the security office.

"Did Professor Amram have an appointment with a rabbi?" she asked.

She waited while the security office manager checked his log.

"I just saw a rabbi walking out of the professor's office. He may be a thief. He is in the elevator now."

"I'll alert the security officer on duty."

The security officer saw a rabbi carrying a briefcase, entering an ancient Peugeot, and driving away. He ran to his old Citroën and followed while reaching for his mobile phone.

"I have to leave immediately. I am following a man who may be a thief. I will contact you later." He left a message at the answering machine of his supervisor.

The Peugeot and the Citroën took Route 4, traveling south from Haifa. After passing the Arab village Freydis, the Peugeot turned west on Route 70 followed by the Citroën. The Peugeot entered the six-lane Highway 2, moving southward toward the Arab village of Jisser-Al-Zarka at a very high speed.

The third car joining the chase was a traffic police vehicle with a siren and blinking lights. When he caught up with the Citroën, he signaled the driver to pull over and stop. The security driver spent the next ten minutes defending his driving at 150 kilometers per hour.

*   *   *

The old Peugeot entered the Arab village. Mahmood abruptly stopped his car at the village square, ran into one of the homes carrying the red envelope, and gave it to a tall, husky dark-skinned man with a large black moustache.

A minute later, a young man came out, drove the Peugeot into a paint shop, came out, and locked the door.

Bashir was pleased after opening the envelope and finding the parchment, but he was more interested in the engraved stone. He called his Tunisian friend in Paris, Professor Muamar Abdul, the scholar specializing in ancient languages who had published several articles on ancient engraved sarcophagi found in Egypt and Jordan.

"Muamar, I need your expertise. I'll send to you by fax a photograph of a stone engraved in ancient Hebrew. I can't read it."

"You have many scholars in Jerusalem who can read ancient Hebrew, You don't need me."

"I know. But I don't want to use a Jewish scholar. It is a confidential matter. I will be grateful if you could decipher it for me."

* * *

Three hours later, when Bashir received the response from Paris, he called Mahmood again.

"I have another job for you," he said when Mahmood entered his office. "The small parchment that you brought to me was found with two engraved stones. Omar brought one stone and I want you to get the other."

"Do you know where it is?"

"I don't know. But I rely on you to find it and bring it to me."

Mahmood was a loyal operative. Bashir knew him well as the one who is determined to demonstrate his dedication to the cause.

He always follows orders. He'll find the stone.

* * *

Mahmood returned to the sixteenth floor of the Haifa office building. This time, he wore a sport summer shirt and a jacket.

He saw a different secretary sitting at the desk in front of Professor Amram's office.

"Is the professor in the office?"

"Is he expecting you?"

"No. But I was referred to him by Professor HaLevy from the Sorbonne."

The Secretary checked with Avner, invited Mahmood to enter the office and closed the door behind him.

"Professor Amram, I am here on a special mission. We know about your findings at Yodfat. We already have possession of the parchment and one engraved stone. I am instructed to get the other stone."

"Who are you? Who sent you?" Avner asked.

"It's not important. All you have to do is give me the second stone. You will certainly cooperate to secure the safety of your grandson. We have him in a safe place. He will be released after we get the stone."

"You kidnapped him?"

Visibly disturbed, Avner got up from his chair while pressing the red button below his desk.

"Let us say that he is our temporary guest."

Mahmood never knew what hit him. He collapsed facing the floor with a security guard sitting on his back. Avner pressed the red button again. Another security officer entered with an Uzi sub-machine gun and handcuffed Mahmood.

"Surely you will cooperate with our security officers," Avner addressed Mahmood. "You will tell us where my grandson is held and where the stone and the parchment are hidden—if you still want to have the pleasure of meeting Bashir in prison."

CHAPTER 37

2015 The Two Discoveries

THE *WALL STREET Journal* published an article on two
significant discoveries in two excavation sites in Israel.
An Israeli government spokesman refused to confirm or deny the
existence of such findings, stating that the president of Israel does
not comment on rumors.

Avner approached the age of eighty-five. His hair had turned
completely white, but he was determined not to retire. When pressed
by friends and colleagues to explain why, he responded with his
standard answer: "What would I do if I retire?"

When pressed again by suggestions that he would be free to do
anything he wanted to do, he followed up with his second standard
answer: "This is what I want to do. I want to continue my research
in archaeology and write another book."

The International Biblical Archaeology Society chose Jerusalem
as the city for its annual conference. When Avner was invited to
deliver the keynote address, he declined the honor, indicating that

there were many archaeology giants whose achievements dwarfed any of his accomplishments. The president of Israel intervened and convinced him to reconsider because it was important for Israel to have the keynote address delivered by an Israeli researcher.

Sitting at his desk trying to master ideas for his keynote address, Avner scanned his life to search for outstanding achievements. His two successful careers in electronics and archaeology were important to him, and he was proud of his professional contributions in both fields. However, he could not forget his participation and his contributions in his youth to the struggle of the Jewish people for the creation of an independent Jewish state after two thousand years of exile.

Avner's mind took him back to the events of the prestate struggle in fighting the British prior to their departure from the country and to the Israel War of Independence in 1947 and 1948. He closed his eyes and tried to remember his life in the Irgun.

> *1944—* *British naval destroyers prevented Holocaust survivors from entering the country and sent them to a concentration camp in Cyprus.*
>
> *1945—* *The Holocaust and the British actions generated a wave of pride, inspiring youth to join underground forces to fight the British.*
>
> *1946—* *The British discovered my Irgun membership, forcing me to leave town and drop out of school.*
>
> *1947—* *The Tel Aviv Irgun training*
>
> *April, 1948—The Irgun battle in Jaffa when my three Irgun companions were killed next to me, and my subsequent injury in that battle*

*1948— When Menachem Begin disbanded the Irgun,
I joined the Israel Defense Forces as a
lieutenant.*

Those were great achievements.

Avner opened his eyes, finding himself back in 2015.

*   *   *

The 2015 International Biblical Archaeology Conference
was held at the Jerusalem Waldorf Astoria Hotel. The religious
leaders attending the opening session included the Dalai Lama,
the imam of Lhasa, and the two chief rabbis of Israel. Delegations
and history professors came from several universities in Europe
and North America.

Avner walked slowly to the podium accompanied by his wife,
Daphna, his son, Benjamin, and his four grandchildren. He accepted
the framed certificate presented to him and gave it to his grandson
Avner Ilan Amram for safekeeping, congratulating him for passing
the Israeli Bar after completing his studies at Bar-Ilan University
School of Law. When his family members returned to their seats,
he started to deliver his address:

It is a great honor and a pleasure to stand here before
such a distinguished group of prominent religious and
political leaders—rabbis, priests, ministers, an imam,
representatives of the pope, the Orthodox patriarch, and
the archbishop of Canterbury, prominent scholars, and
researchers. I am humbled by the presence of such great

wisdom surrounding me. I am only a researcher of the past standing before greater and wiser men and women who are dedicated to serve others for a better future.

It is said that memory belongs to the past and understanding to the future. We can remember the past, but we certainly cannot remember the future. The main way with which we can understand the future is by extrapolating from our knowledge of the past. I only hope that my work has contributed something to that.

To the uninitiated, the life of archaeology researchers is a web of confusion leading them astray to unplanned and unintended side issues. They can never plan their work, for it is contingent on new and mostly unexpected discoveries. To the researchers, their life is extremely colorful. It is a life of travel to excavation sites, different countries, different cultures, diverse technologies, libraries, conventions, laboratories, ancient parchments, and, most importantly, the past. They travel through the history about which they are so passionate. For archaeologists, these journeys are what give their lives meaning.

Before I tell you about our recent discoveries, I must emphasize that most of the credit does not belong to me. None of them would have been possible without the collaboration, the hard work, and the dedication of many individuals. Allow me to mention just a few.

I would not be here today had I not received continuous encouragement and advice from my idol, the late Professor LeCorbellier of the Sorbonne University in Paris.

I am greatly indebted to the late professor Shimon Mizrachi, the former dean of archaeology at the Hebrew University. He urged me to pursue a career in archaeology, which led to the discovery of the famous Tel Dor parchment and to the recent discovery on which I will elaborate shortly.

I cannot forget the late general Yigal Yadin, whose claim to fame was not being a brilliant general in the Israel War of Independence; it was his anthropology and archaeology research. General Yadin warned me about the obstacles that I could face in my work—especially obstacles caused by fraudulent artifacts. His warning saved me from being fooled by fraudulent parchments.

It is a great pleasure to honor the Dalai Lama, who is present here today. He donated to the Jewish people the ancient parchment that was discovered in a Tibetan cave. Its inscription was critical in our decision to initiate the Yodfat excavation site.

The most important participants in all my research are the archaeology professors and students at Harvard University, at the Sorbonne, and at the Hebrew University. They labored at the excavation sites, digging, retrieving, and evaluating the artifacts.

Finally, allow me to thank my wife, Dr. Daphna Amram, who performed most of the carbon 14 dating tests on the parchments and artifacts and who provided the encouragement to continue my research even at my advanced age.

Our team of researchers established a process for evaluating parchments. It is not limited to just carbon dating and deciphering inscriptions. It is also aimed at understanding the society in which the inscriptions were written. The process starts by placing all aspects of the puzzle squarely on the table.

Before the evaluation of any ancient documents is started, a research system is established to identify each fragment and to prepare an inventory of all fragments to be examined. Each item on the inventory could be a complete parchment or document, sometimes referred to as a folio, or it could be a small fragment of a folio, which may include only a few words. Some folios have deteriorated so much that only small fragments of the page are found, some as small as one or two inches in size. Often, many fragments of a page are completely lost. Each folio and each fragment is photographed or microfilmed. In many cases, when the inscriptions are not readable by a naked eye, we use digital ultraviolet photography.

The cataloging of each fragment and the carbon 14 dating process are well-known and relatively routine compared to the work required to reconstruct a page by fitting the many small fragments together. A new computer software program facilitated this reconstruction process. It has a unique algorithm developed by Professor Moshe Levi at the Technion Computer Science Department. It is a recipe that enables an archaeology researcher to move and rotate with ease an image of a fragment on a computer screen to match it with the image of another fragment or with an image of a larger group of fragments. This tedious labor is an important task for deciphering inscriptions on ancient parchments.

In most cases, the resulting collection of fragments is analogous to a slice of Swiss cheese. Few are the ancient parchments found intact without missing sections. The challenge for the researcher is filling in missing words and sentences in the holes of the Swiss cheese. It requires knowledge of the ancient languages. In our research, it was mainly ancient Hebrew, Talmudic Aramaic, ancient Greek, and Middle Age Castilian Spanish. Naturally, we had to consult with experts who have specialized in these languages.

Our project of deciphering the inscription on the Tel Dor parchment was particularly challenging. The missing words and sentences in the holes of this piece of Swiss cheese would not have been filled in without the assistance of Dr. Solomon Buzaglo, who is with us today. He enabled us to complete the reconstruction of the whole parchment inscription.

The evaluation of the treasure chest, which was discovered near the Shikmona Oceanography Research Center by Professor Alphonse Halevy of the Sorbonne University, deserves a special mention.

It took our research staff four years to unravel the saga of the treasure chest. It was found buried deep below the seabed south of Haifa, not too far from the Tel Dor site. I will not belabor you with the details of the struggle to solve the mystery. I will just present our conclusions.

Professor Halevy believes, and we concur, that the gold coins found in the chest belonged to the much larger treasure of the Temple and that it was taken out of Jerusalem before the arrival of the Romans. It was part of the accumulated gold gathered by the

Hasmonaean Dynasty over a period of over one hundred years. We also believe that Herod sealed the gold coins in the cast-iron box and intended to ship it to Rome to serve the emperor. We are still not sure if the box was intentionally placed in a deep hole twenty feet below the seabed or if it just sank due to its heavy weight over time.

Avner stopped talking and looked around to savor the reaction of his audience before continuing.

Today we received permission to make public the information about the two most important results of our findings. The first one is about the Tibetan parchment, and the second is about our new discovery at the Yodfat excavation site.

The Tibetan parchment was dated to the time of King Hezekiah, the king of Judea before the destruction of the First Temple of Jerusalem. We concluded that Hezekiah wrote it after the Assyrian armies of Shalmaneser successfully invaded the northern kingdom of the ten tribes of Israel, but before the Assyrian king Sennacherib failed to capture the southern kingdom of Judea. In the parchment, the king noted that the ten northern tribes renounced the laws of Moses and allowed the worship of idols. He predicted that the ten exiled tribes would assimilate into other nations. They had discarded the laws of Moses, renounced their tradition, and adopted a life of extravagance for the rich and injustice for the poor. He stated that they would be lost. King Hezekiah deserves the credit for coining the term *ten lost tribes*. He was the perfect prophet when he wrote this prediction.

Here we are, twenty-five centuries later, and we still have no idea what happened to the Ten Lost Tribes.

The second announcement is the news about our Yodfat discovery.

During the last two centuries, numerous biblical archaeologists have been looking for artifacts from the time of the Roman Empire. Many were guided by the information provided by Josephus Flavius. In his book, Josephus wrote that the Romans took the Jerusalem Menorah and displayed it during the triumphal march of Titus as he returned victorious to Rome. There were many speculations claiming that the Menorah depicted on the Titus triumphal arch in Rome represents the original one. Others claim that it was a fake Menorah built by Titus himself. Most of the excavation sites of the twentieth and the twenty-first centuries were in several locations in the Holy Land, including the site known as Tel Yodfat, the fortress built and commanded by Josephus Flavius before it fell to the Roman assault.

During the last three summers, our excavations were primarily at an area near the Yodfat fortress in the lower Galilee. The site is on the northern ramp of the Atzmon Mountain south of Yodfat.

We discovered a well-concealed chamber in the mountain. It included artifacts apparently hidden by Josephus Flavius prior to the forty-seven-day siege by the Romans. The project yielded important information that led us to an extremely important conclusion. I am announcing this conclusion while I am inviting other researchers to either confirm it or prove it wrong.

Our analysis led us to conclude that Josephus Flavius was a very clever and courageous commander of the

Yodfat fortress. He managed to mislead the Romans. The Menorah taken to Rome for the Titus triumphal march was not the original Menorah of the Temple. Josephus personally provided the Romans with information on the location of the hidden Menorah to divert their efforts from searching for the hidden Ark of the Covenant. He knew that it was a replica of the original Menorah. He allowed the Romans to take the fake Menorah, which they thought was the original one, and thus satisfied them to the extent that they gave up the search for the Ark. It was a plan that worked. It seems that he had saved the original Ark, wherever it is today.

If I am right in my analysis, and if it is confirmed by other archaeology researchers, Josephus succeeded in saving and preserving the most important relic of the Jewish people, the Ark of the Covenant. In that case, his name should be cleared in the annals of Jewish history. Some researchers consider him to be a traitor because he survived the battle of Yodfat and wrote his book under the tutelage of the Roman emperor. Josephus Flavius was not his real name. The Roman emperor gave it to him. His real name was Yosef ben Matityahu of a priestly family in Judea. We actually have a hero and not a traitor. If I am right, he used the ingenuity of the Maccabees even in the midst of a defeat by the Romans.

You would surely ask me on what basis we arrived at this conclusion. What proof do we have?

Distinguished guests, it is a privilege and an honor to present to you the proof. We certainly would not reach such a conclusion without proof cast in concrete. And my proof is here with me, proof that was found by my son, Benjamin, in the Yodfat excavation site at Mount Atzmon.

Professor Amram turned around, picked up a small box of polished wood with a glass front in which there were two slabs of stone and a small fragment of a sheepskin parchment. The box was marked September 2012. He turned back to face his audience and lifted the box.

> This is the proof that is cast in stone, in hard stone—surely harder than concrete. You are looking at the two tablets of stone on which are engraved the Ten Commandments in ancient Hebrew. They are replicas of the original tablets that were in the Ark of the Covenant. They are replicas of the engraved stones on which the Judeo-Christian world is based. Yes, they are replicas. We did not find the original ones, but our tests indicate that the Ten Commandments were engraved on these replicas at the time of Queen Shlom-Zion. She is another example of the Maccabee ingenuity. In addition to creating replicas of the Menorah and the Ark, she also created these two replicas of the two original tablets in the Ark.
>
> Near the two stones, we found a very small parchment on which was written the following three words: YOSEF BEN MATITYAHU. The fragment is inside this box for you to inspect. This small parchment was stolen by Bismillah. But it was found on the body of Bashir after his arrest.
>
> I must again give credit to the Tibetan people who donated the Tibetan parchment to the city of Jerusalem in 1982, whose inscription led us to the Yodfat project.
>
> Our work is not done; it is just beginning. Other independent researchers must confirm our conclusions. The president of Israel has indicated that, with the consent

of the two chief rabbis of Israel, the two tablets will be on display at the *Heichal Hassefer*, the Shrine of the Book, at the Israel Museum in Jerusalem, together with the Dead Sea Scrolls, the parchment from the Judah Maccabee scroll, and the Tibetan parchment.

I strongly believe that the last Maccabee has not been born. He may never be born. There will be many other followers of the Maccabee ingenuity and bravery.

Before I conclude, I want to highlight the presence of Christian, Muslim, and Buddhist friends who came here today to participate in this conference. It is an achievement when representatives of different religions meet to work for a peace among nations and among religions. The presence of the Dalai Lama here demonstrates a friendship of Buddhists to the Jewish people. The presence of Christian delegations demonstrates that the Christian Jewish history of great conflicts is delegated to the annals of history. The presence of our Muslim guests today indicates that the Muslim Jewish history of conflicts may be headed to a similar chapter in history. Your friendship is of supreme importance to the Jewish people.

In closing, allow me to mention the driving force that propelled me and my colleagues to pursue our search for Jewish history. It is the centuries-old belief in the prophecy of Isaiah on the days when peace will be the law of the land.

The longed-for prophesy of Isaiah is "At the end of time, nations shall beat their swords into plowshares. No nation shall lift its sword against another nation, and they shall not learn war anymore."

CHAPTER 38

2015 Not the Last Maccabee

W HEN Dr. DAPHNA Amram approached the podium, Avner froze, not knowing what to expect. He stepped aside and waited.

"I am not scheduled to talk," Dr. Daphna Amram addressed the conference.

"However, I am certain that you will be interested in the results of another research program.

"I am not a DNA scientist, but my daughter, Dr. Dvora Danielli, is a geneticist. During the last five years, she has been conducting DNA research at the Hadassah Medical Center in Jerusalem. The Sheba Medical Center and New York University have a comprehensive gene-mapping project of the Jewish people to trace their wanderings to and from Israel and in the Diaspora. My daughter's work was much more limited. Its central objective was to obtain DNA links between the twenty-first century Sephardic Jews and the Jews who lived in Spain prior to their expulsion.

"Her work is not a subject for an archaeology conference, unless it relates to my husband, Avner. I kept the information of her findings from him until today.

"In 2009, she read an article about a Tel-Aviv resident who retained a geneticist to research her roots in Catalonia, the north eastern region of Spain. Using up-to-date DNA technology, the researcher traced his client's family to the year 1368, to a person who lived in Barcelona carrying her maiden name.

"Among the many discoveries of my daughter's project, she traced the family link of my husband Avner. She authorized me to make the following announcements:

"Professor Avner Amram is a direct descendant of Rabbi Moshe de Leon, who compiled the Bar Yochai *Book of the Zohar*.

"But the second discovery is more significant. It is my pleasure to announce that Avner Amram is a direct descendant of Shlom-Zion, the Hasmonaean queen.

"We can now confirm that the last Maccabee has not yet been born."

EPILOGUE

T HE PARCHMENT FROM the Judah Maccabee scroll, the Monastery parchment and the Tibetan parchment were placed on public display next to the Dead Sea Scrolls at the Shrine of the Book in the Israel Museum. The two engraved stones found at Yodfat were displayed in a sealed glass cabinet at the Knesset Building.

The Dalai Lama sent a message proposing the Tibetan parchment be renamed the Josephus Flavius parchment. His proposal was rejected in favor of the Dalai Lama parchment.

The city of Jerusalem named a street Yosef ben Matityahu Street in honor of Josephus Flavius.

After resigning from his position as the manager of the Bismillah Istanbul chapter, Farid moved to Jerusalem where he changed his name to Shmuel Ben Avraham and joined the yeshiva of Rabbi Ohayon.

Ali returned to his Bedouin family at Abu Jamda, never to volunteer again.

The International Biblical Archaeology Society published an article on the Yodfat discoveries. It caused an unprecedented controversy in the world of biblical archaeologists who questioned the authenticity of the two stones. It spawned new investigations by a generation of young biblical researchers. Professor Avner Amram predicted that it might take decades for a consensus to be reached. He declared the new wave of studies generated by the controversy comparable to the Tunguska projects in Siberia, a series of investigations that still have not resulted in a consensus. After 100 years of research, there are 150 theories to explain the cause of the 1908 explosion in Siberia, which resulted in 1,000 square miles of devastation. The theories included an explosion caused by a large meteorite from outer space, an asteroid, an explosion from a dormant volcano, a UFO, an exploding antimatter, and even a black hole.

After retiring at the age of ninety, Avner prepared a will in which he included a page listing names of individuals whom he identified as having a reasonable probability of being members of the Amram family. They all traced their family origins back to Toledo, Spain. His list included Alberto Maimon of Rome, Dr. Solomon Buzaglo of Curaçao, Dr. Emanuel Angel, Rabbi Toledano of Amsterdam, Rabbi Sasson of Istanbul, and Rabbi Shlomo Ohayon of Jerusalem. The document urged his descendants to continue searching for other members of the family.

AUTHOR'S NOTE

THE HIDDEN SCROLL is a historical fiction. It includes names of prominent individuals who made history from the time of Hezekiah, the king of Judea, to the time of the president of Israel and the two Dalai Lamas of the twentieth and twenty-first centuries. Except for a few prominent public figures, all other names in the book are fictional names. Any resemblance to the names of actual persons—living or deceased—is coincidental.

The Bismillah organization is fictional. It is an imaginary organization created to describe obstacles encountered by the archaeologist Avner. It reflects the actions of the real grand mufti of Jerusalem, Haj Amin al-Husseini, who dedicated his life to fight against the Jews anywhere in the world.

I have not requested permission from any hotels to use their names in the novel.

I included chapter 32 to dramatize the thirteen years in a cave where Rabbi Shimon Bar Yochai kept the hidden scroll.

The inclusion of imams and emirs in the novel was intentional to express my hopes for peace and to emphasize the need to urge the silent majority in the Islamic world to isolate the radical Islamic terrorists whose actions are detrimental to the Islamic cause.

LIST OF MAJOR CHARACTERS

1. Haj Amin al-Husseini   (See "Historical Notes")
2. Benjamin   Avner's father
3. Avner   archaeology professor
4. Thubten Gyatso   the thirteenth Dalai Lama
5. Tenzin Gyatso   the fourteenth Dalai Lama
6. Ahmad Ibn-Najad   first director of Bismillah
7. Bashir, son of Ibn-Najad   second director of Bismillah
8. Farid   elder son of Bashir
9. Colonel Menachem   Avner's brother
10. Young Benjamin   Avner's son
11. Young Avner   Avner's grandson
12. Elaine   Avner's first wife
13. Daphna   Avner's second wife
14. LeCorbellier   dean of archaeology at the Sorbonne
15. Halevy   archaeology professor at the Sorbonne
16. Mizrachi   archaeology professor at Hebrew University
17. Bar David   archaeology professor at Harvard University

For additional information about this book, visit my website at www.anouchi.org

ACKNOWLEDGMENTS

W ITHOUT THE SUPPORT of my family and a pool of friends, this book would never have reached the printing press. It would have remained a manuscript collecting dust printed on a laser printer.

I owe thanks to Daniel Silva. His *Silent Server* inspired me to write this historical novel.

I thank professors Joseph Eaton and Alex Ohrbach of the University of Pittsburgh who reviewed the earlier draft of my manuscript. Their constructive criticism resulted in a major rewriting to the extent of changing the title of the book. They were both generous in offering to review my final manuscript.

I am indebted to John DeBoer and Archie Hooton for editing many chapters and Nandita Menon for editing the complete manuscript. They were generous with time and encouragement.

I consulted dozens of history books and articles to gather critically needed information for the novel. I owe special thanks to my brother, Danny, who assisted me in gathering historical details related to the 1967 and the 1973 wars in Israel.

Finally. my wife Patricia, deserves special thanks for reviewing my first draft and for her patience during the months of writing and rewriting the manuscript.

HISTORICAL NOTES

MANY OF THE events described in this fiction include references to historical events, but I took the liberty of ascribing imaginary actions to many of the characters, molding them in the interests of the plot. Most readers will be familiar with the names of many historical figures such as Judah the Maccabee, the Hasmonaean Queen Shlom-Zion, Rabbi Akiva, Rabbi Shimon Bar Yochai, and Menachem Begin.

The notes in this section are intended to outline the known facts and historical background around which the novel was written..

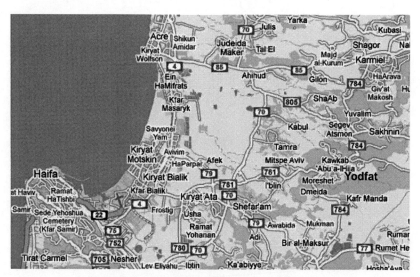

Map of Haifa Bay and Yodfat

1. THE MACCABEES

Following the death of Alexander the Great, his empire split with the land of Judea falling under the control of the northern Seleucid Greeks. During a ceremony in the town of Modi'in, Greek soldiers forced a Jewish man to worship the Greek god Zeus in public. A Jewish zealot killed the man and the Greek soldiers. It triggered a revolt by the local Jewish priest, Matityahu and his five sons, and volunteers who joined them. They are known as the Maccabees, an acronym of the Hebrew words meaning "who is like you among the gods, O Lord."

Judah the Maccabee, their first commander, fought for and won independence from the Hellenistic Seleucids in 164 BCE. The success of the revolt against the mighty Greek army earned the Maccabees fame, a success brought about through the use of ingenious tactics planned by Judah the Maccabee and the outstanding bravery of his fighters. After the defeat of the Greeks, the Maccabees entered Jerusalem in triumph and cleaned the temple that had been desecrated by the Greeks. It was reconsecrated by Judah as a Jewish Temple. Every year, Jews celebrate Hanukkah, which means dedication to commemorate the Judean victory.

After Judah the Maccabee's death in battle, his younger brother, Jonathan, succeeded him. At Jonathan's death, his youngest brother, Shimon the Maccabee, assumed command of the Jewish army as well as the position of high priest, thus founding the Hasmonaean Dynasty. Jewish independence lasted until 63 BCE, when the Romans entered Jerusalem.

2. QUEEN SHLOM-ZION

Shlom-Zion, known also as Queen Salome Alexandra, was the last of the Hasmonaean rulers. She brought peace and prosperity to the country for nine years, shortly before the Roman takeover of Judea. She became queen at the age of sixty-two, after the death of her husband, Alexander Yannai, who was a tyrannical ruler closely associated with the Sadducees. Once she assumed the throne, Shlom-Zion instituted a wide range of reforms in conjunction with Rabbi Shimon Ben Shetach. Praised in the Talmud for her piety and her care for her people, Shlom-Zion's reign initiated public education, the marriage Ketubah, and reform of the Sanhedrin. She is credited for maintaining peace with the neighboring countries and ruling over a time of great abundance and fairness.

A parchment before and after treatment

3. TITUS

Titus was the military commander in Judea during the revolt against the Romans between 67 and 70 CE. Originally, his father, Vespasian, commanded the campaign against the Jewish revolt until he became emperor after the death of Nero. Titus completed the campaign in the year 70 CE by besieging the city of Jerusalem and destroying it with its temple. The senate honored him for the success of his campaign and built the triumphal arch named after him in Rome on which are depictions of the treasures brought back from the temple in Jerusalem. It still stands today. Upon Vespasian's death, Titus succeeded his father as emperor. His reign lasted only two years, and he died in 81 CE.

Titus Triumphal Arch in Rome

4. RABBI AKIVA

Rabbi Akiva was one of the greatest sages of the Talmud era. He was both a scholar and a revolutionary. In the year 70 of the common era (CE), the Romans destroyed the Second Temple and the Jews were exiled from Jerusalem. The emperor promised to rebuild the city, but his plan was to rebuild it and rename it Aeila Capitolina, dedicating it to the Roman god Jupiter. This edict, along with the harsh laws forbidding the study of Torah and the observance of Jewish laws, led to the Bar-Kochva Revolt over sixty years after the destruction of the Temple in the year 132 CE.

While Shimon Bar Kochva was the military commander of the revolt, the spiritual leader was Rabbi Akiva. Devastated by the death of his pupils and the failure of the Bar Kochva revolt, Rabbi Akiva persevered and continued teaching his surviving students.

Rabbi Akiva ignored the Roman prohibitions against the Jewish people and their practices; he was declared a criminal for teaching the Torah wherever he could and was eventually captured by the Romans. He was one of the ten rabbis who were tortured and executed in public. While under torture, he called out joyfully, "All my life, I've been waiting to fulfill the commandment of the Shema Yisrael, 'You shall love your G-d with all your heart, with all your soul, and with all your might.' Now I finally do it." Rabbi Akiva died a martyr's death, but he left behind dedicated students to continue his work. One of the most important disciples was Rabbi Shimon Bar Yochai.

5. RABBI SHIMON BAR YOCHAI

Rabbi Shimon Bar Yochai was one of the most prominent rabbis of the Mishnah scholars known as the Tannaim. He lived in Israel after the destruction of the Second Temple of Jerusalem in 70 CE. He was the most dedicated disciple of Rabbi Akiva and is considered the author of *The Book of the Zohar*, the central document of the Kabbalah Jewish Mysticism.

According to the Talmud, Bar Yochai preached against the Roman government. His anti-Roman sentiments led to his condemnation by Varna in 161 CE. He escaped this doom by hiding in a cave with his son and eight other rabbis. They stayed in hiding thirteen years, studying the Torah and its philosophical teachings.

Bar Yochai is credited with interpreting a large body of Jewish laws. In many disputations between rabbis, his decisions are frequently cited. To him are attributed the important legal decisions in the documents called Sifre and Mekhilta and, above all, *The Book of the Zohar*, the main work of the Kabbalah.

In the Talmud, a reference to Rabbi Shimon without further qualification signifies Rabbi Shimon Bar Yochai.

Rabbi Shimon Bar Yochai is buried in Meiron, near the city of Safad, in Israel, where many devout Jews gather once a year to celebrate the Lag ba'Omer festival in his memory.

6. JOSEPHUS FLAVIUS

Yosef ben Matityahu was a commander in the Jewish Army of Judea during the first century CE. At the age of twenty-nine, he was appointed general of the Jewish forces in Galilee with a task of defending Galilee from the Romans. He fortified the town of Yodfat and the surrounding area. In his last stand at the fortress of Yodfat, he held back the Romans during a siege lasting forty-seven days until it was captured by Vespasian's forces. The defenders committed suicide, but the Romans captured him. Having been a member of the priestly family in Jerusalem, he was first taken to be an eyewitness to the destruction of Jerusalem and the Second Temple by the Roman army in 70 CE. Titus then took him to Rome where the emperor Vespasian renamed him Josephus Flavius.

Josephus wrote the historical book *The War of the Jews Against the Romans*, documenting his participation in that war. Some historians consider his book as essential to our understanding of the war with the Romans.

The Menorah on the Titus Arch

7. TIBET

Tenzin Gyatso, the fourteenth Dalai Lama, who was born in China, was installed in 1940. He assumed full powers in 1950 after a ten-year regency.

In 1950, Tibet became a "national autonomous region" of China under the traditional rule of the Dalai Lama, but under the actual control of a Chinese Communist Commission. The Communist government introduced far-reaching reforms that sharply curtailed the power of the monastic orders. After 1956, scattered uprisings occurred throughout the country, but a full-scale revolt broke out in March, 1959, prompted in part by fears for the personal safety of the Dalai Lama. The Chinese suppressed the rebellion, but the Dalai Lama escaped to India, where he established headquarters in exile.

8. HAJ AMIN AL-HUSSEINI

Muhammad Amin al-Husseini was born in 1893 in Jerusalem, Palestine, a province of the Ottoman Empire. In 1922, Sir Herbert Samuel, the high commissioner of Palestine, appointed Haj Amin as the grand mufti of Jerusalem. In his book *The Rape of Palestine*, William Ziff described the life of the mufti:

> Implicated in the 1920 disturbances was a political adventurer named Haj Amin Al-Husseini. Haj Amin, was sentenced by a British court to fifteen years hard labor. Conveniently allowed to escape by the police, he was a fugitive in Syria. Shortly after, the British allowed him to return to Palestine where, despite the opposition of the Muslim High Council who regarded him as a hoodlum, the British High Commissioner of Palestine appointed him the Grand Mufti of Jerusalem for life.

> Once he was in power, Haj Amin began a campaign of terror against anyone opposed to his policies including many Arabs. In 1929, he instigated Arab riots against the Jews of Palestine. The riots began when Al-Husseini falsely accused Jews of defiling the Al-Aqsa Mosque. The call went out to the Arab masses to slaughter the Jews. After the Hebron massacre, the Mufti distributed photographs of the slaughtered Jews, claiming that the dead were Arabs killed by Jews.

According to records from the Nuremberg and Eichmann trials, the German SS helped finance al-Husseini's efforts in the 1936-39 revolt in Palestine. Adolf Eichmann visited Palestine and met with al-Husseini at that time. In 1940, al-Husseini requested the Axis powers to help him settle the Jewish problem in Palestine along the lines similar to those used to solve the Jewish question in Germany.

Haj Amin spent the rest of World War II as Hitler's special guest in Berlin, advocating the extermination of Jews in radio broadcasts back to the Middle East and recruiting Balkan Muslims to form the infamous SS "mountain divisions" that tried to wipe out Jewish communities throughout the region. At the Nuremberg trials, Eichmann's deputy, Dieter Wisliceny, testified.

The Mufti was one of the initiators of the systematic extermination of European Jewry and had been a collaborator and advisor of Eichmann and Himmler in the execution of this plan . . . He was one of Eichmann's best friends and had constantly incited him to accelerate the extermination measures. I heard him say that, accompanied by Eichmann, he had visited incognito the gas chambers of Auschwitz.

Hitler meets with Haj Amin

Haj Amin al-Husseini meets
Muslim Nazi soldiers in Germany

Later, Haj Amin was among the sponsors of the 1948 war against the new State of Israel. He arranged the assassination of Jordan's King Abdullah in 1951. He died in 1974.

9. THE MARRANOS

Who were the Marranos? The Jews who were forced to convert by the Inquisition. The first known forced mass conversion of Jews to another religion took place in Minorca in the year 418 under Bishop Severus. Other famous early mass conversions took place in Auvergne, France, in 576 followed by King Dagobert Edict in 629, ordering Jews to accept baptism or be expelled from the country. One of the essential elements of Marranism is the practicing of Judaism in secrecy and passing the practice from generation to generation. The victims continued to practice Judaism in secret and took the first opportunity to revert back to their faith. The church did all it could to prevent any association between the converts and the professing Jews. During the First Crusade of 1096, many Jews saved their lives in Germany by accepting forced baptism and later were encouraged by Rashi to return to Judaism. In the Muslim world, we find many cases of forced conversion of Jews like the Daggatun in the Sahara or the Domneh of Salonica or the Jeddidim who are descendants of forced converts in Persia during the seventeenth century.

The classical land of secret Judaism is Spain. As far back as the Roman period, the Jews in Spain were numerous and influential. Many claimed to trace their descent to the aristocracy of Jerusalem, which was exiled by Titus.

When Spain adopted Catholicism in the sixth century, the Jews were the first to suffer. In the year 616, the church ordered the baptism of all the Jews under the threat of banishment and loss of property. Nineteen thousand Jews were baptized against their will. This practice continued until the Arab invasion in 711, when the converts returned to their faith. Under the Arab rule, the Golden Age of the Spanish Jews was initiated, first in the Caliphate of Cordova and later in other regions. The Jewish communities increased in numbers, in culture, in religious and secular literature, and in wealth. This era included Jewish giants such as Hasdai Ibn Shaprut (915-970) the famous vizier of Cordova. Under his leadership, the world center of Jewish culture was transferred from Sura and Pumpedita in Babylon to Spain. Under the encouragement of Shlomo-Ibn-Gvirol, another Jewish vizier, a renewed surge of Jewish culture took place in Granada. The writings of Shlomo Ibn Gvirol, Yehuda Halevy, and Moses Ibn Ezra are with us today. The highest level of scholastic interpretations of the Torah was achieved by Avraham Ibn Ezra and by the Rambam in his *Mishne Torah* and *The Guide to the Perplexed.*

The tolerance of the Jewish flourishing in Spain continued until the twelfth century, when the Almohades Moorish sect took control. Both Judaism and Christianity were banned, and most Jews fled to the Christian North, but many were put to the sword or sold as slaves. After the Reconquista of Spain by the Christians, the Jewish scholarship continued to flourish under the church until the fourteenth century. On Ash Wednesday 1391, a crowd broke into the Jewish quarter of Seville, and four thousand Jews were massacred. Similar massacres followed in Cordova, Toledo, Barcelona, and other cities. Fifty thousand Jews were massacred in one month. Large bodies of Jews accepted baptism en masse in order to escape death. Of these converts, many returned to Judaism either when the danger passed or when they could flee to North Africa. Many remained in Spain as pseudo Christians who were referred to as conversos. Outwardly, they lived like Christians. They baptized their children, but immediately washed off the ceremonial water when they returned home. They married in church and immediately followed up with a Jewish ceremony at home. They were Jews in all but name, and Christians in nothing but form.

Many circumcised their sons, and the majority married among themselves. On occasions, they visited synagogues, and their gifts were generous. Many were successful in passing the Jewish laws to their children for transmission to their children. Some were not successful and were eventually assimilated to become Catholic, whose descendants are found today throughout the Spanish society. The Christian community called the conversos *nuevo Christianos*, but the masses called them Marranos.

THE INQUISITION

It became obvious to the church that the mass conversions did not make Spain free of Jews. Baptism converted Jewish infidels outside the church into heretics inside it. It was evident that most conversos were Christians in name only. The conversos were declared incapable of holding public office or bearing testimony against Christians.

In 1480, the church established the Inquisition to inflict punishment for heresy. The Inquisition launched its career of blood. In February 1481, six Marranos were burned alive in public in Seville in the first auto-da-fé (act of faith), and a sermon was preached at the site. Many Marranos fled to surrounding territories, but they were captured by the nobility and returned to the Inquisition. The marquess of Cadiz alone sent back eight thousand Marrano refugees, and the dungeons of Seville became overcrowded. In November 1481, 298 persons were burnt publicly, and their possessions confiscated by the church. Many conversos who confessed on the understanding that they would be spared were paraded as penitents. In one march, fifteen thousand conversos were paraded.

In 1482, the queen's confessor, Thomas the Torquemada, was appointed as chief inquisitor, and immediately, tribunals were set up outside Seville, and the auto-da-fé practice spread to most cities and towns in Spain. Luis de Santangel, who was knighted by King Juan II, was beheaded in public. Famous family names appeared in the list of auto-da-fé records: Santangel, Sanchez, Caballeria, and others, while professing Jews now lived in Spain without serious problems. The situation became illogical: a Marrano would be burned alive for performing in secret what his unconverted relative was performing in public without punishment.

In 1492, after Granada was captured from the Moors, the religious zeal in Spain was at its peak, and the Spanish monarchs decreed the expulsion of all nonconverted Jews from the country.

10. THE EXPULSION EDICT

In 1492, King Ferdinand of Aragon and Queen Isabel of Castile issued the expulsion edict. It was not made public until March 31 of that year so that the final date would occur just before the Ninth of Av, the date of the destruction of both Temples of Jerusalem. The following is a translation from the Hebrew version of the edict, which was published by Professor Reinhart of the Hebrew University in Jerusalem, a scholar on the Spanish Inquisition. The English version is not an exact translation, but it is very close to this original document.

THE EXPULSION EDICT

> Don Fernando and Donia Isabel . . . to the Prince Don
> Juan, our dear and most beloved son, the Infantis,
> to the Priests and to the Jewish communities in
> this city of Avilla, and to all the cities, the villages
> and the places in this region, and to all the other
> cities, villages and places in our kingdoms and our
> possessions, peace and greetings.
>
> Know yea, and you must know, that, because we
> were informed that in our kingdoms there were bad
> Christians who converted to Judaism and betrayed
> our Catholic faith, and the main reason was the close
> connection between Jews and Christians.
>
> In the *cortez* (royal court) of the year 1480, we
> ordered the separation of Jews in all the cities, villages
> and places of settlements in our kingdoms and in our

possessions, and we ordered to give them the Jewish
neighborhoods and places for them to live in, with the
hope that in separation, the matter would be corrected.
And we also gave an order that an Inquisition be set
up in our Kingdoms and possessions. And this, as
you know, was done more than twelve years ago,
and with which many sinners were discovered by
the Inquisitors and by the men of the Church and by
laymen as well.

And now is revealed in public the great damage that
was done to Christians from their associations, their
contacts and their conversations that they had, and
that they have, with Jews. And, because it is proven
that the Jews always try, in every ways and means in
their possession, to destroy and pull away from our . . .
Catholic faith, the believing Christians, to attract them
to their faith and their damaging views, in teaching
the Christians their ceremonies and religious customs,
in gathering them in meetings, where they teach them
and their children, by giving them books with which
they pray their prayers, and declare their fasts, in
gathering them to read to them and to learn the stories
of their Torah, and in declaring their Holidays on time,
and in informing them what religious laws they must
observe, in giving them and in taking out of their
home all the matzot and the meat that was slaughtered
according to their ritual, and in convincing them that
there is no other faith outside their faith. And this was
proven by their declarations and confessions, those of
the Jews themselves and of those who were misled by

the Jews. And all this brought upon us great damage and harmed our . . . Catholic faith.

And although all these things were known to us before, and we knew that the true remedy to all these damages and all this evil thing, is to terminate the contact between the Jews and the Christians and to expel them from our kingdoms, we were lenient by ordering the Jews to leave the cities, the villages and all the settlements in Andalusia, where, as was said, they caused very heavy damage, because we believed that such an order would be sufficient, so that those who live in these cities and villages will stop sinning as mentioned above.

And because we knew that this thing, and all the punishments that were given to some of these Jews, who were discovered as great sinners in these crimes against our . . . Catholic faith; after we heard that this step is not sufficient as a complete remedy—for the purpose of stopping these crimes against our Christian faith, that every day it is found that the Jews continue and increase their bad intentions which cause damage where they are, and in order that there will be no more crimes against our faith, both at those who were not affected and those who failed, repented and returned to the mother church—what would happen due to our human weakness and to the actions of the Satan who constantly struggles against us, something that easily could happen—if the main reason for it is not removed, and it is: the expulsion of the Jews from our kingdoms,

for when a crime is performed in any society, there
is sense that those lower ones be removed, scattered,
and suffer for the sake of the important ones, the
fewer for the many. And those that destroy the good
and decent life in the cities, in the villages with the
means of contamination that will hurt others, that they
be expelled from the settlements, and even for very
unimportant cases that could cause damage to society
it is customary to act that way, so much more for a
large crime like this one.

That is why, at the advice of several members of
the church, the higher and the lower priests in our
kingdoms, and people of science and consciousness
from our advisory council, after having thought about
this matter seriously, we agreed to expel all the Jews
and Jewesses from our kingdoms. And never shall
any of them return. And we, therefore, issued this
edict; and we so order all the Jews and Jewesses of
all ages, those that were born in our kingdoms and
those that were not born here, that until the end of
July of this year, will depart from our kingdoms and
our possessions, with their children, servants and
maids, all the members of their families, old and
young, and they should not dare to return and live
in the places where they used to live, for if they will
not obey this order, and if they will be found living
in our kingdoms, they will be sentenced to death and
to the confiscation of their possessions in favor of
our court and the treasury of the kingdom: and these
punishments will be given to them based on their

action without a trial, without a court hearing and without a declaration.

And we decree and say, that no-one in our kingdoms, of any standing or rank, will dare to receive, to give shelter, to house and defend, not in public and nor in secrecy, any Jew or Jewess after the end of next July, and for ever, not in their lands and not in their homes and not in any part of our kingdoms and our possessions, under the penalty of punishment of losing all their property, the servants in their possession and the fortresses and all other things that pass in inheritance, and they will also lose anything that we have given them, all in favor of the court and the royal treasury.

And, in order that these Jews and the Jewesses will be able in this period, until the end of July, to sell in good manner their possessions, for this period we take and receive under our royal protection, them and their possessions, so that, in the designated period until the end of July, they will be able to walk and to stand securely and will be able to come and sell, exchange and transfer from their ownership and their possessions and their lands, to decide on them freely and under their free will. And during this period, no damage will be done, and no evil will be performed or any injustice to these men and to their property against the law, under the penalty of punishment, in which are judged those who act against the security of the kingdoms.

And thus we give permission and authority to these Jews and the Jewesses to take their possessions outside our kingdoms by sea or by land, as long that they will not take any gold, silver and metal coins, or any other items that are forbidden by the royal laws, except for trade items that are not forbidden, and paper contracts. And we also ordered that all the councils, courts, leaders of the kingdoms, the Caballeros and the Escodrerros, the clerks and the good people in this city of Avilla and in the cities, villages and other places in our kingdoms and our possessions, and to all the vassals under our control, and to the natives, to keep and perform this order and everything that is written in it, and that they should give all the assistance to anyone who requires it, under the penalty of punishment of losing our protection and the confiscation of their property in favor of the court and the Royal treasury.

And, in order that this order reaches the knowledge of everyone, and that not a single person could claim that he did not know, we order that this decree will be declared in the usual places and city squares in this city and in the major cities, villages and all the places of the church, by a town crier and in front of a notary public. And not these or other things will be done against the law.

Given in our city Granada, 31 March in the year 1492, I the King, I the Queen, I, Juan de Coloma, Secretary of the King and Queen our masters, wrote as he was instructed.

Get Published, Inc!
Thorofare, NJ 08086
11 December, 2009
BA2009284